ARTIFACTS, DRAGONS,
and other
LETHAL MAGIC

— Dowser 6 —

ARTIFACTS, DRAGONS, and other LETHAL MAGIC

Meghan Ciana Doidge

Published by Old Man in the CrossWalk Productions
Salt Spring Island, BC, Canada

www.madebymeghan.ca

Author's Note:

Artifacts, Dragons, and Other Lethal Magic is the sixth book in the Dowser series, which is set in the same universe as the Oracle series.

While it is not necessary to read both series, the ideal reading order is as follows:

Cupcakes, Trinkets, and Other Deadly Magic (Dowser 1)
Trinkets, Treasures, and Other Bloody Magic (Dowser 2)
Treasures, Demons, and Other Black Magic (Dowser 3)
I See Me (Oracle 1)*
Shadows, Maps, and Other Ancient Magic (Dowser 4)
Maps, Artifacts, and Other Arcane Magic (Dowser 5)
I See You (Oracle 2)*
Artifacts, Dragons, and Other Lethal Magic (Dowser 6)

Other books in both the Oracle and Dowser series to follow.

I See Me (Oracle 1) contains spoilers for Dowser 1, 2, and 3. *I See You* (Oracle 2) contains spoilers for Dowser 4 and 5.

For Michael

For always finding me when I'm lost

I wasn't even remotely interested in collecting the third instrument of assassination. It was far better for everyone involved — and for Warner, specifically — if I just let it be. And since I was the only one who could retrieve the artifacts, I figured it was my call to make.

I was wrong.

And though that wasn't unusual, I was just so … so … wrong … about everything.

I was wrong about who I was protecting and why. I was wrong about who and what I could control. And I was wrong about who I was becoming.

Baker of cupcakes, maker of trinkets, half-witch, half-dragon, dowser, alchemist …

Why couldn't I just be Jade?

Chapter One

I massaged the pineapple-and-coconut-scented shampoo through my hair, enjoying the steaming hot water pounding against my shoulder blades. That morning's baking session had felt longer than normal. Every year, the holiday craze felt as though it hit earlier and earlier, then lasted longer and longer. Usually, business in the bakery was quiet through the end of December and into the new year, with just a slight bump around New Year's Eve. But it was three weeks into January already, and I'd had to bake extra *Hug in a Cup* — a buttercream-topped dark-chocolate cake — and *Lift in a Cup* — a delicate white cake with coffee buttercream — when we'd sold out an hour after opening.

I'd also had to explain why I didn't have a pumpkin-spiced, latte-flavored cupcake to fourteen different people throughout the day. At the end of January. And by people, I meant thirtysomethings on their way to midweek brunch, sipping from their personalized Starbucks mugs and —

A formal summons from the treasure keeper interrupted my thoughts when it materialized before me with a puff of smoky dragon magic. I squeaked at the appearance of a golden envelope in the steamy air, flinching harshly enough that the sudsy curls I'd piled on top of my head toppled down into my face. I might be half-witch/half-dragon, but shampoo in my eyes still stung.

"Son of a freaking hell." I spun away, evading the envelope as I lifted my eyes and face to the showerhead. The summons remained suspended behind me, patiently waiting for me to pluck it out of the air. It was the fourth such missive I'd received in the last three months, and I still couldn't figure out how they were getting through the magical blood wards on my apartment.

And speaking of brunch, I had dim sum with Warner on my mind, and was therefore in no way interested in 'freeing the magic of Shailaja, daughter of the mountain,' which had been the gist of the last three missives from the treasure keeper. The summons that had appeared two weeks ago had actually been signed 'By order of the Guardian Council.' A year or so ago, that single sentence would have had me quaking in my boots. But I knew there was no way the Guardian Council had gathered over anything as mundane as a rogue dragon — even one who'd been a bad girl over five hundred years ago, and who'd wound up with her magic locked away because of it.

You had to drag a greater demon into the dragon nexus to rouse all nine guardians at once. Trust me, I knew.

The simple remembrance of all that power gathered in one room still made my bones ache. The combined might of the guardians had obliterated every taste, sound, and sight, overwhelming my dowser senses and scrambling my brain.

Shailaja was beneath their combined notice. Whether she was the treasure keeper's new pet or not.

The envelope started vibrating as I rinsed the last of the conditioner out of my hair. I turned off the water and reached for a towel, knowing that if I moved more than two steps away, the envelope would follow. The second summons had done so. Then it exploded all over me when I ignored it for too long. It had taken me two days and too many expensive chocolate bars to clear the smoky taste of its magical detonation from my mouth.

I toweled off, grumbling to myself about having a well-earned moment of relaxation interrupted. Wrapping my hair in the damp towel, I reached up and tapped the bottom edge of the envelope.

Its thick golden paper unfurled, exposing a thin piece of parchment and Pulou's handwritten demand.

Jade Godfrey,
Daughter of the Warrior, Treasure Keeper's Alchemist,
your presence is required in the Chamber of the Treasure
Keeper immediately.

I didn't bother reading any further. Same old yadda yadda. I hadn't set foot in the nexus for over a year, and I wasn't about to do so for some rabid koala who had a thing for my boyfriend. By which I meant Shailaja. My default disposition might be 'nice' with a swirl of 'blissfully ignorant,' but I wasn't a complete moron or a glutton for punishment.

A glutton for chocolate and cupcakes, yes.

A glutton for endangering my friends and family, no.

I touched the edge of the summons and firmly intoned, "I will not be attending."

The parchment and envelope crumbled, raining gold glitter and ash all over the tiled bathroom floor in a seriously flashy RSVP.

Dragons loved sparkly magic.

But then, who didn't?

Dim sum at Sun Sui Wah was always a delight, but it turned into a fifteen-course extravaganza whenever I had a dragon seated beside me.

Specifically, a six-foot-four-inch, broad-shouldered, dark-blond, blue-green-eyed sentinel who had a serious thing for Chinese food.

Impromptu dim sum outings had become almost a weekly ritual for Warner and me over the previous year. We'd tried just about every restaurant in Vancouver, returning to our first choice after we'd decided it was the tastiest.

The linen-swathed table we were currently occupying in the middle of the restaurant was designed to accommodate groups of eight or more. The host never bothered to seat us at any of the smaller tables that ringed the large open room and were designated for parties of two. It hadn't taken long for us to gain a reputation. It probably helped that Warner ordered in fluent Cantonese. The sentinel was relaxed and jovial when surrounded by good food and large crowds of people.

Even on a Thursday the restaurant was more than half full and noisy. The management had recently installed two massive TV screens, but none of their clientele appeared to pay attention to whatever sports game was playing at any given time.

Thankfully, brunch or lunch was an easy time for me to get away from work, and Sun Sui Wah was open seven days a week. Because even as stable and predictable as my schedule was, Warner had taken over patrolling the territories of Chi Wen, the far seer, working alongside Haoxin and Qiuniu, the guardians of North and South America. Apparently, it was commonplace for the younger dragons to do so — further training and whatnot — but I was suspicious that it might also be my father's way of keeping Warner and me from getting too cozy. Either way it meant that the sentinel came and went without much warning.

His unpredictability didn't bother me as much as I would have thought, though. Probably because it was obvious that he made an effort every single time he walked through the portal in the bakery basement.

Of course, it could also be that he had a knack for picking the perfect shade of green or blue whenever he manifested his clothing. Today, he was wearing a deliciously thin-knit kelly-green merino wool sweater that barely encompassed his shoulders and hugged his ribs and abs just enough to make it difficult to not continuously stare at him.

We'd actually set this rendezvous far enough in advance that I also had the option of making a bit of an effort with my appearance. I opted to wear a new long hoodie of gray cashmere over a dark pair of straight-leg Citizens of Humanity jeans, with a black tank top underneath my T-shirt for extra warmth. The jeans showed off my vintage Fluevogs — golden-brown Giulias with their stacked three-inch heel, from the Fluevog Operetta family. My Christmas presents from Gran — a charcoal silk and cashmere hand-knit triangle scarf, a matching set of wrist warmers, and a ribbed, slouchy hat — were all I needed to add to the outfit to make it outdoor ready. So far, the winter had been mild in Vancouver.

"I thought the wolf was coming back after Christmas?" Warner asked as he reached across the table, expertly picking up a prawn dumpling with his slick plastic chopsticks.

"I texted this morning," I said. "Haven't heard back."

I hadn't seen Kandy for more than a couple of days in a row since I'd left her in Portland. She'd been in Mississippi last July with the oracle, Rochelle, and her shifter boyfriend, Beau. Something had gone down there, but aside from grousing about how she'd 'saved the oracle's and the kitten's asses' she hadn't given me any details. Though being close-mouthed was typical for the green-haired werewolf, I couldn't shake the feeling that something had happened in Mississippi that she didn't want me to know ... or that she was trying to figure out a way to tell me.

I just hoped like hell it wasn't that she'd laid eyes on a sketch of one of Rochelle's visions and it was freaking her out. You know, something like my death rendered in charcoal.

Still chewing the dumpling, Warner dipped half a shrimp-and-garlic spring roll in the Worcestershire-type sauce that came with the dish. He popped the crunchy roll into his mouth whole, then raised an eyebrow at me.

"Same with Kett," I said.

Warner grunted. "The vampire is under house arrest."

"Sorry?"

"You were worried about the vampire. He's in London. His elder wasn't too pleased to find me knocking on his door."

I stared at Warner, mouth hanging open and everything. "You knocked on the door of the big bad of London because I was concerned?"

Warner shrugged. "It's good to keep them a little shaken up."

"How shaken?"

Warner grinned wickedly. "Well, he's going to have to rebuild a tower that was probably seismically substandard anyway."

"You ... destroyed the big bad's ... castle?"

"Destroyed is such a harsh word."

I started laughing.

"Damn vampire didn't want to come with me. I had to formally request permission from the fire breather to enter her territory, then the cold bastard didn't even want to be rescued."

"Oh my God … you told Suanmi you were rescuing a vampire and she gave you permission?"

"I might have used the term 'hunting,' but yes."

I attempted to stifle my laughter. I was already drawing attention from nearby tables, which was saying a lot in a huge room filled with large groups of boisterous families.

Warner grinned at me. His chopsticks were poised over the gai lan in garlic sauce.

I wiped tears from my face. "What does house arrest mean?"

Warner shrugged again. "Kett isn't exactly verbose. But apparently, it's voluntary … or self-imposed. He seemed pissed that he'd have to cover the cost of the repairs, then sneered at the gold I offered."

"Kettil, the executioner and elder of the Conclave, is difficult to please."

"I wasn't trying to please him." Warner topped up my tiny mug of jasmine green tea, then lifted his gaze to meet mine.

"Thank you," I whispered. I'd come to adore the blue starburst that edged the green of his irises. Under the right circumstances, flecks of gold appeared in his eyes as well.

He pushed the final prawn-and-chive pan-fried dumpling — my favorite — across the table toward me, touching the back of my hand as he withdrew his arm. The neck of his sweater opened up just enough that I could see a hint of the dragon tattoo across his collarbone.

Yeah, I was doing that staring thing again. Instead of acting embarrassed, I kept eye contact and slowly curled my lips in a smile.

Warner laughed, low and husky and for my ears only. "Later. We have another stop first."

"Oh?"

"We're going somewhere else for dessert. It's a surprise."

"Well, apparently you just stormed a castle to rescue my vampire BFF who didn't actually want to be rescued, so I'll let you have your dessert secret. For now. But don't push it, sixteenth century."

Warner laughed, then raised his hand for the bill.

I finally tore my gaze away from him, dipping the prawn-and-chive dumpling in soy sauce. I'd never been so enamored with anyone before, and certainly not for well over a year. Usually, a couple of weeks were all it took to send me packing. My former boyfriends all had habits ... deal breakers ... and well, just weren't ... enough.

Some days, being around Warner was almost too much. Too consuming. Thankfully, he had his dragon duties, I had the bakery to distract me, and we met somewhere in the middle every few days.

Still, I wondered if there were just some people you couldn't get out of your system. Not that I was interested in trying.

Warner and I were tucked behind a white-painted lattice panel at the rear of the tearoom at Notte's Bon Ton Pastry. The lattice, which divided the tearoom from the glass bakery counters, was attached to fake pillars and woven through with fake ivy. The unusual design aesthetic was punctuated by small brown tables of marble laminate and delicate-looking wrought-iron chairs with cushions wrapped in cream-colored vinyl. Though customers were constantly coming and going from the pastry and confectionary itself, only one other table was occupied in the tearoom. Four well-heeled women in their midforties were enjoying tea and a chat a few tables away.

I was perched on the edge of my seat, with my hand hovering over an artfully arranged pillared glass plate of delectable French pastries. I'd been indecisively thinking about which buttercream-filled sample of goodness I should select from the bounty arrayed before me.

But now, I was staring at a diamond-crusted, rune-carved platinum box nestled among the pastries.

A platinum box that looked as if it might contain an engagement ring.

I'd been staring at it for a while.

Staring.

Without talking.

"Jade?" Warner asked.

I was fairly certain he'd been speaking before, but I'd missed his actual words.

Smoky dragon magic sparkled off the box.

My tea was getting oversteeped. I wasn't usually a tea drinker, but when invited to afternoon tea, you were generally expected to sip at something. Even if it was simply a way to justify the pound of buttercream and pastry you were about to consume.

I'd gone for Earl Grey, with every intention of being liberal with the cream and sugar.

None of this was remotely relevant.

I withdrew my hand, lifting my gaze to meet Warner's.

He looked concerned. "For your necklace," he said. His tone implied that he was repeating himself. "They were my parents' betrothal rings. Blossom unearthed them for me."

I stared at Warner, lightly touching my necklace and its collection of wedding rings, and feeling their magic roll beneath my fingertips. Magic I couldn't taste because it was my own. Or, more specifically, it was magic I had claimed by drawing on the residual power present in the wedding rings when I first collected them, then added them like charms to the necklace. I'd wound the chain twice around my neck today, though I usually wore it wrapped three times. When shorter, it didn't get in the way so much. You know, for when an inevitable knife fight broke out.

"Blossom?" I echoed Warner rather than actually responding to him. "She's ... cleaning for you?" Blossom was the brownie who had repaired my bakery after Shailaja the rabid koala had trashed it a year ago. She continued to keep the place sparkling clean, asking only for cupcakes in payment.

"My parents' home in Stockholm needed some repairs and reorganization."

I nodded. Right. Stockholm ... Sweden. Warner owned a townhouse in Gamla Stan. Or, rather, he'd inherited that townhouse, though I gathered he mostly bunked in the dragon nexus.

I reached across the table and lifted the box away from the neighboring pastries. Its spicy dragon magic danced underneath my far-too-tense grip.

"The vampire contributed to your personal warding. I figured it was fair to do the same."

I blinked rapidly.

"You appear frozen in fear, Jade."

"Ahh ... I ..."

I couldn't articulate anything, probably because I still wasn't thinking terribly clearly. So I lifted the lid of the platinum box instead. Two gold rings crusted with tiny gems were nestled within a velvet lining of dark gold. One ring was smaller than the other. Tiny incomprehensible runes were carved on the inner edges of both bands.

"Wedding bands," I murmured.

"Betrothal," Warner said, repeating himself for what I was pretty sure was the third time. "Have I made a mistake? Are they not ... right somehow?"

The age-darkened gold and the well-worn runes on the rings simmered with dragon magic. I'd never felt such a strong residual from a simple ring before. Though knowing that one of the bands had been worn by the guardian of Northern Europe for who knows how many hundreds of years, it was easy to guess that an Adept of her power was bound to leave more than a trace.

A smear of buttercream marred the edge of the platinum box. Most likely from the rectangle of *Jealously* — a wafer-thin, delicate pastry layered with buttercream and fluffy sponge cake — that it had been hidden behind. I wiped it off, then sucked on my fingertip.

"They're perfect ..." I whispered.

"But?"

"But I ... are you ..."

"Am I perfect?" Warner laughed. "I'd like to think I am."

"That's a huge lie."

"Jade. I'm ... I've obviously upset you. Perhaps I should have given them to you for Christmas. But I was worried about the ... significance of the time of year. I wouldn't have sprung them on you now, but I know you feel that your necklace has diminished since ..."

I didn't prompt him to finish his thought, choosing instead to brush my fingers across the rings and allow the silence to stretch between us.

"Since Shailaja," I said finally.

Warner nodded reluctantly, obviously wishing he hadn't steered the conversation toward the rabid koala.

Well, I wished he hadn't either.

"I know you think she stands between us," Warner said. "She doesn't."

I curled my fingers over the rings, gathering them into the palm of my hand and feeling the residual magic intensify when the bands touched each other.

One of these rings had been worn by a guardian dragon for centuries. It was a staggeringly significant gift, even if it wasn't accompanied by the marriage proposal I'd been expecting the moment I laid eyes on the box.

The rings were a gift I wasn't ready to accept. Not with Shailaja hovering in the background of our lives.

But I wasn't ready to refuse, either.

"Thank you." I raised my eyes to bravely meet Warner's blue-green gaze. "I'll add them to my necklace tonight."

He smiled, settling back in his chair. "Aren't you going to introduce me to the sweets?" He gestured toward the platter of pastries between us.

He was going to let the subject drop.

For a moment, I thought about picking it up again, but I wasn't sure what I wanted to say. Was I going to push for the marriage proposal I had thought was happening? Even knowing it was a proposal I couldn't figure out how to accept?

"The *Diplomat* cake is Notte's signature dessert," I said. "You can get it with or without rum. Most people order it as the base for their wedding cakes ... or for baby showers ... "

Why did it suddenly feel as if the table between us was just an illusion covering a yawning chasm?

I gestured toward the pastries prettily piled on the glass cake stand before me. "They're sized for individual servings. Most are filled with buttercream and pastry like the *Diplomat*, but with different flavor combinations ... "

Warner reached across the table, snagging the hand I was holding over the pastries like I was some sort of dessert tour guide. He ran his thumb across my palm, sending sweet shivers up my wrist and forearm. "I've upset you," he said.

"No. Shailaja upsets me."

"You got another summons."

"I did. And I already know how you feel about it, so we don't have to talk about that, either."

Warner laughed quietly, but his amusement was tinged with bitterness. Instead of dropping my hand, he squeezed it.

I closed my eyes, attempting to calm myself. "I'm all riled up," I muttered.

"And we're nowhere near a bed."

I laughed, answering Warner's leer with one of my own. I leaned forward suggestively.

He did the same, matching my body language.

Holding his gaze, I reached into the collection of pastries and extracted my favorite. "The *Florentine*," I said. "Three individual Florentines sandwiched together with chocolate buttercream."

Freeing my right hand from Warner's grip, I broke the pastry in two, but the crisp, caramel-coated shaved almonds and candied fruit didn't snap cleanly. Rich buttercream squished out and over the broken edges. I licked the chocolate goodness from my fingers.

Warner grabbed my left hand along with the other half of the Florentine, pulling it across the table and completely ready to give it the same treatment with his tongue. Then, realizing we were in public, he growled and took a bite of the pastry instead.

With the cocoa creaminess of the buttercream in my mouth and Warner holding my hand, I felt more grounded.

We consumed the rest of the pastry, enjoying the treat in comfortable silence.

"We're going to need a box of those," Warner said.

"Oh, yeah. At least one box."

We strolled out of Notte's Bon Ton, laughing and laden with bakery boxes filled with more pastries, along with a seven-inch *Diplomat* cake for Gran. The betrothal rings were tucked safely in my moss-green Peg and Awl satchel, though I swore I could still taste their magic despite the containment spell that sealed the bag. Granted, that spell was mostly to stop things from falling out of the satchel and not necessarily to dampen magic.

Warner went abruptly still.

My father Yazi — the warrior of the guardian nine — was sauntering toward us from the corner of Trutch and West Broadway.

My laughter died on my lips. I simply stared at my demigod father as he closed the space between us.

Other shoppers brushed past us. West Broadway was a busy street even on a Thursday afternoon, but the pedestrians skirted my father as they passed. The overly intense gaze of his light-brown eyes didn't break from me. Except for that eye color, he was my exact twin ... well, a brawny, better-tanned, masculine twin.

I hadn't seen my father since he'd saved the rabid koala from a killing blow from my knife, at the site in Peru that I'd come to think of as the temple of the centipede. He'd stopped me from becoming a murderer that day. Yet I'd responded by shoving his Christmas present, unopened, underneath my bed. I was holding onto my grudge, hard and tight. It was unlike me.

My father smiled as he stopped beside us. I fought the instinct to smile back. He wore a hand-knit scarf of blue and green looped around his neck, a sky-blue T-shirt, and a pair of well-worn jeans. The scarf looked suspiciously like my Gran's knitting.

"A jacket might have been a good idea," I said.

Yazi cast his gaze over my somewhat-cold-weather-appropriate attire, then shrugged. So much for being careful to not stand out.

"Sentinel," he said, addressing Warner without looking at him.

"Warrior."

"You are dismissed."

Wait, what? No freaking way.

Warner immediately stepped to the side, but then he seemed to fight off the impulse to leave with a jerk of his shoulders.

Yazi glowered at him.

"We're on a date." I ground the words out between clenched teeth. "How dare you —"

"I dare," my father said. "We have things to discuss."

It was certainly obvious — even to me — where my penchant for childish retorts had been inherited from.

"I'm not remotely interested —"

"I have some errands to run." Warner interrupted the rant I'd been gearing up on. "I'll meet you back at the bakery."

"Your courtesy is noted, Jiaotuson," Yazi said.

In response to the formality of his last name, Warner bowed — though stiffly and shallowly — in my father's direction. Then he tugged the boxes of pastries out of my hands. He squeezed my wrist lightly while doing so, and the comforting taste of his black-forest-cake magic tickled my taste buds.

I just nodded, worried about making things worse if I opened my mouth.

Warner turned away, and I quickly lost sight of him on the busy sidewalk. His disappearance was due to his chameleonlike magic more than anything else. Physically, he towered over everyone, even my father.

"The boy dares too much for you," Yazi said.

It was an observation, not a critique, but I still bristled at it. "His name is Warner. Calling him Jiaotuson is just a cheap way to remind him —"

"Of his lineage? His duty? His bow was at least five inches shy of acceptable, yet I let him walk away without reprimand —"

I pivoted on my heel, turning my back on my father and following Warner's path back to the bakery.

Yazi effortlessly fell into step beside me.

Catching a break between the slow-moving cars circling the block for parking, I jaywalked across West Broadway. Then I cut north along Balaclava until I hit the sidewalks of West Sixth Avenue, where the traffic was almost nonexistent. The street was lined with refurbished Craftsman-style and Cape Cod-inspired family homes, as was the norm for the area. Most of the houses in Kitsilano had been renovated and redesigned into duplexes and triplexes in an attempt to combat the ever-rising price of real estate in Vancouver. The bid for density wasn't really working, though. Gran's house on the water in Point Grey was considered a mansion these days and was worth an ungodly amount of money.

Turning east, I wrapped my cashmere hoodie tightly around me, stuffed my chilled hands in the pockets, and tucked my chin into my scarf against the cold.

The warrior didn't leave my side, and neither did his muted but still potent spicy dark-chocolate magic. No matter how much dim sum I ate, I still couldn't place the spice that imbued my father's power. My own magic must be similarly flavored, since all the shapeshifters I knew insisted that I smelled of Chinese food.

"It's not raining," Yazi mused. "Doesn't it always rain in Vancouver?"

I stopped in my tracks, rounding on him. "I will not discuss the weather with you!"

"I understand that you are mad —"

"I'm freaking livid. I see Warner maybe once a week, because all the other times, you have him off doing hell knows what —"

"There are territories to walk," Yazi said mildly. "If you —"

"No."

"No?"

"No. I will not unlock your sweet little girl's magic for her."

Yazi frowned as if he had no idea what I was talking about.

"And yeah, I get why you don't want Warner and me together."

"And why is that?"

"Because you think I'm not ... enough."

"Enough? Enough what?"

I clamped my mouth shut. The conversation was veering off in unexpected directions. I was actually managing to confuse myself in the process of venting.

I began walking toward the bakery again. Sections of the sidewalks were becoming slick as the afternoon cooled, and I wasn't wearing great shoes for long-distance urban walking.

We'd crossed Trafalgar, then Larch, before my father spoke again.

"I would have thought ..." he said, then corrected himself. "It was my understanding that the sentinel intended to propose ... with my blessing."

"He hasn't."

"Because you wouldn't accept him?"

"Listen, just because you slept with my mother once and accidentally made me, that doesn't make you my father."

"It most certainly does."

"Biologically, maybe."

"In every way."

"You can't be my dad if I won't let you."

"Watch me."

Jesus, it was like arguing with myself. Except with an Australian accent. "No. You don't get to choose the rabid koala —"

"This rabid koala is Shailaja?"

"Yes, and you don't get to choose her over me ..."

"When did I choose her over you?"

I stopped to face off with him. "You don't get to say you're my father, then play the 'I'm so busy I've forgotten carrying a crazy teenager out of a mountain and leaving my flesh and blood behind' card."

Yazi's frown deepened. "I asked you to come."

"You demanded —"

"Yes, when the portal was closing and I feared for your safety."

"You cradled her in your arms to protect her from me. You called her 'child.' "

Yazi tilted his head, genuinely perplexed. "I am not so old that the command of modern English eludes me. It was you I was speaking to. I called you 'child' and informed you that the treasure keeper couldn't hold the portal open for long. I picked up the rabid koala, as you appropriately call her, because it was the quickest means to remove her from the situation. Had you followed me through the portal, I would have had no concerns about you continuing to fight with her. If that was what you deemed necessary."

I stared at him. Then I shook my head. "She's crazy," I muttered.

"Yes," Yazi agreed.

"But you're still here to demand I return to the nexus, unlock her magic, and hunt down the last instrument of assassination."

"Request, yes. And as for the instrument, only if you wish to do so."

"I don't wish to do so … any of it."

Yazi glowered at me.

I glowered back at him.

He looked away.

Silence stretched between us, and even with the heat of my anger, I began to get cold.

"The sun sets early in this part of the world," he said.

And we were back to the weather. "Only at this time of year."

I started walking toward the bakery again. We were only a few blocks away, and I yearned to be back within its sweet, comforting aroma.

"I've never been anyone's father," Yazi said. "I alternate between wanting to let you achieve your destiny and wanting to shield you from it. Then I say nothing at all."

"I'm not going to unlock her magic."

"The healer believes that her magic being corrupted is what is making her ... rabid."

"Qiuniu is a soft touch."

"Is that why you haven't accepted Warner Jiaotuson? You have feelings for the healer?"

"Absolutely not."

"Good, because —"

"But I'll marry who I want to marry."

"Yes. Fine. But —"

"No."

"No?"

"Yes, no."

Yazi thought about my refusal while we turned north on Balsam toward West Fourth Avenue. "I could demand it. I could command it."

"Let's see how that works out for you."

"The disturbed fledgling creates an imbalance —"

"No."

"You are being childish and wasting everyone's time."

"Double freaking no, then."

Yazi rolled his shoulders, opened and closed his mouth ... and then stilled as if listening to something.

Right. Something more important was happening in the world. Something more important was always happening.

"Nice chat, daddy," I said, erecting a barrier of sarcasm before he could tell me he had to go.

"Jade …"

"Just go."

"All I'm asking is for you to do your best when requested."

"But my best will never be enough, will it? Shailaja ran circles around us last time we fought her off to keep her from seizing an instrument of assassination. And she wasn't anywhere near her full power."

"You have to trust your elders."

"Yeah? The same elders who didn't even know Shailaja or Warner still existed in some suspended form?"

"Information gets lost over hundreds of years. We adapt."

"It's one thing to adapt. To endure. Sure, I can do that as well. It's a completely different thing to barrel blindly into situations I have no hope of controlling."

Yazi reached out, gently tugging me to a stop a few feet from the dry cleaner's on the corner. Ahead of us, traffic moved slowly up and down West Fourth.

I reluctantly turned to face my father.

He brushed his fingers down my upper arm. Even through my cashmere hoodie, I could feel his dampened magic. I didn't want it to be comforting, but it was. The caress was also a gesture ripped off from my mother, Scarlett.

"Control is beyond any of us, Jade. You walked the earth for twenty-three years before I knew you existed."

"Yeah." I dropped my gaze to somewhere around his chest. The scarf he was wearing was frayed along one edge, as if he'd caught it on something, then pulled away without realizing the delicate cashmere had snagged.

He dropped his arm, sighing regretfully. "I must go."

I nodded.

"She cannot harm us, Jade," Yazi said. "She doesn't have the means to do so. And neither the treasure keeper nor I will allow any harm to befall you."

"The instruments."

"Which only you can wield."

"She'll figure out a way around that."

Yazi's gaze became distant again. He was listening to a voice I couldn't hear. A guardian was calling him, which was something they never did lightly. And I was the brat holding up the quashing of a demon rising or some other earth-shattering event that needed his attention.

"Go," I said again, but I was nicer about it this time.

He nodded. Then, without another word or admonishment, he disappeared around the corner faster than any human could run.

Pretty much oblivious to my surroundings — because I seriously had too many things to think about all at once — I slowly wandered the last block and a half to the bakery.

Chapter Two

I slipped into the bakery kitchen from the back alley entrance, avoiding West Fourth Avenue by routine. Then, caressing my pristinely clean, stainless steel workstation as I passed, I wandered into my tiny office, pushing the door mostly closed behind me so I could access the large, heavily warded safe that sat behind it.

After doing a bunch of research, I'd decided to replace the safe I'd had repaired after Warner cracked it like it had been overbaked meringue. The squat model now bolted to the concrete floor was about five feet tall and two-and-a-half feet wide. Its steel casing was layered with so many magical protection wards that I wasn't sure it could actually hold any more. Thankfully, though pure iron wasn't particularly receptive to magic under normal circumstances, the safe's steel alloy accepted my alchemist power readily.

I reached through the layers of warding and spun the five-digit combination code into the dial lock. It was old school, but electronics and magic didn't pair well.

The safe door was easily three inches thick. Completely excessive for a bakery, but quite possibly still not enough security for what it held. Namely, the dragonskin tattoo map that led to the third and final instrument of assassination. A map that supposedly only I — or another alchemist like me — could unlock and read. A tattoo that had once been inked onto the back of a guardian dragon by another alchemist — then had been skinned from that dragon after he'd passed on his mantle.

Pulou had inherited the map, along with the powers and responsibilities that came with being the treasure keeper of the guardians, about four hundred years ago. Then he'd handed the map over to me, a year and a half ago now. Which was crazy — both the time that had passed, and the freaking responsibility of collecting the only three known items that could kill a guardian dragon.

Though I'd opened the safe to tuck the betrothal rings into it, I was suddenly hesitant to part with them after retrieving them from my satchel. Adding rings to my necklace wasn't as easy as soldering trinkets together, not even with my second bedroom vacant and feeling more like the craft room it had once been. My mother had moved into Kandy's apartment while the werewolf was gone — to give me space. Or so she'd said once I figured out she'd been gone for more than a week. But after clapping eyes on my father wandering the streets of Vancouver, I wondered if there was more going on.

I snagged the map out of the safe and wandered with it over to my underutilized desk.

Dropping the strap of my satchel over the back of my desk chair, I sat down and contemplated the betrothal bands. As I rolled the rune-etched rings around in my hand, I could taste echoes of Warner's black-forest-cake magic within the residual traces of power in the gold and gems of the rings.

Once again, the significance of the gift was overwhelming. And I still wasn't sure about ... anything. I still felt solid in my decision to walk away from the nexus and the treasure keeper's tasks, which had made me feel used and unappreciated. But the conversation with my father made me feel childish and selfish rather than self-assured.

I opened the dragonskin map with my free hand, leaning across the desk and gazing at the incomprehensible pools of blue and green that made up the bulk of the tattoo. The blocks that I'd moved to create the centipede that had been one of the keys to the map had disappeared over a year ago, after I'd collected the second instrument of assassination.

The tattoo's flower-and-leaf motif still remained tangled across one side of the map. The white blooms that decorated almost-barren branches were reminiscent of cherry or apple blossoms, but they wouldn't simply be flowers from a fruit tree. As with the other items previously represented on the tattoo — the five-colored silk braids and the metallic centipedes — there had to be something deadly about the flowers and the light-green leaves. Or perhaps it was whatever they represented that was malicious. I just didn't know what that was yet.

What I did know, and had known for some time, was the process that would let me unlock the final map. I hadn't bothered to figure out where the map was trying to lead me, but I probably could have if I'd wanted to. Well, after I determined the first location. That was how the other maps had worked. Figure out the country, narrow it down by the nearest portal, then trigger the map.

I ran my fingers along the edges of the dragonskin. When Warner or any other dragon touched the map, lettering appeared along its top edge. 'Where dragons dare not tread.' But we'd figured out that warning wasn't necessarily true. Not if the dragon was a rabid koala accompanied by shadow demons of her own creation, for instance. Or not if the dragon was accompanied by an alchemist.

Forget the 'unlocking her magic' crap. The final instrument of assassination was what Shailaja really wanted from me. With the braids and the centipedes tucked safely away in Pulou's treasure trove, she needed me to collect the final weapon for her. How she expected to wield it, I had no idea. When I'd nicknamed her 'rabid koala,' I didn't know how well the name would fit or how unbalanced she really was.

Shailaja wanted to live forever, and she needed a guardian's magic in order to do so. How I could be the only one who understood that — just a cute-but-silly, ignorant, half-blood abomination of nature, according to certain guardian dragons — was beyond me. But maybe everyone else was just too powerful to see Shailaja as a threat.

Except that wasn't my problem anymore. It actually never had been. I just needed to keep reminding myself of that.

I leaned farther over the map, blowing on the cluster of blossoms tattooed along its top left edge. The flower petals fluttered as if stirred by an early-morning spring wind. Magic sparkled from the stamens in the center of each bloom, like pollen caught up in the breeze. That glittering pollen sprinkled down over the center of the tattoo.

Then the map shifted to reveal a vast land mass — specifically, a ridge of mountains denoted by black triangles of varying sizes, but with no blue bits to indicate lakes or nearby oceans. If this was a country, I couldn't distinguish it from any other landlocked country. At least nothing I recognized from Google Maps.

And I wasn't interested anyway. Was I?

I brushed the sparkling magic away from where it had settled over the triangles and the darker edges of the landmass. It scattered underneath my hand, tickling my dowser senses as it dissipated. The map shifted back to its default mottled blue-green aspect.

Sitting at my desk and playing with magic. That wasn't childish at all.

"Switzerland?" a reedy voice asked from the right front corner of my desk. "The Alps?"

I flinched, though I tried to suppress the reaction. No one magical snuck up on me these days. Ever.

Except Blossom.

I lifted my gaze to find the brownie hunkered down on my desk. Peering at the map with her large hands folded across her bent knees, she resembled an olive-skinned gargoyle, except less craggy.

I nodded, catching a hint of her lemon verbena magic. "I thought that too. The mountain formations look wrong, though."

Blossom nodded sagely, lifting her miniature-muffin-sized dark-brown eyes to mine. Then she deliberately lowered them to look questioningly at the betrothal bands.

"Warner said you found them for me," I said. "Thank you."

She narrowed her eyes at me, then straightened and ran her hands across the pink Cake in a Cup apron she wore as a dress. "I've been tidying the house in Gamla Stan for him," she said, playing with the ruffle on the edge of the apron. "I planted some of your favorite flowers there ... the chocolate ones."

"Cosmos? Do they survive year-round there?"

Blossom snorted, as if the idea that any flowers she planted wouldn't be perennial was preposterous.

She glanced at the rings a second time, then at the half-open safe door.

"Is something wrong?" I asked. "Something you want to tell me about the rings?"

She shook her head. "No. I see I have been hasty. I must go."

"Um ... okay."

Blossom disappeared before I could say goodbye.

The brownie was difficult to figure out. She mostly kept to herself, though she'd expanded her cleaning territory to include my apartment, then Kandy's/Scarlett's apartment, and then Gran's house, all without asking. Pearl had yet to actually catch Blossom in the act of cleaning, though.

I had figured out pretty quickly that the brownie preferred it when I left dirty dishes in the sink rather than running the dishwasher, and that she loved my lemon or lemon-frosted cupcakes best. But other than that, I didn't know where she lived or whether or not she had any family. It was difficult to chat with someone who could slip around me unnoticed.

And now something was going on with Blossom and the betrothal rings, but I was apparently too thick to figure it out.

I sighed. Then I rolled up the map and carefully placed the betrothal rings in their platinum box.

A gentle knock came on my mostly closed office door. Bryn, my alternate baker and full-time employee, poked her head through the gap.

"Jade? You available?"

"For you? Anytime."

Bryn pushed the door open a bit more, chuckling softly. Her straight dark hair fell over her eyes. She'd had it cut last week and the stylist had been a bit scissor happy, so now it wouldn't stay tucked back.

"It's for a customer actually. A new customer ... who's very ..." Bryn bit her lip, contemplating her next words.

Well, that was interesting. I'd never seen her at a loss before.

"She's just ... very, very."

"Okay, then." I laughed. "I'm either being entangled in some nefarious plot or about to win the lottery."

"It could go either way," Bryn said, perfectly straight-faced. Then, breaking into a grin, she turned and headed back through the bakery kitchen and into the storefront.

The double doors into the store swung shut behind her as I locked the map and the rings in the safe. I didn't spot any 'very' looking customers before they closed.

But when I stepped through those doors myself, Suanmi, the fire breather of the guardian nine, stood before the glass display case in the middle of my bakery storefront. She was gazing at the chalked list of cupcakes on the back wall.

Yes, Suanmi.

The fire breather.

In my bakery.

My knees went a little bit to jelly at the sight of her.

Her dark hair, which was usually pulled back in a severe-but-perfect bun, was braided at both temples, then joined into a single braid at the back of her head while the remainder of her unruly mane cascaded over her shoulders. She was wearing an utterly gorgeous, slim-fit cashmere cardigan in royal blue, which fell all the way to her ankles. The sweater was held closed by a single button over a deep-charcoal turtleneck and vintage black skinny jeans.

And ... her boots.

Suanmi scared the crap out of me, yet I was salivating over her knee-high black leather Louboutins, with their two-and-three-quarter-inch heels, industrial red soles, silver spikes across the toes, and thick silver chains at the back of the ankles. Yes. The fire breather had paired crazy expensive biker boots with cashmere.

And on top of the massive change in her costume? I couldn't taste a single drop of her magic. Not a single drop of the guardian power that had once thundered around me so intensely I feared it might crush me.

She had walked right through the bakery's blood wards and they hadn't even stirred.

All the hair rose on the back of my neck.

"I'll take one of everything chocolate," the fire breather said. Her French accent was a sultry melody. "And a triple espresso."

"Um ... to go?" Todd, my part-timer and espresso wizard, was staring at Suanmi like she was ... well, very. Very, very.

"Non," she said in French. Then she turned dismissively from the counter to survey the tables by the front windows.

Oh, God. She was looking for a seat.

Slipping in behind Bryn as she was serving the next customer in line, I whispered fiercely in Todd's ear, "Get one of the silver platters we use for bridal showers."

"What?" he mumbled. He was still staring at Suanmi, blinking at her through his horn-rimmed glasses as if he wasn't sure she was real.

I bumped him with my shoulder. "And make that the best freaking espresso you've ever brewed."

"Right. Cool."

Todd crossed to his skookum espresso machine and began sorting through frothing pitchers, grinders, filters, and ... well actually, I had no real idea what the equipment was or how it all worked. We only served fancy coffees at Cake in a Cup because of Todd — and even then, only while he or Tima, my other part-timer, were on shift. But Bryn and I could make a fierce hot chocolate.

Suanmi settled onto a stool at one of the high round bistro tables by the middle window. She reached up and brushed her fingers over the trinkets hanging beside her. With her outfit cutting at least ten years off the appearance of the forty-five-year-old woman she usually pretended to be, the fire breather stuck out among my Lululemon-clad clientele like ... well ... like one of the most powerful Adepts in the world had wandered into a bakery on their day off.

Yeah, the guardian of Western Europe was slumming.

I combed my fingers through my hair, then tugged down the exposed edge of the tank top I layered underneath my long-sleeved T-shirts in the cooler months. My brand new cashmere-and-jean outfit looked like grubby rags next to what the fire breather was wearing.

Thus smoothed, I crossed out from behind the counter to greet Suanmi. Since I was certain that the summons and Shailaja were beneath the guardian's notice, I racked my mind for whatever transgression I'd committed that was so atrocious that the fire breather had felt compelled to come after me, hoping with each step I took that I wasn't about to be burned to a crisp in my own place of business.

I stopped a couple of feet away from her table. Then, as she turned her golden-flecked hazel eyes on me, I took a half-step closer. I nodded in her direction, casting my gaze onto her folded hands on the table and her prettily French-manicured nails. I couldn't exactly bow while surrounded by customers in my freaking bakery, now could I?

Suanmi lifted a hand, casually gesturing toward the empty stool across from her.

Jesus, she wanted to chat.

Give me spells and sorcerers and demons from hell. Those, I could handle. But cupcakes and coffee with the fire breather? Not so much.

I sat, woodenly perching on the edge of the stool so my feet remained planted firmly on the ground.

The corners of Suanmi's red-glossed lips lifted in a light sneer.

Todd appeared beside the table, first sliding the triple espresso in front of the guardian, then following up with a silver platter packed with cupcakes. 'Everything chocolate' was practically one of each item on the Cake in a Cup menu.

"Hot chocolate, Jade?" Todd asked.

"No. Thank you."

"No?" Todd seemed exceedingly puzzled. And he was right to be so, because that might have been the first time I'd ever refused chocolate in my life.

"Please, indulge," Suanmi said.

I swallowed and nodded to Todd. Frowning, he looked back and forth between us, then returned to his machine.

"Guardian," I said. "Your presence is a blessing —"

"Oui, oui," Suanmi said dismissively. "No one expects formalities from you, alchemist."

Lovely.

"The cupcakes?" Suanmi asked. "What is your favorite?"

"Um ..." Oh, God. Why did I name my freaking cupcakes so freaking provocatively?

"You do not know your own favorite?"

"*Lust in a Cup.*" I blurted the name so loudly that I had to smile away the glances from customers at the neighboring tables. I modulated my tone as I gestured toward a cupcake on the edge of the platter. "Dark-chocolate cake with dark-chocolate cream-cheese icing."

"Hmm." Suanmi carefully lifted the cupcake, then held it aloft as if it were a glass of fine red wine.

Todd returned with side plates and napkins, along with a sixteen-ounce hot chocolate for me. The napkins were printed with my bright-pink Cake in a Cup logo, the white version of which embossed my pink mug. With the platter of cupcakes at its center, there was barely room for the extra plates on the table.

"Good first choice," Todd said to Suanmi. "Personally, *Buzz in a Cup* is my favorite."

The fire breather turned her elegant sneer on him. He fled.

I grabbed the hot chocolate and took a swig, burning my tongue but not caring one bit as the thick, bittersweet ganache hit my tummy and grounded me.

Suanmi took a bite of the *Lust.* She tilted her head to the side contemplatively while chewing, nary a speck of cake or icing on her red lips.

"Delightful." She placed the cupcake down on her plate, then looked at me expectantly. "And another?"

"Ah ..." My mind was a complete blank. I stared at the dozen or so cupcakes in front of me for inspiration.

"Perhaps Drake's favorite?"

I lifted my gaze to meet the fire breather's. Was Drake why she was here?

"He likes them all."

Suanmi laughed. Her amusement sounded like sweet chimes.

My heart rate picked up. I took another swig of hot chocolate to calm down. If Suanmi was going to reprimand me, she would have done so already. All of this was ... polite conversation. Terrifying but polite conversation.

The fire breather wanted something from me.

"*Thrill*," I said. "Drake is partial to *Thrill in a Cup*." I gestured toward the mocha-buttercream-frosted white cake at the center of the silver platter.

Suanmi snorted softly as she retrieved the cupcake. "Not surprising."

I laughed.

Yes, I let my guard down for one second, laughing as if I were friends with the fire breather and commiserating about Drake, her fifteen-year-old lovely terror of a ward.

"The heretic ..." — Suanmi spoke between delicate bites of the *Thrill in a Cup* and tiny sips of her triple shot — "... can remove the tie that binds the sentinel to the instruments of assassination."

I stopped chuckling. Actually, my brain froze.

Suanmi waved her free hand. "Shailaja," she said, supplying the name as if it was utterly beneath her to utter it. "Daughter of Pulou-who-was. She offers you this trade."

"Shailaja can remove the sentinel magic?"

"So she says."

"To you?"

Suanmi raised an eyebrow at me. She switched out nibbling on the *Thrill in a Cup* for the *Lust in a Cup* without breaking her gaze from mine. "I have not spoken with her directly."

"You're no one's messenger."

Suanmi crooked her lips into a smile. "Observant, warrior's daughter."

"She lies."

Suanmi shrugged, somehow making the casual gesture look epically classy. "Make the removal a condition of your cooperation. Prior to unknotting whatever contains the fledgling's full potential."

I'd already 'unknotted' the rabid koala's magic once, under extreme duress, by shifting the power contained within my necklace into her. Apparently, she needed the help of an alchemist to do so, which unfortunately made me uniquely qualified.

"Why would you want to help Shailaja?"

"I don't."

"Why would you want to help me?"

"I don't."

"Well, consider me confused."

"Guarding the fledgling has become an increasing pain. Release her magic, and she becomes useful again … or not. Either way, she'll be out of the nexus."

"The sentinel magic … couldn't Pulou remove it if Warner wanted it removed?"

Suanmi shifted her focus to the cupcakes. Her plate was empty. She'd consumed every last crumb. "Another?" she asked.

I swallowed past whatever emotion was clogging up my throat. Was I feeling fear? Frustration? Hope? Confusion?

"Did you prefer the *Thrill* or the *Lust*?" I asked.

"Both were lovely," Suanmi said, slipping into a low, soft purr.

My belly squirmed. The fire breather was … buttering me up. And every hint of that was more terrifying than her condemnation ever could have been.

"*Rapture in a Cup,* then." I fished the cupcake out of the dozen on the platter. Carefully touching only the paper, I lowered the offering onto Suanmi's plate. "A swirl of chocolate and lemon cake topped with chocolate-cream-cheese frosting."

I locked my gaze to the fire breather's, allowing a slow, teasing smile to spread across my face.

Two could play at this game.

I withdrew my hand, but Suanmi caught it before I'd moved more than a couple of inches. She ran her finger across the outer edge of my palm, then let me go.

She lifted her hand. A streak of chocolate frosting marred one creamy fingertip. Maintaining steady eye contact with me, she sucked the icing off her finger.

A wave of dizziness crashed over me, along with a realization.

It was all for me.

The outfit, the boots, the platter of chocolate cupcakes ... and the offer. An offer that would free Warner from Shailaja.

I was being seduced by the fire breather.

No. Correction.

I had been seduced.

My heart thumped once.

Suanmi's perfectly red lips twisted into a smile.

My heart thumped a second time. Fear rolled in my belly.

And I knew. I knew that whatever the fire breather wanted, she got. She didn't have even an ounce of the charm my mother wielded so expertly, but she called to the deep, dark recesses of my heart. If she smoothed back the black silk sheets that I was sure adorned her bed, then crooked her finger at me, I'd climb in ... and it wasn't about sex. It was about possession and control — all enforced by the most destructive element on earth. Fire.

"Water," I blurted.

Suanmi frowned. "Quoi?"

I shook my head. Water trumped fire. The thought cleared my mind enough for me to continue the conversation.

"Who says no to you?" I whispered, my voice catching in my throat even as I spoke the words.

Suanmi laughed. It was a low, husky sound, full of confidence and fury — and nothing like the chiming chuckle I'd heard from her only moments before. A wicked grin spread across her face, and for a moment, I swore I could see fire dancing in her hazel eyes. Her guardian magic rolled up and around her, tasting of chocolate-cream-filled eclairs and toasted hazelnuts, with a fiery finish of sooty whiskey that burned its way down my throat.

The bakery wards reacted instantly, pressing tightly around us.

The fire breather gasped, delighted.

Then the taste of chocolate and hazelnut-whiskey truffles was gone. Just like that. Her control was epically terrifying.

The wards retreated, settling back down into the walls and floor.

"Impressive, alchemist," Suanmi whispered.

I nodded, my mouth too dry to speak. I took a gigantic swig of my hot chocolate.

The fire breather returned her attention to her cupcakes and espresso.

"You didn't answer my question," I eventually said. "Can Pulou remove the sentinel magic?"

Suanmi shrugged a single shoulder, prettily. "Knowledge is sometimes lost."

"So I hear."

"As such, doing so is beyond Pulou. But if you insist upon it as a condition of your service, the feeble fledgling will be forced to teach the treasure keeper the spell that might break Warner's bond to the instruments of assassination. In order to keep her end of the bargain."

"If Warner agrees to any of it."

Suanmi lifted her head, shifting her gaze over my shoulder.

I pivoted on my stool, tasting Warner's magic a second before he stepped through into the storefront from the kitchen.

As he caught sight of Suanmi and me, he paused. Then he leaned back into the doorway with his arms crossed, reverting to intimidating sentinel mode.

Well, that wasn't going to be great for business.

"Do you think he will say no to you, alchemist?" Suanmi murmured. "With all your sweet treats and tasty magic?"

I bristled, wanting to insist that I possessed finer qualities, but Suanmi leaned closer as if about to whisper a secret.

"He crossed through my territory for you, Jade. To check on the well-being of a … vampire." She enunciated the word 'vampire' in the exact way someone else might sneer 'demon scum.'

I changed the subject. "The far seer has taken to calling me 'dragon slayer.' Maybe it's not such a good idea for me to be anywhere near the nexus."

Suanmi waved her hand dismissively. "The far seer has no relative sense of time. And even he would admit that the future is fluid. He could be speaking of hundreds of years from now."

"Hundreds of years?"

"You're the warrior's daughter. Your magic will burn bright until it consumes you or flares out."

"That's comforting."

"You mistake me, alchemist. We aren't friends. You are a means to an end. And, unfortunately, Drake has a soft spot for you … and Warner. You are dragons of an age."

"And Shailaja isn't?"

"No," Suanmi said.

And with that single-word answer, I felt as if I'd been dismissed.

The fire breather ate the last half of her cupcake in silence, pausing only for sips of her espresso. Then she lifted her gaze to Warner a second time.

"I'll leave you with this thought. An exchange, if you will."

Oh, Jesus. I was being entered into some bargain with the fire breather, and I had no idea how to refuse her … or if I even wanted to refuse her.

"Adaptation," she said. "This is the key to living a long life. Take the sentinel. He wakes five hundred years in the future. Does he cling to old beliefs and rhythms? No. He forms an attachment with you, trains with Drake, and walks through this world with interest. He anchors himself in the now. Shailaja, as far as I've bothered to figure out, doesn't. The inert cannot survive."

Yeah, I had no idea what to do with that info except smile and nod.

Lifting her espresso for a final sip before she rose, the fire breather gestured to the remaining cupcakes on the platter. "I'll take these to go."

Sliding gracefully away from the table, she crossed toward the entrance of the bakery. "But first, I would walk. It's been centuries since I've been in this part of the world."

I'd pivoted in my chair with her exit, so that I was forced to pivot back in order to watch her walk past the front window. Moving west along West Fourth Avenue, Suanmi slipped on a pair of animal-print, butterfly-shaped Dolce & Gabbana sunglasses.

Thoughts ... ideas ... concerns rolled around in my overly full head. Honestly, I hated thinking so much. I hated my need to dissect every word and gesture, hoping to find some kernel ... of what? Wisdom? I wouldn't recognize wisdom if I did find it. Stability?

Warner stepped up beside my chair. I tilted my head back until I could meet his gaze.

"Jade?" he asked, concerned.

I nodded. "I'm overreacting." My voice sounded oddly detached.

"I doubt that." Warner slipped away, brushing his fingers across my hand as he passed. Then, stepping out the door, he followed the fire breather down the sidewalk.

I stood, moving woodenly through the process of bussing the table and boxing Suanmi's remaining cupcakes.

I'd been seduced by the guardian of Western Europe. It was the oddest feeling, but the acknowledgment of it didn't change anything.

She was right.

I wanted the link between Warner and Shailaja severed. I needed it severed, though that need was utterly selfish and probably rash. Exactly the emotions and actions I'd been so painstakingly avoiding for the past year.

But still, the idea resonated deeply ... enough so that it had penetrated the darkness clouding my heart. Darkness born from the loss of my sister. Darkness fostered by the fear of my capacity for violence and retribution. Darkness that kept Warner confined and hemmed into a tiny portion of my affections.

It was just an idea ... a pinhole of light ... but I pushed away everything else that had been disturbing about Suanmi's visit, and I clung to that glimmer of possibility.

Maybe ... just maybe ... there could be a happy ending for Warner and me. Or, rather, a happy beginning ...

Chapter Three

bsolutely not!" Warner bellowed. "Even if Shailaja could do it. It's just another power bid of some kind. Why would she relinquish any hold she thinks she has? You should know by now —"

"Yeah, and that's what this always comes back to," I said cuttingly. "Me being stupid."

We'd been standing in my apartment fighting over Shailaja — again — for the last ten minutes. Warner had been gone just long enough for me to get myself all worked up … the kind of riled I got when I knew I was about to get all emotional and irrational and demanding but couldn't see any other way forward.

"How could you have possibly gotten that out of what I just said?" Warner glared across the granite kitchen island at me. "Jesus, Jade. You know I don't —"

"Don't say 'Jesus' like that. You only say 'Jesus' like that because I say 'Jesus' like that. You wouldn't have said it five hundred years ago."

"Christianity was around when I was —"

"And now we're back to me being stupid."

Warner threw his hands up in the air, then stepped into the living room and began pacing around my worn leather couch. "I don't even know what we're fighting about anymore."

I pressed my palms to the cool granite of the counter, hoping to calm myself. But then I blurted out the next thought whirling around in my head instead. "You're only with me because I anchor you!"

Warner stopped pacing to stare at me, completely confused.

And in that pause, I heard myself ... my mental switchbacks and my muddling of issues. So I made a concerted effort to get us back on track. "The fire breather wouldn't back the rabid koala if —"

"And now you take advice from your sworn enemy."

" 'Sworn enemy' is a little harsh. I thought it was more like we shared a mutual loathing." I tried to laugh, but my terrible attempt at a joke fell flat. I threaded my fingers through the wedding rings on my necklace, seeking a bit of grounding. Then I tried to be reasonable ... again.

"Okay, fine," I said. "I get that this whole thing is off."

"Off is an understatement."

"Can you try to not be an asshole?"

"Obviously not, because I wasn't aware that defending my life, my position, and my responsibility made me one."

I clamped my mouth shut. Then I decided to try a different tactic. "Shailaja can manipulate you through the sentinel spells." And by 'manipulate' I meant making me think she'd killed Warner by magically shoving him back into his sentinel stasis mode. Which was yet another thing Warner and I avoided talking about.

"And knowing that, you want me to allow her to perform more magic on me?"

"No. Suanmi says the treasure keeper can remove the spell."

"Then why hasn't he approached me with the offer?"

"He doesn't know yet. Shailaja needs to show him how to do it. Suanmi suggested bargaining —"

"With my life." Warner's voice was suddenly low and deadly.

"It ... I ... it didn't feel that way. And once he knows how, perhaps Pulou could adapt the sentinel magic and make it his own. Alter it somehow, so Shailaja can't access it."

"I chose to become the sentinel of the instruments of assassination over four hundred and fifty years ago. I didn't take on that duty lightly. Though she cannot wield the instruments, Shailaja is a proven threat —"

"I know."

"Let me finish."

I nodded, loosening my grip on my necklace and forcing myself to focus on Warner rather than my own jumbled thoughts.

"I might have followed in my mother's footsteps. I might have taken on the mantle of Jiaotu to become guardian of Northern Europe. I wondered ... for many years ... I wondered if that was the only reason she'd had me. It was insecure of me, really. She was far too young to even be thinking of relinquishing her guardianship. But I might have walked in the treasure keeper's footsteps. Before any of that could come about, Pulou approached me with the sentinel commission. He was gravely concerned, and my magic, specifically my ability to adapt, made me the best candidate among the dragons. My mother was ... proud."

Warner paused. I wasn't sure if he was thinking or upset. I stayed silent either way.

"This is who I am," he said finally. "I know no other way to be."

I nodded. Then I pulled the platinum box containing the betrothal rings from my satchel. I'd retrieved it from the safe on my way up to the apartment, knowing Warner would join me there once Suanmi left the city. My hand was shaking as I placed it on the counter between us.

Warner stared at the box, then looked at me.

"You've mistaken me, Jade," he whispered tensely. "I know you're not ready —"

"It's not that I'm not ready. It's that you're not available."

"You'll leave me if I don't submit?"

"No. Never," I cried. "But I can't accept the responsibility of the gift. Even if you didn't mean it as a proposal." The tears I'd been trying to contain spilled over my cheeks, and I swiped them away viciously. I didn't want to appear weak in front of Warner, not now, not with this on the line. "I don't want you to be anyone different. I just can't ... I can't ... just ... give me a second, okay?"

Warner nodded stiffly.

I fled the kitchen, making a beeline back through the apartment and ducking into my bathroom for Kleenex. I took a fistful from the decorative box on the back of the toilet, wiped my face, and blew my nose.

After a few calming breaths, I stepped back into the hall. Then I ducked back quickly, deciding that I should bring the box of tissues with me.

But as I turned back to the bathroom, I glanced through the open doorway into my bedroom. I saw an oddly dark spot there, standing out on the periwinkle-blue bedding, just below the pillow.

I stepped into the bedroom, crossing toward the perfectly made queen-sized bed tucked against the far wall. The room tasted of Blossom's lemon verbena magic, which wasn't unusual. But the chocolate cosmos half-tucked underneath my pillow was completely out of place and season.

I picked up the flower. Its delicate petals were like dark-brown velvet. I inhaled its scent deeply. Even plucked and abandoned on my bed, it still smelled of vanilla and chocolate. In the summer, I grew cosmos in my window boxes along with a few strawberry plants, but I had no idea what a single flower was doing on my bed in January.

"I'll do it."

A sharp ache shot through my chest. I slowly turned toward the hall.

Warner was leaning in the doorway to the bedroom. His expression was troubled as he contemplated the spotless hardwood floor somewhere around my feet.

"No," I said before I'd even made the decision to blow my own argument to hell. "I could never … force you to do …" And then I was crying like an idiot again. I was trying to be so adult, so rational. And I was failing miserably.

Warner lifted his blue-green eyes to meet my gaze. "You know what the only good thing about being the sentinel of the instruments of assassination was? The only good thing to come from five hundred years of service, whether I was awake for it or not?"

I wiped the tears from my cheeks, attempting once again to stem the flow. "What?"

"You, Jade Godfrey. You."

I started blubbering again. "You don't know what it was like, thinking she'd killed you. And that was before … before this …" Unable to supply any additional words, I swept my hand to indicate the bedroom. My disjointed movement cost me my hold on the chocolate cosmos, and I had to scramble to catch the flower before it hit the ground.

"Blossom had hundreds of flowers in here," Warner said. "Strewn all across the bed. I'd spoken to her about the possibility of planting some for you at the townhouse. She must have anticipated my giving you my parents' betrothal rings today. And interpreted it to mean ..." He trailed off, then stepped forward to brush his fingers over the chocolate cosmos carefully cradled in the palm of my hand.

"Were ... are the rings a proposal, then?"

"There was a moment, that morning when you brought me back, that I didn't recognize you."

"I know."

"I never want that to happen again. The rings are a promise. A promise to never leave if it's in my power to stay. So I'll consent to having the sentinel magic that ties me to the instruments and the map severed. For you. For me."

I lifted my arms. Warner swept me off my feet before I finished the movement.

I wrapped myself around his neck, clinging to and kissing him fiercely. He always felt indestructible to me in our most intimate moments. As if nothing could knock him off his feet. As if he was steady as a mountain in the midst of a storm. Even if that metaphor cast me as the storm. And he would actually be indestructible once he was freed from the sentinel spell. Shailaja could never send him away again.

Then he'd be bound only to whatever he chose to be bound to. And after the magic tying him to the instruments and the map was removed, I hoped like hell it was me he wanted to be with. By choice. Not just because I had been tasked to collect the instruments, or that my magic was 'tasty' as Suanmi had suggested.

Warner slipped his hands through my hoodie and underneath my T-shirt-and-tank-top combo, drawing my attention firmly into the present and away from any sense of what-might-be.

I groaned as his magic followed in the wake of his touch. I pressed my tongue to his, then sucked at the tip lightly before releasing it. I inhaled all of his chocolate goodness, allowing his sweet cherry and creamy whipped cream to fill every empty bit of me.

He slipped his thumbs underneath the edge of my bra just as I attempted to pull his sweater off over his head. We ended up laughing through a tangle of clothing and limbs and drying tears.

Then our touch became heated, intense, as more of our skin was exposed. I adored the way he held me — firmly, without fear that I'd bruise or break.

He bowed over my breasts, my nipples hardening before he even made contact. Then he slipped his hand between my legs, drawing a low moan from me. I clung to his shoulders, arching back as pleasure lapped up and over me from my core.

"Warner ..." I whispered.

"I've got you, Jade."

"I know."

I leaned down, breaking his concentration on my breasts, and wrapped my hand around the length of him. He was a warm, enticing combination of silky skin and firm flesh. It was his turn to groan.

"Now I've got you ..." I snagged his earlobe with my teeth.

He laughed, sounding a little too in control. So I increased the speed and pressure of my stroke.

Warner picked me up and threw me onto the bed. I fell back willingly, laughing breathlessly. He wrapped his hand around my ankles, dragging me closer to him at the edge.

Then he knelt down and applied his tongue to where his fingers had just been dancing.

Ah. Well, that was one way to divert my attention.

I groaned. "Warner ..."

He gathered my legs closer together, narrowing his available space but increasing my pleasure. Warmth spread from between my thighs, up across my pelvis and lower belly.

I wanted to beg him to stop teasing and simply mount me. I wanted him deep inside me, but I knew he wanted to pleasure me first.

He slipped his hand upward, caressing my belly to start, then reaching higher to pinch my nipple between his fingers.

I cried out, convulsing with an almost painful pleasure.

He didn't stop.

Instead, he slid his free hand underneath my ass, lifting me a few inches off the bed while he increased the rate of his tongue's ministrations and rolled my nipple between his fingers.

I orgasmed, writhing as the pleasure crashed over me, fiercely and almost without warning.

Warner rose up over me, replacing his tongue with his fingers. His touch was soft, teasing the last few convulsions from me.

"One," he whispered, kneeing my legs apart and slipping into my wetness.

I cried out again, clinging to him from the intensity of being entered so quickly after climaxing.

He slowly withdrew, careful and sweet. Then he swiftly slipped back inside me.

"Jade ..." he whispered into my hair.

I gasped and clung to him, seemingly incapable of doing anything else in the moment.

"Jade," he whispered into my neck.

I turned my head toward him, pressing my lips behind his ear. Then I reached down to grab his ass, pulling him tighter and deeper within me.

"Jade." Warner kissed me softly, reaching his own end with a few more strokes and a quiet groan.

He collapsed over me.

"One," I said smugly.

He laughed, rolling off me. His delicious magic bounced against the blood wards that coated the walls all around us, then reverberated back. I almost orgasmed a second time as that tasty power flowed over and around me.

My nipples tightened even further. I lifted myself half off the bed, throwing my leg over Warner. I straddled him with my hands splayed across his chest. I could feel his heart pounding.

Leaning over to deliberately brush my nipples against his chest, I slowly kissed my way along the simple lines of the black dragon tattoo etched across his collarbone and over his shoulder.

I bit his neck lightly. He groaned, bucking underneath me.

"Seconds?" I asked teasingly.

Cocooned in a tangle of cotton sheets and Warner's warm body, I drifted in the aftermath of our intense lovemaking session. I never felt quite as relaxed as I did after three orgasms. Of course, coming three times in one evening hadn't been a habitual thing for me. Not until Warner.

"You know she left that flower on purpose," Warner murmured.

"Blossom?"

"Yes."

"Smart."

"Yeah. You'll leave her extra cupcakes?"

"I'll bake a batch just for her. I'm pretty sure her favorite is *Delight in a Cup.*"

"Lemon buttercream?" Warner smacked his lips, sleepily appreciative.

I laughed quietly. "And white cake."

"Fluffy ... sweet ... moist cake." Warner grunted his approval. Then his arm became heavy across my back as he drifted off to sleep.

I curled around him, allowing myself a moment of bliss. Tomorrow, I'd have to face Shailaja. But if that meant being able to break the weird bond between her and Warner, then I was cool with it.

Plus, if it came down to it, I knew I had no problem skewering her. Even she knew my jade knife was a serious threat.

As sleepy as I was, a slow, wicked smile spread across my face.

Yeah, I was the big bad she'd fled from in Peru.

Okay ... so maybe I had gotten a little bored over the past year.

Cupcakes and dim sum kept a girl content for only so long. Maybe it was time to get my hands just a little bit dirty.

While Warner slept through the early-morning hours, I slipped into the second bedroom and added the betrothal rings to my necklace. The room was still decorated in piles of silk and goose down, as it had been when Scarlett was living in the apartment full time. It felt empty, though.

I hadn't casually made trinkets for a long time. Ever since I discovered they could be used for dark magic ... or that they were magic at all. But I missed the process of stringing the unusual items I'd collected for years onto lengths of silver chain, then melding tiny bits of residual magic together to make something pretty. Something pretty and potentially deadly.

Now, the bits of magical things — knickknacks, polished jade, and chipped figurines — lining the shelves gathered dust while I spent my days at the bakery and every available evening with Warner. Well, they would have gathered dust if Blossom hadn't seemingly claimed every personal space owned by a Godfrey as her territory.

I settled at the desk underneath the window. The blinds were open, and the lights of West Vancouver and North Vancouver along the North Shore Mountains beckoned from across the inlet. The cloudless sky was almost as dark as the craggy, snowcapped peaks.

I freed the betrothal rings from their platinum cage. Untwining the necklace, I lifted it off over my head and stretched out its full length on the dark, worn wood of the desk. Years ago, it had taken me eight months to pay installments on the thick-linked gold chain from a pawnshop downtown. It hadn't come with a drop of magic. Nor had I understood then how over the course of every day I wore it and every wedding-ring charm I added to it, I was creating something so powerful.

Some deep part of me believed that magic needed a purpose — even the residual magic unintentionally left behind by a powerful Adept. For anyone else, the rune-marked betrothal rings were simply beautiful gold bands. In my hands, they would become something more.

Maybe that was egotistical, but I didn't think so. It was an acknowledgment. A celebration of magical energy once trapped and now released.

Adding the rings to my necklace was more about magic and strength than soldering or melting points or casting metal. But it still took me a couple of hours. I wanted to shift a few of the wedding bands around so that I could keep the betrothal rings together. I wanted them to rest over my heart when I wore the necklace wound twice.

As I worked, dragon magic danced beneath my fingers. Tiny hints of witch and sorcerer and vampire magic rose up to tickle my taste buds. Traces of power kissed my skin as I smoothed and coaxed the gold necklace and the gem-crusted rings into a cohesive whole.

I was happy.

Settled. Content. Unified within.

I missed creating in this fashion. Baking cupcakes every day was satisfying. I felt productive and valued in my role as a baker and small-business owner. But my alchemist magic worked on another level. It brought a lightness to my very being.

I missed creating magical items. Maybe I'd even forgotten who I was in some fundamental way. Any alchemy I'd performed in the last two years — most of it under duress — had been rushed and purposeful. Even when adding the wedding rings Kett had given me to my necklace, I hadn't immersed myself in the process. I had only been trying to quickly repair the damage Shailaja had done while draining the necklace's power.

Something had changed since then.

I had changed.

Maybe it was the glimmer of hope that Suanmi's strange and terrifying visit had triggered. Maybe it was that I could almost see the future for the first time since Sienna left me. Or, rather, that I knew I was close to getting a glimpse of that future. Right after I got Warner away from Shailaja.

I put the finishing touches on my necklace. The taste of residual dragon magic abated.

I lifted the chain over my head and twined it twice around my neck. The newly added energy flowed through it, topping up its magical reservoir and strengthening the protection the necklace could provide if I called upon it.

Shailaja had drained the chain a year ago. But thanks to Kett and Warner — and to dancing in an Adept club in San Francisco — it felt more powerful than ever.

I would never voluntarily hand my necklace over to anyone. Never again. And if they did manage to get it off me? They'd have to kill me to keep it.

The pool of people who could actually inflict bodily harm on me was getting rather shallow. Except for the one I was about to add to the list, unfortunately. But if the warrior said he had Shailaja under control ... well ... who was I to question one of the nine most powerful people in the world?

Especially because all I wanted to do was snuggle back into bed with my hunky boyfriend for a final hour of sleep before my alarm went off.

Priorities.

It was good to keep them straight ... if only minute by minute.

The chocolate cosmos and a handwritten note were resting on the pillow where Warner's head had been cushioned. I reached out and brushed my fingers across the slightly bruised petals. I wondered where it had fallen during our lovemaking.

And the fact that Warner had retrieved it and placed it so I'd see it when I woke?

Well, let's just say I was learning that some things were better than chocolate.

Blasphemy, I know.

The note read:

I've gone to chat with the treasure keeper.
See you there. — W.

I played with the rough edges of the paper, curling it in my fingers as I contemplated the note. Warner had fished what appeared to be a brown bank envelope out of the recycling bin, then had written on one torn half of the back. His black-inked scrawl was thick and barely discernible.

I wondered how he was feeling about having the sentinel spell removed. Ready to have that part of his life over with, presumably, based on the fact that my bed was empty.

My alarm went off.

Time to bake.

Then later, I'd help my sworn enemy become even more powerful.

Life was weird like that.

Chapter Four

After my shift in the bakery, I showered, scrunched my hair until it was a halo of golden curls, and brushed on some makeup. But I hesitated as I dug my dragon leathers out of the closet. And not because I was afraid they wouldn't fit. I'd actually been training. Yes, voluntarily. Mixed martial arts, mostly. I went to three different studios — I was cheating on my trainers — to cover my unnatural endurance. And I only really tested my strength and my sword skills when Warner and I sparred in Gran's garage.

No. I hesitated over what to wear because I wanted to look like I didn't give a crap.

I tossed the leathers aside, opting for an older pair of skinny-leg Seven jeans, a black tank top, and knee-high black leather boots — my classic Cece Fluevogs. I added my wildly appropriate 'Attempted Murder' T-shirt to the ensemble, even though a section of the hem was loose.

Then I smirked at myself in the full-length mirror.

The entire outfit was a disdainful middle finger.

Except the boots. They just rocked. I wasn't about to compromise my footwear — not for fashion, or utility, or deadly grudges.

I stopped at the safe to shove the dragonskin map into my satchel, reminding myself I had every intention of giving it back to the treasure keeper when whatever fiasco I was about to participate in was done. Then I hightailed it out of my office.

Crossing through the pantry and down into the bakery basement, I didn't bother with the overhead light. I jogged down the wooden steps, quickly crossing the dirt floor to stand before the brick and concrete of the east wall. Warner used the portal weekly, but I hadn't been in the basement for over a year.

Calling up the golden magic of the portal was like accepting a bear hug from a long-lost beloved friend.

I crossed through the buoyant magic. One moment, I was standing on the dirt floor of the basement. The next, I was stepping onto a white marble floor. As the portal snapped shut behind me, my senses were momentarily scrambled by the intense amount of utter power that imbued the curved walls, the nine intricately carved doors, and the gold-leafed pillars that marked the center of the dragon nexus.

Chi Wen, the guardian of Asia, wandered through one of the two archways that led to the residences. The ancient far seer was wearing a ridiculously large green T-shirt. It was printed with an image of three leering cartoon bananas, along with the rhetorical question *Eating Out?* Paired with his white robes, gold sandals, and neatly combed white hair, the ensemble was just ... wrong.

I was absolutely certain the T-shirt was a gift from my green-haired BFF. The werewolf had a weird obsession with kinky fruit T-shirts. I never got any of the jokes ... if they were jokes at all.

The far seer didn't appear to notice me as he crossed toward the ornate door that led to his territories in Asia. The oriental-inspired etchings appeared to be coated with gold paint, but I had always suspected that the door itself was solid gold.

"You are expected, dragon slayer." Chi Wen spoke in his heavily accented English without looking at me.

I grimaced, then quickly dipped my head and shoulders in a low bow. "Far seer," I said, intending to follow through with some other nicety. But as I raised my head, he was suddenly standing far too close to me, so that I ended up flinching away instead.

"When you request your audience, it is customary to bring a gift of magic." Chi Wen blinked up at me as if trying to focus his eyes. Then, as though he'd spotted what he'd been looking for, he grinned. "Balance must always be maintained."

"You … I …" I tried to make sense of what he was saying, then gave up. "I don't understand."

"When you visit the oracle in Washington state." He pronounced 'Washington' deliberately, as if it was a new word for him.

"I won't be requesting anything from Rochelle's mind … or magic. Ever."

Chi Wen's grin widened. "You are not all the oracle sees, warrior's daughter."

"Okay." I shuffled my feet.

"The green-haired werewolf gave me this T-shirt. But you don't like it."

"I … it seems a bit irreverent."

"Yes. I like that. She survived, but she is not happy about the circumstances. She blames me. The shirt is a punishment."

"Sorry? What circumstances?"

Chi Wen reached out and patted my forearm. Thankfully, the gesture wasn't accompanied by a blast of his seer magic. "We will have time to chat later. I will explain all."

Oh, God, no. That sounded like a terrible idea.

Chi Wen turned to shuffle back in the direction from which he'd just come.

"Um, far seer?" I called after him, though I was seriously glad his attention had shifted elsewhere. "I think you were just leaving ... before, I mean. Before I got here."

"Yes, yes," he said without looking back. "But now you are here."

I blinked and he was gone. Chi Wen was stronger and faster than he liked to appear. But he couldn't completely disguise his potent magic from me. At least not in the nexus.

I glanced around, realizing I had no idea where I was supposed to go. Not for the first time, I wished cellphones worked in the nexus. And that Warner actually carried one.

The guardians used the portal magic anchored to the nexus as a communication device. And while I was fairly certain at least one dragon had to be in the nexus in order to make a connection, I wasn't sure I could access the magic the same way. Other than calling the treasure keeper to me ... and I wasn't really interested in summoning anyone. I just wanted this over and done with.

So I could wait around for Warner. Or —

The summons! "Right," I said, annoyed at myself. Even though I could blame my current distraction on the far seer, I was dreadfully slow sometimes. "I have no idea where or what the chamber of the treasure keeper is."

I said it out loud, though I wasn't actually expecting a direct answer. But a blank door tiled in smooth, white metal to my far right blew open with a blast of glacial air. All the hair in my nose instantly froze.

"Jesus," I muttered, shoving my hands in my pockets and blinking rapidly to ease my suddenly dry eyes.

The chill abated. When no one immediately stepped through into the nexus, I slowly wandered toward the open door. The portal's magic glowed invitingly, but I didn't want to be in anyone's way if they were coming through. I glanced at the doors on either side. The one on the right led to South America. I knew that because I'd walked through it a year ago and ended up in the mountains of Peru. The door on the left was the door Chi Wen had been shuffling toward a moment before.

I had no idea where the portal standing open before me led. Obviously, I knew Pulou's territory was technically Antarctica, but I'd assumed that was just an honorary title. Because who wanted to go for a walk in a vast, frozen continent? Though … that might explain the treasure keeper's ever-present fur coat —

How much longer are you going to dither, Jade Godfrey? Pulou's British lilt sounded in my head, conveyed through the portal's power. He was amused.

Great. I loved entertaining guardians. Not.

"An idea of a destination might be nice," I muttered, stepping into the golden magic.

I passed through into a chamber that was almost identical to the nexus, except it appeared to have only one door. Well, one door that I could see. The endless, gravity-defying mountains of magical artifacts and treasures that spread out before me might have been obstructing or obscuring other exits.

I stumbled under the unexpected onslaught of magic emanating from the treasure trove. I was out of practice shielding my dowser senses. I never really needed to do so anywhere but in the nexus. But the chamber of the treasure keeper was every bit as intense.

Every type of magic I'd ever tasted bombarded me from all directions. With a single inhalation, I could taste the power inherent in witches, sorcerers, dragons, shapeshifters, and vampires. But all of that was intermingled with countless other sources for which I had no context or classification.

A massive concentration of blood magic and black magic gathered among the more benign items, making my stomach curl sourly. It made sense that such malicious power would be contained in the trove, though. The treasure keeper's primary function — after maintaining the portal system — was to hold and protect any artifacts that might be dangerous in the wrong hands.

The haphazard piles of gold and gems, weapons and jewelry, statues and vases weren't sorted or stored in any sort of logical fashion. Not that I could figure out, at least. Apparently, Blossom hadn't expanded her territory to include the treasure keeper or his chamber.

"Welcome to Antarctica." Pulou's voice boomed through the room rather than in my head, but I couldn't actually see him yet.

"Thanks," I muttered, straightening my shoulders and coaxing my necklace to shield my overwhelmed dowser senses. "But it's actually my second visit. Though it's a hell of a lot bigger than I remember."

I might not have known that a door led to it from the nexus, but I recognized the chamber of the treasure keeper now that I'd stepped into it.

While hunting down the first instrument of assassination, I had reached into the dragonskin map and plucked an artifact from the treasure trove. At the time, I'd thought I was somehow standing inside the enormous fur coat Pulou always wore — and whose extradimensional pockets held all kinds of magic in ways I didn't understand. Maybe I was back inside that coat right now. The metaphysics of magic were way beyond me. Good thing I was super okay with not actually knowing one way or the other. I had no interest in cluttering my head more than it already was.

Warner stepped around a distant mountain of treasure, managing to avoid kicking the gold coins pooled across the floor. He was dressed in his dragon leathers. And they fit him so, so well.

A saucy grin spread across my face, and I cocked my hip sexily before I met his stony gaze. The soon-to-be-ex-sentinel was not a happy camper.

He promptly closed the space between us, reaching out for my hand. Then, changing his mind, he swept me into a bruising kiss.

Magic exploded against my chest, spreading out where my necklace wrapped around me — but pooling most intensely where the betrothal rings rested above my heart.

I gasped.

For a brief, painful moment, it felt as if I were bleeding … torn … on fire.

I wrapped my arms around Warner, holding him as tightly as I could. He thrust his tongue into my mouth, and I met him with equal intensity.

Whatever crazy energy had flared up between us settled back into my necklace, leaving the metal warm even through the layers of my T-shirt and tank top.

Warner loosened his hold on me just enough to drop his gaze to my chest. A grin eased the strife that had hardened his face. "You added the rings."

I nodded. "Did you feel them?"

"Yes." The single word was full of satisfaction and pleasure. He brushed his fingers over the two betrothal bands. Then — not one to let a perfect opportunity pass — he managed to cop a healthy feel.

I laughed huskily.

Snarky female laughter rang out across the room.

Freaking Shailaja was somewhere close by.

Warner growled, releasing me reluctantly. "We're waiting on the healer and the warrior, but I'd rather just get this over with." He turned back the way he'd come. "I'm glad you took the time to add the rings. All the better for the battle you're about to undertake."

I jogged a couple of steps to catch up to him. "That's not ominous at all."

He grunted, then navigated us around the curve of a wall of treasures to our left. I stopped myself from trailing my fingertips along the arm of a large gilded throne that teemed with magic as we passed. Its red velvet seat was shredded as if clawed by a large beast. Next to it, a dozen or so oil paintings were propped against a pile of variously sized wooden chests overflowing with gems, chalices, and daggers. I couldn't actually see a ceiling other than a vast wash of white-gold light that illuminated everything within the chamber.

I had no idea how Pulou — or anyone else for that matter — would ever be able to find any specific item within the chamber. I coaxed more shielding from my necklace, feeling the onslaught of magic ebb to a multi-flavored trickle.

The room opened up before us, revealing that only the entrance was constructed in a similar design to the nexus. A glance back over my shoulder still gave me the impression of a rotunda, though, so there was most likely some sort of space-altering magic built into the chamber. That wasn't unusual with buildings of dragon construction. If we were actually in a physical building at all. Though Pulou's mention of Antarctica seemed to support that hypothesis.

I had always thought that the treasure keeper also being the guardian of Antarctica was weird. Did penguins really need a full-time guardian? But it made sense that a vast frozen continent would be a great hiding place. Its remoteness would add to the chamber's magical security.

A large stone table stood before us, rune carved and smooth edged. The area around it was cleared, as if the surrounding artifacts and collectibles had been shoved back a few feet to leave a vaguely circular space.

"Why is it always with the altars?" I muttered to Warner.

He snorted. "Magical anchors."

"There isn't any bloodletting on the agenda, is there?"

"Well, there wasn't in the initial application of the binding. But Shailaja hasn't been forthcoming about the process of its removal."

Pulou stepped out from between two mounds of treasure behind and to the right of the altar. As broad and beefy as a grizzly bear in his fur coat, he was carrying a gold-banded porcelain bowl and an ornamental serpentine dagger. At least I was hoping it was ornamental.

When the treasure keeper spotted us, he held up the bowl. "Found it."

Shailaja snorted from somewhere behind Pulou. Though I hadn't even laid eyes on her yet, she set my teeth on edge. It wasn't just that she was currently in the form of a tiny teen. It was because she was petite and snotty. Petite, snotty people irked me in general. As petty as it was, I found myself hoping she returned to her adult form with some exotic, incurable skin condition when I unlocked her magic.

"The bowl, the dagger, and the altar were used in the initial binding," Warner said. He spoke quietly, though the other dragon ears in the chamber would have no difficulty hearing him.

"I must insist that the alchemist aids me first," Shailaja said. She spoke to Pulou, ignoring Warner and me as she stepped up beside the guardian. Her accent was a slightly stronger and far more prissy version of the treasure keeper's British lilt. "It's far too dangerous to perform the unbinding improperly trained."

I mentally amended my wish list for Shailaja to a painful bout of syphilis. The STD had been incurable in the sixteenth century, right? The rabid koala needed to be taken down more than a few notches.

Pulou grimaced, but he otherwise ignored Shailaja's 'insistence.'

As the rabid koala finally turned to eye me up and down, I couldn't help but smirk. The treasure keeper clearly wasn't her biggest fan — telling a guardian that he didn't have the training to pull off a spell really wasn't a great idea. And if my father and Suanmi couldn't stand her, then Shailaja didn't have many friends in the nexus.

"That's what you wear to perform great magic?" she asked, clearly perturbed by my jeans and T-shirt.

Me: one. Rabid koala: zero.

"The T-shirt seemed appropriate given our last encounter," I said, gesturing toward the two crows and the 'Attempted Murder' emblazoned across my chest. "Seeing as how I kicked your ass."

Shailaja narrowed her muddy-brown eyes at me. She was wearing a navy-blue chiffon-silk dress with a scooped neck, and it was practically falling off her bony, pallid shoulders. The fabric of the dress gathered underneath her breasts and pooled at her feet. It was made for a much taller woman.

She wasn't wearing anything underneath the reams of thin silk. That was somehow even creepier than the altar.

The silence hanging between the two of us stretched. Warner was a statue at my left side, ready to back me in an instant. Pulou was fussing with the placement of the bowl on the altar. We were making him uncomfortable, which was almost amusing.

I upped the wattage of my smile, dancing my fingers across my jade knife. It was currently snug at my hip in its invisible sheath, but could be drawn and at the rabid koala's throat in a heartbeat.

Shailaja's hand strayed down to a silk tote bag she wore slung over her shoulder. I hadn't noticed it against the dress because it was almost the same shade of navy blue. The tote looked full.

"You think you have anything in that bag that could beat me in here?" I whispered. I swept my left hand to encompass the treasure chamber. "With all this power at my beck and call?"

I turned to address Pulou. "Even so, it's probably not a great idea just letting Miss Crazy wander around here unchecked."

The treasure keeper cleared his throat. Now I was the one questioning his abilities.

"Sorry," I muttered.

"This was where the spell was first performed," Shailaja said smugly. "Removing it here gives Warner the best chance of survival."

Warner snorted. "Removing the spell will not harm me."

"Well, not if I perform the ceremony," she purred. "In my hands, there would be absolutely no chance of you coming to harm. Anything else is a risk, though. I want you at my side, Warner. Not in the ground."

"Boring," I said, stretching the word out in a sing-song manner.

"I would prefer to await the healer," Pulou said, ignoring our inane banter. "Sentinel?" He nodded to Warner. "You are sure?"

"I am. Though ..." Warner turned his stony gaze on the rabid koala. "Binding or none, I will still be the sentinel of the instruments of assassination."

"I wouldn't have it any other way," Shailaja said, giggling breathlessly.

I snorted. "Stuck in the past," I muttered, recalling what the fire breather had said to me in the bakery. "How about utterly delusional?"

Warner stepped forward, stripping off his leather vest to give me a delightful view of miles of skin, broad shoulders, and a torso that tapered to highlight his leather-encased ass.

Yeah, I still enjoyed ogling him behind his back.

He turned and winked at me.

Okay, so maybe I was a little obvious.

Shailaja stepped up to stand beside Pulou on the opposite side of the altar. Her head came only halfway up to the guardian's shoulder.

Warner climbed up on the altar; then he lay down on it, face up. The shoulder that bore his dragon tattoo was directly next to the bowl where Pulou had placed it.

"Um," I said. "That doesn't really help with the whole creepy aspect."

Warner chuckled.

"I repeat my objection," Shailaja said, sounding seriously concerned. Her face was far too close to Warner's gorgeous chest for my liking. "The alchemist should first aid me in unlocking my reserves. Then I will free the sentinel from the ties that bind him to the instruments."

"Yeah, right," I said. "Because you're so trustworthy."

Shailaja lifted her gaze from Warner's stoic profile to meet mine. I stepped up to face her across the altar. She smirked but didn't answer me.

Now that I was closer, I could feel the power thrumming off the stone table. Though its edges were rounded, the top slab was constructed out of rough-hewn granite and was framed with an intricate border of images and runes. I didn't recognize the etchings, but I was fairly certain that one of the four carved stone legs was intended to be a Chinese guardian lion, typically seen on temples, palaces, and … tombs.

Pulou spoke. "With the table unearthed and the artifacts used to cement the binding identified and re-covered, plus the notes from the journal you discovered, Jade, I feel confident in my ability to perform the ritual."

Shailaja looked surprised. Then her face twisted into a grimace. "You have one of my father's journals." Her voice was flat.

"Indeed." Pulou didn't even spare her a glance.

"You seem surprised, Shay-Shay," I said. "Like maybe you thought they'd all been torched for some reason."

"I'd like you better if you couldn't talk," she said spitefully. "You're useful but annoying."

Pulou rolled his eyes. "Let me see what is keeping the healer."

I waited, expecting him to leave. But when he didn't move away, I realized he was having the conver-sation in his head. "Don't you need to physically be in the nexus to communicate with him?" I asked.

Pulou glowered at me. "I am the master of the portals."

Right. Don't question the ways of a supreme guardian. Check.

Shailaja wiggled her fingers to draw my attention. She was hovering her hand over Warner's chest. She made a grab for one of his nipples, but he seized her wrist roughly before she could touch him.

Bones snapped. She … giggled.

"Oooo, Warner. I do like this new coarser, lustier version of you. I guess I can thank the alchemist for that as well. Since I assume you've modeled yourself after her."

Warner released her. He turned his head slightly to look at me, deliberately cutting Shailaja out of his line of sight.

I twined my fingers through his.

"Don't," Shailaja hissed, suddenly deadly serious. "Don't touch the altar."

I pointed a finger at her, then gestured back to the words on my T-shirt. Attempted. Murder.

"I don't get it," Shailaja snarled. "It isn't funny or smart if I don't get it. It's just stupid and childish."

"Well, this is going as well as expected," Qiuniu said from behind me. The second after the healer announced his presence by speaking — his Brazilian accent was almost as yummy as he looked — I could hear the light strains of music he carried with him everywhere. Considering how heavily I was having to shield myself from the magic in the chamber, I wasn't surprised that I hadn't felt him approach.

I turned, allowing myself to simply stare at the most gorgeous man I'd ever laid eyes on. Even though I was gaga for Warner, I could admit that Qiuniu was damn pretty. If you liked that sort of thing. And it seriously didn't help my concentration that he was currently swathed in samurai-inspired combat gear, similar to my father's but with burgundy accents. Though he wore no helmet and wasn't currently carrying a sword, he'd obviously just come from somewhere he had deemed more dangerous than usual.

"My apologies, treasure keeper," he said, stepping up to my right. "There was an incident that needed the warrior's and my attention." His decidedly unfriendly gaze rested on Shailaja.

The rabid koala appeared to be examining the runes carved on the border of the table. Though as I eyed her, her lips twitched as if she was fighting a smirk.

"Thank you, healer." Pulou's tone was an odd mixture of weariness and displeasure. He shifted, standing across from the healer and directly beside Warner's shoulder and the gold-banded porcelain bowl. "Your time and energy are always appreciated."

Qiuniu nodded, his gaze still on Shailaja. "Alchemist," he said conversationally. "I would love to examine your blade. At your convenience, of course. Healing the wounds you inflicted with it was most challenging."

Shailaja's head snapped up at his benignly uttered but antagonistically directed words. She wasn't smirking anymore.

"Of course," the healer continued, still needling the rabid koala, "that could be due to your unique magic, not simply the knife."

So I'd hurt Shailaja badly? I caught Warner's gaze and raised my eyebrows. He nodded almost imperceptibly. My gag order on anything related to Shailaja should have included a clause excepting good news.

"I'd be happy to oblige, healer," I said. "Perhaps if you have a moment after the unbinding?"

"I'll make the time."

Shailaja glowered, glancing between Qiuniu and me.

"Shall we?" Pulou said.

"As you please." The healer touched Warner's forehead lightly. The music that always accompanied him increased in volume, then abated as he removed his hand. I thought he might have been checking Warner's vitals.

"The dagger is key," Shailaja said begrudgingly. "With it, the binding was carved. With it, the spell will be undone." She turned her attention to me, her teeth grinding on her words. "I want some guarantees from the alchemist. She's not as stupid as she looks, but she is stupid enough to attempt to renege."

Pulou and Qiuniu looked at me, waiting.

Gee, thanks for jumping to my defense, guys.

I hated entering into verbal bindings, but I would do it for Warner without even thinking. Though I could still be careful about how I chose my wording. "If you successfully guide the treasure keeper through the process of lifting the binding that ties Warner Jiaotuson to the instruments of assassination, and that ties him to the dragonskin tattoo map that belonged to Pulou-who-was, and if you do so without harming him or anyone else in any way, then I will aid you in removing that which contains your dragon magic."

"As you did in the bakery," Shailaja said.

"As I did under duress in the bakery. But you may not utilize my necklace or any object of power I have created."

"No matter. I have a few options selected for the occasion."

"Do you accept my proposition?" The words felt dry and dirty coming out of my mouth.

"I do."

Magic passed between Shailaja and me. It was nothing heavy, but even a light connection to the rabid koala would bother me until I got rid of it.

Pulou picked up the dagger. Now that I was closer, I could see that it wasn't snake-shaped as I had originally thought. Rather, the pommel, grip, and cross guard were a dragon's head, body, and folded wings. The dagger's curved blade was meant to mimic the tail. Seen up close, the weapon bore a striking resemblance to Warner's tattoo.

"The binding must be lifted from the sentinel with the dagger, then affixed to the bowl," Shailaja said. She gave a disinterested shrug.

"No," I said. "It can't possibly be that easy."

"It isn't," Pulou said gruffly. "The fledgling can be so flippant only because the sentinel binding was created by the former treasure keeper, and now I am he."

Shailaja smirked, then took a deliberate step back from the altar.

I met Warner's gaze.

He nodded. "I'm ready."

I took a step back from the stone table, summoning my jade knife into my right hand and twining the fingers of my left hand through the wedding rings on my necklace.

The treasure keeper held the dagger over Warner's shoulder, gathering the black-tea-and-heavy-cream flavor of his magic around him. The golden hue of his guardian power flowed over the weapon, coating the carved hilt, pommel, and blade. With no words or incantation, he brought the tip of that curved blade toward the dragon tattooed on Warner's chest. The tail tip of the dagger cut into the corresponding tail etched onto Warner's skin.

Then, jerking the dagger a few inches away, Pulou siphoned half of the dragon tattoo into the blade.

Warner arched upward on the stone table. His jaw was fiercely clamped shut as he refused to scream in response to whatever torment he was suffering. It was as if Pulou had somehow grabbed the magic of the binding spell sealed to his skin. His dragon magic rolled over his eyes; then he slammed back down onto the altar. Every tendon and vein in his neck and torso bulged. Blood streamed from the wound on his chest. Yet he didn't utter a word.

"Oh, God ..." I cried out before I could muzzle myself.

Pulou pulled at the magic of the tattoo again.

Warner curled forward — away from the assault on his chest and shoulder — then slammed his head back onto the altar. The stone underneath his skull cracked. The runes all along the edges of the altar awoke with a flash of golden light.

"He's fighting it," Pulou muttered to Qiuniu.

My heart dropped into my stomach. If Warner was fighting the removal, that meant —

"No," the healer said. "You simply don't quite have the tenor ... the frequency. Try touching the bowl with your other hand. Perhaps the transfer needs to be grounded."

Pulou grasped the edge of the gold-banded bowl.

The tattoo disappeared.

The treasure keeper immediately twisted the blade and the captured binding spell away from Warner, then jabbed the dagger toward the side of the bowl. The dragon tattoo reappeared across the banding, as if it had been etched there all along.

"Holy crap," I said.

"Energy must be transferred," Qiuniu said. "It cannot be destroyed. As you know, of course, alchemist. If we aren't exactly sure how the spell was created in the first place, it is safer to simply contain it within another vessel. Even better when that vessel was instrumental in the initial spell."

I locked my gaze to Pulou's for a brief second. I knew all about 'transferring energy.' I had stripped every last iota of magic from my sister Sienna, then stored it in my katana what felt like centuries ago. Pulou had taken and stored the mangled sword somewhere in his treasure trove. I'd seen it decorating the head of an ivory Buddha the last time I'd inadvertently visited.

The treasure keeper had pretty much sworn me to secrecy about it all — both the existence of the sword and my ability to create such a terrible object of power.

I stepped up to the altar.

Qiuniu held up his hand. "Wait. The protection spells have been activated. Warner must have unintentionally done so when the binding was ... well ... tearing him apart."

Delightful. It was probably better that I'd missed the severity of Warner's suffering. I didn't think I could have been trusted to stand by and simply watch him be tortured, not even in the presence of two guardians.

Warner sat up with a groan, then swung his legs off the altar. Attempting to stand, he stumbled.

The healer had Warner propped up on his shoulder before I could close the space between us. I stepped up to place his free arm around my neck. Warner evaded my attempt to help him, though, brushing the back of his fingers across my cheek instead.

"Everything is okay," he murmured. "Just don't do anything crazy without me."

"Nah," I said flippantly. "Who could be crazy without you?"

The healer snorted. "Let me get Warner settled. He'll be fine after a few hours of sleep. That was a rather intense binding spell."

"I'm coming with you."

"No, you're not," Shailaja said. "I want this done."

She glanced at Pulou for support. He pointedly examined the newly decorated gold-banded bowl. She curled her lip in a silent snarl, then visibly calmed herself. "I've held up my end. Fulfill your promise, alchemist."

The verbal agreement we'd entered into tugged me toward her. Apparently, the rabid koala could trigger it on demand.

Fantastic.

Qiuniu cleared his throat. "I would rather be here."

"So return quickly," Shailaja said. "We've done this before without you. I barely even need the alchemist. She's simply a tool."

Pulou and Qiuniu stared at her, silently unimpressed.

"Fine," she sneered. "I promise to not harm a single golden curl on her golden little head. Happy?"

Pulou laughed. "That's an exceedingly specific promise masquerading as a broad statement, fledgling."

"I need the alchemist. She is useful. I shall not harm her if it is in my power not to do so."

"And if she attempts to kill you?" the healer asked. I thought he sounded more amused than he should be when discussing attempted murder.

But then, I was the joker wearing the T-shirt.

"Then naturally, all deals are void."

Pulou tucked the bowl and the dagger into the pocket of his fur coat. I imagined them reappearing somewhere in the chamber behind or beside me. But that made my head hurt, so I thought about the expensive chocolate waiting to be consumed in my satchel instead.

"Do try not to kill anyone while in the chamber," the treasure keeper said casually. "You are here only at my invitation, and … the artifacts might react badly to murder. Anyone's murder."

Right. Good to know.

A wicked smile spread across Shailaja's face. "Yes. Balance must always be maintained, Jade Godfrey."

I opened my mouth to sneer right back at her, then decided I was done maintaining the boring nastiness between us. Instead, I pressed a kiss against Warner's lips.

"Just prop me in that corner," Warner said.

"No way," I said teasingly. "The healer says you need a nap like a good boy. I'll bake you cookies."

"Cowboy cookies?" Even exhausted, the sentinel was game to play along.

"Anything you want."

Warner grinned, brushing his hand against mine. Then he nodded to the healer.

"I'll be gone only moments," Qiuniu said.

He walked away from any further discussion, Warner still propped over his shoulder. Though I was pleased to see that my boyfriend was holding up most of his own weight.

"It's going to be okay," I whispered to myself.

Then I caught sight of Shailaja. She was watching Warner leave. Her expression was unfiltered, raw. My stomach soured with the realization that the rabid koala might actually be in love with him. Which was seriously twisted, given that she wanted the instruments of assassination so badly, and given how long he'd been firmly standing in the way of her acquiring them.

And now there was me.

I was the obstacle between her and Warner now. As well as between her and the instruments of assassination.

She turned her gaze on me, then sneered.

Yeah, I wasn't stepping aside.

Chapter Five

Shailaja hopped up and sat cross-legged on the altar. She lifted her silk bag onto her lap and thrust her hand into it — much deeper than the bag appeared to be. Then she pulled out a medieval-looking jeweled crown constructed out of some sort of silver-gray metal. She twirled the crown on her finger. It wasn't particularly pretty, and the jewels appeared almost utilitarian — if jewels could be such a thing — but I could taste the sorcerer magic emanating from it even with my senses dampened.

"There once was a man who thought he would be a benevolent king," Shailaja said. "But then, as the legend is told, he loved the wrong woman."

I narrowed my eyes at her. I really wasn't interested in story time with a psycho. On the other hand, I was seriously jealous of the apparently magically bottomless bag.

"There's a sword that goes with the crown as well, but the treasure keeper said I couldn't use it." Shailaja pouted in Pulou's direction.

I gathered this was supposed to be a fetching expression. It wasn't.

"Shall we continue here?" I asked the treasure keeper.

The guardian nodded. "As best a place as any. Contained."

"It's just a little ... overwhelming."

Pulou nodded, then tilted his head deliberately left and right. The piles of treasure and artifacts pushed back from us another six feet.

His redecoration exposed the Buddha I'd seen the first time I unknowingly visited the chamber. The three-foot-high ivory statue was still joyfully holding his round belly, and was wearing my mangled katana like a lopsided crown.

I realized that Shailaja was following my gaze.

"What is that pretty?" she asked.

I ignored her, pulling my eyes away from the sword. "My apologies, treasure keeper, but I believe I must ask you to step back as well."

Pulou nodded, taking a few steps away and placing himself between us and the exit. Smart man. Then, rather amazingly, he gathered all the magic in the chamber toward him, drawing the energy farther away from Shailaja and me.

I stepped up to face her, standing almost nose to nose.

"Had I known you'd replenish your necklace so ... voluptuously," the rabid koala whispered, "I wouldn't have bothered with this old thing." She waved the crown offishly. "I still remember the taste of your blood, alchemist."

"And my knife? Do you remember that as well?"

"Intimately." She pursed her lips and kissed the air between us.

I blinked, just once. But when her smile grew, I found myself wishing I hadn't reacted at all.

"What else have you got in the bag, Shay-Shay?"

"Come find out, Jade."

Shailaja lifted the crown between us. She held the artifact by forefinger and thumb on either side, so that her fingers were carefully spaced on four of its jeweled points.

I placed my fingers on the four points nearest to me. One point remained empty.

Shailaja tilted her head, studying the artifact we held. "A solar or radiant crown such as this would indicate some sort of adherence to or study of Greek mythology. But the magic is sorcerer-based alchemy, yes? Some sort of protection, with perhaps the power of persuasion mixed in. Using nine jeweled points is rather obvious, though. Who do you suppose was the would-be-great king's benefactor?"

"Not interested," I said.

"What does it take for an object to wind up in the chamber of the treasure keeper?"

"You're here. I would think the parameters were pretty clear to you already."

"But I can leave whenever I want. What is that?" She nodded over my shoulder toward my mangled katana.

I was careful to not even blink in response.

"Just take the magic," I said between gritted teeth. "I don't want to be this close to you ever again."

"Then give it to me, alchemist. Nothing can simply be taken. Balance must be maintained."

"You took the magic from my necklace. Drained it dry."

"You offered it to me first."

I hissed, seriously tired of playing games with her. I focused my attention on the power contained within the crown we held aloft between us. Its sorcerer magic was unmistakable, tasting of loamy earth, sweet potato, and some sort of truffle. I couldn't immediately make out the purpose of the alchemy — and whether or not it offered the wearer magical protection and power of persuasion. But I was assuming that Shailaja's history lesson might have just been a guise to test the extent of my dowser abilities, and that she was guessing about the crown's origins herself.

I reached out to the magic contained within the artifact, coaxing it with my own alchemist powers. Teasing it to stir and blend with my own magic. But I didn't claim it, as I did with the magic I added to my necklace or my knife. Instead, I simply gathered the power of the crown into tiny cyclones underneath each of my fingertips. Then, with a bit more of a push than it needed, I released each miniature storm toward Shailaja.

The rabid koala gasped, then giggled.

Damn. I should have known she'd like that.

She licked her lips and purred. "Again."

I grabbed more of the energy contained within the crown and systematically started filtering it to Shailaja. I could actually see the dark-blue magic as it began twining around her fingers, then spreading up her hands and wrists.

Shailaja inhaled deeply. All her snarky attention was diverted to the crown and siphoning its magic.

I felt it the instant she started pulling the sorcerer-based alchemy toward her. The blue streaks of magic twisting around her forearms slowly drained of color, then turned into a golden sheen as she somehow converted their power.

Even watching it happen a second time, I still had no idea how she did it. Somehow, she gathered all the magic I gave her and pulled it up and around her like …

Like a cloak.

Like the treasure keeper's fur coat … which was actually a manifestation of his guardian mantle.

I met Shailaja's gaze.

She smiled.

Then she tried to reach through the crown and grab my own magic.

It hurt, like having the tips of my fingers latched onto by a gigantic leech … a sensation that was exceedingly similar, in fact, to how Shailaja's shadow leeches siphoned magic.

Still grinning like a maniac, Shailaja smacked her lips. "Just a little sip, Jade."

I ripped my fingers from the now-drained crown and backhanded her across the face.

She flew off the altar, and for a brief moment, the protection wards etched into the edges of the stone table reached up and grabbed my arm, pinning me in place.

Shailaja — cackling like the crazed teen she was — rolled ass over head. She crashed into a pile of treasure, knocking the Buddha over and sending my mangled katana flying.

The pile of artifacts collapsed over her in an avalanche of gold and platinum and gems, burying her from my sight.

"Was that necessary?" Pulou asked mildly from behind me.

I looked back over my shoulder at him. "Yes."

He shrugged, not even remotely concerned.

The pile of treasure shifted. Shailaja stood, coins and jewels cascading from her head and shoulders as she stepped out from among the artifacts. She was coated in all the magic that had been contained in the jeweled crown.

She stumbled toward me, not laughing now. Her eyes were ablaze with golden dragon magic.

"Alchemist," she gasped, pained. Her upper lip was bleeding. It hadn't yet healed from my slap.

We'd reached the point of no return. I wondered if I chose to break my promise at this vulnerable point, whether or not the magic siphoned from the crown would consume the rabid koala. Or whether she'd just suffer until it faded, unabsorbed.

"Now," she demanded. "Now!"

She lunged for me, grabbing my upper arms. Though she was far too strong for her size, I could have shaken her off.

I glanced over at Pulou.

He nodded wearily.

I reached up and grabbed Shailaja's face. Her skin was oddly moist, so much so that I nearly let go of her. She convulsed, losing her grip on me. Her eyes rolled back in her head.

"Please," she whispered.

I pushed. I pushed every drop of the magic she'd gathered like a gossamer cloak around her into the core of magic that was … simply her. I forced the power from the crown to unite with what I felt was Shailaja's magical essence.

She screamed in pain.

She screamed in delight.

She ripped herself away from my hold, magic rippling up and over her arms, legs, torso, and face.

She began to grow. To expand.

First a year, then two. An eighteen-year-old stood in front of me, then a twenty-year-old.

The magic surrounding her began to settle, to fade.

Then Shailaja — easily twenty-five years old in appearance, practically my height in bare feet, and skinny as a goddamn cinnamon stick — threw her arms in the air and screamed in triumph.

She opened her glowing golden eyes, locked her gaze to mine, and whispered, "Time to play."

I pulled my knife, but she grabbed me far quicker than even I had expected her to move. She pinned my knife arm, then slammed her mouth across mine.

Yes ... she ... kissed me. If I could even call it a kiss. It was a brutal assault.

I slammed the heel of my left hand up underneath her chin, snapping her head back hard enough that she lost her hold on me.

"That's enough!" Pulou bellowed. Guardian magic blasted through the chamber, as if he'd just released everything he'd been holding at bay.

The magical tsunami washed over me. I stumbled to maintain my footing.

Only a few feet away, Shailaja twirled in the magic, her silk dress lifting up around her knees.

I shielded myself with my arms just in time to block the kick I saw coming. Her foot slammed across both my forearms, throwing me back into the pile of treasure behind me.

"An eye for an eye, sister!" she shrieked.

I scrambled to my feet, attempting to throw myself clear, but my legs were tangled among treasure chests and armored breastplates and golden chalices.

Uncounted centuries' worth of hoarding collapsed over me. Something heavy hit the back of my head, followed by a few hundred more unidentifiable but weighty items. I fell, curling into a ball and protecting my head as best I could.

The avalanche settled over me.

An eye for a freaking eye. Freaking bitch. I was going to have to dig myself out.

The weight of the treasure lifted off me. The entire pile flew back, leaving me curled in a ball on the cleared white marble floor.

Shailaja giggled. Then she was abruptly silenced.

I peered through the arms I still held crisscrossed over my face. The treasure keeper was holding the rabid koala by the back of her neck and head. His arm was ramrod straight, held at an angle that forced Shailaja to dance on her tiptoes. Pulou was barely allowing her feet to brush the floor.

"Alchemist?" Pulou asked.

I rolled to my feet. "All good. No problem."

"She started it," Shailaja said jokingly.

"Still rabid," I muttered.

Pulou nodded and released Shailaja. She stumbled forward, falling to her knees in front of him.

"Look at me," the treasure keeper said.

Still on her knees, Shailaja pivoted and lifted her chin.

"Shailaja, daughter of Pulou-who-was," the treasure keeper intoned. "You shall be brought before the Guardian Council and judged for your past crimes against humanity. Then, I have no doubt, you will meet your end at the edge of the warrior's sword."

What? That was the plan? Restore Shailaja's magic, only so they could try her for —

"No," the rabid koala said.

No? Interesting choice. I was pretty damn sure that begging was probably the way to go in this situation.

"You think to stand against me?" Pulou asked, clearly amused by her defiance.

"Of course not, treasure keeper." Shailaja slipped her hand into her bag. "I intend to take my rightful place."

"We shall see." Pulou folded his arms as if he didn't appreciate the potential danger kneeling before him.

"I intend to take your place."

Pulou frowned.

I called my knife into my hand, already stepping toward them. Why hadn't I started moving the second Pulou freed me from the treasure? I was so slow. Compared to a full-blood dragon, at least.

Shailaja pulled a small box out of her bag, opening it and flicking it toward the treasure keeper in the same forward motion.

I managed another step.

It was a platinum box, encrusted with raw diamonds. Deadly magic exploded in the chamber. The taste of metal instantly clogged my senses.

Pulou already had his shortsword with the huge emerald embedded in its guard raised. He would easily knock aside the assault.

My foot hit the marble a third time. Jesus, I'd only managed three freaking steps? Though it was a tiny bit sad that the rabid koala was insane enough to attack a guardian. And that I was stupid enough to believe —

Portal magic sizzled through the air between Shailaja and the treasure keeper. Portal magic that inexplicably tasted of cream cheese and sugared carrots and cinnamon.

Shailaja's magic had always tasted of burnt carrot cake. Now, fully restored, that cake was paired with delicious cream-cheese icing. The portal was her creation, not Pulou's. This was the magic I had helped her reclaim. The magic she must have inherited from her father as the former treasure keeper.

I caught sight of a gleam of silver and a series of spiked legs at the edge of the box, then it and the evil it held at bay popped into the portal and disappeared.

I slammed into Shailaja, lowering my shoulder to check her directly in the ribs and throw her aside. Pivoting back, I tasted the magic of Shailaja's miniature portal a second time.

"Treasure keeper," I screamed, lunging and lifting my hand toward the magical bloom that was behind him now. But I was too far away … too late … too slow.

I was always going to be too slow.

The box flew out of the miniature exit portal, completely blindsiding the treasure keeper. It smashed into the side of his head.

The last time I'd seen that box, it had been in the hands of the far seer, with the silver centipedes I'd collected in Peru safely contained within it. It had been sent on to the treasure keeper, who would have put it into his coat for safekeeping. Into the chamber of the treasure keeper. Where we were standing right now.

But the instruments of assassination weren't contained any longer. The three silver centipedes tumbled out of the box, instantly latching onto Pulou's shoulder and neck.

Pulou fell.

Just like that. No stumbling or preamble. It was as if he'd been hit with some sort of uber-powerful binding spell.

The marble floor underneath him cracked, throwing me up in the air and a few feet back. Unfortunately for Shailaja, I landed on my feet. Still running.

I threw myself toward the treasure keeper. The centipedes were twined around his neck and moving steadily upward. Pulou was frozen in the midst of a full-body convulsion. His face was twisted in pain, every vein and tendon stretched and distended.

I reached out with my dowser senses for the metallurgy — the magic that had created the centipedes — even as I stretched my fingertips across Pulou's mountain of a chest. The taste of metal flooded my mouth. I just had to claim it —

Shailaja kicked me in the back. I flew over the treasure keeper, rolling forward onto both feet, then spinning around in a low crouch to meet her next attack. But that attack never arrived.

The treasure keeper was holding the leg that Shailaja had kicked me with. She was struggling to get away from him.

He gurgled a terrible, frustrated fury.

Taking the opening Pulou was holding for me, I ran, completely primed to thrust my jade knife deep into Shailaja's heart.

A centipede slipped into the treasure keeper's nose. He began to convulse, foaming at the mouth and bleeding from his eyes.

A second centipede slipped into his ear.

He lost his grip on Shailaja.

She flipped backward and away from my killing strike. I only managed to cut her across the chest.

She rolled away, then settled on her haunches like a cat. "Too late. It's done, now. And you'll have to help me with the next part, or his magic will be lost forever."

Keeping my blade raised between Shailaja and me, I dropped to my knees by the treasure keeper. He'd gone terribly still, but his magic was undiminished. I couldn't see the third centipede anywhere, but it must have been … inside him. With the others. Ripping through his brain.

Choking back a sob of fear, I placed my free hand on the side of his face. His potent power ran up my arm, instantly setting my nerves on fire.

Ignoring the blistering pain, I reached for the magic of the centipedes. The iron-bright taste of their metallurgy flooded my mouth once again.

I didn't know what else to do ...

I wasn't a healer. But I was a dowser and an alchemist.

I captured the metallurgy of the centipedes and held it fast. "Mine," I whispered. Then I yanked that magic toward me.

"No!" Shailaja screamed.

Answering my call, the centipedes ripped out of Pulou's face, spraying blood and flesh and brains all over his chest and my knees.

Just as they'd done in Peru, the three gore-covered centipedes clicked into place on my necklace and went instantly dormant.

Pulou's face was destroyed. He was completely missing his left ear. But I could already feel the power that he'd been radiating shifting to concentrate on healing him. I just had to hope he'd managed to call out for help before he fell, and keep Shailaja occupied until the big guns arrived.

I reached up to touch the three silver centipedes looped through individual wedding rings on my necklace. Interestingly, they'd attached on the left as far away as they could get from the betrothal rings. I lifted my gaze to meet Shailaja's.

"He's dead," she said, but her tone suggested she didn't believe the words.

Pulou took a shuddering breath.

"You want to play with the instruments of assassination?" I whispered. "I'm game."

Rising to my feet, I tickled my fingers across the centipedes. They dropped into my left hand, then slowly began curling around and around on my palm.

Across from me, Shailaja rose, pulling a wickedly pointed runed-etched rapier out of her bag.

I stepped around the treasure keeper's body, placing myself between him and whatever else Shailaja had stashed in her bag. "Let's see what happens when I murder you in the chamber of the treasure keeper," I said, not worried in the slightest at my own viciousness.

"I hate, hate, hate you," Shailaja snarled.

But she didn't attack. Actually, she backed off a few steps. Unfortunately, I couldn't press her without leaving Pulou vulnerable.

"The miniportal trick is cute," I said. "But probably only good once against a guardian."

Shailaja sneered. "You think you can hold me off, alchemist?"

"I think the warrior is about to walk through the door."

She laughed. "You're so utterly stupid. If it wasn't for your tasty magic, I'd think Warner was completely addled."

"Enlighten me."

"Even guardians have to be invited to walk here ... each and every time." The all-grown-up-but-still-rabid koala took another step toward the pile of artifacts by the laughing Buddha. The mangled and malformed katana it had once worn as a crown was lying among the scattered treasures a few feet away. "No, you'll step aside and allow me access to the treasure-keeper-who-never-should-have-been ... and who soon won't be anything at all."

"Meaning what? You're going to take his place?" I laughed harshly. "If it didn't mean more pain for Pulou,

I'd like to watch you die trying. And Shay-Shay? You're wrong about the warrior being locked out. Yazi already had an open invitation to this particular party."

Somewhere behind me, the door to the chamber slammed open. Portal magic blasted through, lifting my hair from my shoulders and rippling Shailaja's silk dress around her ankles.

With his warrior magic stirring the chamber's smaller treasures and artifacts, my father strode toward us. His timing was freaking perfect ... well, if I ignored the fact that Pulou was seriously injured.

Shailaja dove behind the pile of treasure she'd been creeping toward. I let her go. She wasn't my problem.

I turned to kneel back beside Pulou, adhering the centipedes to my necklace again as I leaned over him. I lifted my gaze to the warrior of the guardians as he came into view — and realized only in that moment that it might look as if I was the one who'd attacked the treasure keeper.

Seeing my father in full warrior gear was like looking into a hurricane. Or what I imagined a F5 tornado would look like. Except with golden magic in place of rain and cloud — gold wind, gold thunder, gold lightning.

The warrior raised his broadsword. The golden blade and its pearl-and-gem-encrusted pommel were the flashiest thing about my father ... and the deadliest. The magic emanating from the weapon made my eyes water ... or maybe they were bleeding.

I raised my now-empty hands, ready to profess my innocence, yet knowing I wouldn't be able to get a coherent word out before he ran me through.

"Where ... is ... she?"

I stared at my father, mouth hanging open to plead for my life. He was glaring down at me. I could barely think. The portal to the nexus was still open, and combined with the magic of the chamber, the treasure keeper, and my father, it was all scrambling my brain.

"Jade?" he asked again. "Where is she?"

I threaded my fingers through my necklace, pulling more of its protective magic around me like a dampening cloak. Then I raised my hand and pointed toward the spiced carrot cake I could just barely taste, behind and to the left of me.

Yazi stepped over Pulou, brushing against me as he passed.

"Dad," I said with a sickening realization. "She might have the braids."

The warrior's gaze dropped to the centipedes on my necklace. He nodded. "Even if she does, she's incapable of holding them herself long enough to kill me."

"But she can do this miniature portal thing. That's how she hit Pulou. It tastes like her magic right before it opens."

Yazi's lips curled into a smile full of pride. "Yes. Drake is not the only one envious of your dowsing abilities." He stalked away, drawing his power with him.

My head cleared further. I placed my hand on Pulou's chest. He was breathing, but the dreadful wounds on his face hadn't begun to heal yet. I glanced around as my father stepped between piles of artifacts and out of my sight, the loose coins rattling as he passed. There had to be some sort of fabric nearby that I could staunch the treasure keeper's wounds with. I eyed, then dismissed, a rolled carpet propped against the ebony statue of a multi-armed deity I couldn't readily identify. Even I knew mixing magical carpets and the blood of a guardian was a seriously bad idea.

My mangled katana was gone. I was certain it had been lying on the ground just beyond the laughing Buddha.

I scrambled to my feet, then … I hesitated.

I shouldn't leave Pulou until the healer arrived. My father was capable of handling the rabid koala, even if she had armed herself with the katana. He was the freaking guardian of the guardians.

Except … except … except Pulou had locked the katana away. He'd taken it from me without discussion. Then a breath later, he had declared the sacrificial knife I'd created with blood magic a trifle. And it was a secret between us. The terrible secret of how I could drain all the magic from an Adept.

My father stepped out from between the piles of treasure to my right, exactly opposite from where he'd entered. He glanced over at me, then made a decision.

"I'll stand over Pulou," he said, turning back toward me. "You go for the healer. He was called away again. Apparently, the heretic set up multiple distractions with her demon leeches." He curled his lip derisively.

"She's crazy but smart. Wily."

Yazi snorted. "Go. Even with Pulou unconscious, the healer will hear you if you call for him from the nexus."

I rose, turning away. Then I tasted sugared carrots.

"Dad!" I shouted as I spun back. But I was too slow.

Another miniature portal opened up, this one about a foot from my father's head. My mangled katana spun through it in a maelstrom of multicolored magic, as if it had been thrown like a Frisbee.

The warrior was moving even before I'd finished shouting my warning. He lifted his sword to knock the katana aside, but he only caught its edge.

The twisted blade clipped him in the forehead.

He stumbled.

He stumbled.

My father stumbled.

Blood flooded down across his brow, obscuring his left eye. For a brief, mind-numbing moment, I saw the white bone of his skull. Then the gash on his forehead began to knit together.

As it ricocheted off Yazi's head, the katana disappeared into another flash of carrot-cake-imbued magic.

Shailaja laughed, stepping out from the shelter of the artifacts piled behind the ivory Buddha. She was holding the mangled katana.

"Come play, warrior." She giggled.

Crazy, stupid bitch.

Though I could say one thing for her. When she went all in, she stuck with it.

My father moved in a blur of golden magic. He had Shailaja by her neck and off her feet before I could take a second step.

She gurgled another giggle as I ran toward them.

The warrior had played right into her hands.

Another portal opened over their heads. A small, diamond-crusted gold box dropped from it, breaking open as it smashed onto the warrior's head. Three rainbow-colored silk braids tumbled from the box. Sorcerer alchemy, tasting faintly of moss and honeysuckle, trilled through the chamber.

Shailaja's face was turning pink.

I would have sworn I was running as fast as I could, yet somehow I wasn't moving at all.

Another portal opened underneath the tumbling braids. Winking in and out of existence, it swallowed the instrument of assassination, then deposited the braids on the warrior's neck, directly into the gap in his hard-shell armor.

Yazi went stock-still. Then he began to convulse.

Shailaja's face was turning purple. Despite the effect the braids were having on him, the warrior was still strangling her.

I was three steps away.

The rabid koala swung wildly, bringing the katana into play. She sliced the edge of the twisted blade across the warrior's neck.

Blood spurted.

He dropped her.

Shailaja fell, sprawling across the marble floor and gasping for breath.

I kicked her in the face.

Her head and shoulders snapped back. Slack jawed and completely discombobulated, she spun away across the smooth floor.

I stalked toward her, raising my jade knife for a killing blow.

Then the warrior fell.

The marble underneath my feet buckled. I lost my footing. Shailaja found hers, slamming a kick to my gut that threw me tumbling back over my fallen father.

I scrambled to my hands and knees as Shailaja dove away. She rolled, gaining her feet and dashing beyond the nearest pile of artifacts.

I threw myself at my father, plucking the braids from his neck. They had burned through skin, muscle, and tendon to reveal the white of his spine. He was foaming at the mouth, but he stopped convulsing the moment I got the instrument of assassination off him.

I shoved the braids into the front pocket of my jeans, then pressed my hands to the other wound in his neck.

My katana … my katana could cut a guardian. And not just cut. It could actually deal a blow that could cause my father to stumble.

The idea was ridiculous.

I could taste Shailaja's magic. She was nearby, refocusing. The wound at my father's neck wouldn't stop bleeding. And Pulou felt as though he was miles away.

I couldn't protect both guardians.

Hysterical laughter bubbled through my throat and past my lips before I could stop it. It really wasn't the right time to realize that being the only one standing over defenseless guardians was utterly paralyzing.

I yanked my T-shirt off and clumsily tied it around Yazi's neck. Then, forcing myself to ignore the undeniable fact that I wasn't strong enough to do so, I grabbed his ankles and started dragging him back toward the treasure keeper.

Each step was excruciating. His guardian magic fought me over every inch I tried to move him. It was as if he was anchored to the marble floor.

Shailaja's magic bloomed to my left.

I ducked.

A thick chain flew by my head. Without thinking too much about it, I grabbed for its magic — a weird combination of watermelon and mustard — and shoved it toward the rabid koala just as she appeared to my right.

Having lost its momentum, the chain hit Shailaja at the knees, wrapping around her legs. She shrieked in frustration. But she didn't throw the katana she still held.

I managed another step closer to the treasure keeper.

She could have taken me out with the sword, yet she'd tried chaining me instead. That didn't make any sense. I was the only thing standing between her and two incapacitated guardians.

I gained another step as Shailaja wrestled with the chain around her knees.

Realizing I wasn't seconds away from death gave me a second to think rather than just react.

I gathered my father's guardian magic around me. He was the fount for my magic — or at least the dragon half of it. Dowsing might be a witch thing, but my alchemy was born from my dragon heritage. My knife was like my father's knife. His magic was my magic.

The guardian power shielding my fallen father accepted that I was friend, not foe. My burden lightened suddenly, and I crossed the remaining distance to the treasure keeper in three more steps.

I carefully arranged my father alongside Pulou, head to toe, ignoring Shailaja as she slipped passed to my right.

Freed from the chain, the rabid koala crossed to stand about twenty feet away. She was between me and the exit. The portal to the nexus still stood open beyond the stacks of treasure behind her.

I placed my hand on my father's chest, then on Pulou's, confirming that both were still breathing.

They were alive.

I rose, stepping around the fallen guardians.

Shailaja raised the katana, primed to throw it. She held it sideways by the hilt. Every edge and surface of the weapon was imbued with deadly witch and sorcerer magic, including the containment spell that Blackwell had hit me with in his castle. The twisted blade was filled with every last drop of magic that Sienna had stolen from her dozens of victims, some of whom had been uniquely powerful. And all of it was coated and sealed in my own blood.

Unfortunately, clarity was usually an afterthought for me. Standing in the chamber with my father fallen behind me, I understood why Pulou had chosen to lock my terrible creation away.

And now it was in the hands of the rabid koala.

Karma was a crazy bitch, and she'd been after my ass for a while now.

Honestly, I was getting a bit tired of it.

I raised my knife. "You've run out of instruments of assassination, Shailaja."

"Not quite yet," she said, grinning at me as if we were best friends forever.

Then, inexplicably, she blew me a kiss, spun away, and ran for the portal to the nexus.

God help me, I followed her.

We leaped through the portal. Momentarily held within its golden magic, I was close enough to Shailaja that my outstretched fingers brushed her hair. But as our feet hit the marble floor of the nexus, she grabbed my forearm and broke my wrist, just as easily as I snapped the spun sugar I used to garnish *Vixen in a Cup*. The holidays and my salted-caramel-frosted chocolate-gingerbread cake often made me whimsical.

Pain radiated up my arm. I stumbled but didn't fall.

My sense of whimsy was so, so far away. I doubted it could ever make the long trip back.

Shailaja was across the rotunda and reaching for the door to Western Europe before I completely gained my footing.

I almost let her go.

Fleeing into Suanmi's territory was the absolute worst thing the rabid koala could do. And for one blissful moment, I imagined walking away and letting Shailaja fall to the fire breather.

Then the far seer wandered in through the adjacent archway. He spotted me first, offering me a cheerful smile even though I was just standing there, stupidly cradling my wrist and watching the rabid koala make her escape.

He turned his head and found himself face to face with Shailaja.

"No!" I yelled.

Shailaja chuckled triumphantly, placing the mangled katana over Chi Wen's head almost delicately. "Hello, far seer. Perfect timing."

Frowning, he cranked his chin down and peered at the twisted steel around his neck. Then his face brightened. "Oh! Is today that day?"

Oh, God.

No.

Shailaja yanked the door to Western Europe open. Portal magic flooded the rotunda. She tugged the loosely lassoed far seer closer to her, and he followed like a sheep going to slaughter.

My wrist healed.

"Fetch me the third instrument of assassination, Jade Godfrey," Shailaja said.

"I already have these two. Why would I need a third?"

ARTIFACTS, DRAGONS, AND OTHER LETHAL MAGIC

The rabid koala glanced behind me. Then, grinning, she stepped into the open portal.

Behind me, I could feel my father moving through the portal from the chamber of the treasure keeper. Shailaja wasn't going to stick around to chat.

"They won't let you out with those two, stupid," she said cheerfully.

"I am not the only one who sees," Chi Wen said, paraphrasing himself from before everything went all to hell ... well, Shailaja's party version of hell.

"Shut up, old man," Shailaja hissed. Then to me, she said, "And I'll spare your father. I find you very useful."

"The warrior doesn't need my protection."

"Is that why you were standing over him just now?"

Yazi staggered through the door behind me. I didn't have to glance back to know that he probably shouldn't have been on his feet yet. His magic tasted ... burned.

"I'll see you soon, alchemist." The rabid koala wagged her chin toward Chi Wen as if she was making some lame joke. Then she dragged the far seer into the portal.

Absolutely inexplicably, he went with her.

"Jade ..." My father's voice rumbled through the nexus.

I glanced over my shoulder. He was leaning on a gilded pillar near the door to Antarctica. He looked as though he'd aged twenty years.

The sight utterly enraged me. She had Chi Wen. She had my freaking sword. And she'd hurt my dad, badly.

Could the mangled katana kill a guardian? Was that why the far seer was calling me dragon slayer? Was that why Chi Wen hadn't fought the rabid koala?

Shit.

"Leave it, Jade." Yazi pushed away from the pillar, attempting to steady himself and failing.

The portal began to close. I spun away from my injured father. I dove into the waning magic, slipping past the door seconds before it shut.

"Jade!" My father's warning was swallowed as I tumbled through the golden transportation magic.

I had no idea where Shailaja was taking us, but I was completely prepared to show up primed and stab-happy.

Chapter Six

Except I didn't show up anywhere. The portal magic just went on and on. My run slowed to a walk. Then I wasn't sure I was moving anywhere at all, so I stopped.

I peered forward, then looked back. I couldn't see anything. No door behind me or in front. No ... nothing.

Just miles and miles of endless portal.

Or maybe ... just a sealed-off pocket of portal magic.

Was I trapped?

I shook the silly thought off. I couldn't get trapped in a portal. Its magic wasn't a here-and-now location. It was just a means to pass through.

I focused my thoughts on Shailaja. It wasn't a difficult task. I'd never hated anyone so fervently. I walked toward that focus.

And ... went nowhere.

I started panicking. I could feel hysteria creeping up, threatening to clog my throat and muddy my thoughts.

I threaded my fingers through my necklace and held my knife at the ready. I called on all the magic I held in both. I pushed the panic away.

I focused on the nexus. The carved doors, the golden pillars. The marble floors, the rounded walls. The mind-shattering magic it held.

I walked toward it.

I went nowhere.

I focused on the bakery basement. I focused on my kitchen, on my apartment, my bed, my mother, and my grandmother. But then I remembered that the particular portal I had just tried to walk through was tied to Western Europe, and therefore it didn't lead to any of those things.

I tried to think of London, then Scotland. But I couldn't recall specific places or … or … or …

I was trapped.

Somehow, I was trapped in the portal. I couldn't move forward or back.

The golden magic that I'd always found so inviting and buoying was slowly suffocating me. Which was ridiculous. Magic couldn't choke me. I was an alchemist. I could control magic.

But … not this magic. It wasn't my magic. Portals were the treasure keeper's magic. And, to a lesser degree, the magic of the daughter of the treasure keeper before Pulou.

Somehow Shailaja had caught me … ensnared me. Maybe doing so was as simple as closing the portal before I could pass through it.

My father's bellowed warning echoed through my overwrought mind.

I had to calm down. I just had to figure it out.

The portals were tied to the treasure keeper's magic. Some doorways were permanently anchored within the natural magic of the world, tied to specific grid points across the globe. Other doors, only Pulou could open and walk through. Those portals were ties created by the treasure keeper … ties anchored by the treasure keeper. So … what happened when the treasure keeper wasn't on duty?

It was possible that Pulou was still unconscious in the chamber of the treasure keeper. With half of his face … his brain … ripped out. Shredded by me in an attempt to stop the centipedes from killing him.

Was that why my father had asked me to not follow Shailaja?

Then …

Then I was going to die.

I was going to drown.

I was going to suffocate.

My magic wasn't going to burn bright until it consumed me or burned out. It was going to be slowly snuffed out.

I started clawing at my neck and chest. I knew I shouldn't, but I just couldn't breathe.

I couldn't breathe. I couldn't breathe.

I was going to die alone. Suffocated by magic I thought I had some mastery over. I'd gone from being simply ignorant and uneducated to being stupidly arrogant.

White dots appeared before my eyes.

Jesus. I was having a panic attack.

I stumbled.

I fell.

The golden vista around me went black.

I was dreaming of chocolate … dark, creamy chocolate with sweet cherry midnotes and a slightly smoky aftertaste …

I was dreaming of Warner.

And for a moment, I thought I was snuggled in the comfort of my bed. Safe. Adored.

Except Warner was angry. Scared and viciously angry. The taste of his magic intensified ... the sweet cherry overwhelmed with deep, dark cocoa and soot.

The intense emotion jolted me awake.

My heart was thrumming as if it had been shocked with adrenaline. I opened my eyes to the endless golden magic of the portal.

I was still trapped.

I had no idea how long I'd been passed out.

I was lying on my back. The betrothal rings on my necklace were resting near my heart. And just for a moment, I thought they felt warm, giving off a glimmer of the energy that had passed between Warner and me when we kissed in the chamber of the treasure keeper.

I pulled myself into a lotus position, choosing to ride the flood of emotion that had woken me, instead of collapsing back into my pathetic wallowing.

Maybe feeling Warner's anger was just part of a dream. Or maybe he was looking for me.

I slipped my fingers through the betrothal bands, reaching for a taste of the residual dragon magic that had lived within the metal before I absorbed it into the necklace.

I couldn't taste it.

I couldn't taste anything but the omnipresent portal magic.

I squeezed the rings, gritting my teeth against the pain as they bit into my fingers.

I shouldn't have jumped into the portal. I shouldn't have asked Warner to put himself anywhere near Shailaja. I'd assumed she had some plan, but I ignored my intuition because all I could see was the goal line.

Specifically, Warner freed. Free to be with me.

And I'd quashed his marriage proposal. I'd been scared and childish and ...

No.

I was too young for regrets. Hell, I was too stupid for regrets.

I wasn't done.

I gathered all my magic — all my fear, all my anger — and I focused it on the rings cutting into my fingers.

I stood, even though I shouldn't have been able to find purchase in the magic. I didn't know up from down. I didn't know forward from back.

I shut everything else out except the rings in my hand, and Warner. I opened my mind and heart to the possibility of a future.

Then I reached out my free hand. I reached out for the promise Warner had made when he gave me the rings. I reached for the dream. For the energy that had passed between him and me.

I wanted more.

I wanted it all. Every day.

And I'd fight for it. I'd burn for it.

I'd kill for it.

I stepped forward.

A firm, warm grip grasped my outstretched hand.

"Jade ..." Warner whispered through the portal, his voice resonating through my head and my heart.

Still completely blind within the golden magic, I loosened my hold on the rings, reaching out and up to wrap my hand around the back of Warner's neck.

He pulled me forward into a crushing, fierce, far-too-brief kiss. Then he scooped me up and lifted me out of the portal.

We crossed through into the nexus. I could taste the shift in the magic around me, but I still couldn't see anything but an endless wash of gold.

"Can you stand?" Warner asked.

I nodded and he put me down. I felt the solid marble underneath my feet for only an instant before I was crushed into a brutal, sooty, Chinese-spiced, dark-chocolate hug.

"I thought I'd lost you," Yazi said, pressing his lips against my temple hard enough to bruise me. He let go before I could respond, though. "Healer? Her eyes?"

The magic of the portal snapped shut behind us.

I felt Qiuniu brush his fingers across my temples. I could barely taste his magic, having to strain to hear the music he usually carried with him.

I blinked, my eyesight clearing enough to make out his lovely face and his strained, dark eyes.

"What's wrong?" I murmured.

"Your magic is overwhelmed, and my own is tasked elsewhere," he said. "I'm sorry, but it will take time for you to regain your equilibrium."

"That's not what I meant … something besides me is wrong."

The healer turned away without comment, hunching down over a large figure propped up beside the door Warner had just pulled me through.

A large, fur-cloaked figure.

Pulou.

I blinked a few more times, but my sight remained hazed in gold.

The treasure keeper was slumped over his knees. The healer pressed his shoulder and he shifted back against the gilded wall behind him.

I took a step toward Pulou and stumbled.

Warner caught me just as I realized that my perspective was oddly skewed. The floor had felt a lot closer than it actually was. "How long was I … gone?" I asked.

"A few hours," Yazi said, crossing to the healer and the treasure keeper. He moved as if nursing multiple injuries. The braid burn at his neck was an angry series of red, swollen welts.

Hours? And the guardians were still behaving as if they'd just been attacked and injured? They should have been fully healed. If not instantly, then certainly within an hour or two.

I looked at Warner for confirmation. My eyesight had cleared enough that I could plainly see the stress etched across his face and his stiffly held shoulders.

"More than a few hours," he said. "I couldn't get to you. We couldn't get to you without the treasure keeper. So … the healer woke him … upon request."

Qiuniu snorted. I gathered it was the 'request' part of Warner's declaration he found suspect.

The healer and Yazi hunkered down, placing Pulou's arms over their shoulders as they lifted him between them. It wasn't an easy task.

I was starting to shake. I grasped my necklace and fought the impulse. It wasn't a good time to break down, not in any noticeable way. Not in front of a bunch of seriously injured demigods.

"Jade …" the treasure keeper muttered.

"You found her," the healer said. He lifted his free hand and placed it on Pulou's neck as if checking his pulse.

The treasure keeper's head lolled to the side. His face was a raw mass of barely healed, bright-red scar tissue. He was still missing an ear.

My father stumbled as if more weight had just shifted onto him, catching him off guard.

I reached for Warner's hand. He met me halfway. Gripping him and my necklace helped to steady my trembling limbs. I hated seeing my father diminished. It didn't … fit. It didn't click with my worldview.

"Pulou sleeps again," Qiuniu said. "As should you, warrior."

Yazi ignored the younger guardian. "Jade, you are not to leave the nexus."

"Sure thing, Dad."

His fierce gaze fell to the centipedes attached to my necklace. "You have the braids as well?"

I dug the five-colored silk braids out of the pocket of my jeans, holding them across my open palm.

Warner squeezed my other hand a little too hard.

Qiuniu flinched.

And I couldn't taste a single drop of the magic that bothered them all so much. Pulou had told me that my magic masked the power of the instruments when I held them, but obviously even the sight of the braids disturbed the healer and Warner.

"The sentinel is officially reinstated," my father said. His tone was unyielding.

"What?" I cried.

Warner shook his head, just once. "Without the spell."

Yazi scowled at the interruption. "He will collect the instruments from you and give them to the treasure keeper. You will not leave the nexus. You will leave the hunt to me."

"She holds the far seer," I said. "She's made ransom demands that you can't fulfill."

"Chi Wen's participation in all of this is … confusing, but ultimately his own choice. Perhaps he thought to draw her away from you … from us."

"Or perhaps he had a deadly weapon at his neck."

"What?" Warner asked.

I locked my gaze to my father's. Tension ran along his jaw.

Warner and Qiuniu glanced between us.

When neither of us elaborated, the healer shifted Pulou higher onto his shoulder. "Warrior," the Brazilian guardian said softly. "We must —"

"I know," Yazi snapped.

Warner turned to me, holding a plain platinum box in his hand. I made a show of dutifully depositing the braids into it. He snapped the rune-etched lid closed.

I met my father's gaze a second time. "I don't need the instruments to take out the rabid koala. I believe I've proven that my knife will do just fine."

Warner closed his eyes and shook his head. The healer quashed an involuntary laugh.

"Jade." My father gnashed his teeth on my name. "You're making it personal."

"It is personal."

Yazi tried to take a step toward me, then realized he couldn't do so without dragging Pulou and Qiuniu with him. He looked to Warner. "Sentinel?"

"I'll do my best, warrior."

I tamped my mouth closed on any further retort. I was being childish again. Being ordered around by a parent evidently brought out that reaction. However, it obviously wasn't the right time for overt feistiness. My father needed a dose of whatever healing power Pulou had gotten from Qiuniu to make him sleep, so I needed to shut up and agree ... for now.

Yazi eyed me for another moment. Then he and the healer turned to carry the treasure keeper out of the nexus.

"My time and reserves are already overtasked," Qiuniu said without looking back. "Until the other guardians return to the nexus, we will be ... lesser."

"I understand, healer," Warner said.

"Warner is not the boss of me," I muttered to my father's retreating back.

"Excuse me?" Warner said quietly.

I looked up at him. "Nothing. I just had to get it out. What do you 'understand'?"

"The healer has given us permission to pursue the ... Shailaja. But we won't have any guardians at our backs until this has all been sorted. If we choose to act against the warrior's wishes, we are on our own."

"Geez, you pack a lot into an understanding. I didn't hear any of that."

Warner reached up and ran his fingers through my hair, tugging on the curl that Pulou had chopped in half over a year ago. That lock was longer now, and though Warner liked to tease my vanity over getting it snipped, he wasn't being playful.

"I know now," he said. "I know how losing you feels. How you must have felt in the temple of the centipede when you thought ..."

I closed the space between us, pressing myself fully against him and lifting up on my toes. He met me halfway, but it was my kiss.

I kissed him for all the pain I'd caused him. I kissed him for almost leaving before we'd really begun our life together. I kissed him because I didn't say yes.

Energy from the betrothal rings ran between us. And though it seemed cheesy to even think of it in those terms, it felt as though that magic connected us, heart to heart.

"You found me," I whispered against his lips.

"I thought it was you who found me."

I laughed softly. "Well, that's impossibly perfect."

"I guess I can't make you promise not to do it again."

"Could you promise such a thing?"

"Doubtful."

"There you go."

Warner brushed his lips against mine again. Then we both caught a movement in our peripheral vision.

Drake was waiting, watching us from a few feet away. He was in his dragon leathers, and was taller than he was the last time I'd seen him. Pushing six feet now. His dark hair was cut almost too short, making him look older than his almost-sixteen years. Older and angry. I'd never seen him look so fierce.

No, not fierce. Vengeful.

"I'm going with you," he said, once he had our full attention.

"No," Warner said.

"All right," I said.

Warner glared at me sternly, which was difficult since we were still both intimately wrapped around each other. "Even if we are going after her —"

"We are."

"Even if, the fledgling —"

"Who is stronger and more resilient than either of us."

"Not everything is about magical amperage. Training and knowledge —"

"Chi Wen is my mentor," Drake said, stepping closer. "He's my responsibility."

Warner dropped his arms from around me, running his hand through his hair with much frustration. "Jesus, there's two of you."

I swallowed my smirk. Now really wasn't the time to be amused.

"You've got that backward, fledgling," Warner continued. "You are his responsibility. Our responsibility."

Drake turned his dark gaze on me. "If you leave me, I'll follow."

"I know," I said. Then to Warner, I added, "If we're all ignoring guardian directives, we might as well be together." Suanmi had almost fried me for taking Drake to London when I'd been hunting Sienna, and Shailaja might actually be crazier than my blood-crazed sister. But the fledgling guardian was safer with Warner and me than he would be hunting on his own.

Warner growled a string of curse words in German under his breath. He yanked a second rune-carved box out of his pocket and held it out to me.

"If we're leaving," he said. "If. We won't get out of the nexus without giving the instruments to the treasure keeper. I think they might have been part of the reason I couldn't find you in the portals."

"Uncollectable by dragons," I said. "Though Shailaja managed to get her hands on them."

"She touched boxed instruments. Though why the hell Pulou let her spend enough time in the chamber to find them —" Warner clamped his mouth shut, then slid his eyes toward Drake. The fledgling was listening to everything with great intensity.

Being pissy about the guardians was obviously a line Warner was unwilling to cross around a guardian-to-be.

I tickled my fingers underneath the centipedes twined around my necklace, and they obligingly dropped into my hand. Then I deposited them into the box Warner held.

He snapped the lid closed, almost clipping my fingers.

I raised my eyebrows at him challengingly.

He narrowed his own eyes at me. "Do I have to drag you with me?"

"We won't go anywhere without you," I said. "You're the boss. Remember?"

"Who made him the boss?" Drake asked. "I thought the removal of the sentinel spell was successful?"

"It was," I said.

"The warrior," Warner said, just a split second after me. "And I didn't need to be reinstated. I chose to have the spell removed, but that doesn't mean I intended to abandon my duties."

I narrowed my eyes at the so-called sentinel. I wanted him away from Shailaja, and … crap. Well, here I was, threatening to go after her and forcing him to come with me.

Drake frowned. "If anything, I should be the boss. The far seer is my mentor —"

"No." Warner and I said it in unison.

Then, swallowing more inappropriate laughter, I brushed my fingers against the back of Warner's wrist. He was holding both boxes in one hand. It should have been impossible that such terrible, destructive artifacts could be contained in such small packages.

"I won't go anywhere without you."

"The portals are shut down, Jade. You wouldn't get very far before I caught up."

"And then you'd be pissy and sullen for hours," I said. "I'm cool with avoiding that."

Warner's growl was playful. Then he turned away to stride off in the direction my father and the healer had taken Pulou.

"You have an odd method of communicating with the sentinel," Drake said.

"It's called flirting."

He looked doubtful. "Is it?"

"Hush, fledgling." I grinned.

Drake nodded thoughtfully, then reached over his shoulder and tugged a rolled piece of thick parchment out of a leather backpack he wore. The pack blended so perfectly with his dragon leathers that I hadn't seen it before. He was also armed with his golden sword. Its plain, serviceable hilt and pommel protruded from just behind his shoulder. Its sheath was built into his vest.

"I have a map of the grid point portals," he said. "They should all still be active. Though the ride might be bumpy."

Bumpy? How about suffocating? Or terrifying?

Delightful.

"So we can't go directly back to the bakery?"

"Not without Pulou to open a specific portal." Drake eyed me. "You should know that. You always come and go with Pulou's help, don't you?"

"Ah …"

"Is there a permanent portal in the bakery?"

"Maybe …"

"And you didn't tell me?" Drake forgot his gruff new persona in order to be genuinely upset for a moment.

"It's a secret."

"Oh." Drake unrolled the map, looking mournful.

"You're thinking of all the cupcakes you could have eaten."

"I am."

"That's why I didn't tell you."

"Plus the secret part."

"Right."

"I understand secrets."

"Any you'd like to share?"

"Nope."

Drake grinned at me, but neither of us could maintain the levity for long.

"If the portal to the bakery is of Pulou's construction, it will no longer be active," he said.

"It is Pulou's."

"Even the guardians are stranded right now. With only Pulou, Yazi, and Qiuniu in residence. The other guardians will know something is wrong. If they can abandon whatever they're doing, they'll make their way to a grid point and return to the nexus."

"How long does that usually take?"

"I don't know. This hasn't ever happened before."

"Ever? Like never ever?"

"Yeah. Never."

"Okay, then. That's not daunting."

"Nothing daunts the warrior's daughter."

"A brave face isn't necessarily a sign of courage. In my case, it could simply be pure stupidity."

"I disagree."

Our conversation was interrupted by Warner striding back into the nexus. He was outfitted in a backpack similar to Drake's, though he was armed only with the sacrificial knife I'd modified for him as a Christmas gift two years ago.

Oddly, he also had a wad of jade-green silk scrunched in his hand. As he drew near, he flicked his wrist to fan the fabric out. It was a gorgeous, gold-embroidered, quilted silk jacket with a short Asian-inspired collar.

He handed the jacket to me. Apparently, Warner had noticed I was wearing only a tank top.

I accepted the pretty thing, smoothing my fingers admiringly over the dragon motif on its front panels.

"Thank you," I murmured sedately, though I was grinning like a gushing idiot.

"I didn't want you to be cold. I looked for a set of leathers, but found nothing usable. Not quickly."

"Who does it belong to? I'm just going to end up ruining it." I sighed.

Warner shrugged. "It was abandoned in the healer's chambers. I doubt anyone is coming back for it."

I laughed. "I doubt the owner is being invited back." Anyone who went around laying blistering kisses on unknown half-witches, like the healer was prone to doing, didn't spend many evenings alone.

Warner snorted.

Drake was glancing back and forth between Warner and me. "I don't get it. It's a somewhat useful garment. Why would the owner abandon it?"

The sentinel shook his head at the fledgling, then gestured at him to spread out the grid point portal map. Black-inked continents, lighter colored-in countries, and crisscrossed lines of longitude and latitude inscribed the ancient-looking parchment.

I slipped on the jacket. It was silk lined and felt absolutely delicious against my skin. I had been a little chilly. God, I absolutely adored Warner. Did everyone have issues with not completely pawing and gushing all over their boyfriends every second of the day? Maybe it was just me.

"I have the dragonskin map," I said. "So if we get close enough to the final instrument, I might be able to get the map to reveal the temple or whatever. If it works the same way as it did before."

Warner flicked his eyes to mine, stoic and unyielding. Apparently, all I had to do to ruin the cozy feelings that had settled between us was to open my mouth.

"We are not collecting the instrument," he said, looking down to Drake's map.

"How else are we going to lure her out?" I asked mildly, attempting to not be a complete brat. "She can track me, but we can't track her. Apparently, no one can. Right? That's why we got all the way to the temple in Peru before the warrior found us."

Tension stiffened Warner's shoulders. He didn't look at me. We didn't talk about Peru much. We didn't talk about Shailaja, or the guardians' previous failures in apprehending her. But I was fairly certain that Warner had engaged in endless conversations about it all with Pulou and my father.

I prodded him. "It's the shadow demons, isn't it?"

"What shadow demons?" Drake asked.

"Shailaja somehow bound the souls of a sect of eternal-life sorcerers to a demon entity that feeds on magic," I said. "They're like leeches."

"That's concise." Warner snorted.

"I do think about these things, you know." Apparently, I was only capable of not being a brat for about a minute.

"There is some … conjecture that Shailaja created the sect," Warner said. "Gathered followers and so forth."

Jesus. "That was in the former treasure keeper's journal?"

Warner nodded. He was still studying Drake's map, probably memorizing every grid point he didn't know.

"Are these your notations?" Warner asked Drake, pointing to a series of newly inked Chinese characters. About three-quarters of the rectangles scattered across the continents had been labeled.

"Yes," the fledgling said. "An exercise for the treasure keeper. Homework, Jade calls it."

Warner grunted in acknowledgement, then continued eyeing the map.

"And these leeches are what? Familiars?" Drake asked. "Soldiers?"

"They allowed her to move through the temple of the braids in the Bahamas," I said. "Stripping through the magical protections ahead of her, until she triggered the final trap. The rabid koala needed the braids for her master plan, but she couldn't use the shadow demons to collect them. They would have drained them. I think. They can also leech magic from Adepts. Anyway, she was trapped there for five hundred years, give or take."

"She also uses the demons as some sort of transportation," Warner said. "Pulou isn't sure, but he thinks they might pull her in and out of this dimension. Making her difficult to track."

Bingo. And just as I'd thought.

"And her master plan?" Drake asked.

Warner glanced at me.

"Immortality," I said.

"By way of the mantle of the former treasure keeper," Warner added. "Pulou-who-was."

"She was going to kill her own father?" Drake asked, aghast.

"Apparently. Just as she attempted to kill Pulou today."

The fledgling returned his attention to the map he held while he chewed over the information we'd dumped on him.

"Do you have your cellphone?" Warner asked.

"Yeah. Though whether it will work after being in the nexus … and the portal … is always a crapshoot."

"Passport?"

"Nope. I've got some Canadian cash and my Visa card."

"But the heretic will come for the warrior's daughter?" Drake asked.

Warner sighed. "Yes, she'll come for Jade."

"She needs me to wield the third instrument," I said. "She intends to take the far seer's mantle. I guess Chi Wen will do as a fallback."

Drake snorted. "His guardian magic will consume her."

"Maybe," Warner said. "But the far seer will die either way. Hence, the necessity of leaving the third instrument where it lies." He looked at me pointedly.

"She's got Jade's broken sword," Drake said.

"How do you know?" I asked.

"I listen."

"So do I," Warner said … again, pointedly. "And no one mentioned a sword to me."

I cleared my throat, trying to formulate the right words. Not only about how I apparently had created a weapon that was capable of harming a guardian, but also how in the process of mangling the katana, I had revealed my ability to drain every last drop of magic from another Adept. Permanently.

Warner raised an eyebrow at me. Drake shuffled his feet. The fledgling was almost as bad as I was about filling in the silent bits of conversations.

I pressed my fingers to my eyes. My vision still wasn't great, and I certainly wasn't thinking completely clearly. I was scared and trying to hide it. I was confused and trying to talk my way out of it.

I dropped my hands, then pointed to a sort-of-familiar rectangle on the map. I wasn't talking about the sword. Not yet.

"That's our entry point."

"Alberta?" Warner asked.

"Those look like the Rocky Mountains to me," I said, drawing my finger down a line of hand-drawn mountain peaks to the left of the grid point I'd suggested using. "So the portal must open somewhere between Edmonton and Calgary?" The cities were identified, but unfortunately I didn't read … or speak Chinese. None of the North or South American portals were tagged with any of Drake's notes.

"Yep. It's the nearest grid point to Vancouver," Drake said helpfully. "Over land."

"Over land is a necessity for the alchemist," Warner said. "She doesn't like to get her feet wet."

I narrowed my eyes at him. Apparently, two could play the pissy game.

"Who does like getting their feet wet?" Drake said, interrupting the tongue-lashing I was about to apply to my snarky boyfriend. "You're either in the pool or not."

"Fine," Warner said. "The walk from Alberta to Vancouver will give you plenty of time to tell me the tale of a sword powerful enough that it has given the guardians something to talk about."

"Yeah," I said. "But we'll have to figure out transportation and passports quickly, because we're going to Portland first."

"I thought we were going back to the bakery," Drake said. "Vancouver would be a solid base of power. A good place to lure the heretic."

"Shailaja isn't going to follow me to Vancouver. She's annoying and seriously screwed in the head, but she's not stupid."

"She'll only follow if she thinks you're going after the instrument?" Drake asked.

"I don't think she'd risk coming after me under any other circumstances."

"But if we stay somewhere long enough," Warner said, thinking out loud, "she might show up simply to see what you're doing and give you a push. Actually, Vancouver might be the best choice."

"But I still don't think she'd show in Vancouver. She might not be able to track me behind the wards on the bakery. So even if I had already collected and secured the third instrument, she wouldn't know it. Plus, Gran and Scarlett kicked her ass once already, and now they're forewarned."

Warner scrubbed his hand across his face. "She knows you don't hold the third instrument."

My heart pinched ... just a tiny irrational pinch. "Because you told her?"

Warner grimaced, then sighed. "She caught me off guard. Her questions seemed ... innocuous at first, then concerned for your well-being."

"My well-being?"

"Jade ..."

I opened my mouth to interrogate Warner about when, where, and why a conversation had taken place between the rabid koala and him, but he looked so pissed at himself that I didn't articulate any of it.

Blithely ignoring the weird tension ebbing and flowing between Warner and me, Drake spoke. "How is Portland any better? That's pack territory."

"The far seer isn't the only one who sees," I said. "As he was annoyingly insistent about earlier."

Warner rolled his shoulders but kept his mouth shut. I told myself I wasn't going to feel guilty, like I was withholding information. It wasn't as though he gave me a detailed list of his daily activities. Plus, we hadn't exactly had time to chat, what with removing sentinel spells and getting trapped in the portal system.

A grin spread across Drake's unusually dour features. "Chi Wen gave you a clue?"

"A clue to what?" Warner asked.

"We're going to see the oracle!" Drake hooted.

"Yeah," I groused. "Freaking delightful. And apparently we're walking from Alberta."

"The vampire owns a jet," Warner said, blithely ignoring my sarcasm.

"Yeah, the idea of you and Drake in a jet shutting down the engines and the navigation system with your magic isn't scary at all. Plus, we can't use Kett. That's … rude."

"I was thinking more that his immortality is definitely a bonus when facing an unstable and unpredictable opponent. And he's bored. Bored elder vampires aren't a good thing in general. So we'd be doing the world a service by inviting him."

"And dragging him into all this mess … again? Shailaja practically killed him last time. And I'm not sure his snack break actually slowed her down at all."

Warner shrugged. "I doubt you'd hear him complain."

"I like the vampire," Drake said. "He's cool."

I laughed, completely involuntarily. "You can say that again."

"Why? You clearly heard me the first time. And what do you mean by snack break?"

Warner shook his head, grinning despite being in stern sentinel mode. "If we're going to move, we need to go now. Before any of the guardians return." He eyed Drake, then me. "Going now might be overlooked. Breaking out is entirely different."

"We're going to need snowshoes," I muttered, turning to the door that led to the grid points in North America. Needing snowshoes might be a huge exaggeration, but for a West Coast girl, the idea of trekking through Alberta in January was seriously daunting.

I really, really wasn't looking forward to walking through the portal. I hadn't quite shaken the lingering effects of my last attempt to cross through the nexus's transportation magic. Plus, I was seriously aware that I was still riding an adrenaline high triggered by the sight of my father and Pulou so badly diminished. But that fear wasn't going to get me far.

Warner wrapped his hand around my waist, leaving my right hand free in case I had to pull my knife.

Drake reached for my left hand.

Thus flanked and more than well supported, I nodded and opened the door before me. "Alberta. Here we go."

*

Chapter Seven

Warner, Drake, and I stepped through the magic of the portal, hand in hand. Apparently, the three of us commanded its power so definitively that I didn't even have time to build up to a panic attack. The portal magic wasn't going to trap me, cage me, confine me, swallow me, drown me …

Okay, maybe I had enough time to freak out a little. At least for the brief moment that I could feel my left foot behind me on the marble of the nexus and my right foot ahead of me, hovering over nothing. Then I completed the step and found my boot buried in about seven inches of snow.

Drake dropped my hand and immediately began casing the snowy, tree-shielded hollow we'd arrived in. The light-blue sky was clear. And while the immediate area was covered in snow, it was not as deep as I'd imagined it would be in Central Alberta at this time of year.

It was, however, cold.

Warner had pulled his knife sometime during the crossing, but as the portal snapped shut behind us — and since we weren't immediately attacked by some nefarious force — he sheathed it.

The curved blade of the knife always reminded me of the atrocious things Sienna had used it for, and the fact that I had then altered the weapon with blood magic to free the fledgling necromancer Mory from certain death in London. But Warner was meant to wield that knife. I had smoothed the wicked curve of the blade and added to its magic in the hopes of tempering it, but it was Warner who'd tamed it. So much so that I could taste only his magic now whenever he held it.

I rarely had any reason to manually sheathe or unsheathe my jade knife these days. It just magically came and went from my right hand as I willed. Just as Shailaja had inherited her miniportal trick from her father's guardian magic, I had apparently created a similar bond with my knife in mimicry of how my father wielded his weapon. Of course, Yazi's broadsword was a manifestation of his guardian power. My knife was carved from a pretty green stone I'd found on the edge of a river.

Following the scattered path of my thoughts, and before I spent any time taking in our surroundings — other than to note that it was cold and everything around us was blanketed in snow and teeming with natural magic — I turned to Warner.

"Shailaja can open miniature portals and throw things … weapons … through them."

Warner nodded. "The warrior mentioned that. And by weapons do you mean some mysterious sword that apparently everyone knows about but me?"

I swallowed, then cleared my throat. "Not everyone. Just Pulou and me. And my father … as of a few hours ago."

"I'm listening."

"My katana. Or at least it was a katana until I twisted it around my foster sister's neck, then drained every last drop of her magic out of her and into the blade."

Warner raised both his eyebrows. His green-blue eyes were a vibrant contrast to the white background of snow-covered trees behind him. "All of her magic?"

"Everything she'd stolen from the Adepts she killed ... and also all her natural magic ... her binding powers ... her witch magic. She was purely normal ... human ... when I was done."

From the corner of my eye, I saw Drake prowling the line of trees behind us. Though I'd faltered in recounting the sword's creation, it seemed terribly important to keep my gaze locked to Warner's.

"That's ..." He hesitated but didn't break eye contact with me. "That's unprecedented."

"That's why the treasure keeper took the mangled katana. That's why he suggested I might want to keep that information to myself."

"How many Adepts did Sienna kill?"

"I don't know ... I'm not sure all the bodies were recovered. Too many."

"And now Shailaja has this sword. She used it against a guardian? Successfully?"

I nodded, then forced myself to elaborate. "She threw it like a Frisbee. Except, you know, a Frisbee created through blood magic bound to a deadly sharp blade."

"A Frisbee." Warner echoed the word, carefully mimicking my pronunciation. He did the same thing every time he heard, then immediately learned, a new word or phrase.

"Like a chakram," Drake said. "Only larger. It's about double the typical size."

"Sorry?" I asked. "A chakram? And how do you know?"

"A circular throwing weapon with a sharpened outer edge," Drake elaborated. "From India. And I overheard the warrior discussing it with the healer. The cut was deep."

My stomach squelched at the thought of bringing harm to my own father. A cut deep enough that a healer as powerful as Qiuniu would question its origin was … disturbing.

Warner nodded thoughtfully. Happily, he still wasn't running away screaming.

"Okay. A chakram, then." It was my turn to carefully pronounce the foreign-sounding word.

"Shall we text the vampire?" Warner asked.

"That's it?"

"Do you have more to tell me?"

"Not that I can think of."

"So, yes. That's it."

I stared at Warner. "But …"

"But?"

"Jade thinks she's evil," Drake said oh-so-helpfully from somewhere above and behind me. "Because she created this evil thing. And now the heretic has use of it."

I turned away from the intense huddle I had going with Warner, looking up to see that Drake had climbed a large winter-bare, snow-shrouded tree.

I shivered in my quilted silk jacket, turning back to Warner and seeing him watching me.

"Evil?" he asked softly.

I shrugged, glancing toward the ground. But then my gaze caught on his knife. Another of my wicked, thoughtless creations.

"Ignorant, maybe," I mumbled. "That's worse, isn't it?"

Warner huffed out a laugh that I thought was terribly inappropriate.

I glared at him.

He grinned down at me. "You're cold. Text the vampire."

"There's no point in texting. First, the magic around here will probably fry the phone. Second, I doubt there's any signal. Third, we don't even know where the nearest airport is. We'll probably need to jack a car and drive into Calgary or Edmonton."

"Jack?" Warner asked, laughing.

"Yeah, you know. It's best to sound tough when discussing criminal activity."

"We could always ask her for directions ... or a car," Drake said. Effortlessly, he dropped some twenty feet out of the tree, landing with his hand pointing behind me.

I spun, but I saw only more trees.

"She's coming from the farmhouse. They'll probably have a phone." Drake took off in the direction he'd indicated.

Warner choked back another round of laughter.

I gave him the evil eye.

He smirked at me, then shrugged. "The gatekeeper. I didn't expect her to necessarily be so close."

I absolutely adored looking like an idiot in front of my boyfriend. I knew the grid point portals usually had gatekeepers who watched over them, such as Amber Cameron in Scotland. But the portal in Peru hadn't, so I had factored in the fairly remote location here and decided that this one probably wouldn't either.

"Peru didn't," I said snottily as I turned on my heel to follow Drake.

"Actually ..." Warner started to contradict me, but he swallowed his words when I rounded on him. "Right. Peru didn't."

I laughed at his too-obvious lie.

He smiled. Then, wrapping his arm around my shoulders, he tugged me forward to press a soft kiss to my lips.

I allowed myself to breathe in his warmth, just for a moment. I was still jumpy, and my dowser senses felt wonky from having been immersed in the portal magic for too long. Warner's black-forest-cake magic was a tasty comfort.

"There isn't a speck of evil in you, Jade Godfrey," he whispered as he brushed his lips across my cheek.

He released me. Then he took a few quick steps to catch up to Drake, who had ducked between the trees and out of sight.

Warmed within and without, I smiled and followed, telling myself that we all had our own definitions of good and evil. I knew how close I walked the line between the darkness and the light. Hell, I leaned toward the light as fervently as others embraced the darkness. Cupcakes, trinkets, chocolate, Warner, Drake, Kandy … and even Kett were my anchors.

I just needed to remember to remind myself of that … like, constantly.

A woman was striding toward us across a wide stretch of land that I assumed was usually filled with fields of wheat or canola. In the distance to either side of us, fences crisscrossed more pasture and grasslands. Out from among the trees, the blue sky appeared endless. And without a wisp of cloud cover, the morning was cool. Maybe around minus six degrees Celsius. The bright orb of the sun was near enough to the eastern horizon behind us to hazard a guess at the time of day.

The hollow in which the portal was nestled was surrounded by a grove of trees, then encircled by a split-rail fence that seemed most likely erected to bar access to the cattle in the far-off neighboring fields.

The footprint trail through the snow that the stranger left in her wake led back to a well-kept and rather large blue-gray farmhouse. A similarly painted barn stood farther off to the east, as did a grain silo. A curl of smoke rose from the chimney.

The woman's heavy jacket hung open, as if she'd pulled it on in haste. Her chin-length dark-blond hair lifted in the breeze that also ruddied her pale cheeks.

She was also a witch, through and through. Her magic was an extrapolation of the natural power that emanated from the ground beneath my feet. All hay and fertile earth and something with eggs ... milk custard? No. Panna cotta, maybe.

The witch carried a second jacket, which was a considerate gesture since any guardian who walked through the portal probably wouldn't need one, except in a blizzard or perhaps to blend in. She shielded her eyes from the sun as we neared.

I wondered how long it had been since a dragon walked through the portal she watched over. Maybe Haoxin, the guardian of North America, came here once in a while. I could see free-ranging chickens scratching in the snow in a wire-fenced area at the rear of the farmhouse. What little I knew of Haoxin suggested she was something of a foodie, so fresh eggs might be a big draw for her.

Drake and Warner dropped back to fall into step behind me. The woman striding toward us faltered, stumbling slightly.

I smiled, calling politely, "Hello. Gatekeeper?"

The witch nodded, more hesitant as she closed the final dozen feet between us. She eyed Drake and me, but seemed mostly concerned with Warner. I didn't blame her. I might find the sentinel sexy, but I was fairly certain that everyone else got stuck on his intimidating size and gruff demeanor.

"Thank you for greeting us," I said, ignoring that she was clutching the extra coat she carried as if it were a life jacket. "I'm Jade Godfrey. This is —"

"Godfrey?" the witch blurted. "Pearl's granddaughter?"

"Yes."

"But ..." She eyed Drake and Warner again, then snapped her mouth shut on her unasked question. She wanted to know how a witch had walked through a portal owned and operated by dragons. But asking about magic was considered rude in the Adept world. It was an odd rule of etiquette, but I'd been thankful for it pretty much every day since the discovery that my father was one of the guardian nine, and not some anonymous Australian backpacker like I'd always thought.

The witch thrust the jacket toward me. "Marigold Albrecht. Mari."

We stared at each other for a moment, but the witch didn't elaborate. Apparently, I was becoming far too accustomed to Adepts who insisted on listing all their titles and accomplishments after introducing themselves.

Warner stretched his hand out toward Mari. "Warner."

She hesitated before shaking it.

"Drake." The fledgling stepped forward to offer his hand. "Is this your farm?"

"My family's." She raised her chin proudly as she shook Drake's hand. "We've held this land since it was first settled."

"We are well met, Marigold Albrecht," I said. "We're also unfortunately in a bit of a hurry. We have to sort out … transportation."

She nodded. "It's breakfast. Saturday, January 23rd. Just … in case you didn't know. I was making French toast. Would you join us while you … make your calls?"

As I glanced at Warner, my traitorous stomach grumbled. Yes, practically loud enough for the chickens and cows to hear. Though, between fighting off Shailaja and getting trapped in the portal, I'd apparently gone without food for twenty-four hours, so it really wasn't surprising.

The sentinel threw back his head and laughed. Drake, who never missed an opportunity for mirth, instantly joined him.

Though I swore I could feel the rumble of their combined magic underneath my feet, I ignored them as I addressed Mari primly. "That would be lovely."

She nodded. Her eyes were wide and edged with fear at the casual power held in Warner's and Drake's laughter. She turned stiffly, leading the way back to the farmhouse.

Warner's laugh ebbed into a chuckle.

I pulled on the puffy winter coat Mari had handed me as I kept pace with the witch. "It's not as chilly as I expected," I said. "Less snow."

"Yes," Mari said. "The weather has been unusually warm. We're hoping for more snow, of course. To get water into the ground for spring. The drought was bad last year. Hay has gone from forty dollars to a hundred and fifty a bale."

I glanced over my shoulder at Warner. He nodded in response to my look. He'd leave some gold for Mari and her family when we departed.

"Not that I'm complaining," Mari said. "It's a good life."

"Of course not." With our Canadian duty of discussing the weather fulfilled, silence fell between us.

What were Adepts supposed to talk about if not magic?

"The vampire?" Warner asked, stepping up beside us.

Marigold stumbled, then gasped when Drake appeared out of nowhere to catch her elbow.

I dug into my satchel, pulling out the lead-lined case I stored my phone in to protect it from the magic of the nexus and the portals. "Will I get a signal out here?" I asked Mari.

"You should."

The witch picked up her pace as we reached the yard and passed the chicken coop, which was a miniature replica of the farmhouse. Beyond the main fence, pure white hens scratched around the edges of the wire-encased run attached to the coop, while a large white rooster with bright-red, low-hanging wattles eyed us warily.

Just beyond a back porch built of graying cedar, a tiny toddler clad in overalls was pressed against the kitchen window. A wide, low set of wooden stairs led to the back door. A blond-haired man appeared behind the child, coaxing the now-madly waving boy away from the window.

I fell back a few steps as Mari jogged up the stairs, pausing to activate my phone and give her some space to explain our appearance to her family.

She entered the home, leaving the door open. Three pairs of gumboots were neatly lined up by the back door, along with a galvanized metal bucket filled with tiny plastic gardening tools.

Something about that hint of a tidy, regular life made my heart pinch. I turned away from the hushed conversation Marigold was having with her family just a step inside the kitchen. The toddler was tucked behind her leg, watching the strangers on the doorstep. Mari's hand was tangled in his already-mussed hair. She was leaning into the man, who I assumed was her husband. Their body language was easy and intimate.

My phone powered up successfully. I opened the messaging app, selected the thread tied to Kett's mobile number, and applied my thumbs to the keyboard.

Hey. We're in Alberta. About to go hunting. How about a lift?

I looked up from the screen.

Drake had hopped the fence and was sneaking up on the chickens in an attempt to pet them. The rooster was not pleased with the fledgling's antics.

Warner was watching me. Too closely.

"We shouldn't stay," I said. "Now that I'm not in the nexus …"

"Shailaja will be tracking you," Warner said, finishing my sentence. He tilted his head. The sun kissed his face, glinting off the lighter strands within his two-day-old stubble.

My heart pinched again. And then I was suddenly struggling to hold back tears.

"Life is not always so … fraught," Warner said quietly.

"No?" The word came out twisted with doubt and fear. I tamped down on the foolish irrationality gnawing at me as I growled, "Prove it."

A grin transformed Warner's stern face. "I plan to."

"Hey!" Drake shouted. "Egg!"

We turned to see the fledgling holding his prize aloft. He'd raided the nesting boxes on the outside of the coop. Apparently, the rooster had decided he wasn't a threat before wandering off with a group of his girls. The other hens at Drake's feet appeared more interested in the possibility of treats than egg snatching.

"Drake!" I hissed. "Don't steal other people's food."

"That's all right," Mari said from the porch behind me. "He's welcome to it."

I turned to find her holding the toddler on her hip. The tableau made my heart wrench.

"I'm sorry," I said. "We can't stay. We may be tracked here, and … well …" I swept my hand to indicate the house and the yard. "I wouldn't want to bring any harm in our wake."

Mari sniffed. "No one is tracking you through my wards." She lifted her chin proudly. Then she reached back and placed her hand on the exterior of the house, next to the door.

Witch magic swept up and around the house and yard, slipping underneath my feet and tingling against my skin. Mari had triggered protection wards. The powerful, deep-rooted magic filled my mouth with the taste of a creamy, grassy-finished cheese similar to Camembert.

"You are welcome to join us," Mari said, repeating her invitation.

The magic of the wards settled around me, leaving only a comforting hum.

"Thank you," Warner said. "Your hospitality is appreciated."

"Hello," I said to the boy as I stepped up to the patio. "I'm Jade."

"Garnet," the chubby cherub answered gleefully, as if he lived to tell people his name. Then he held out his hand.

I hesitated, suddenly concerned about touching the boy. About hurting him … just by being in proximity to him. What the hell? It wasn't like I was poisonous.

I reached out, cupping his hand in mine and getting most of his forearm in the process. He grasped me firmly, without trepidation.

"I'm three and thirty days today," he declared.

His magic tickled my taste buds. It was a combination of the witches — his parents — standing silently and proudly behind him, but also uniquely his.

"I can taste your magic, Garnet," I said, leaning closer. My necklace swung forward to capture the toddler's attention, though he didn't grab for it.

His mother went very still, holding her breath. Even having two Adept parents wasn't a guarantee that a child would manifest any magic.

"Does it taste like French toast?" Garnet asked. "Or pancakes? Sunday is pancake day."

I laughed, letting go of his hand and wishing I had a reason to keep hold of his soft, unblemished skin a little longer. "Your mother tastes like panna cotta … like yummy custard. Your dad?" I lifted my gaze to the silent figure looming in the open doorway.

"Brick. Brick Albrecht," he said, his tone suggesting he was still unsure of the strangers on his doorstep. "I took Mari's family name."

I nodded, then turned my attention back to the child. "Your dad's magic tastes of frothed milk edged with some sort of spice … sweet, yet strong with a hint of earthy licorice … caraway?"

"And me?" Garnet asked.

"And you?" I held out my hand to the boy again, palm up. He placed his hand on mine without hesitation. His gaze was full of trust and curiosity.

That was what I'd been missing.

That was what I'd been walling myself off from. What I'd come to believe didn't exist any longer. Not in my world, at least.

"Your magic tastes like vanilla cream pie, baked meringue and all."

Mari let out the breath she'd been holding.

"Pie!" Garnet exclaimed, wiggling free of his mother. "That's dessert!"

Apparently, tasting of pie wasn't particularly satisfying to the toddler. Though he appeared unfazed as he ducked between his parents' knees and stormed happily into the house.

I looked at Mari. "I guess pancakes would have been better."

She laughed, then caught herself. "Thank you," she whispered. "We didn't know. We weren't sure he had any magic."

I wasn't overly pleased about the edge of reverence in her tone, so I shrugged. "It's customary, isn't it? To give a gift to your hosts? Normally, I'd bring cupcakes."

"Oh!" Mari exclaimed. "Yes. You're that witch."

Drake snickered behind me. I turned back to give him the evil eye as Mari and Brick stepped back into the house and invited us in.

My phone pinged.

Drake followed the Albrechts inside. Just beyond the kitchen table, he kneeled down to present Garnet with the perfect brown egg he'd collected.

I glanced at the text message that had appeared on my cellphone.

> *Nearest airport?*

Right. Our mission … whether we chose to accept it or not. Obviously, Kett was on board.

Warner stepped past me, brushing a kiss to my forehead while he glanced at the text. "See?" he murmured. "Bored. And too powerful to be."

He stepped into the kitchen, reaching out to shake hands with Brick before I could respond.

I sighed, then followed. Thankfully, a fire was roaring in a potbelly stove between the kitchen and the family room, because we'd just let all the warm air out of the house.

Apparently, Mari and Brick's place was just off Range Road 203, and a fifteen-minute drive east of Bashaw, Alberta, by way of Highway 53. We were a little under two hours from Edmonton, but Bashaw did indeed have an airport.

The area was known for wheat, canola, and beef, as I'd guessed, but fruit and fishing were the primary industries closer to Buffalo Lake just to the south. Brick was chatty and rather proud of their heritage, once he had food in front of him and we were all seated around the kitchen table. I quickly figured out that the farm itself and the portal gatekeeper responsibilities were passed through the matriarchal line to Marigold, though, rather than through his family. Hence him taking the Albrecht name.

The French toast was brilliant. Crispy on the outside and chewy in the middle. Doused in single-pressed maple syrup, it soothed away the residual anxiety I'd carried through from the portal incident.

Haoxin did drop by the farm, about once a year. She'd been doing so for the past hundred and fifteen years. Though, based on my rough math and basic understanding of the guardian ascension timeline, I estimated that she'd only been the pretty, petite swathed-in-silk blond that I knew for approximately twenty-five years of that stretch.

Mari's family documented the visits in a family chronicle that would have made Gran's fingers itch. The witch pulled the leather-bound book out after cooking breakfast, and asked us all to spell our names for her so she could add us to that history.

I asked her a few more questions as she wrote the information down. Apparently, Haoxin did take a couple of dozen eggs back to the nexus with her after each visit — yeah, I had her figured. The guardian also kept a Jeep in one of the barns close to the main road, which I hoped she didn't mind us borrowing.

I exchanged a flurry of text messages with Kett, Scarlett, and Gran while Warner questioned Mari and her husband about everything from the acreage of the farm to their magical fortifications and security protocols. Drake played with Garnet, matching the toddler's energy effortlessly — and all the while, picking up every word Warner uttered.

I wanted Gran and Scarlett behind the blood wards on my apartment and bakery. And if Shailaja and her renewed magic could walk through those wards like Suanmi had? Well … I'd have to worry about that later. Technically, Gran was the gatekeeper of the bakery's basement portal, though that was one of Pulou's own portals and not on a grid point. I should probably trust that she would be able to hold Shailaja at bay.

Two hours with a three-year-old made it very clear that my weird emotional scene at the back door wasn't about having kids. It was about my wanting to lead a 'normal life,' where crazed dragons weren't trying to kill my father and mentor. So, my 'normal.' Not anyone else's. Which was the rub, wasn't it? Because what if this was my normal now?

"We should go," I said.

Warner slid his hand up my thigh underneath the well-worn wooden table as he reached for the final, and probably cold, homemade sausage from the platter of meat that Mari had already replenished once and left out for picking at as we chatted. "How close is the vampire?"

"Um … it's an eight- or nine-hour flight from London, isn't it?"

Warner shrugged. "Not in his jet. And not if he wasn't in London when you texted." He turned his attention to Mari as she stood to clear the table. "My … nanny used to make sausage like this. They're delicious."

Mari bobbed her head. "A family recipe."

"Germans make the best sausages," Warner said.

"They're Canadian," I said teasingly. "And have been for a long time."

He grinned. "The only Canadians are the First Nations. Everyone else is an import."

I laughed. "You are such a snob. The same could be said for Europe."

"Nah. I can trace my family back for … many years." Like his use of the word 'nanny' a moment before, Warner checked himself on 'many.' Which made me wonder how many thousands of years he actually meant.

I snorted, trying to figure out some smart retort. Then my phone pinged.

> *An hour and a half.*

Warner leaned over to read the screen, then rose from the table. Drake instantly joined him from the living room, tousling Garnet's hair when the toddler protested his leaving.

"You'll keep the wards activated once we are gone?" Warner asked.

"Yes," Mari said. "I understand. We will not approach the portal again until either you or Haoxin tell us it's safe."

"We're being overly cautious," Warner said. "I would ask you to leave ..."

Mari straightened up as she spoke. "The portal is mine to watch over."

We were right to be cautious, but I seriously doubted that Shailaja would follow us to Alberta. And if she did, I doubted she would pay any attention to the gatekeepers. They were beneath her notice. Purely a function of the guardians, or as Shailaja would see them, simply servants of the guardians and —

From far out across the empty fields around the house, I felt the magic of the portal tickle my taste buds.

For a moment, I assumed I was having a weird flashback to the endless time I'd spent trapped in the portal's golden magic. Then Warner was moving so fast through the back door — Drake hard on his heels — that the kitchen window beside it cracked under the pressure of his passing.

Jesus.

I scrambled out of my seat, barking, "Stay here," to our hosts. Then I was running out into the snow while attempting to pull on my boots.

I was so, so stupid. Why had I let us linger? I was wrong to have trusted that Shailaja couldn't track me through the witch's wards. I should have walked to the freaking airport and waited there. We'd be hungry and cold, yes. But then the sweet boy in the farmhouse wouldn't be in danger and —

Warner and Drake were standing before a petite figure in full warrior gear. I tasted her intense magic — a blend of basil and smoky, sweet tomatoes — before I could clearly distinguish her face.

Haoxin had arrived.

I should have been expecting her. The last time we'd used a grid point portal into North America, she'd popped by. It was her territory, after all.

Her blond hair was held tight against her head in a series of intricate braids pulled into a low bun. She carried a katana almost identical to mine, before I'd used it to drain Sienna's magic. My weapon had been a gift from my father, and for the brief time it took me to catch up to the group standing in the snowy field, I wondered if hers had been as well.

"Jiaotu and I have returned," the guardian of North America was saying to Warner and Drake as I stepped up beside them. They were both barefoot in the snow and didn't appear to care. "Being best suited to combat the problem, we will remain in the nexus in case the heretic returns."

"What do you mean, 'best suited'?" I asked, offering the guardian a short bow and catching my breath after my dash from the farmhouse.

Haoxin grinned, sheathing her sword over her shoulder. "The healer mentioned that Shailaja has a new trick. Jiaotu and I are difficult to sneak up on."

"And the others?" Warner asked before I could request further clarification.

Haoxin shrugged. "Some of the older guardians are … amused and not at all surprised."

"The same guardians who weren't in favor of collecting the instruments of assassination in the first place?" I asked.

"Yes. And the guardians who were walking the earth when Warner and Shailaja first disappeared."

"Those incidents are not connected," Warner said gruffly.

"No?" the blond guardian asked archly.

"Suanmi?" Drake asked.

Haoxin shook her head. "As far as I know, she hasn't returned."

Drake looked relieved. Then he squared his shoulders when Haoxin smirked at him. Despite being one of the guardian nine, I doubted she smirked when Suanmi was in the same room.

I probably should have been relieved as well, but with the adrenaline from thinking Haoxin was Shailaja still coursing through my veins, I was a little preoccupied. I'd have to worry about dealing with the fire breather later.

"I must return," the guardian said. "How will you contact us when you locate Shailaja?"

"We won't," Warner answered. "But Pulou and Yazi can track Jade."

"Of course. Let's hope they wake soon. The healer is currently calling the shots, which is obvious since you're all here and not in the nexus where you probably should be." Haoxin eyed all of us, one at a time. "Jiaotu might not stand for it much longer. He is not amused to see Qiuniu in charge."

Haoxin was the youngest guardian, followed by the healer, Yazi, then silver-tongued Jiaotu. With the nexus under siege, I assumed that age equaled seniority.

"I am the sentinel of the instruments of assassination," Warner said caustically. "My duties are clear and cannot be countermanded."

Haoxin shifted her stance, losing every drop of her easygoing humor in the process.

I wasn't a fan of the transformation.

"It is your companions who are questionable, sentinel."

"That could be debated," I said. "Endlessly."

Haoxin shifted her blue-eyed gaze to me briefly, then returned her attention to Warner. "You're defensive, my friend."

Warner didn't answer.

"We're not going back," I said.

"You won't be moving forward terribly quickly without the portals. I understand your prey doesn't have that restriction."

"She'll come to us when it's time," Warner said.

Haoxin tilted her head, regarding him in silence for a moment. Then she let the subject drop.

"Jiaotu and I will listen for you through the portals that remain open," she said. "Whatever help that will be."

She pivoted, leaving us so quickly that I felt the magic of the portal flare from dozens of feet away before I saw her walking through it.

"Jesus," I muttered.

The guardians were a scary bunch. And our task was even more daunting when backed by the remembrance that Shailaja had incapacitated two of them. She had used the instruments of assassination and my katana to do it.

And if we could locate it, I was about to hand the final instrument over to her. Or at least I was going to pretend to hand it over. Just long enough to … to what?

Pulou had mentioned a trial and a possible judgement leading to the edge of my father's sword. Was I meant to replace the jury and the executioner?

Chapter Eight

The Bashaw airport consisted of three small outbuildings and one runway. One grass runway, currently plowed but still covered in hard-packed snow.

"Um," I said as I peered through the windshield of the army-green Jeep Wrangler we'd borrowed from the Albrechts. Well, from Haoxin, really. "Is that runway long enough?"

"Long enough for what?" Drake asked from the back seat.

Warner tucked the Jeep against the gray-sided building nearest the runway. There didn't appear to be a parking lot.

"For a jet to land."

Warner shrugged, turned off the engine, and dropped the keys in the glove box at my knees. "I assume the vampire wouldn't have said he'd pick us up here otherwise."

True. Except Kett's definition of 'safe' might be slightly different than mine.

"I've never flown on a jet before," Drake said, a trace of glee breaking through his serious demeanor. Though his mentor was still being held hostage by a rabid koala, so I certainly couldn't blame him for being grim.

"You'll sit at the very back," I said, unclipping my seat belt. "As far away from the engines and the cockpit as possible."

Warner was able to interact with most technology without blowing it all to hell with his magic, though long-term use would presumably be a problem. But I'd seen the fledgling guardian shut down a car engine just by laughing.

Thankfully, the Wrangler was heavily warded against both magic and magical detection, similar to the vehicle Warner and I had borrowed in Peru. That meant that Shailaja still couldn't track me.

Drake hopped out of the Jeep, letting a glacial gust of air inside as he tumbled out into the snow to explore.

"Speaking of Chi Wen," I muttered, watching the fledgling investigate the empty service buildings. "Who coordinates the air traffic? There isn't even a tower here."

"It's not that kind of airport, Jade," Warner said kindly. "It's also not the sort of thing you usually worry about."

"You're right." I brushed my fingers across the wedding rings on my necklace, reassured by the tingle of magic that rose at my touch. "I just didn't want to be here."

"I know."

"Sometimes it feels as though life contrives to mess with you … with me. Is that what destiny feels like?"

Warner fell silent.

Just sitting quietly with him in the comfortable warmth of the car, I realized I was exhausted. Physically drained, yes. But it was the emotional baggage I was lugging around that was the true weight.

"No one is infallible," Warner finally said. "Even the guardians have been caught unawares."

"Have they?"

"Do you know different?"

I shook my head, then stopped. "Can he hear us?" I asked, nodding toward Drake as he circled the building third from the end.

"Not through the wards on the Jeep."

I pressed my fingertips to the window beside me, leaving smudges on the chilled glass. I was careful to not screw with any of the spells that protected the vehicle … and us, though I could taste their power. Guardian magic. Haoxin's, specifically. I wondered if the nine guardians really knew each other, even after hundreds of years.

"Chi Wen just went with her," I said. "He didn't even try to get away."

"I thought you figured that was because of your katana?"

I turned to look at Warner. He glanced at me but kept his gaze on Drake.

"Could she take him by force?"

"No."

An empty pit opened up in my stomach. "I'm being played somehow. Aren't I?"

Warner shook his head immediately. But then he paused to think about it. "If you are, then we all are. And what could possibly be the endgame? No. The guardians were simply sloppy. Arrogant."

"Whoa, sentinel. No need to commit treason."

Warner snorted. "The far seer is old. He had planned to relinquish his guardianship to Drake's mother, but now he needs to wait until Drake's magic is fully realized."

"But that happens, right? The sword master was the previous warrior's apprentice, until he was injured too badly to inherit his mantle. Then he trained my father, who's a hundred years younger than him."

"Thankfully, dragons have long lives. The transfer of a guardian's power isn't tied to a certain period of time."

"But Pulou talks about his predecessor as if he wasn't totally with it by the time he passed his mantle on. Was that because Shailaja was to inherit? Then was deemed unworthy?"

"Could be."

"But you weren't supposed to be the guardian of Northern Europe? And take your mother's place as Jiaotu?"

Warner had brought the subject of his possible inheritance up before, back when we were fighting in my apartment. I was rather distraught at the time, though.

"No. The timing wouldn't have been right. She was too young."

"So you took the sentinel job."

Warner reached over and squeezed my knee. I stroked the back of his hand. We had talked about this all before, but the repetition would help me feel as if I had the pieces collected and sorted.

"And now?"

"Now what?"

"Will you be the next far seer?"

Warner started, as if the possibility hadn't occurred to him. But then he answered without hesitation. "No."

"But Drake is too young, and Chi Wen's actions make it seem like … like he's altered. Or … maybe my father is right, and he was simply drawing Shailaja away from the nexus."

My phone pinged. I tugged it out of my satchel, glancing down to see a text message from Kett.

> *Look up.*

Warner leaned over to read the screen, then snorted. I cranked my neck to gaze up at the clear sky, but I couldn't see the jet anywhere.

"We can fly back to Vancouver and stay put," Warner said. "We can head back to the nexus. There are always options."

"If we do, Drake will go after her alone," I said.

"He might. Or he might enlist Suanmi to help him."

I shook my head. "He wouldn't ask. She'd lock him away. Rightfully so."

I applied my thumbs to my phone.

Safe landing.

Then I leaned across to brush a kiss against Warner's lips before I climbed out of the Jeep.

Snow crunched underneath my feet. Drake joined me at the nose of the vehicle, grinning and pointing overhead. "I think they're circling."

I peered up at the sky, finally catching sight of the sleek white jet as it squared off with the end of the runway and started its descent.

"Please don't crash," I murmured. I wasn't sure whether or not a vampire could survive a plane crash, but I knew his human crew wouldn't.

Warner joined me, leaning back against the Jeep. We watched in silence as the jet swooped down like a majestic pure-white bird of prey. Its wheels hit the runway at the first possible point. I held my breath as the plane barreled toward us. Then it barreled past us.

"Jesus," I swore under my breath. I clutched my arms across my chest in fear.

The plane stopped something like a dozen feet from the end of the runway, then attempted to use the remaining space to awkwardly turn around. It didn't really fit, sending its nose wheel into the surrounding fields a couple of times. Thankfully, the snow wasn't too deep.

I tossed my borrowed jacket into the Jeep and locked the doors from the inside. Though I was instantly crazy cold, I didn't want to steal Mari's coat or get it destroyed. Collecting instruments of assassination was seriously hazardous to my wardrobe.

By the time Warner and I stepped onto the runway, Drake was already at the side of the dual-engine jet. As far as I could tell, it was the same plane that had flown me out of Peru a year ago. A custom-painted Learjet that appeared almost predatory with its long nose and tipped wings.

Directly behind the cockpit windows, the door of the plane popped open and slid to the side. Stairs slowly descended. Kett stood in the opening, grinning down at the fledgling pacing beneath him. His hair and skin were practically as white as the snow surrounding us. He was wearing dark wash jeans, a deep-tan cashmere V-neck sweater, and his typical, ridiculously expensive, dark brown wingtips.

"Hail, vampire!" Drake called up to him. "Permission to board?"

Kett threw his head back and laughed.

Taking that as his answer, Drake grabbed the railing the moment the stairs touched the ground. After quickly scrambling up, the fledgling shook hands with the vampire at the top of the stairs. Then he disappeared into the jet.

I paused at the base of the stairs, grinning up at my friend. I hadn't seen him since Peru, though we texted often. Warner waited a step behind me.

"I thought you might have trouble landing," I said.

Kett grinned. He was acting unusually jovial. "It's the takeoff that might be an issue."

Delightful.

"Not to worry, alchemist. We are light on fuel, so all will be well."

Jesus, it was just getting worse.

Kett tilted his head, looking at me, then to Warner, and then back to me. The smile slipped from his face, leaving only his ice-carved, almost-inert features behind.

I didn't mind his stillness. I might have, once, but now I was coming to understand what walking through centuries could be like for an Adept.

I gripped the cold metal of the railing. I had one foot up on the first step but didn't follow through with my other foot.

"I'm … I'm not sure what I'm getting you into," I whispered, knowing he could hear me even though the engines were still powering down.

Kett nodded. "You look cold, Jade Godfrey." Then he retreated into the plane.

I really was chilly. And though that didn't seem like a great excuse to drag a friend into danger, Kett seemed comfortable with it. And who was I to argue with a practically indestructible being?

I woke up to find a vampire watching me sleep.

It wasn't as creepy as it sounded. Of course, it helped that the vampire in question was one of my BFFs, and that he had a possible allergy to my blood.

I scrubbed my hands across my face, feeling worse than I had before I'd succumbed to blissful slumber.

"How long was I out?" I asked, straightening my plush white leather seat.

"Not long enough," Kett said. "We refueled in Calgary and are just crossing the border now. You should try to nap longer. You look anemic."

I snorted, making the easy assumption that 'anemic' was probably the worst thing a vampire could say about you.

I cranked around in my chair. Kett and I were seated across from each other in the middle of the six-passenger, wide-aisled jet. Warner and Drake were sprawled across the back two seats. They'd fallen asleep watching a movie, and the pop-up monitors on their side shelves were reflecting some sort of action sequence across their peaceful faces. The jet's interior design was white on white … on more white. It was definitely calming. Which I imagined was the point. Otherwise it was simply a damn expensive customization on a whim. And Kett wasn't prone to whimsy.

I turned back as a dark-haired steward made his way toward us from the galley at the front of the cabin. I recognized him from the last time I'd flown Vampire Air in the aftermath of thinking I'd lost both Warner and Kett in Peru. As he had then, he wore a pristinely pressed navy suit and a crisp white shirt. Still no name tag, though.

"Tea? Hot chocolate?" the steward asked. His voice was pitched low so as not to wake Warner and Drake, but I could have told him not to bother. They were seriously out cold. "We have real whipped cream."

He held a small silver tray toward me. It contained three hot towels and a tiny silver ramekin of what appeared to be lotion.

I eyed Kett. "Please tell me that's not my regular face cream."

"It is."

"You know, other girls would find you seriously creepy."

Kett reacted to my teasing about as much as a statue would have.

I took the tray from the steward, who apparently practiced the art of ignoring his passengers' small talk on a professional level. "I don't know your name," I said.

"Mark, ma'am."

"I'm not a ma'am, Mark."

The steward nodded.

Then I felt awful for being pissy. "Hot chocolate with real whipped cream would be lovely." I balanced the tray on the arm of my chair.

"Food would be better," Kett said.

I narrowed my eyes at him as I unrolled a hot towel and wrapped it around my hands. "You aren't the boss of me."

"Perhaps a fruit and cheese plate?" Mark smoothly interjected. "Or I could put together a lunch of sandwiches and a salad?" He glanced up at Warner and Drake, who were still conked out behind us.

"The fruit and cheese would be nice," I said while giving Kett the evil eye. "And the hot chocolate."

Mark laughed softly. "Of course, Ms. Godfrey." Then he took off up the aisle.

I turned to Kett. "Tell me what happened to you after Peru," I said bluntly.

Kett looked out the window instead of answering me.

We were flying in a light-blue sky over an endless swathe of fluffy white clouds, somewhere above the northern United States. Alberta was a large province, but I doubted it would take us long to get from Calgary to Portland in Kett's jet.

"We've spoken about it," Kett finally said. His tone was aloof, as if he hadn't almost died in the temple of the centipede. "At length."

We hadn't, though. Not anything more than him mentioning that he'd survived. Every query I'd sent by text was met with a response about some interesting magical fact he'd uncovered. He was currently studying alchemy and dragons, of course. Though the lore he was seeking was difficult to track down and not terribly plentiful. Which wasn't surprising since it was sort of the treasure keeper's job to collect, if not suppress, anything he believed fell under the guardians' purview.

Perhaps I was meant to read something into his interests, as a means of coming to some sort of understanding about his well-being?

"Warner said something about voluntary house arrest."

Kett waved a pale hand dismissively.

"And destroying a castle?"

"Hardly."

The conversation was going absolutely swimmingly. "I'd like to know that you're okay." My heart felt as if it were stuck in my throat, but I swallowed it away.

Kett turned his cool, ice-blue gaze on me. "I am as I always will be ... simply more than I should be, for the moment."

I nodded as if I understood. Then, realizing I didn't have any idea what he was talking about, I stopped myself. "More than you should be? So you're locking yourself away because ... you might be dangerous?"

"I have a decision to make," he said. "It isn't the sort of thing to rush into. I'm not retreating from the world out of injury, Jade. You haven't broken me."

"Yeah, well, you're kind of unbreakable."

"Indeed. Might I suggest you keep that thought in the forefront of your mind."

"You know I can only think of so many things at one time."

Kett twitched his eyebrow disapprovingly.

"Fine." I sighed. I unrolled the second hot towel and pressed it to my face. Then after it had cooled, I bathed my face and neck with the third towel, finishing the process by smoothing some of the face cream across my cheeks and forehead. The ritual was soothing, and perhaps even more refreshing than the nap had been. The vampire always knew best. And yes, I knew how ridiculous that sounded, even in my own head.

"I like your dragon," Kett said. "He is adapting well to the twenty-first century."

"It's a talent of his."

"And the new wedding bands? The ones with the runes?"

I glanced down at my necklace. Kett had wicked eyesight if he could see the tiny runes carved on the inside of the rings.

"A gift from Warner," I said.

A slow, soft smile spread across Kett's face. It was an unusual expression for him ... almost wistful. "Most long-lived creatures must continually walk the earth," he said. "To maintain a connection to the ages. A grounding."

"The fire breather indicated the same."

"Did she?"

Kett leaned forward eagerly. Which is to say, he tilted his chin toward me and lifted one eyebrow slightly, so I interpreted that as him being keen for any gossip I might indulge in about the guardian nine.

I grinned as Mark dropped off my hot chocolate, along with the fruit and cheese. I plucked a red grape from the bunch on the silver platter, popping it obligingly in my mouth as I raised my eyebrows in Kett's direction.

He chuckled under his breath.

See? I didn't have to be a brat all the time.

"The fire breather?" he asked, prompting me a second time.

So I filled him in. And why shouldn't I? He was putting his ass on the line for the guardians a second time, and they wouldn't ever offer him a single word of appreciation. Other than not ending his immortal existence. Though that was presumably a huge boon for a vampire when dealing with guardians.

I got the idea that Kett and I were supposed to be some sort of bridge between the vampire Conclave and the guardians. Though if things came down to it — say, if the 'it' was the edge of my father's blade or a fiery whisper from Suanmi — I was pretty sure my opinion wouldn't be a factor in whatever happened.

Showing up at Desmond's front door unannounced probably wasn't a great idea. But I had no idea where Rochelle was, and I was pretty certain that if I gave the pack too much of a heads-up, they'd make an effort to block me from seeing the oracle.

Even I could read between the lines of Kandy's absence from Vancouver and her stilted text messages. I was persona non grata among the West Coast North American Pack.

Well, freaking bully for them.

I'd let them say no to my face. Then I'd set Drake and Warner on them. Following up with a peppermint-powered vampire, if it came to it.

Okay. I might have been feeling slightly defensive.

One of Kett's massive SUVs was waiting for us at the Portland International Airport — a Range Rover, according to what was printed on the nose of the insanely expensive-looking vehicle. In the afternoon light filtering in through the open bay doors of the private aircraft hangar, both the SUV and the jet appeared to be exactly the same shade of white. I wondered idly whether the vampire had all his vehicles custom painted.

Warner, Drake, and I climbed into the cushy leather seats of the behemoth vehicle without speaking. We made the drive to Desmond's home in silence, with Kett at the wheel.

There really wasn't anything to plan. I was hoping Rochelle was in the immediate vicinity. Though the far seer had mentioned Washington, and Drake thought the oracle preferred to be on the coast.

I couldn't argue with that. But, even in the off-season, a couple of hundred campsites along the American west coast was a couple of hundred too many to search. And even if I had Rochelle's or her boyfriend Beau's phone number, I had a feeling they wouldn't take my calls voluntarily. Not even at Kandy or the far seer's behest.

It was weird to sort of be a bad guy for some people. Or at least an avoid-at-all-costs-then-duck-and-run guy. We should have stopped in Vancouver for cupcakes to soften our sudden appearance, but the last time I'd been face to face with Rochelle, I'd had to practically force her to eat one. Force-feeding wasn't exactly a balm to my soul.

We parked across the street from Desmond's tall laurel hedge. It had easily grown two feet since I'd sat on the front steps with Audrey, discussing the fact that Kandy would have to stay with the pack to heal properly.

I'd had no idea that meant my green-haired best friend would never return to Vancouver.

Exiting the SUV at the same time as everyone else, I slipped from the back seat and closed the door. I stood on the sidewalk, trying to get a glimpse of the house beyond the driveway.

Drake was anxious, shifting from side to side. Then he followed Warner's lead when the elder dragon folded his arms and leaned against the SUV's rear hatch.

Kett joined me on the sidewalk.

"Maybe I should have texted," I muttered, glancing around at the high-end neighborhood.

A luxury car slowed as it passed us on the left, speeding up after Warner waved casually to indicate we belonged. We were the only vehicle parked on the street. Each pristine lawn in the immediate vicinity boasted a tiny sign declaring its house's security system provider. It was that sort of community.

"Maybe I should text now?"

Kett lifted his face to the cloudy sky. A slight breeze ruffled his white-blond hair across his wide brow. "Wolf moon," he whispered.

I followed his gaze. It was too early and too cloudy to see the moon yet. "You mean the full moon? Tonight? Is that an issue?"

Kett turned his gaze to me, though I couldn't see his eyes through his dark sunglasses. "Not for you." He flashed his teeth at me, laughing silently.

I huffed, grabbing my phone out of my satchel as I crossed the wide boulevard. Other than the car that had just passed, the upscale neighborhood was quiet for a Saturday afternoon. Or maybe everyone just generally kept to themselves, whatever the day of the week.

I paused at the foot of the driveway and texted Kandy.

Hey! Surprise! I'm at the door.

Then I lifted my head, surveying what appeared from the front to be a wide, brown-sided seventies-style rancher set back on the lot behind a wide front yard. The house was actually two levels, with a modern open floor plan. However, the way it perched on the hillside made it appear smaller. Two black SUVS — not quite as expensive as Kett's — occupied the driveway, blocking the three-car garage. Even though it was January, the large front yard was green, well mowed, and well hidden from the street by the hedge.

The house looked exactly the same.

The magical wards, however, were new. By the taste of the earthy midnotes, the protection coating the house was of witch construction, but I had no idea if the wards were meant to keep magic out … or in … or both. Not until I tested them, of course.

Kett stepped into my peripheral vision, then tilted his head questioningly. Grinning, he slipped into the shadows gathering at the edge of the laurel hedge and disappeared.

"Cool," Drake murmured.

Warner snorted, though he quirked his lips in a brief smile when I glanced back.

"I should have worn the T-shirt Kandy gave me," Drake said.

Something else shifted in my peripheral vision within the shadows, but before I could focus on it, it was gone. A hundred to one, Shailaja had just sent a shadow leech to check up on me. Now that we were away from the protection of the wards in Alberta, it certainly hadn't taken her long to find me.

"Any T-shirt from Kandy won't go with the sword," I said to Drake, distracted as I turned onto the front walk and crossed toward the house. Standing before the front door, I glanced down at my phone to confirm that my text had gone through.

It had. So maybe Kandy wasn't in Portland.

I was being a complete ninny. Freaking out about seeing Kandy just because something was going on with her that she didn't want to discuss. The werewolf had always been incredibly private. I probably should have been more worried about coming face to face with Desmond.

I glanced back at Warner and Drake, who had crossed the street to stand at the mouth of the driveway. Judging by the peppermint emanating from the hedge to my right, Kett was about twenty feet away, slipping around the side of the house. The wards had intrigued him.

What did the alpha of the West Coast North American Pack need with wards?

I reached up and tapped the knocker at the center of the large wooden door. Three light taps. The wards didn't react to my proximity.

The door blew open.

A hulking, hairy beast wearing a cowboy hat tackled me to the ground.

We rolled across the front lawn before he managed to pin me. I slammed the heel of my hand up and underneath the beast's chin — right before he tried to rip my throat out with his two-inch-long incisors. Then I held him off in a chokehold with the same hand while I tried to get a look at him.

He'd lost the cowboy hat. He also appeared to be … well, a werewolf. As in, the mythological half-human/half-beast monsters from the old horror films. I'd assumed he was a shifter in half-form, but now, getting a better look at him and tasting his magic, I was pretty sure I was wrong. His eyes were blue, not awash with the green of shapeshifter magic. And his magic tasted of ... brown sugar and pecans and pastry ... paired with some sort of ripe berry fruit. Something was wrong, yet terribly familiar, with that mixture of flavors.

As the werewolf struggled against my chokehold, a great gob of saliva hit me in the forehead. Just freaking gross.

I could hear Drake giggling.

Damn it.

Plus, I was getting grass stains on my new silk jacket.

I tossed the werewolf off me, rolling to my feet in the same motion.

He flew across the front lawn, slamming into the side of one of the SUVs with a pained whelp. Then he fell onto all fours, panting with discomfort.

The SUV was seriously dented. As in, I doubted whether either of its passenger-side doors would ever open again.

Whoops.

Warner started coughing, covering his laughter.

I glared in his general direction, picking up the cowboy hat off the lawn and feeling badly about hurting the beast.

But what the hell?

Kandy jogged through the open front door. Despite the fact it was January, the green-haired werewolf was clad only in bright-blue cropped leggings and a pink-printed white Cake in a Cup T-shirt.

"Henry ..." she hissed under her breath. She sounded as though she might be looking for an escaped dog, while trying to hide the fact that he'd escaped in the first place. "What are you —" Then she spotted me on the lawn and a smile took over her fierce face. "Jade!" she cried.

Drake barreled across the yard and attacked her. She didn't even see him coming, and the fledgling was bigger than her by far. They went down in a tangle of limbs, both laughing manically. Gold glinted from the three-inch-wide rune-carved cuffs Kandy wore.

With a confused but eager howl, the werewolf leaped across the lawn to pile onboard the tussling match.

I sighed, then wandered into the fray to grab the werewolf and toss him back inside the house.

Yeah, I'd put two and two together, and had come up with the idea that a movie werewolf brawling on the front lawn was a bad idea if you wanted to maintain a good relationship with your neighbors.

I made an easy guess that the werewolf's presence also explained the new wards.

Henry tumbled into the tiled entranceway beyond the wide front doors; then Desmond filled the open doorway. Literally. His shoulders pretty much brushed the doorframe to either side, though he was shy of six feet. While he glowered at the scene in his front yard, his brunette beta, Audrey, appeared behind him, holding Henry in check. At least I was hoping I'd read the situation correctly, and that the werewolf was the Henry who Kandy had come out to look for.

Desmond's magic — smooth dark chocolate with a strong citrus finish — rolled through the front yard.

Kandy tossed Drake away, rolling to her feet in front of her alpha with her head bowed.

Drake slipped back to flank me.

Desmond glared at the two of us, one at a time. Shards of his green shapeshifter magic danced in his brown eyes as he gave a momentary glance to Warner, who had come closer to lean casually against the dented SUV.

The alpha then returned his gaze to me, flinching as Kett appeared at my other side.

Desmond bared his teeth. It wasn't a pleasant greeting. "Jade Godfrey."

"Desmond Charles Llewelyn," I said, "Lord and Alpha of the West Coast North American Pack. We come with a request."

"Of course you do." Desmond curled his lip in a snarl. Then, after glaring at all of us for another moment, he turned and walked back into the house.

"Wow," Drake muttered. "He's seriously peeved."

Kandy spun, throwing herself between Kett and me and lacing her steel-muscled arms around my shoulders. She pressed her face into my neck, inhaling deeply. Then she whispered, "Take me with you. I'll even promise to not eat any of your chocolate."

"Wow. That's, like, totally crazy."

"You're right. I take it back. You do have chocolate, right?"

Audrey stepped through the front door, scanning all of us arrayed on the lawn and driveway as though we were peons who should be falling to our knees in worship before her. The dark hair cascading over her shoulders was a sharp contrast to the tailored, pinstriped collared shirt she wore tucked into a sleek pencil skirt. She looked as though she'd just brokered a billion-dollar business deal in between bouts of giving some lucky dude the best sex of his life.

Except the werewolf peeking over her shoulder completely ruined the effect.

I fought a smirk, drawing Audrey's attention.

"He's worried about his hat," Kandy whispered.

"What?"

"Henry. He's worried about his hat." Kandy elbowed me, drawing my attention to the cowboy hat I still held.

I looked at the werewolf behind Audrey, then lifted the hat questioningly. The werewolf nodded his head, then opened his maw in what was most likely supposed to be a smile. Silhouetted in the doorway behind Audrey, he appeared to be seconds away from chomping off the petite beta's head in a single bite.

Something in the back of my mind screamed, *Toothy monster! Run! Run!*

Instead of fleeing, I returned the werewolf's smile.

Audrey frowned. And the more I upped the wattage of my grin, the deeper her brow furrowed.

"I could play this game all day, beta," I said coyly. Then I blew her a kiss.

Her mouth quirked. She swallowed the involuntary smile, covering it with a heavy sigh that seemed to suggest doing anything else was better than conversing with me.

"The West Coast North American Pack welcomes the alchemist and friend of the pack Jade Godfrey, along with Kettil, elder and executioner of the Conclave, and ..." Audrey's formal invitation faltered as she eyed Warner and Drake.

"Warner, the sentinel of the instruments of assassination," Kandy said, barely missing a beat. "Drake, apprentice to the far seer."

Audrey nodded to Warner and Drake.

They returned the gesture.

"Please," she said, stepping back and sweeping her arm into the house. "Enter, make your request, and we will do our utmost to accommodate you."

Trying to not smirk like a brat at all the formality being thrown around, I stepped into the entranceway, passing Audrey, then pausing before the werewolf. Kandy was still glued to my shoulder.

I handed the cowboy hat to the werewolf. He took it, but didn't put it on.

"Henry," Kandy said. Her voice was pitched low and fierce. "You don't leave the house. And you don't attack visitors. If that hadn't been Jade at the door, you could have killed someone. You're lucky she didn't gut you."

The werewolf snapped his mouth shut and nodded. When he did so, his jaws were perfectly aligned and his blue eyes were startlingly human. My nose came up to his fur-covered Adam's apple.

I definitely wasn't looking at a transformed werewolf in his half-beast/half-human form.

He was a sorcerer and a werewolf.

And then, with the taste of Kandy's chocolate-berry magic in my mouth, I clicked together the missing piece of the puzzle.

"Hi, Henry," I said. "I'm Jade."

"He can't talk," Kandy said.

"Why does his magic taste like pecan pie paired with a weird berry coulis on the side?" I turned to lock my gaze to my best friend's. "Why does his magic taste like yours?"

She instantly cast her gaze to the gray slate tile underneath our feet. The submissive gesture made my heart pinch.

Henry was Kandy's secret.

"He's mine," she muttered. "He's bitten."

I turned to look at Henry, about a hundred different questions at the ready.

"Perhaps save the stories for later," Audrey said as she brushed by us. "I imagine that even you don't lay siege to an alpha's home unless it's important, alchemist."

She crossed through the entranceway into the living room beyond. Desmond was standing at the front picture window, gazing out to where Portland spread below the hillside on which the house was perched. The afternoon was waning, and the cloud-covered sun cast a light-orange hue along the horizon.

"Laying siege?" I muttered. "Dramatic much?"

"Is it?" Kandy glanced over her shoulder at Kett, Warner, and Drake, who were spread across the entranceway and effectively blocking the front door.

I opened my mouth to protest, then clamped it closed. I should have thought about how much magical power I was dragging around with me as if it were an everyday occurrence. Most Adepts went a lifetime without ever laying eyes on a vampire, or learning that dragons were more than a myth.

Kandy reached across and patted Henry's exceedingly hairy arm. "Wards or no wards, that's a lot of magic for a newborn to handle," she said soothingly. "Now go practice."

Henry took off to the left, toward the house's gym and offices. His toenails clicked across the slate but were muffled when he hit the hardwood of the hallway.

I looked questioningly at Kandy.

"Later," she said gruffly. "Audrey's right." She cocked her head toward Desmond, then added in a hushed whisper, "Henry's stuck like that for the days around a full moon. He's practicing quelling the magic. But we're … sort of trapped here for the week."

My heart lightened at this pronouncement. I had dozens of more questions, but now I knew my friend had a reason for her absence in my life. A reason she was embarrassed about, though I wasn't sure why.

The green-haired werewolf hustled into the living room to stand off to one side of her alpha. As she passed,

Lara rose off the square-edged gray leather couch, which was a new addition to the otherwise sparsely furnished room. She winked at me over her shoulder. Then, pursing her purple-glossed lips, she shucked her purple suede ankle boots and padded over to join Desmond by the window.

Flanked by his two enforcers, the alpha didn't bother to turn around.

Audrey stood by a low, round glass-topped table, which appeared to be constructed out of some sort of large steel-edged, wooden-spoked wheel. Desmond had finally replaced the glass coffee table, which had a way too regular habit of getting broken.

The beta was the only one fully facing us as we wandered into the living room. Warner and Kett fanned out behind me on either side. Drake was tucked in behind my right shoulder.

The beta eyed the coffee table beside her, then took a deliberate step away from it.

The pack was ready to rumble. But I seriously hoped it didn't come down to claws versus fists.

I stared at Desmond's too-broad shoulders, waiting for him to acknowledge us. When he didn't turn, I stopped myself from gritting my teeth as I looked pointedly at Audrey.

"Your request, alchemist?" she asked.

I eyed Desmond a moment longer, then nodded formally to Audrey. "We request an audience with the oracle, beta."

Desmond finally glanced over his shoulder at me. His magic glinted from his eyes. I kept my gaze on Audrey.

She chose her words carefully. "The oracle is a protected member of the pack —"

"We've been sent by the far seer," I said.

Desmond's shoulders stiffened.

"Shit," Kandy muttered under her breath.

Audrey swallowed, then looked to Desmond for guidance.

Okay, so something had happened between the pack and Chi Wen? I glanced back to Drake. The fledgling guardian stepped up beside me, shaking his head once to indicate that he didn't understand the shapeshifters' concern — even as I could practically taste it wafting off them.

"No," Desmond said.

"No?" I echoed. An involuntary grin spread across my face. I definitely hadn't been looking to fight, but I would if I was pushed. And I'd enjoy it. It would feed the darkness I kept at bay with chitchat and chocolate.

Audrey took a step back from me.

Kandy and Lara each took a step closer to their alpha, clearly indicating I'd have to go through them to get to Desmond.

I tried to subdue my sudden need to wrap my hand around the hilt of my knife.

"My apologies," I said, though my words were stilted. "The last few hours have been a trying time for us. I mean no aggression. I understand the pack protects its own. We mean the oracle no harm."

"That's what you say, Jade Godfrey," Desmond said. "But your actions rarely match your words."

I clamped my teeth together.

Audrey winced.

From behind me, Kett spoke. "Perhaps it is time that you mend your relationship with the alchemist, alpha." His cool voice was like a balm.

"I don't take orders from a vampire," Desmond snapped. "Elder of the Conclave or not, you don't outrank me in my territory." His steely gaze swept across all of us. "The oracle is under my protection."

Kett stepped up to my left, then deliberately angled his head toward me, as if to exclude the shapeshifters from his next suggestion. "The beta and the enforcer in purple are aware of the location of the oracle."

Desmond snorted. "Try asking them directly."

Kett laughed, breathing his peppermint magic across my neck and shoulder. "Blood doesn't lie."

All the hair rose on the back of my neck. I shuddered, licking my lips. "That is perhaps an unnecessary step, executioner. For now, at least." Vampires could read people's minds while feeding on them. Or maybe it was just an ability of Kett's. Not that I had any direct experience, but Kett had threatened to get permission to bite me for my 'blood-truth' the first time I met him.

"This ..." Desmond spat as he shouldered past Kandy and Lara. "This is who you align yourself with."

I lifted my chin. "What alliance do you offer, alpha? You've already killed a member of my family."

"A black witch —"

"Who I'd already rendered harmless."

"It was pack justice, Jade."

"And I'm not pack. You made sure I never could be."

Desmond glanced at Drake, then over my shoulder at Warner. "That was never an option. Your magic made it so."

"The guardians are under threat," I said, deliberately and perhaps provocatively locking my gaze to Desmond's. "We seek the oracle to counter that threat. There is a possibility we bring harm in our wake, but I understood that Rochelle and Beau are mobile."

Desmond didn't answer. But he didn't drop his eyes from mine, either.

"We're sent by the mentor of the oracle," Drake said. "You have no right or cause to stand between us and her. We all walk the path of our own destinies. This is Rochelle's."

Desmond glanced at Drake. The fledgling was actually taller than the alpha, though probably barely a third of his width.

"The guardians have left the oracle in your protection, alpha," Drake added quietly.

"Are you threatening me?" Desmond growled. "I expect such disrespect from the alchemist, but I'm surprised to hear it from a dragon."

Warner laughed. "You think we're interested in bandying words with you, shapeshifter? You think anything but Jade Godfrey's presence holds us in check?"

"This is my territory!"

"And the world is ours." Warner's tone dripped with quiet condescension.

Desmond took a step back — not from fear, but to open up a clear path to Warner. "I didn't hear guardian in your title."

"But you heard apprentice to the far seer in mine," Drake said softly.

A muscle in Desmond's neck clenched. And not knowing why I did so, I slowly lifted my hand and stepped forward to brush my fingers against his shoulder. I deliberately kept my gaze lowered and any and all aggression out of my move. "Kett is right," I murmured. "Don't take what's between you and me and hold it between us and Rochelle. This is too important."

"It's always about saving the world with you, Jade," Desmond said. Not unkindly, though.

He pulled his gaze from Warner to look at me. I didn't drop my hand.

"It was never going to be between us," I whispered. "You don't even like me. I never should have kissed you."

Desmond dropped his gaze to my hand on his shoulder, then looked past me. But he was staring into his own thoughts and remembrances, rather than into the dining room and kitchen. "I never should have forced a binding on you," he said quietly. "But Hudson ..."

"Hudson was worth it," I said, pleased that the thought of the former beta no longer triggered a well of sadness for me.

Desmond touched the back of my hand gently. "I don't take the protection of my pack lightly."

"It's your life."

He lifted his gaze to meet mine. "Yes."

"And this ... apparently ... is my life."

Desmond nodded. Then he stepped away.

My hand fell from his shoulder.

Something had shifted between us. I might never be able to fully forgive him for Sienna's death. But I could recognize why those actions had been necessary in his eyes.

"Audrey?" Desmond said as he moved back to his post by the window.

"They were in Astoria yesterday," Audrey said, pulling her phone out of her pocket. How the hell it hadn't been ruining the line of her skirt, I had no idea. I silently cursed her for this bit of fashion wizardry.

"Oregon?" I asked.

"They've left Astoria," Drake said. "We're looking for a Washington location."

Audrey huffed out a sigh, then started texting.

"Once you've got that sorted," a deep voice drawled behind us, "I'll drive."

I had tasted him approaching, but I was still surprised to see a brown-haired, wiry man in his early thirties — rather than a werewolf — in the entranceway behind me. He'd paired his cowboy hat with a brown suit jacket, blue jeans, and honest-to-goodness well-worn cowboy boots.

"Henry," Lara purred from her position by the window. "You clean up nice."

Henry chuckled, running a hand through his short hair before he dropped his cowboy hat on his head. "The oracle owes me a favor. I think it's time to collect."

"Marshal," Kett said, slipping across the entranceway and offering his hand to Henry. "The wolf moon has been good to you."

Of course Kett knew who Henry was. I met Kandy's gaze and shook my head.

She mouthed the words, *Know-it-all.*

"Westport," Audrey said, continuing to text.

Kandy looked at Desmond.

He nodded to her. "Go, then. Come back intact … please."

"I've never met a bitten werewolf," Drake said, calling my attention back to Henry's surprising human reveal.

The marshal, as Kett had called him, held his hand out to the fledgling guardian with an easy grin. "Henry Calhoun. I've never met one before, either. Or a dragon, for that matter."

Drake shook his hand.

"The bitten don't usually survive," Kett said coolly. Then he slipped out the front door.

Henry turned to me. "Alchemist," he said. "I've heard a lot about you."

"All good, I hope."

His blue eyes danced with mirth as he tilted his head, grinning at me instead of responding. Then his gaze fell to my necklace and got stuck there. Typical sorcerer.

"Ah," he said, remembering to speak. "I understand you might be open to fixing something for me." He lifted his hand to reveal a set of gold handcuffs hanging off his index finger.

"Oooo," I said. "What are these pretties?"

Kandy started guffawing behind me. Drake joined her.

Warner snorted, then exited to follow Kett.

Okay, so sorcerers weren't the only ones who lost all sense when it came to tasty magic.

I lifted my chin, covering my eagerness to lay hands on what appeared to be magical handcuffs. "What have you got to trade?"

Henry grinned. "I own the property that Rochelle and Beau use when they're in Westport."

I nodded sagely, as if I was giving the deal some great consideration. Then I pretty much snatched Henry's cuffs out of his hand in agreement.

So I liked wielding my magic. Who didn't?

Chapter Nine

By the time we'd flown into the regional airport in Olympia, Washington, then rented cars and drove the hour or so to Westport on the coast, it was just after eight o'clock in the evening. The dark sky was partly cloudy, but it wasn't threatening to rain ... yet. In this part of the world, precipitation didn't come with much warning.

We'd split up for the drive. Henry was in front with Kandy, Audrey, and Kett in a hulking black Cadillac Escalade. Warner was driving a smaller green Ford Escape, following with Drake and me. Apparently, Kett hadn't had enough notice to insist on white vehicles only.

Although getting trapped within the portal certainly hadn't been any sort of picnic, traveling that way was a lot less hassle than either flying or driving. It probably didn't help that I was still exhausted.

I was disappointed that I wasn't traveling with Kandy, but she was concerned about Henry's newfound ability to take human form even under the full moon — and was even more concerned that he might suddenly revert. Kett's fascination with the whole bitten werewolf/sorcerer thing — of course and always — had inspired his tagging along in the shapeshifters' SUV.

Audrey hadn't wanted Kandy or Henry to set foot out of the house, let alone go anywhere near Rochelle.

The beta had been seriously snitty about it, in fact. Supposedly, their presence in Mississippi had 'only made things worse,' and the oracle and Beau were under Audrey's supervision.

The beta had also balked over 'flying in a jet owned by a vampire.' But she didn't have much say about it after we'd all driven to the airport and boarded without her consent.

The road cutting west away from Interstate 5 wasn't treacherous, but it was seriously dark and underutilized. I'd expected the area to be similar to Vancouver Island or Squamish — a mostly single-lane highway weaving through rocky cliffs covered in mossy fir and cedar trees. But the land was fairly level, and for the most part, sparsely dotted with trees and foliage. At least, as far as I could see in the dark.

Drake was sprawled out lengthwise in the back seat. I'd managed to refrain from chiding him about putting on a seat belt, though I had mine securely fastened. Warner wasn't a bad driver, but he operated the vehicle like someone with insane reflexes and the ability to walk away from a pileup without a scratch. Occasionally, I had to remind him that cars were built for regular humans. Following behind Henry kept him in check. Though he grumbled about the snail's pace every fifteen minutes or so, we were still cruising twenty or more miles an hour over the posted speed limit.

I was slowly savoring the last few squares of a silky smooth bar of 75 percent cocoa from Akesson's — part of the supply of chocolate I'd made sure was packed in my satchel before I entered the nexus what seemed like a lifetime ago. The single-origin bar from Madagascar somehow evoked a fruity tartness — citrus and red berry notes at the same time. Identifying the subtleties at play within its deep cocoa flavor was a great way to force myself to take a time-out.

In order to keep the new treat all to myself, I'd given Drake one of my favorite bars — Manjari from Valrhona, an exceedingly fresh and fruity 64 percent cocoa with a finish of roasted nuts. Drake had accepted the treat, but he didn't go all rapturous about it. Apparently, even great chocolate couldn't fully revive his jovial nature.

"Do you think she sees us coming?" I asked Warner as I leaned toward him, holding my second-to-last piece of chocolate in front of his lips.

He opened his mouth and I pressed the chocolate to his tongue. "The oracle?" he asked, lightly sucking my fingertips before I withdrew my hand.

"I don't think Rochelle can quite tap in like that yet," Drake said. "Or focus her sight."

"I was just thinking how terrifying it would be for her to see us bearing down on her like this," I said.

"She's made of steel," Drake said. "Or some sort of flexible metal at least."

I glanced over my shoulder. The moonlight filtering in the side window above his head illuminated Drake's face just enough for me to discern that he had his eyes closed. His half-eaten chocolate bar was resting on his chest.

"A person can be scared and fierce at the same time," I said.

He didn't answer.

Warner lifted his hand from the gearshift to caress my knee. "Kandy texted," he said. "They know we're coming."

"Yeah." I laughed wryly, straightening in my seat. "But is knowing better or worse?"

"If this is where the far seer told you to go, then this is where we go," Drake said. A reprimand edged his tone.

"I'm heading there, aren't I?"

"Yes. But you question everything, warrior's daughter. Fate guides our feet."

"Well, I'm glad that's so clear to you."

Drake snorted. "It is to you as well. Though you clearly get some sort of perverse joy out of pretending otherwise."

"That's enough." Warner lifted his gaze to the rearview mirror, glaring at the fledgling guardian being sulky in the back seat. "You are with us only because the dowser has a generous heart. Either you're a distraction or a support. And a distraction will get Jade hurt. Pick one so I know what to do with you."

"My apologies," Drake murmured. "I just don't like this sense of uncertainty. Jade's questions exacerbate that."

"Talking things out is a valuable tool," I said. "So is chocolate. Eat the rest of yours."

"But then it will be gone. You taught me to savor."

"There are times to savor and times to consume."

Drake snapped a piece from his bar and popped the chocolate in his mouth.

Ahead of us, Henry came to a stop at a fork in the road. The headlights of the Escalade lit up a road sign: "Westport — 9 miles."

I rolled my window down a few inches. Though I could faintly hear the crashing surf ahead of us, I couldn't see the shoreline.

Henry turned right.

Warner eased on the gas to follow, rolling through the stop sign.

"The last official record placed the population of Westport at two thousand and ninety-nine," Drake said. He'd sat up as we rolled to a stop, and was now leaning forward between the front seats. "It's located on a peninsula, which is supposedly the farthest west we can go and still be on the mainland of the United States. Its public marina is the largest on the outer coast of the United States' Pacific Northwest. And it houses a large commercial fishing fleet, as well as several recreational charter fishing vessels."

"Thanks, Drakepedia," I said. "Did Kandy let you borrow her phone? You know your magic is going to ruin it."

"Her iPad. And I Google fast," he said smugly. "Swift and indomitable, as is the wind that stirs the waves breaking on yon seashore."

Warner and I burst out laughing.

"What?" Drake asked. "Kandy says I need to practice being inscrutable."

"Guardian poet." I giggled.

"Actually, that's Qiuniu's job," Drake said.

I looked from Warner to him, cranking my neck in my surprise. "Sorry, the healer is a poet?"

He nodded. "Poetry, music, the written word."

"That's why his healing magic is accompanied by music?"

"Excuse me?" Warner asked archly. "Are you saying you hear music when the healer kisses you?"

Grinning madly at Warner's sarcasm, I countered, "You were the one who swooned in his arms earlier."

"Yeah," Drake said. "That's what makes him so dreamy."

I lost it, laughing so hard that my stomach hurt. Warner joined me, filling the vehicle with his tasty magic and deep-bellied guffaws.

"What?" Drake said, aghast. "Haoxin says so!"

The engine of the SUV sputtered, then died.

Silence fell as the vehicle slowly rolled to a stop.

"We killed the car," I whispered.

More hysterics ensued. If it was inappropriate to wallow in our circumstances, laughing was really the only thing we could do.

Red taillights lit up ahead of us. Henry had just figured out we were no longer following him.

"I really hope it isn't a long walk from here," Drake mused.

I wiped tears from my face, struggling to get myself under control. The road was narrow enough that Henry had to execute a three-point turn in order to head back toward us.

"I think the beta might make me sit on her lap," the fledgling continued. "Not the other way around as it should be. I'm twice her size, but she's pretty dominant."

I choked, still weeping with mirth.

"I don't think it will come to that, fledgling," Warner said with a straight face. He turned the key in the ignition. The engine started, then settled into a gentle purr.

Henry slowly drove by us. His and Kandy's faces were pale blurs in the front and back driver's-side windows of the black SUV.

Warner lifted his hand, waving as they passed.

Henry turned around once more, then passed us to take the lead again. As he slid by, the back door of our SUV opened. Kett slipped into the back seat beside Drake.

Warner hit the gas before the vampire had fully closed his door.

"Cool," Drake said.

"Show-off," I groused. "Did you even bother telling Henry you were leaving while you were moving?"

Kett settled in with a shrug.

"You probably scared him."

"If the sorcerer wants to run with the West Coast North American Pack, he'll need to get used to being scared," Kett said coolly.

"I don't think he was bitten by choice," Drake said.

The vampire slowly turned his ice-blue gaze on the earnest fledgling. A slow smile spread across his face. "Being there was his choice."

Drake tilted his head, considering the vampire's logic. Then he nodded, grinning.

Warner snorted.

"I'll step out as we move through Westport," Kett said.

"You're leaving?" I asked.

"For a moment."

"Not a fan of oracles?"

Kett's grin was more a flash of teeth than a smile, but he didn't offer an answer.

Warner was eyeing the vampire in the rearview mirror. "We don't have time to ... monitor you, Kettil."

"I'll endeavor to not kill anyone, as always."

"Excuse me?" Though I wasn't totally following the conversation, I was uncomfortably aware that they might be talking about feeding. Specifically, Kett's dining requirements.

The vampire drummed his long, pale fingers on the armrest to his left. The uncharacteristically nervous movement was a blur in the moonlight. "I find the mode of transport and the proximity of the shapeshifters chafing, alchemist. No more than that."

I nodded, turning back as the first buildings of the town of Westport appeared on either side of the road before us. Most of the single and two-storey structures appeared to be business oriented, and were all long-closed for the evening. At first glance, the tidy seaside town appeared more functional than quaint. Maybe the fishing that Drake's Googling had highlighted took precedence over tourism.

"I have less need of sustenance lately," Kett murmured.

I didn't look back at the vampire. If he was in a sharing mood, it was better to let him talk than to question him. But when he didn't continue, I spoke. "Since London?"

"More since Peru."

"What happened in Peru?" Drake asked.

"I ... I bit the rogue dragon," Kett said. "It was ... ill advised."

Warner laughed under his breath, like he sensed how that was the closest the vampire would ever come to admitting a mistake.

"You drank dragon blood?" Drake asked. "And you still ... function?"

Kett didn't answer. But I knew — based on the past few hours we'd spent together and his absence over the previous year — that the answer might be a question of what his continuing to function actually entailed. He had mentioned some sort of pending decision during our conversation on the jet. And I got the feeling he was being forced to make it.

"The oracle is young, yes?" Kett said, ignoring Drake's question. "I thought it best if she wasn't ... inundated."

Kett was a collector. I would have thought he'd be eager to meet Rochelle. But maybe he wasn't all that interested in the possibility of coming face to face with his future. That made two of us.

"Jade can open the conversation," Warner said in agreement.

"Rochelle knows me too," Drake said.

"Also, Audrey isn't going to stay behind," I said.

"We three will set up a perimeter," Warner said. "If we're lucky, Shailaja will show her face, and this will be all over quickly."

"After we find Chi Wen," Drake added.

I glanced at Warner. I was still worried about the far seer's state of mind — and about what finding him altered might do to Drake.

The sentinel nodded imperceptibly.

"As you say," Kett murmured. He sounded unsettled, though. Almost fretful. I was pretty sure that no one but me or maybe Kandy could pick up the different nuances in his cool, poised tone.

I reached my hand back through the seats. Kett brushed his fingers against my palm without looking away from his window. Drake wrapped his warm hand around both of ours, creating an odd — but definitely not awful — peppermint and honeyed-almond sandwich.

"I'm glad you survived, vampire," Drake said. "Thank you for your aid and friendship."

Kett looked surprised. Then he lifted the corners of his lips in a smile of acknowledgement. "I am at your disposal … as you require."

Satisfied, Drake released us.

A comfortable silence fell as we rolled through the tiny town of Westport. A few restaurants and a gas station were open, but the single main street was quiet. Sleepy. Which I wouldn't mind being for the next twelve hours or so.

Beyond the final buildings in the main section of town, Henry flicked on the left-hand indicator of the Escalade, then turned. We followed, moving closer to the sound of the surf.

"No other guardian is friends with a vampire," Drake said conversationally. "Especially not an elder of the Conclave. There is strength in this diversity."

I grinned a little, catching Warner doing the same out of the corner of my eye.

"Indeed," Kett said. His tone was as cool as ever without any hint of sarcasm at the fledgling's suggested alliance. But then, ancient vampires played the long game.

I wouldn't have been surprised to learn that Kett plotted centuries ahead. Though the fact that those centuries could possibly now include me — according to Suanmi — still unnerved me. My whole life, I'd been expecting nothing but an ordinary, mortal existence.

Of course, I still had to survive the next confrontation with the rabid koala to have any kind of existence at all.

A vintage-1970s Brave Winnebago was parked beside a tiny cabin on a sparsely treed acreage, about a dozen feet from a long, narrow, gray-sand beach. Well, at least it was gray in the moonlight. Momentarily mesmerized by the reflection of the full moon shimmering across the dark surf of the open coast, I climbed out of the SUV.

The age of the RV was easy to estimate, just based upon the exterior color scheme of cream, orange, and brown. Though what I could see of the cabin windows were dark, the Brave was ablaze with light. It was an easy guess that Rochelle and Beau were pulling power from the cabin but staying in the RV. All the curtains had been drawn throughout the midsection of the Brave. I wondered if they drew them every evening, or if this was a reaction to our impending arrival.

Henry had parked the black Escalade in a spot behind the cabin, though it was a tight fit between the building and the large oak tree that backed it. It was the type of tree that might have held a tire swing at one point. I wondered how long Henry had owned the property, and whether or not it was a family cabin.

Warner had parked twenty feet or so back on the dirt drive, pretty much blocking the exit. I imagined that was a deliberate choice. Kett was already gone, having slipped silently out of the Escape five minutes before we'd arrived, with the main street of Westport still in the rearview mirror.

Interior lights illuminated the neighboring homes through the sparse pine and fir trees on either side of the lot. The houses were near enough that I could see a family of four watching TV in the living room to the north, and smoke curling upward from the chimney to the south. But they weren't so near that the neighbors would hear or see anything untoward transpire. Unless they were Adepts, of course. And I seriously hoped to avoid anything transpiring.

However, untoward things tended to happen around the oracle and me. Hell, bloody and nasty things tended to happen around me and any other Adept.

Pine needles and dry sand crunched underneath my feet, but none of the stealthy shapeshifters, the dragons, or the sorcerer made a sound. I suspected Henry employed magic on his loafers to gain the effect.

Warner and Drake melted into the darkness to case the area, while Kandy and I paused beside an empty firepit about a dozen feet from the Brave's side door, closer to the beach than the cabin.

Audrey crossed toward the RV, lifting her hand to knock. Henry hovered a few feet back from her.

"Henry's family owns the lot?" I asked Kandy. "There aren't any discernible wards on the cabin ... or the RV."

The green-haired werewolf shrugged, keeping her eye on Henry. He had lifted his gaze to the moonlit sky above the crashing surf.

"Problem, sorcerer?" Kandy's voice rang out through the dark night, causing Audrey to pivot away from the door.

Henry shook his head. Then he shook it again and grinned. "Nah."

A large shadow percolating with dark-chocolate magic landed silently on top of the Brave, which dipped under its weight. There, it perched over Audrey, mimicking a watchful gargoyle.

For a split second, I thought it was Desmond's magic I was tasting. Then I caught the hint of cayenne pepper.

Beau.

Not knowing if I was witnessing some sort of shapeshifter game or not, I could only watch as Audrey turned, ready for an attack, seconds before Beau dropped on top of her. In his massive double-fanged, orange-pelted half-beast/half-human form, he was easily three times the size of the beta. I'd never seen him in either his tiger or his half-form, and both abilities were unusual. Werewolves were the dominant species among the shapeshifters. Big cats were rare, and tigers even more so.

Audrey intentionally fell backward, flipping Beau over her head and rolling both of them closer to Henry.

The beta's magic rose up as she transformed. Her terrifying, seven-foot-tall, dark-gray-furred half-beast form was apparently constructed solely out of muscle, tooth, and claw. Audrey's expensive outfit wasn't going to come out of this looking so perfect anymore.

As they tussled, the two of them chortled a cacophony of absolutely dreadful monster noises, trying unsuccessfully to pin each other.

There was a more immediate issue, though.

Henry, who was still standing between the wrestling monsters and us, was shaking. Moaning, he tore his fevered gaze from the growling mass of teeth and claws to stare up at the full moon.

"Kandy ..." I breathed.

"I see him," she said curtly. "Henry?" She padded closer to the moonstruck sorcerer.

I stepped back.

Henry lost whatever battle he was fighting in his mind. His skin split — tooth and claw and hair ripped through his human visage. His jacket and jeans ripped through at the seams. His precious cowboy hat tumbled away as he threw his head back, howling in pain and frustration.

"Ah, shit," Kandy muttered. Her shapeshifter magic rolled up and around her while she hurriedly started tugging off her sneakers, leggings, and T-shirt.

Henry attacked her before she could finish undressing — or transforming. And there was nothing playful about the claws he raked across her. Though he'd been aiming for her ribs, she spun away from him to take the vicious blow across her back.

Audrey tossed Beau aside. He tumbled past the cabin and the SUV parked behind it, disappearing into the more densely wooded area at the back of the acreage. He snapped a couple of good-sized trees in half as he went. Then, scrambling, he leaped forward to catch them before they toppled into the cabin or the RV.

Henry lifted his bloody claws to his wolfed-out face. He licked them lovingly, moaning as he did so.

Kandy transformed, shredding her remaining clothing and filling my senses with bittersweet dark chocolate and ripe red berries.

Henry lifted his snout to the sky and howled. It was a terrifying, hair-raising cry full of anger and torment.

I was wrong. The neighbors were definitely going to hear that.

Drake stepped into my peripheral vision.

"Let the shapeshifters handle him, fledgling." Kett's cool voice sounded out from the deep shadows beyond the driveway behind me.

Audrey wrapped her hairy, muscular arms around Henry, pinning him. He struggled, thrashing and growling. Then Kandy stepped up to lock her gaze to his. In her half-beast form, she was taller than the bitten werewolf by half a head.

A terrible, rippling snarl emanated from her misaligned jaws.

Henry pressed his ears back against his head, struggling to hold Kandy's gaze. Then his snarling turned into a whimper, and he dropped his chin to his chest.

Audrey released him. He fell to his knees.

"He needs to run," Audrey said. Her words were perfectly formed, though harsh and guttural. The beta was exceedingly skilled at wielding her shapeshifter magic. According to Kandy, talking while in half-form was difficult to master. There was something tricky about keeping human vocal cords intact while transforming.

Kandy's answering snarl sounded like a negative response. But then she and Audrey both swiftly transformed again, taking on their wolf forms. Kandy was the smaller of the two, and her pelt was a lighter gray than Audrey's. They would blend in better in their animal forms, though it seemed doubtful that Westport had many wolves roaming its beaches. However, even among the trees, the werewolf was going to be a little obvious.

Audrey leaped over Henry and disappeared into the woods. Kandy circled the crouched werewolf, then slammed her shoulder into him, pushing him after Audrey.

He followed the beta, with Kandy literally nipping at his heels.

"He's embarrassed," Drake said. "Embarrassed about being bitten?"

"No," I said. "Embarrassed about not being able to control his magic."

"But it's new to him. He'll learn."

"He's an adult. He has expectations of himself. Being … clumsy makes us feel stupid."

Drake looked doubtful, but then shrugged his shoulders.

Kett's peppermint magic moved away behind us. The vampire was tracking the shapeshifters from a distance. Or maybe he was simply patrolling the area.

Drake followed Kett back through the woods. Warner appeared on the dirt driveway just as the fledgling guardian was swallowed into the darkness on the far side of the acreage.

I smirked at him over my shoulder. The two of them couldn't have planned the transition better.

The sentinel grinned at me but didn't approach, choosing instead to lean against the front of the Ford Escape that was blocking the drive.

I crossed to the Brave. Beau was back in his human form, wearing low-slung black sweatpants and giving me an eyeful of his gorgeous mocha-colored, well-muscled chest. Well, as much as I could discern by moonlight. With the green of his shapeshifter magic overriding the normal bright blue of his eyes, he contemplated the sentinel over my shoulder while guarding the door to the Brave.

"Jade," he said, acknowledging me but clearly not happy about it.

"Beau." I hit him with one of my blinding smiles.

He smirked, but then looked upset. "Was that my fault? With Henry?"

"I think the sight of the moon was already swaying him," I answered carefully.

"But I put him over?"

"Probably."

He nodded, but didn't move away from the door.

"I'm here to see Rochelle."

"I got that."

"Do I have to go through you?" I said it as a joke, but it fell flat. Unfortunately, when I seriously outclassed someone magically, just about anything coming out of my mouth sounded like a threat.

"Who's the guy?" Beau asked, nodding over my shoulder at the sentinel glowering at him from the driveway.

"Warner," I answered. "Kett, a friend of ours, and Drake are walking the perimeter."

"The vampire and Chi Wen's apprentice?"

"Rochelle's expecting them?"

"Not exactly. I'm just putting stuff together," Beau said. "Is Warner a dragon too?"

"Yep."

"His magic smells different than Drake's."

"His magic is different. But we mean you no harm."

"But you expected to be followed? Kandy texted that we should be ready to be mobile."

Beau was young — a few years my junior — yet he was crazy perceptive.

"Yeah," I said, sorry to admit it. "Maybe not, but …"

"But." Beau huffed out a sigh. "I'll get us unhooked."

He stepped away from the door. "Rochelle's waiting on you. She …" He shook his head at whatever caution he'd been about to voice. "Tell her I'm taking care of the Brave."

I nodded.

He crossed around the front of the RV toward the cabin.

Then, dreading every step, I reached up and unlatched the door before me. Willingly climbing into an RV with an oracle waiting for me was seriously low on my to-do list.

More accurately, it was seriously high on my never-do list.

Rochelle was seated facing the door at the far side of a tiny, bright-green dinette table situated on the passenger's side of the Brave, across from the kitchen area.

The slight-framed oracle was clad in her typical uniform of a black hoodie, worn black jeans, and white-framed, bug-eyed tinted glasses. Oddly, though, only the lower five inches of her hair was dyed the jet black it had been the first time I met her. Her two-inch roots appeared to be pure white, with one full, thick streak of white running the length of her long wedge cut, from her center part to her blunt tips.

Rochelle's hair made me wonder about the far seer's hair. I'd assumed that Chi Wen wore the visage of an old man by choice. All the guardian dragons appeared capable of halting their ageing process. I hadn't even thought about his white hair being connected to his oracle or seer magic.

I'd seen a trace of white in Rochelle's hair after her vision in Portland and just hadn't connected it back to her oracle magic. I'd been rather distracted at the time, helping her sneak away and being pissy with Desmond. So did oracle magic wear on the Adepts who wielded it? Differently than a witch's or sorcerer's magic?

The thought was disconcerting, especially when factored in with Chi Wen inexplicably tagging along with Shailaja. Was the far seer losing it? Did seeing the future take a serious toll on an Adept's mind?

Though Rochelle's face was relaxed, her hands were clenched over a large, thick sketchbook.

I'd been staring at her for too long. "Hey," I said as I stepped fully into the RV. "Rochelle."

"Jade." She lifted her hand up to touch the thick rose-gold chain that rested at her collarbone. The remainder of her necklace — along with the massive raw diamond that I knew hung from it — was hidden underneath her hoodie. The magic of the necklace and Rochelle's oracle power tasted of freshly harvested apples — tart and juicy on first bite, but sweet and complexly flavored underneath.

"May I come in?"

"Please do."

I reached back to shut the door behind me, aware that I was scaring the crap out of Rochelle but having no idea how not to do so.

"Beau said to tell you he was taking care of the Brave."

Rochelle nodded stiffly, but didn't respond further. Maybe mentioning that my uninvited visit was going to force them to move wasn't a great lead-in.

I stood a few feet away, smiling as I kept my hands in plain view. When that only upped the tension that was already threatening to overwhelm the small space, I opted for a benign topic of conversation. Of course, all I really had to talk about was cupcakes, chocolate, and magic.

"There's an apple festival at UBC in the fall. Usually in October." I crossed to squeeze into the dinette across from Rochelle. Living full time in the Brave would be rather confining for me, but it apparently suited the oracle perfectly.

"Yeah?"

"They offer over sixty varieties of apples. You know, for tasting." The RV was warm. I unbuttoned my silk jacket. "I usually just hit the marketplace. People bring toy wagons ... you know those red plastic ones? I think they convert into a bench seat? That's how many bags of apples they buy. I've been known to drop over a hundred dollars myself."

"I can't taste my own magic," Rochelle said, unimpressed.

I faltered, aware that I was rambling. The tiny girl — woman — across the table from me made me nervous. I could probably crush her without really trying. Well, if I sat on her.

"I'm here about the far seer," I said.

"About? Not for?"

"No ... at least I don't think so. Jesus. I don't know. Maybe this is some sort of weird quest he's sent me on."

"And you need to know if I've seen anything relevant."

I nodded.

She spread her hands across her sketchbook.

I flinched. I couldn't help it.

"So do you have any sketches of the far seer?" I asked optimistically. I was seriously hoping to do an end run around getting blasted with oracle magic.

"No."

She removed her glasses, carefully placing them to the side, then lifted her oddly pale-gray eyes to meet my gaze.

I tried to smile. The expression felt instantly false, so I dropped it.

"I ... I didn't bring a gift," I said, not knowing I was going to say it until I voiced the thought.

"That's okay. I don't really need anything."

She turned her left hand palm up, then slid it half-way across the table toward me. Charcoal dusted her fingertips. I wondered if she'd been drawing before we arrived, or whether the tint was permanent.

"No," I said. "It's ... proper. A formal exchange." I lifted my gaze from her hand to her necklace. "I'll fortify your necklace. As I promised in Portland."

Rochelle instantly withdrew her hand, touching her necklace protectively.

"You won't have to take it off."

Relief flushed her face momentarily, but she quickly replaced it with a scowl. "Not necessary," she muttered.

"I can't reach properly over the table. Come stand here." I swung my legs off the edge of the bench seat so that Rochelle could stand before me without anything in between us. Then I waited for the oracle to make her decision.

She slowly straightened from behind the table, keeping one of her hands curled around her necklace and one pressed over the sketchbook.

"It won't hurt. You probably won't even feel it."

"I can feel you. Before you even entered the Brave. I can feel your energy. Your magic."

That was surprising. I didn't know oracles could sense magic that way. I closed my eyes, giving my neck a roll. Then I inhaled to center myself, coaxing my necklace to absorb and dampen my magic. I'd never thought to do so around anyone else before, and I wasn't certain how successful I'd be at it.

Energy thrummed through the chain currently twined three times around my neck. I opened my eyes. "Better?"

Rochelle nodded, stepping over to stand before me. Her fingers hesitated at the zipper of her hoodie. "What do you mean by 'fortify?' "

"What do you want?"

"Can you hide my magic? Like you just did with yours?"

"No. I don't think so, anyway. I think you have to learn to do that yourself. But I think your necklace would already be receptive to that."

"Learn how? You just closed your eyes and breathed."

"I … um … Well, I'm not sure it works the same for you. It might be part of my alchemist powers. But I think it's a matter of focal points. You know, grounding your energy within the energy of the necklace."

Rochelle nodded thoughtfully. Her gaze was cast somewhere around my left shoulder, but I didn't think she was treating me warily, as she would a shapeshifter. She was simply thinking about her magic.

"What fortifications can you offer, then?" she asked.

"I can make sure no one but you can remove the necklace. I can lay protection spells on it so that it helps deflect any malicious magic flung your way."

Rochelle shifted her feet. "But you can't take away the visions."

Something in her tone put me on edge. "I wouldn't."

"But you could," she whispered. It wasn't a question.

"So you've seen? In the past or the future?"

"The past, I think. With the black witch on the beach."

I nodded, not sure what to do about Rochelle knowing my secret. Though the knowledge that I could drain the magic from an Adept really wasn't that much of a secret anymore, now that Shailaja had my mangled katana. The oracle probably knew a lot of things about me that I would rather she didn't.

"I'm not sure what you're asking," I said carefully. "I won't harm you."

"I know. But if I asked?"

I shook my head vehemently. "No. I would never steal your magic. I'll never do it again. I'm not certain I was wholly aware I was doing so the last time."

Rochelle looked at me for a moment. I wasn't sure what she was thinking. The only times she appeared truly engaged were when Beau was around, and when she was wielding her oracle magic.

"I'll show you what I know," she finally said. "What I've seen of you. And you'll lay protection spells on my necklace so that no one can take the chain from me or harm me with magic."

"I can't guarantee the second part. I can't block against specific spells, but I can create a shield of sorts. A personal ward."

"I understand your stipulations."

I laughed. "Who have you been making deals with?"

Rochelle stiffened her shoulders. "It's important to be clear on our terms."

"Okay."

She reached for her necklace.

"Leave it on. I'll use your magic to tie it to you."

She bit her lip, then unzipped her hoodie.

I reached up to place my forefinger and thumb on the chain, leaving my other fingers splayed on her upper rib cage and collarbone.

I smiled. "I'm going to need some apple pie after this," I said jokingly.

Rochelle nodded, completely serious. "I'll warm some up for you. It's not homemade, but Beau liked it."

I laughed.

Rochelle cracked a rare smile.

Then I set to work on her necklace, tangling her magic with the magic already bound to the gold and the diamond. Smoothing it all with my own magic.

I informed the necklace that it belonged solely to Rochelle and no one else. But I got some sort of feedback. "Huh," I muttered. "Has anyone ever tried to take the necklace?"

"No."

"I doubt they could have. When I tuned it to your oracle magic, I guess I already created that protection. Or it was inherent to the necklace."

"It was my mother's."

Right. I'd known that. Rochelle's mother had died — while possibly wearing this necklace — at the moment of her birth. I wondered if those coinciding events had magical ramifications as well.

I turned my attention back to my alchemy, tugging magic from my own necklace and channeling it through my fingers into Rochelle's chain. Then I blended it all, fusing it together to create a magical shield tied to the oracle.

"Your eyes are glowing," Rochelle murmured. Enamored, she brushed her fingers through my curls and got them tangled. "And your hair. Like you glow in my visions."

I lifted my hands away from the necklace, disengaging myself from Rochelle's magic.

She looked startled, as if only just realizing she was touching me. Hastily, she withdrew her hand. "Okay. My turn."

"Sure," I said, attempting to not grind my teeth at the thought of having her oracle magic invading my mind.

Rochelle zipped up her hoodie, hiding her necklace. Then she spread her feet slightly as if to anchor herself. "I'm still practicing," she said apologetically.

"Delightful."

She touched her fingertips to my forehead.

Nothing happened.

She pressed a tiny bit harder.

Still nothing.

"I … I don't understand."

I sighed. "I do." Casting my dowser senses outside, I tasted honey-roasted almonds more distinctly than black forest cake. I raised my voice slightly. "Drake?"

A brief murmured exchange occurred outside the door between Beau and Drake. Then the fledgling guardian opened the door and climbed into the RV.

"Hey, Rochelle," he said, grinning ear to ear.

The smile she offered him was fleeting but genuine.

204

I took my necklace off and held it out to Drake.

Rochelle stepped to the side, allowing Drake space to kneel before me. I looped the chain with its wedding rings around his neck twice. Then he rose.

"Should I step out?"

"I think so."

Drake flashed Rochelle another toothy grin, then left as quickly as he arrived.

"Try again," I said.

Rochelle swallowed. Then she touched my forehead tentatively. The taste of apple intensified in my mouth.

"Be specific," I said. "Just show me exactly what you think is relevant."

"Easy for you to say," she muttered.

Then the oracle electrocuted my brain.

Okay. It wasn't quite that bad. But she did shove a series of images at me so quickly that I couldn't see or hear anything else.

"Jesus!" I cried out without meaning to.

Rochelle gasped, removing her hands and curling them into fists.

"Just do it, oracle," I growled as I squeezed my eyes shut.

Her cool fingers touched my temples. Then I was standing ankle-deep in the snow on a smooth stone pathway, looking at a doorway carved into a mountain.

I'd been there before.

"This is wrong," I said, realizing that it was the time of day that was wrong as I spoke. I'd assumed I was looking at the door to the temple of the centipede, but the mountain before me was illuminated by evening light. It was too dark to have been that day in Peru. The snow was too plentiful as well. And as the vision grew clearer, I saw that the door was carved into the granite, not simply outlined by glowing runes.

Leaves and flowers were embossed into the stone of the doorway, which was easily fifteen feet high and eight feet wide. I couldn't see a handle or hinges.

I blinked. Then I found myself looking at Rochelle, who was chewing on her lower lip.

"Stop doing that," I said. "You'll get chapped."

She narrowed her eyes at me grumpily.

I grinned. It was better if I annoyed her. I'd take that over scaring her any day. "Do you know where that door is?"

She shook her head.

"Do you have a picture?"

She nodded as she tugged a folded piece of thick paper out of her hoodie pocket.

"You knew I needed it?"

"Yeah, but I thought I might pick up more, or even something different, if I tried to read you as well. But … you know. I'm still practicing."

I took the paper from her, holding it by the edges and carefully easing it open. It was a detailed charcoal sketch of what she'd just shown me. She must have torn it out of her sketchbook, then carefully trimmed off the ragged edge.

"I know these leaves and flowers," I said.

Rochelle reached for her sketchbook on the dinette, but I was already digging through my satchel for the dragonskin tattoo. Maybe if I compared the sketch to the map, I could work out the location of the door.

"Wait," Rochelle said. "That's … um … that's not all."

I chose my next words carefully. "I only want to know things that are relevant. Things connected to the far seer. Or at least things that will help me find the final instrument of assassination, and therefore draw the maniac who's kidnapped the far seer to me."

Rochelle's eyes widened. "Kidnapped? The far seer? Who could kidnap the far seer?"

Damn. I hadn't meant to mention the kidnapping part. But Rochelle being in my head had severely rattled me.

"It'll be okay," I said, though my words came out more pissy than soothing. "I'm sorry. I also could be wrong about the kidnapping part. It's just that this ..." I waved my hand in the direction of her sketchbook. "This weirds me out."

"I know. You don't want to know if you're going to die."

"Who would?"

"But if you did, would you run? Wouldn't you try to change your destiny?"

I forced a smile, feeling the edges of the sketch I held crumpling underneath my fingers. "What fun would that be?"

"Be flippant all you want, Jade. But I know you. I know why you do what you do. I know you believe. You believe you can only do what you're meant to do."

"Yes, I believe. Will I fail?"

Rochelle shrugged. "I'm not sure what failure would look like in this case."

"Wouldn't me dying be a failure?"

"I don't think so. And neither do you."

I laughed. Rochelle was laying claim to my soul. And laughing was all I could do.

"I don't see death ..." The oracle whispered the words as the white of her magic rolled across her eyes. "But ... I do see ... rebirth."

"That sounds worse."

"Yes."

Great. Lovely. Fan-freaking-tastic.

"There's something else. Something I can't see beyond. Something hidden from me, behind a veil of magic, maybe."

"Delightful."

"I see a … golden fire …"

"Golden fire?"

"Yes."

"And I'm going to be reborn through this golden fire?"

"No."

"That's clear, then. Have you at least got a timeline?"

"I'm trying my best."

Guilt stopped my snark in its tracks.

"I owe you, Jade," Rochelle said quietly. "For fixing my mother's necklace. For sending Chi Wen."

"No one sends a guardian anywhere," I murmured.

"Whatever," Rochelle said. "But I'd just as soon have you out of my head, you know?"

"Sure."

"The golden fire washes you away. It burns the vision of you up. And I can't see anything beyond. I can't even sketch it. It's … too much."

I just stared at the oracle. "I can't do anything with that."

"All you can do is endure."

I shivered. Rochelle was echoing my own thoughts, from all the terrible hours I'd spent staring at her sketches in Chi Wen's quarters in the dragon nexus. It was disturbing.

"There's more ..." Rochelle swallowed her next words. She was rubbing her charcoal-dusted fingers again, as if soothing herself.

"Who is it?" I whispered. "Who's going to die? And can I stop it?"

Rochelle looked startled. "I don't see anyone dying. Any of your friends, I mean."

"Because you don't see them at all?"

She placed her hand on her sketchbook, then gazed out the dark window of the Brave. I hadn't noticed from the outside, but she had pulled the curtains open at some point. Maybe when Henry was losing it. "No ... I've seen them. All of them ... and one other."

Rochelle's hesitation was becoming disconcerting.

"Who?" I said quietly.

She lifted her gray-eyed gaze to me, then stared at my right hip where my knife was invisibly sheathed.

"Don't be mad," she whispered.

"I will be mad," I said matter-of-factly. "I'm going to be mad."

Rochelle nodded, then swallowed hard. She lifted her eyes from my knife and resolutely locked her gaze to mine.

"I would never hurt you," I said.

"Of course not."

"Who, then? Beau?"

Rochelle shook her head, then she flipped open the book to a sketch similar to the one I held. Except I was in this drawing, standing before the leaf-and-flower-carved door. She carefully lifted the edge of the next page and turned it.

I stepped closer to peer down at the newly revealed sketch, which resembled a wider-angle view of the previous image. I was standing in front of the door as before, but five other figures occupied the smudged shadows around me.

"Warner," I murmured, immediately identifying him by his broad shoulders, then by the curved blade he held at the ready.

"Is that his name?" Rochelle asked quietly. She turned the page to reveal a detailed sketch of the sentinel's strong profile.

Despite my anxiety, my heart did a little dance at the sight. There was something utterly titillating about seeing him captured in stillness on the page. I could stare at him forever.

Rochelle flipped back to the main drawing.

"Drake," I said, pointing at the figure positioned just behind my right shoulder.

Rochelle nodded, flipping the pages forward to a detailed sketch of the fledgling guardian. He looked older in smudged charcoal than he did in real life. His Asian features were highlighted in black and white.

Rochelle started to flip back again, but I touched the top of her hand to stop her.

She flinched as if I'd shocked her, though I felt nothing.

"Sorry," I murmured. "But we don't have much time. Perhaps you should just rip off the Band-Aid?"

The oracle nodded, squared her shoulders, and flipped a page.

"Kandy."

Next page.

"Kett."

She hesitated. Then, with her hand shaking, she revealed the fifth shadowed figure.

Son of a bitch.

Blackwell.

"I've texted him," Rochelle murmured. "He's on his way."

I was spinning away from the tiny green-topped table before she voiced her last words. My knife appeared eagerly in my hand. I busted through the door of the Brave, breaking something in the process.

Drake and Warner were standing beside the firepit, overseeing Beau, who was building a fire with paper and kindling. They spun toward me as I leaped from the RV.

My feet hit the ground as the taste of buttered baked potato and sour cream set my mouth watering. Though I hadn't tasted it in over two years, the magic of Blackwell's ruby amulet was unmistakable. And where it manifested, Blackwell appeared. The teleportation power of the amulet was an awesome trick, and with the portals out of order, I was more than a little jealous of the sorcerer's prized possession. That wasn't going to stop me from trying to skewer him, though.

Tracking the amulet's magic, I executed two more quick steps to the left, pressing my knife to Blackwell's neck just as the sorcerer magically appeared in the middle of the clearing.

"Stop!" Rochelle screamed from behind me.

Blackwell's dark eyes widened. His clean-shaven face was unusually gaunt, but he wore his typical ensemble of tailored dark suit and white dress shirt. The sorcerer's taste in clothing was even more expensive than Audrey's or Kett's, right down to his Italian-leather wingbacks. Not that I was currently checking out his shoes.

Before I could press my advantage, the magic of the amulet concealed underneath his dress shirt flared again. Blackwell disappeared.

"You need him," Rochelle shouted.

I spun around, glaring at the oracle, who was hanging out of the busted door of the Brave. It was hanging half off its hinges. A wash of regret momentarily distracted me. I didn't want to be responsible for ruining anyone's home.

Drake and Warner fanned out from the bonfire just as it flared into flame. Their movement called my attention back to the hunt.

Magic bloomed near Rochelle. I lunged. The oracle awkwardly flung herself down the stairs of the RV in a crazy attempt to block my attack.

The sorcerer appeared behind her.

I slid to a stop.

Blackwell scanned the area behind and above me.

"Hiding behind a child, hey, asshole?" I sneered.

"Hey!" Rochelle cried. "I'm, like, practically twenty-one!"

"Warrior's daughter." Blackwell offered me a thin-lipped smile.

"How do I need him?" I growled at Rochelle.

She shook her head, questioning her words even as she spoke them. "Why would he be there? Do you know where the door is? If I see him with you, then maybe he leads you to it."

Blackwell laughed mirthlessly.

I eyed him, warring with every instinct that told me to wipe him from the face of the planet now and forever. Then I sheathed my knife and stepped back.

Rochelle let out a shuddering breath.

"How can I be of service, Jade Godfrey?" Blackwell's smile widened to reveal his teeth.

"Are you sure?" I spoke to the oracle, but without taking my eyes off the evil sorcerer standing behind her.

Rochelle nodded, but it was the utter regret etched across her face that sold it for me. She'd already told me I survived whatever was coming — in whatever form that survival took — so she was concerned she was sacrificing Blackwell.

"Screw it," I muttered. Then I turned my back on the sorcerer. I needed to walk away or I was going to skewer him.

"Show me, Rochelle." Blackwell's tone was muted and kind ... and edged with a sick sort of eagerness. "You have sketches, yes?"

Warner and Drake fell into step with me.

"Who is this?" the sentinel asked.

"Some asshole with a death wish." Pausing my pissy state of stomping away, I turned around and reached up to retrieve my necklace from around Drake's neck.

The fledgling bent down obligingly.

Warner pivoted to face the Brave, presumably studying Blackwell.

"And we'd better warn Kandy and Audrey that he's here," I said. "Or there will be blood."

Drake nodded, then slipped off into the dark woods.

Gazing up at Warner, I settled my necklace over my collarbone. The sentinel's moonlit profile was an aching reminder of Rochelle's sketch. I might have no idea where we were going or what we were getting into, but we'd be there together. There was some comfort in that.

I sighed. "I guess we should patrol."

Warner brushed his hand against mine. "Drake, Kett, and I will patrol. You get caught up with your BFF." He nodded toward the cabin behind me.

I glanced over my shoulder just as Kandy emerged from the woods. She was back in human form, clad only in a sports bra and tattered leggings, and grinning manically. Though whether that was from her run in the woods or news of Blackwell's appearance, I didn't know.

She jogged over to collect her sneakers and T-shirt, then winked at me as she turned back to dig a change of clothing out of the Escalade. Her hair was still green, though it usually reverted to mousy brown when she transformed. Apparently, she'd spent our year apart honing her shapeshifter skills.

"Go," Warner said. "Shailaja will send scouts before she shows up. We'll have warning."

"Yeah," I said. "It really is too bad she isn't an idiot. Crazy, intelligent people are just freaky."

Warner snorted, then stepped off into the trees behind us to join the honeyed-almond and peppermint magic I could taste already roaming the nearby woods. And I crossed the yard for a much-needed gab session with my best friend.

Chapter Ten

Blackwell spent what felt like hours poring over Rochelle's sketches, though it was probably only thirty minutes. When he emerged from the RV, he stumbled on the first step at the sight of the small army arrayed around the bonfire Beau had built.

Good. He should be scared.

Of course, the members of that small army were all roasting hot dogs, which wasn't exactly an act of aggression. And half of them were veggie anyway.

Audrey and Henry had returned from the woods moments after Kandy. The beta reverted to her human form and changed into a tailored collared shirt and slim dress pants, though she remained barefoot. The sorcerer was still in his bitten werewolf form, but he'd happily retrieved his cowboy hat before hunkering down by the fire.

I was surprised that Audrey didn't instantly end up with her teeth at the sorcerer's throat. Though it had been Sienna who'd killed her pack mate Jeremy, Blackwell had been instrumental in setting the stage and luring us into Sienna's trap in the Sea Lion Caves in Oregon.

However, the incident in Mississippi with Rochelle and Beau — which had concluded with Kandy biting Henry — had indebted the pack to Blackwell in some significant way. Apparently, the sorcerer had been helpful. I wouldn't call whatever was going on a truce. But no one was rushing to murder anyone else in the deep night in Westport, Washington.

It was a shame.

Blackwell smirked annoyingly, covering for his moment of hesitation as he descended the steps.

I returned my pissy gaze to the fire as he moved away from the RV. I was going to have to void my practically oath-sworn feud with the evil bastard. If he actually knew the location of the door Rochelle thought we were seeking, then he'd be stupid to settle for anything less. For all his darkness, Blackwell wasn't a moron. He'd probably demand more from me, and I'd have to give it to him. I was just hoping I wouldn't have to agree to an open-ended favor in order to move forward with our task.

The oracle hovered in the doorway of the Brave. "Henry?" she asked worriedly.

The bitten werewolf was crouched on all fours between Kandy and Audrey at the edge of the bonfire. He was gobbling raw hot dogs, though he couldn't quite keep them in his mouth while eating. In response to Rochelle's voice, he straightened, offering the oracle a toothy grin.

Rochelle looked appropriately terrified by his appearance.

Beau slipped out from the shadows between the cabin and the RV. He hadn't joined us at the fire, other than to offer Kandy the hot dogs to roast, along with various condiments sourced from the Brave. Then he'd fiddled with the broken hinge on the door of the Brave until it closed but still didn't properly latch. He reached out to Rochelle and she stepped down beside him. She'd pulled a black, puffy ski jacket on over her hoodie.

"The marshal came to see you, but ..." Beau's explanation trailed off as his attention snagged on something behind us.

I didn't have to turn to taste the peppermint drifting toward me from the sparsely wooded area between the bonfire and the house to the south. Instead, I looked up at the sorcerer, just in time to see Blackwell's expression twist to a grimace that he quickly smoothed over.

"Kettil." The sorcerer acknowledged the approaching vampire with a nod.

"Sorcerer," Kett replied coolly. He crossed to stand a couple of feet behind me.

I laughed harshly. Truthfully, the vampire's unpredictability was really only amusing when it wasn't directly affecting me. But I couldn't help feeling pleased that Blackwell might be worried about whether he was moments from death.

Capturing a vampire as old as Kett in a fog spell — as Blackwell had done while defending his castle from our entry two years ago — might cause that vampire to hold a grudge. It also might garner a certain amount of respect. But respect from a vampire could turn to dismemberment with a misspoken word or a misplaced gesture. Gran called that 'hanging on tenterhooks.'

Beside me, Drake shoved a third hot dog into the bun he'd slathered with mayo, ketchup, and mustard — along with copious amounts of sand. Then he inhaled the concoction.

Yeah, I wasn't big on eating outside. Unless the seaside patio came with umbrellas, heat lamps, and proper tableware, of course.

"Perhaps introductions are in order?" Blackwell asked.

"No," Kett said.

I swallowed a smirk, straightening from the fire to face the sorcerer. "We all know you."

"I won't work with nameless mercenaries."

Warner rose from beside me, eyed the sorcerer, then turned his back on him. I gathered he was opting to walk the perimeter rather than negotiate with Blackwell.

"I don't like relying on such an ambivalent soul," Drake said. His tone was completely benign, though he had just accused Blackwell of being morally challenged. "Is there another way, oracle? Another who can show us our path?"

A vein in Blackwell's forehead pulsed, just once. But it was probably a bad thing that I noticed. I was bloodthirsty when it came to the sorcerer. And also completely aware that I blamed him for things that had most likely been out of his control. Sienna had been beyond all of our control. Even after I'd drained her magic, right up until the moment Desmond had stepped in … until she wasn't anything anymore.

Still, it was easier to hold grudges than admit that I was willfully blind to the faults of the people I loved.

Rochelle squeezed Beau's hand, then loosened her grip to reach out for Drake, beckoning him away from the fire and the hot dogs. "Shall we walk?" she asked. The white of her oracle magic rolled across her eyes.

The fledgling guardian moved to her side so quickly that Blackwell belatedly flinched and stumbled to one side.

"Rochelle," Beau said. "The dowser said we should move, and quickly."

The oracle wrapped her hand around Drake's as she gazed lovingly up at her mate. "I hear you, Beau. But I doubt anyone is coming through them."

Her 'them' was heavy with layers of emotion. Fear. Awe. And a tiny bit of satisfaction. Smugness, even. The oracle might look like a wispy thing, but she had a backbone. Which was good, because anyone friendly with Blackwell was going to need a spine.

With Beau close behind them, Drake and Rochelle turned to walk through the short stretch of wild grass at the edge of the beach. I briefly wondered what Rochelle wanted to show Drake, but I kept my focus on Blackwell.

Blackwell glanced around. "I know the enforcer, the bitten sorcerer, who I'm glad to see survived, and the vampire …" he prompted.

I sneered. "Always ready to deal, aren't you, Blackwell?"

"How is what you do any different, Jade?" he said smoothly. His use of my name was pointedly intimate.

I forced the delightful image of 'accidentally' shoulder-checking the sorcerer into the bonfire out of my head. "This is Audrey, beta of the West Coast North American Pack."

Audrey bared her teeth in Blackwell's direction. He nodded, offering her a tight smile.

"You've met Drake." I nodded toward the trio of moonlit figures on the beach. "Warner is … checking the perimeter."

"Drake and Warner who?" Blackwell asked.

I took a step closer to the sorcerer, seeing firelight dancing in the whites of his almost-black eyes. Kett closed the space behind me. "Do you know the location of the door?"

"I will. I believe I've seen a section of it before. The flower and leaf motif is distinct. Perhaps in an ancestor's journal. I'll have to visit the library at Blackness Castle to confirm."

"Drake is apprenticed to Chi Wen, the far seer of the guardian nine." I paused, waiting for the sorcerer to react.

He tilted his head in acknowledgement but gave nothing else away. It seemed a safe bet that he knew all about the far seer through Rochelle.

"Warner is the son of Jiaotu-who-was. Sentinel of the instruments of assassination."

Blackwell hissed excitedly.

The hair on the back of my neck stood straight up.

"So they do exist," he whispered, speaking more to himself than me.

I didn't answer.

"Is that what lies behind the door, warrior's daughter?" Blackwell's smile as he voiced my title was a brief flash of white in the dark night.

Again, I declined to answer. I'd done the introductions as he'd stipulated. Now it was his turn.

"The information is relevant to my ... recollection," he said, forcing the point.

"How?" Kett asked.

Blackwell glanced from me to the vampire, then back again. "I don't believe we've defined the terms of my participation in your hunt."

"Make your pitch," I said coldly.

Blackwell curled one corner of his mouth into a smirk. Then he thoughtfully cast his gaze over the fire toward the beach.

Drake and Rochelle stood a few feet back from the low surf, the fledgling's dark head bent toward the oracle. Beau was a few feet off to the side, his face lifted to the moon. He took the form of a tiger, so I wasn't sure whether the moon held any sway over him as it did the wolves. As it seriously did with Henry.

"What destinies do you suppose she whispers in his ear?" Blackwell mused.

I looked at him sharply. "You bargain with me, sorcerer, and me only. I speak for no one else."

"Except to guarantee my safety on our ... excursion."

"No one can guarantee that," Kett said. "Not for any of us. Also, we haven't agreed that you will be joining our hunt." His cool words were ominous.

"I believe the oracle has made that part of our agreement preemptively binding," Blackwell said smugly "Jade, you will keep your companions in check. I will not have a blade at my neck ... metaphorically or literally ... during our collaboration."

"Fine," I said.

"I'll get you to the door depicted in the oracle's sketches, if I can. But after that, my participation will have to be renegotiated. I won't jeopardize my life ... or liberty."

I snorted. "As expected."

"And you specifically, Jade Godfrey," the sorcerer continued, "you will drop your vendetta."

I snorted. "You can't make me like you, Blackwell."

"I'm simply tired of watching my back."

"I highly doubt I'm the only one who hates you."

"Be that as it may."

The sorcerer said nothing else. Waiting for my response.

I glanced over to the beach. Rochelle and Beau were standing alone now at the water's edge, the rippling surf only inches from their sneakered feet. Drake had slipped away somewhere, though he was near enough that I could still taste his magic.

"Vancouver is off-limits. I see you there, and any truce is void." I didn't bother to look at Blackwell as I addressed him. I had known he was going to ask for a clean slate. But I didn't have to accept that stipulation without conditions.

"I could demand the same for all of Scotland," he said.

"You could," I whispered. "But could you enforce it?" I turned to meet his gaze.

He didn't immediately back down. Which wasn't particularly surprising. He was always ballsy.

Then he nodded. "I have no need or wish to visit Vancouver."

"I shall no longer hold the crimes of my sister against you, Blackwell," I said.

The sorcerer smiled. I sensed genuine gratitude in the expression, but that didn't stop me wanting it wiped from his gaunt face.

"But we're not friends," I added. "Eventually you'll do something, break some rule. And I'll be there, waiting, to exact justice when you step over the line."

"It's not your place to enforce my choices."

"And who will you complain to, sorcerer? Who has your back?"

Blackwell stiffened, then lifted his chin. "You'll answer to the Convocation. And to the Guardian Council itself."

I snorted. "Good luck getting justice from either."

Blackwell bristled. Finally. "I happen to know that Suanmi, the guardian of Western Europe, is not a fan of yours."

I laughed. "You might want to update your records, sorcerer. Or did I fail to mention the second part of Drake's title? He's the fire breather's ward." Despite my bravado, my stomach curdled in anticipation of the looming, inevitable confrontation with Suanmi.

Blackwell glanced over to the beach, then around the immediate area. He flinched as Drake — possibly summoned by my use of his name — appeared at my left elbow.

"We've stayed too long," the fledgling guardian said. "The sorcerer has already indicated that the information regarding the door the oracle saw us standing before resides in his library. I suggest we go."

Blackwell opened his mouth to answer, but I cut him off.

"That's hundreds of books. Even with Kett with us, it might take weeks to narrow our focus."

"There are many doors in this world," Kett said agreeably.

Drake spun away. I felt sorry for him. Chi Wen was his mentor, and even though the far seer could be rather oblique — even inconsistent — in his teachings, the fledgling wasn't accustomed to waiting around.

I glanced behind me to watch Drake walk away. Warner wandered out of the trees beyond the cabin and clapped him on the shoulder as he passed. Then the sentinel leaned back against the green SUV parked in the driveway, standing guard as always.

"Who are you hunting, warrior's daughter?" Blackwell asked.

"What makes you think I'm hunting anyone?"

"Your company, of course. Warriors all. Strong, fierce … and impetuous."

Kett chuckled. No one was less impetuous than an elder vampire … as long as he wasn't bored, according to Warner.

Blackwell glanced around the area again, thinking out loud. "Or perhaps I've misread the force gathered around you. Perhaps you are the hunted."

"Let's get on with it, Blackwell," I said. "You have a journal to retrieve. And I assume you don't want us ripping through your wards and ransacking your library."

"You are undeniably correct." Blackwell tapped his amulet underneath his shirt. I wondered if he wore it constantly, as I did with my necklace. "Care to accompany me, Jade?"

He held his hand out toward me.

"No freaking way."

"Perhaps I shall accompany you," Kett said. "To make sure you stay on task."

Blackwell looked momentarily ill at the idea of being accompanied by the vampire. Then he smiled tightly. "It shouldn't take me more than a few hours to follow up on my suspicions. I stumbled across something a few months ago, which leads me to believe I'm already halfway there."

He reached into his suit pocket and pulled out a metal rune. A rune that looked like a decapitated stick figure.

It was an exact replica of the runes we'd found on the corpses littered throughout the temple of the braids in Hope Town. It was how we'd identified the skeletons as belonging to a sect of eternal-life sorcerers. A sect that Shailaja had apparently created — and which she had certainly sacrificed to manifest her shadow demon buddies.

"Where did you find that?" I whispered.

Blackwell flipped the rune in his hand, then immediately slipped it back into his pocket. "Is it connected to your current hunt?"

"Only obliquely," Kett replied smoothly.

I had filled the vampire in regarding the story of how Kandy, Warner, and I collected the braids. I couldn't remember mentioning the runes specifically, but the vampire had a fantastic memory.

"I come from a long line of sorcerers," Blackwell said. "My collection is centuries old."

"That still doesn't explain you connecting it to our particular request."

"You should pay more attention to the oracle's sketches, dowser," Blackwell said. "Rochelle's gifts don't frighten me as much as they apparently frighten you."

He was challenging me, but I didn't take the bait. Instead, I put together the pieces and shoved them back in his smug face. "So some granddaddy of yours was an eternal lifer. He was part of a sect of sorcerers seeking the instruments of assassination. Obviously, Rochelle sketched the rune. When? About a year ago? And it re-minded you of what? A book? Then you found the rune in your collection."

Blackwell stuck out his chin. Apparently, he didn't like me undercutting his power play.

I laughed, then turned to Kett. "If you want to join him, I can't stop you."

Kett quirked his lips in a smile. Then he reached over to place his hand on Blackwell's shoulder. In the moonlight, his pale skin was a sharp contrast to the sorcerer's dark suit.

"I assume you aren't staying?" Kett cast his gaze toward the fire and the Brave.

"Well, you know how much I adore camping."

"Keep me apprised of your location," the vampire said. "Sorcerer?"

Blackwell nodded. He swallowed, then brushed his fingers against his amulet.

Magic bloomed, tangling my hair. Then they were gone.

"First friend of yours I haven't particularly liked." Warner's voice cut through the moonlit darkness between us.

Drake snickered as he crossed out of the woods to join the sentinel.

"Did you see the rune?" I asked, crossing to join Warner by the SUV.

He nodded, not at all pleased.

"It can't be one of the ones we collected," I said, attempting to reassure myself. "That would be way too obvious. Right? I mean, I'd love there to be a connection between the rabid koala and the evil jerk. So there's probably no chance of that."

Warner snorted, grinning at me. Ah, it was sweet when your boyfriend thought your homicidal side was cute.

The firelight flickered behind me, then died. I turned to see Beau dousing it with sand. Audrey was speaking to him in hushed tones.

Behind them, Henry — still in his bitten werewolf form — climbed into the RV. The Brave swayed underneath his weight. Rochelle was already inside and putting things away in the kitchen cupboards, preparing to leave.

Kandy jogged out from behind the cabin. She'd retrieved a backpack from the black SUV, presumably containing yet another change of clothing.

"Um ... Henry?" I asked.

"He'll be fine. They're friends."

"Yeah, but they could have left the fire."

"We might as well get some food. Old toothy has a cellphone."

"You just ate."

"You didn't." Kandy crossed around to open the back hatch of the green SUV. Drake wandered after her.

Audrey sauntered over to us, carrying her high-heel pumps in one hand. Other than her change of clothing, I saw no evidence of her recent transformation. The dark-haired beauty was seriously annoying that way. I was already grubby, and I hadn't turned into a monster and gone romping through the woods.

"Henry and I will stay with the oracle. We'll head back to Portland," Audrey said.

"I'm sorry about that," I said. "I know Rochelle prefers the coast."

"The pack will be pleased." She flashed her white teeth in my direction, then smirked.

"Delightful. I'm always so pleased to please the pack."

Audrey laughed huskily, then abruptly returned to her all-business-no-fun tone. "Kandy will accompany you, to protect the pack's interests."

I raised my eyebrows at the beta.

She lowered her voice. "We're waiting for the sorcerer to step out of line. The connection between him and the oracle must be severed. The sooner the better."

"Ah. Kandy will keep you posted?"

"Kandy will enforce, as is her duty." Audrey eyed the back of the Ford Escape over my shoulder, then pitched her voice unnecessarily louder. "Plus, she's driving me crazy. Whining does not become a werewolf."

Kandy snarled an answer, then climbed into the back seat without further addressing her beta.

Audrey returned her attention to me. "The pack thanks you for including us in this matter."

"Right. I'm happy to be helpful."

The beta turned back to the RV without another word.

Warner snorted, then crossed around our vehicle and climbed into the driver's seat.

Beau had temporarily rigged the door to the Brave, creating a latch with a bungee cord from the inside. Audrey tossed her car keys in the air toward him as she climbed into the RV. He caught the keys without question or pause. Then, with a nod in my direction, he headed toward the Escalade parked behind the cabin.

"Beau," I called after him.

He paused, looking over his shoulder at me but not turning around.

"If you ever need anything," I said.

"We know where to find you."

"Right. Okay." I wanted to say something more about Blackwell, and to apologize again for forcing a move on them. Beau wasn't interested, though, so I just added, "Drive safely."

He nodded, then jogged the rest of the way to the Escalade.

Through the windows of the Brave, I saw Rochelle slip into the driver's seat while Audrey joined her on the passenger side. I couldn't see Henry, but I assumed he was sprawled out on the back bed.

A shadow shifted above a tree branch at the edge of my peripheral vision, then stilled. I didn't need to turn my head or judge the angle of the moonlight to know it shouldn't be there. I brushed my fingers lovingly along the invisible blade strapped to my right hip, waiting for the perfect moment to draw and skewer the shadow leech watching me from the darkness.

"I found a waffle place!" Kandy yelled from the back seat.

"Waffles?" Drake asked. "Show me."

The shadow disappeared.

"Come on, Jade," my werewolf best friend groused. "The dragon doesn't know what waffles are. You can mope about doing a deal with a devil while we eat."

I laughed despite myself. Apparently, I was as transparent as plastic wrap over chocolate pudding. I climbed into the passenger seat without further delay. We were blocking the driveway.

"Whipped cream and strawberries?" Drake crowed. "Yes, please!"

I glanced over at Warner, who was waiting for an okay from me. I offered him a blazing smile and buckled my seat belt. "Kandy always knows best,"

"So true," Kandy said. "So, so true. There's always time for waffles ... and cupcakes. But apparently, you didn't bring any of those."

I laughed, trailing my fingers over the back of Warner's hand and wrist as he put the SUV into reverse. "Maybe they'll have cherries and shaved chocolate."

"You know where to find those." Warner leered at me as he backed the SUV out of the driveway. "Anytime, anywhere."

Kandy gagged comically in the back seat. "Tone down the PDA, would you?"

I glanced back at the green-haired werewolf.

She grinned.

God, I was glad to have her back.

Apparently, the local diner Kandy had decided desperately needed our patronage closed at 3:30 P.M. Then the werewolf quickly discovered that everything else within a hundred-mile radius also closed in the early afternoon on a Saturday in January.

Which was how we found ourselves — blurry eyed and grumpy — waiting outside Sweet Iron in Seattle, Washington, at six o'clock in the damn morning.

Okay, I might have been exaggerating about the lack of sustenance on the West Coast. And there might have been some further conversation along the way. But I finally succumbed to the sweet oblivion of intensely needed sleep and Kandy got her waffle wish fulfilled ... all the long way to Seattle.

At least it wasn't raining. Yet.

Also, Kett and Blackwell hadn't returned.

We'd arrived in the city around midnight, then slept in shifts in an underground parking lot a few blocks from the waffle place. Or rather, I slept until Kandy hauled me out of the SUV and dragged me through the hushed, darkened streets to the diner.

As the city woke around us, I begrudgingly admitted that from the exterior, Sweet Iron appeared to have been worth the drive and the wait. The classic Belgian waffle place was situated on the ground floor of a refurbished sandstone-brick building, just in from the corner of Third Avenue and Seneca Street. It was easily within walking distance of the Inn at the Market, where I stayed whenever I attended the Northwest Chocolate Festival. However, with so much yumminess to consume in Seattle, it apparently hadn't popped up on my radar yet.

Drake returned from circling the block. The fledgling was having trouble staying still, but patrolling under Warner's watchful gaze seemed to keep him fairly settled. "The sign says the restaurant doesn't open on Sundays until 8 A.M."

"What?" I mumbled, really not awake or at all ready for bad news yet.

"Never mind," Kandy said, shifting eagerly back and forth on the balls of her feet. "I called in a favor. Six was the earliest they'd open, though. Donation or no donation."

The interior lights flicked on in the diner. A silver-haired man began bustling around the open kitchen behind the glass display counters and cash register.

"You called in a favor and made a donation ... for waffles?" I asked.

Warner snorted.

"These aren't just any waffles, dowser," the green-haired werewolf said gleefully. "You'll be thanking me in about ten minutes. Plus it was a tax write-off for a kid's foundation. That's doubly worth it."

"You know best," I said. We weren't exactly blazing trails to the instrument of assassination, and if Kandy wanted waffles along the way, I wasn't going to argue.

"Always."

A group of club-weary twentysomethings stumbled around the far corner, supporting each other and approaching us on unsteady feet.

"Hey!" a guy in the middle of the group exclaimed. "Are they opening early?"

His friends whooped in delight.

"Keep moving, bub." Kandy curled her lip in a snarl.

The group of friends completely ignored her, stumbling over to form a neat line beside us on the sidewalk. Kandy muttered nastily underneath her breath, but didn't make a scene.

And in the few minutes we waited in the predawn, a long line formed around us. No one even batted an eyelash at our outfits. I could only imagine that we all looked as though we were coming off a hard night of clubbing. Though what club Drake and Warner in their dragon leathers might be coming from, I wasn't sure.

A female employee wedged open the glassed entrance door, releasing the delectable scent of fresh-baked waffles into our eager nostrils. Kandy moaned softly, then began shifting from sneakered foot to sneakered foot. The half-awake employee slowly placed two sets of metal tables and chairs in front of the windows. She had a black semicolon tattooed behind her ear, representing mental health awareness. So I instantly liked her, of course.

Though I seriously hoped there was more seating inside. My aversion to eating in the great outdoors extended to perching on metal chairs in the middle of January.

"She's not an Adept," I whispered to Kandy. "I thought you called in a favor?"

The green-haired werewolf grinned at me. "The vampire isn't the only one with secret ways."

The employee slipped back inside, allowing the door to close behind her. She turned on the red neon 'Open' sign as she crossed back behind the counter that ran the length of the interior of the cafe.

Kandy was inside before the door clicked closed, practically pressing herself against the glass case that shielded piles of hot-off-the-iron waffles from general pawing. We stumbled in after the werewolf.

The menu on the blackboard behind the counter listed a half-dozen sweet and savory options. The diner was simply furnished, with smooth white particleboard tables and white plastic scoop-backed chairs supported on thin metal legs.

"We'll take three of each," Kandy said to the guy behind the cash register. "Plus two coffees, four waters, and an orange juice."

The cashier looked aghast, then cast his gaze at the line forming along the counter behind the green-haired werewolf. "Sorry? Three of which?"

"Three of each option." Kandy carefully and bitingly enunciated each word. "Chocolate dipped, sweet, and savory. Just bring them as you build them."

I snagged two of the two-seater tables, tugging them together in the farthest corner away from the door. The other customers scrambled to fill the tables and chairs around me.

"We'll lose our place," I said, hissing at Drake and Warner, who were still gazing up at the menu.

They appeared seriously confused at the mayhem happening over the seating. Apparently, dragons didn't get the concept of fighting for feeding rights.

"Warner, Kandy is ordering for us." I waved him toward the chair I'd squeezed into the corner by the window. I figured it was the only seat that allowed enough space for his shoulders.

Kandy slapped three hundred-dollar bills onto the counter.

"We just opened. I don't have change for that," the cashier stuttered.

"Just keep them coming and let me know if that runs out." Then she grabbed the bottles of water and the orange juice that the female employee had already placed beside the cash register, turning away from the counter to smile at me.

The older man, whistling merrily away, was systematically filling, then closing, six waffle irons in the kitchen. I knew from experience that his white apron was doomed to be splattered in batter while he dealt with the morning crush.

I missed my bakery. No matter how much work it was every day, I loved opening to a line at the door on a Saturday or Sunday morning.

Kandy's phone pinged as she pressed through the half dozen or so bodies between our table and the cashier. She dumped the waters and the juice in Drake's arms to check her messages.

In an epic juggling feat, the fledgling guardian managed to catch all five bottles before they could strike the white-tiled floor.

I laughed. All those years of dragon training put to perfect use.

"BRB," Kandy said. She shouldered her way back through the crowd blocking the door. Once outside, she stepped off the sidewalk and took a picture of the front of the waffle place. Then she jogged up to the corner to snap a shot of the street signs.

"BRB?" Warner asked. He reached across the table to relieve the female employee — Rachel, now that her name tag was close enough to read — of three of the four plates she was carrying.

Drake snagged the fourth plate, consuming one of the chocolate-covered waffles before he'd lowered himself into the chair across from me.

"It's short for 'be right back,' " I said, wondering what the werewolf was doing. "Oooo, they brought the sweet portion of the menu first."

Two years of serious dragon training, and I was still easily distracted.

After appreciating the pretty piles of waffles covered in chocolate, powdered sugar, strawberries, and whipped cream, I braved the crowd to collect forks and napkins from the self-serve kiosk.

Kandy appeared at my elbow, reaching past me as she grabbed cream and sugar for her coffee.

"Pictures?" I asked, turning back to the table.

Kandy dug into a waffle covered in berry compote before she settled into the seat beside Drake. "Sorcerer needed them," she said around bites. "Is there syrup?"

She elbowed Drake. He levered himself out of his chair and negotiated the crowd in search of golden nectar.

I handed a fork and napkin to Warner, then dropped the rest of the pile at the edge of the table nearest the window. They were less likely to be knocked off there by the feeding frenzy.

Two of the four plates were already empty.

"They're on their way, then?" Warner asked.

Kandy nodded, reaching for a waffle covered in bruleed bananas, caramel, and whipped cream.

Drake returned with the syrup.

I started laughing.

Everyone ignored me.

Kandy, Warner, and Drake continued eating. The customers continued ordering. And food continued to be delivered.

And I laughed.

Shailaja had kidnapped Chi Wen with a sword whose magic was a product of my own alchemy. We were tracking the final instrument of assassination to lure her out. We were waiting on a vampire and sorcerer to return with some clue to some temple, which was most likely filled with magical devices primed to kill anyone who attempted to enter it without the secret password.

But first, we were eating waffles.

I wiped tears from my cheeks, my laughter abating to a pained chuckle. Warner squeezed my knee underneath the table.

"Good waffles," Drake said. Every ounce of his attention was focused on scooping up as much of the syrup pooling on his plate as he could before shoveling a final bite into his mouth.

"Yep," Kandy said agreeably.

I quashed a second round of inappropriate laughter. "I'm okay," I muttered, more to myself than anyone else.

"You're the only one who doubts it, dowser," Kandy said.

Rachel loomed over Drake's left shoulder with more waffles. The savory plates were topped with bacon, brie, and basil; prosciutto, creme fraiche, and green onions; and herbed goat cheese, hazelnuts, and honey. She eyed the fifteen-year-old appreciatively while she swapped out our empty plates. He didn't notice. But then, most people found bacon distracting.

"Hey!" I said to Drake. "It's your birthday soon."

"Tomorrow." The fledgling grinned at me from across the table.

I nodded, finally smiling for a nonhysterical reason. "We'll head back to the bakery as soon as we can."

"And you'll bake me whatever I want?"

"Within reason."

"Whose reason? Yours or mine?"

Kandy barked out a laugh.

Then the vampire and the sorcerer walked into the diner.

They got stared at.

We were crammed into the corner like club rejects, but it was Kett's pale, arresting looks — swathed in pricy jeans and tan cashmere — alongside Blackwell's naturally jet-black hair and custom-fitted charcoal suit that muted the conversation around us.

At first glance, the two appeared to be complete opposites ... but then ... not. Blackwell would have made a good vampire ... depending on what 'good' meant in that context. And Kett had wielded magic before he'd been turned. I had always assumed he'd been a witch, but he might well have been a sorcerer.

Their magic was completely different. Kett's dark-tinged peppermint was embedded in every pore of his skin, even as Blackwell's earthy Cabernet hung back, waiting to be pooled into orbs of navy-blue magic — a blue so dark it was almost black. But they were twins in demeanor and cool charisma. Though obviously, Kett had centuries of practice over the sorcerer. Plus the whole immortality thing.

Blackwell glanced around the waffle place. I would have expected him to be disdainful, but he was carefully neutral.

Kett snagged two more chairs, practically stealing one as its occupant vacated it. She whirled around in surprise. He winked at her and she giggled.

Giggled.

At a vampire.

At an uber-powerful vampire ... who she had no idea was a deadly predator.

No wonder my head was always screwed up. I kept trying to live an Adept life in a human world, and that was just ... skewed.

Kandy shifted her chair closer to the window, then elbowed Drake to snug up against her. Kett placed the two extra chairs between the fledgling and me, but six people really didn't fit well around two tiny tables.

"Coffee?" Blackwell touched Rachel's elbow lightly as she flew toward us with more food. She blushed, nodded at the sorcerer, and deposited another four plates in front of us. In addition to chocolate-dipped waffles, this sweet batch featured Nutella and ice cream, which itself was covered in caramel, chocolate sauce, and peanuts like a waffle sundae.

I sighed. Apparently, only I saw terrifying monsters wherever I looked. Which probably said more about my outlook than anyone else's.

I was losing count of how much Warner, Drake, and Kandy had eaten. But I hadn't had a chocolate-dipped waffle yet, so I snagged one.

Sure, we were pretty much convening a war council, but I was good about keeping my priorities straight. You never knew when you might be consuming the last waffles of your life.

Kett sat down beside me. His knee pressed tightly against mine so that he didn't have to touch Blackwell on the other side.

No one spoke.

As I ate my waffle, I realized suddenly that I was the one everyone was waiting on. When did I get put in charge? That was seriously wack.

"Where are we going?" I asked.

"China," Blackwell said, pulling a leather-bound brown book filled with rough-edged pages out of his suit pocket.

Drake focused on the sorcerer over a plate of waffles topped by roasted turkey breast, Havarti, and raspberry jam. China was Chi Wen's territory. "The final instrument lies in China?" he asked quietly.

Rachel appeared over the sorcerer's shoulder. Blackwell shifted the thick journal out of the way so she could place his coffee down on the only available wedge of table.

"Thank you," he murmured. She followed through with cream and sugar, then reluctantly retreated to tend her other customers.

"China is an exceedingly large country," Warner said.

Blackwell nodded as he made a slow show of adding cream and sugar to his coffee, carefully stirring between additions.

Annoyed, I looked at Kett. "What's to stop us from forcibly taking the journal from him?"

"It's warded," Blackwell replied smoothly. "Keyed along ancestral lines."

I snorted. "Not a problem."

Kett, whose gaze was fixed out the window, cracked a grin. "It's written in a runed language."

"How long would it take us to decipher?"

"Too long."

Damn it.

"Kettil and I have already had this discussion."

"Old toothy doesn't speak for all of us," Kandy snapped.

Blackwell ignored her. "I will be accompanying you."

Warner pushed his empty plate away, leaning back in his chair with his gaze fixed to the sorcerer.

Blackwell swallowed, reaching for his coffee to cover his wariness.

"It's difficult to play cat and mouse with dragons," I said, pitching my voice low but cheerful.

"Indeed," Blackwell replied. "But I'm not playing. I don't have an exact location. My ancestors were armed with charts of the night sky, not GPS."

"Unhelpful in the wrong season," Warner said.

"Obviously, China as a country was distinct even then. That much is clear."

"The Himalayas are difficult to mislabel," Kett said wryly.

Blackwell winced almost imperceptibly. All that attempt at buildup, and the vampire had stolen his finish. "Indeed. A solid landmark by which to guide our journey."

"What is it with the freaking mountain ranges?" I muttered with a glance at Warner.

"All the better to hide massive magical makings," he said, offering me a wry grin.

"Other clues in the text should get us farther along, but we need an entry point," Kett said.

I slipped my hand in my satchel to finger the dragonskin map. I didn't want to pull it out in front of Blackwell or draw the shadow demons to us, though the nonmagicals in the diner would be immune to their leechlike tendencies. But I was hopeful that I would be able to get it working once we were in China. Figuring out the country was key in my previous experiences of hunting the instruments. Then narrowing it down to the nearest portal, and triggering the map. Question was, should I try to ditch the sorcerer before then?

"Transportation?" I finally said.

As I'd expected, everyone eyed the sorcerer. Blackwell sipped his coffee sedately.

"Grid point portal?" I said with a sigh.

The evil sorcerer presumably knew all about dragons and guardians and portals anyway. We couldn't all just sit around in a waffle place silently plotting against him while not moving forward.

"No," Kett said.

"I doubt the sorcerer would survive the trip," Warner said, delivering the threat amicably.

"Airplane?"

"Amulet?" Blackwell countered with a sly grin.

"All have drawbacks," Warner said.

Kandy swiped her finger through a mixture of powdered sugar and maple syrup on her plate, then licked her finger clean. She leaned back and held up four fingers in Rachel's direction. "We'll take four dozen of the chocolate-dipped to go."

"Right," I said. "By jet, then."

Blackwell stiffened in protest. "I won't travel by any mundane mode of transport with …" He trailed off, making his point without outing the dragons sitting around the table with us.

"Then you can teleport ahead and wait for us, sorcerer," I said blithely. "We'll happily plot behind your back for the … what? Twelve or so hours it takes to fly there?"

I glanced at Kett. He nodded.

"Heigh-ho, heigh-ho," I sang under my breath as I got up from the table. "It's off to work we go."

Kandy laughed, shoving past the sorcerer when he didn't move quickly enough. Slipping her arm through mine, she threw her head back and — terribly off key — belted the remainder of the *Snow White and the Seven Dwarfs* song at the top of her lungs.

By the time we settled the bill, grabbed the to-go containers, and made a beeline for the door, Kandy had the entire diner singing.

Apparently, tasty waffles made everyone happy.

Good to know.

Chapter Eleven

We hustled back to the underground parking lot where we'd left the green SUV. As we approached it with the vampire, the sorcerer, and a whole bunch of take-out waffle boxes in tow, Kett triggered the locks on a white SUV currently parked beside our vehicle.

"How do you always know where we are?" I asked. I really knew better than to comment about the vampire's apparent omniscience, but I couldn't help myself. "Do you have a network of valets and pilots and tech providers that just follows you around?"

Kett smiled charmingly. "I'll always find you, Jade."

I narrowed my eyes at him, exceedingly suspicious of his pretty grin.

"He texted," Kandy said. "His one true power is the ability to find and instantly memorize people's cellphone numbers. I think he also might have GPS tracking enabled … like, on everyone. The pack tech guy couldn't do anything about it."

Warner threw back his head and laughed. His magic rolled through the half-empty concrete parking lot.

Directly beside him, Blackwell flinched under the tasty magical onslaught. Well, I found it tasty.

Kett smirked at Kandy. "We're ready to fly out anytime from Seattle International, but I'll need a destination. The pilot prefers to be prepared."

I glanced at Drake, who was climbing into the back seat of our SUV. "Your map might be the best place to start."

The fledgling nodded, reaching over his shoulder to tug the grid point map out of his backpack.

"I'll text you," I said to Kett.

He chuckled as he climbed into the driver's seat of the white SUV.

Warner climbed into the driver's seat of our vehicle, while Kandy opted for the front passenger seat so I could slide in next to Drake.

I paused with one foot in the car, eyeing Blackwell over the open door between us. The sorcerer was standing at the side of the white SUV. He had one hand on the passenger door handle and one hand on his amulet.

"Thinking of leaving?" I asked quietly.

He flicked his eyes to me. I didn't know him all that well, but he looked … worn … thin.

He smiled tightly. "How far do you think I'd get?"

"Isn't that my line?"

He shrugged one shoulder, then turned to open his door.

"I get it," I said.

The sorcerer paused but didn't look back.

"Feeling like you're being swept into something you barely understand, and at the same time, feeling seriously outclassed by the powerful Adepts by your side."

Blackwell turned his dark, expressionless gaze back to me. "We are not the same, Jade. I've chosen to be here. And not one of you is 'by my side.' "

"Yeah, but it's not a real concern for you. You'll get through it without a scrape. Assholes like you always walk away."

Blackwell smirked as if readying some really nasty retort. Then he checked himself and climbed into Kett's SUV.

I slid into the back seat of our vehicle, happily embracing its preheated warmth and the comfort of being surrounded by friendly magic.

Kandy was cranked around in her seat, the green of her magic dancing in her eyes. "Let Blackwell make a wrong step, Jade," she said, teasing yet serious. "I'll be happy to correct him."

"So he didn't save you? During the mystery trip you all took to Mississippi where Henry got bitten?"

Kandy curled her upper lip in derision. "The oracle summoned him. He cleaned up the mess Beau's family made. But no. He helped get me out of a jam. For Rochelle. But he didn't save me ... or Henry."

"Good. The thought of you owing Blackwell anything was making me ill."

Kandy nodded, reaching for her seat belt.

Warner backed the SUV out of its spot, then followed Kett out of the underground parking lot.

"There's only one grid point portal in China," Drake said. His head was bowed over the map in his lap.

"Have you used it?"

"No one does. Except maybe Chi Wen," Warner said, catching my gaze in the rearview mirror. "It's relatively inaccessible. Not conducive for regular patrolling."

"Like Peru?"

Warner shook his head, focusing his attention on pulling out of the lot and onto the city street. "No. Qiuniu does actually use the Peruvian portal. Which is why the buildings and the vehicles were there."

"There's nothing at this grid point. Even the gatekeeper isn't on site," Drake said. "I checked." He pointed to the series of Chinese characters he'd jotted beside the small rectangle denoting the grid point portal in China. "There's sort of a shelter. Nothing you could actually stay in for long, though. It's in the Daxue Mountains, which extend out from the Tibetan Plateau east of the Himalayas. The next nearest grid point is in Japan."

"Or Pakistan," Warner said. "Or Thailand."

"But you walk Chi Wen's territory sometimes," I said.

"Starting in Shanghai, where the nexus is anchored. Then through portals constructed by Pulou in the major city centers."

I shimmied the strap of my satchel over my shoulder and dumped the bag between my feet. "Last time, when we got near enough, the map ... Pulou's map ... led us the rest of the way. I thought I had it working, but I'm not sure now. And I really don't want Blackwell getting a look at it."

"I thought you weren't hunting the ..." Warner began. Then he tightened his grip on the steering wheel and didn't finish his question.

I knew what he was asking, though. "I wasn't. Not before. I was just ... playing with it. Just practicing."

I tugged the dragonskin tattoo out of my satchel, keeping my eyes on the rearview mirror and waiting for Warner to look back at me. When we pulled to a stop at a red light, the sentinel lifted his gaze to the mirror.

I smiled. "I wouldn't have gone hunting for it alone."

"Yeah," Kandy said. "That's why I'm around ... usually."

Warner snorted, offering me a twitch of his lips and a nod in the mirror before returning his attention to following Kett's SUV through the relatively quiet streets. During the week, Seattle's morning rush hour was epic compared to Vancouver's. Not that I really knew much about it. I was exceedingly fortunate that my grandparents had a thing for collecting property years before the real estate market in Vancouver went nuts. I currently lived a dozen steps away from work as a result. Above work, specifically.

I opened the dragonskin map across my knees.

Drake leaned over to peer at it.

"Don't touch it."

"You always say that."

I laughed. "With technology."

"And cupcakes and chocolate."

Kandy chortled. "Well, that's just good sense."

"It actually won't work if you touch it," I said. "Go ahead."

Drake looked surprised, then brushed his fingers against the edge of the tattoo. "It didn't just have these flowers on it before, did it? In the library? I saw it on your desk."

"No," I said. "It still had the sections of the centipede on it then."

An ornately detailed block of lettering, which I'd mistaken for runes the first time Warner touched the tattoo, slowly appeared along the top edge of the map.

"Where dragons dare not tread," Drake said, reading.

"Apparently Shailaja doesn't agree," Kandy murmured.

"She just tried to play the odds," Warner said. "Bring in servants to navigate the difficult sections. The sorcerers, then the shadow demons, and now Jade."

He lifted his gaze to the rearview mirror again, but I refused to acknowledge his concern. We'd had the conversation too many times already.

"It doesn't matter now," Drake said. "Whether or not the sorcerer lays eyes on anything, I mean. We're taking him to the temple, if that's where the door the oracle sees leads. Or he's taking us, whichever way that works out."

The letters faded from the dragonskin tattoo. I sighed. "What's the nearest major city to the portal?"

"Just beyond the eastern edge of the Himalayas ..." Warner said. "Sichuan Province?"

Drake nodded. "Nearest city is Chengdu."

"Then I guess we head there until the sorcerer tells us differently."

Kandy dug her cellphone out of the pocket of her jeans and opened her messaging app to text Kett. And the pack, I presumed.

"The portal is just west of a mountain summit, but I'm not sure which mountain it is ..." Drake was peering at his map again.

"We also need to know what kind of magic we're facing." I leaned down to blow lightly across the blossoms on the dragonskin tattoo. "The braids were some kind of sorcerer-based magic, and the centipedes were metallurgy. So what are these flowers and leaves? Witch magic? Like herbalism?"

"That would be good for us, yes?" Drake asked. "Since you're half-witch?"

"I'm not that kind of witch." I muttered the words, defaulting to my rote response before continuing. "The puzzles magically tattooed into the map were also clues to collecting the instruments, right?"

"I'm not sure I'd call the centipede in Peru a puzzle," Warner said wryly.

"Sure it was ... we just managed to turn it into a really dangerous one."

Kandy snorted.

"But what does a tree … possibly a fruit tree … have to do with the Himalayas … or China?" I said. "And with magic that can kill a guardian?"

No one answered me.

I watched the magic swirl across the tattoo for a moment, thinking. "Maybe it's too soon to figure out that level of detail. But since the far seer is ahead of us on this —"

"What do you mean?" Drake asked. "He knew this was going to happen? But he couldn't have seen his own kidnapping … or even the attack on Pulou or Yazi. Guardian magic doesn't work like that. Even Rochelle can't see her own future. She can only piece events together. Same with the far seer, though he sees on a different level."

"But he sees Jade," Warner said curtly.

I swallowed back the spike of fear that always rose when the subject of my future being tracked by the far seer was brought up. It was easier this time — which unfortunately meant I was becoming accustomed to the idea of being completely out of control of my own destiny. "He was leaving the nexus when I arrived," I said. "But then he chose to stay. When Shailaja grabbed him, he said something about today being the day, like he was slightly surprised. But not completely."

"It doesn't work like that," Drake said, becoming agitated. "He can't see like that."

"I'm just talking about what sort of magic we're seeking," I said. "Trying to be prepared. I just wondered if Chi Wen being connected to it all had anything to do with it. Whether we're about to confront something from Asian magical practices, or seer magic. That's all."

"He was just in the wrong place at the wrong time," Drake said sullenly. "You say it happens to you all the time."

"Yeah," Kandy said. "But he's the far seer of the guardian nine."

Drake pointedly ignored the werewolf. Not that she cared. She was carefully slicing open one of the take-out boxes of waffles with a wolf claw she'd manifested on the tip of her right forefinger. She'd been refining her control over her shapeshifter abilities ever since we met.

"Show me?" the fledgling asked, indicating the tattoo draped across my lap.

The dragonskin map had reverted to its resting state of muddled greens and blobs of blue. I obligingly stirred the pollen within the white blossoms to trigger it again.

Using the knowledge that we were looking at China, combined with Drake's grid point portal map and Kandy's Google-fu, we attempted to decipher the tattoo all the way to the airport.

We came up with zilch.

If the dragonskin tattoo was going to be at all helpful in collecting the third instrument of assassination, it was certainly biding its time.

Sleeping in shifts and huddled in small groups in hushed conversation, we flew from Seattle to Hokkiado, Japan, to refuel, then to Chengdu, China. Initially, no one had wanted to nap or talk around Blackwell, but thirteen hours was a long time to sit around doing nothing.

Kett had switched out the jet. The plane we boarded in Seattle was larger and had orange and gray stripes on its side, as if the vampire hadn't had time to order a cus-tom paint job. The interior of the jet was huge, including a cushy off-white leather couch in the aft stateroom and a glass walk-in shower in the bathroom. Muted grays and dark woods dominated the decor. I presumed the switch was primarily for the longer distance of a flight across the Pacific, but a larger plane would probably also have an easier time compensating for the magical toll that carrying us was about to take on the engines and the electronics.

Either that, or Kett just wanted to be able to sit as far away from the sorcerer as possible.

Blackwell was seated at the front of the plane, alone. He spent the entire flight translating his ancestor's rune-written journal. It was slow going. He occasionally consulted other texts, pulling leather-bound chronicles and handwritten tomes reeking of sorcerer magic out of his always-empty-looking suit pockets.

I was relieved that he was holding up his end. I was also seriously pleased that I wasn't the one attempting to translate the journal. Magically imbued books were not my friends for some reason, and not because I didn't try. Friendly was my default mode. My penchant for stabbing things with my jade knife almost always came much, much later.

We touched down at the Chengdu Shuangliu International Airport, then started slowly trundling toward the private hangars. Blackwell was still working. We had no new information.

I gazed out the windows at the gray-shrouded day and the could-be-any-other-airport-in-the-world, torn between wanting to fret and wanting to wring the sorcerer's neck to see if that would speed up the translation process.

I pulled out my phone instead, checking to see if the time had reset. I swiped down on my screen and noted it was cloudy, six degrees Celsius, and twelve o'clock in the afternoon. Monday, January twenty-fifth.

Drake's birthday.

I swiveled in my seat, grinning at the fledgling, who was sprawled out on the couch and staring miserably at the ceiling. My birthday greeting died on my lips. Now wasn't the time. I'd have to make it up to him with triple the cupcakes when we got through it all.

Drake tugged an earphone out of his ear, sitting up to peer out the window. We'd shoved him at the very back of the plane and given him a box of waffles and a set of earphones so he could watch movies. He accepted the gesture, but he'd kept one ear unplugged the entire flight so as not to miss any conversation.

The steward, Mark, crossed through from the nose of the plane, stopping beside Kett, who was one seat ahead and across from me. "We'll be just a few more minutes," he said quietly. "There's a bit of a queue ahead of us."

Kett nodded. "The items I requested?"

"On location, but waiting on our hangar assignment."

"I don't want to wait any longer than necessary."

Mark nodded, then took off up the aisle, collecting an empty can of Coke from Kandy as he passed.

The mood in the jet was heavy with unreleased tension. I wanted to rally and rage — except I couldn't think of anything that might inspire either of those options. Waiting wasn't a strong suit for any of us. Except maybe Kett.

The jet lurched forward, turning left toward a maze of crisscrossed cement tributaries.

"The shrine of the phoenix," Blackwell said. It was the first time I'd heard his voice in half a day.

Warner, who I'd thought was napping across from me a moment before, snorted. "Myth. A bedtime story, I believe you call it in this century."

I gave him a look. Warner rarely mentioned his age, but maybe Blackwell was putting him on edge. Or maybe the entire situation was. "I hate that 'myth' thing," I said.

"Yes," Drake said. "However, myths only arise when their stories age beyond the mortality of the participants and their ancestors. Storytelling is simply a way of conveying a truth … or what was believed to be true in the time that the actual event occurred."

"We all thought dragons were myths," Kandy said.

"Not all of us were quite that sheltered," Blackwell muttered.

"Not all of us are power-hungry bloodsuckers!" The green-haired werewolf practically spat in the sorcerer's direction. Then she glanced toward Kett, somewhat chagrined.

The vampire merely raised an eyebrow in response.

"The shrine of the phoenix?" I said, prompting the sorcerer for more.

"The phoenix is a mythical immortal who is the antithesis of the dragons," Blackwell said.

Warner shook his head. "Get your stories straight, sorcerer. Or at least your Chinese mythology. The phoenix and the dragon are yin and yang."

"Exactly. Opposites."

"No," Warner said. "I don't know the word in English. Two halves of a perfect unity."

The jet slowed, then stopped. I glanced out the window. Outside, a figure was directing us toward a large hangar. The jet lurched again, turning sharply into the open building.

"Why would this phoenix be associated with one of the instruments of assassination?" I asked.

Warner and Drake remained silent. I wasn't sure if that meant they didn't know — or if they just didn't want to say.

Blackwell shook his head. "As far as I've been able to transcribe the journal, the phoenix is a figure of peace and tranquility ... healing, even. While the dragons are warriors, the phoenix is considered to be a benign, benevolent force."

"Some Adepts require deadly rule," Warner growled.

I hid my grin by unbuckling my seat belt and grabbing my satchel. I loved it when Warner got feisty, but I was pretty sure this was the wrong place and time for any mooning or make-out sessions.

"So, same plan," I said, after reminding myself that I was supposed to be the leader of this expedition. "We assume the shrine is near the grid point like the other two."

Kett, Kandy, and Blackwell climbed out of their seats without responding, moving toward the exit. Everyone was in just-keep-going mode.

I lingered, waiting on Drake as he stuffed some granola bars in his backpack. Warner was still seated, gazing out the window thoughtfully.

Drake slipped past us.

I reached out to Warner, catching his hand in mine and taking a moment to simply look at him.

"Traveling by portal is much more dramatically satisfying," I said.

He chuckled, standing and filling the aisle. "Wet feet and all."

"It was more than my feet that were wet in the Bahamas," I groused.

He leered at me suggestively.

I laughed. "You certainly pick up sexual innuendo quickly for a sixteenth-century boy."

"Sex translates across the centuries rather well."

I lifted up on my tiptoes to press my lips to his neck, just underneath his jaw and ear. He turned his head toward me, tangling his fingers through my loose curls.

"I bet you don't know what the mile-high club is," I murmured.

"I can guess. Then I can ask if a mountain counts."

I laughed, but my chest was starting to tighten. I was delaying stepping out of the plane, knowing that as soon as I did, Shailaja would come into play again.

"Jade ..." Warner whispered against the sensitive skin of my ear.

I shuddered, then sighed. "After ..."

"Always," he said. "There will always be an after for us, Jade. Whatever lies before us."

"She can't possibly get through all of us," I said, attempting to bolster my confidence and justify dragging everyone with me into yet another dangerous hunt. "No matter what side the far seer comes down on."

Warner pulled away from me, just slightly. "You think the far seer is aligned with Shailaja?"

I shook my head. "Not like that ... but ... what if he wants this?"

Warner looked thoughtful. "We are outmatched if we are facing a guardian. But I cannot believe that Chi Wen would do anything to hurt Drake. If he had wanted to choose Shailaja as a successor, he could have just done so."

"And why go after the third instrument ..." I said, thinking out loud. "He had access to the first two. And when he asked me to show him the centipede the night I brought it to the nexus ... well, I thought he was inferring that it would be his death. Except he can't see his own future."

"Questions about the far seer's abilities are best posed to Drake," Warner said. "I've never been apprenticed to a guardian."

I reached up and caressed his face, lightly scratching the short stubble along his jawline. "I'm glad. I'm not sure we would have gotten along if you were a guardian when we first met."

"I certainly would have been displeased about you dragging a demon into the nexus."

I laughed. "I'm sure you would have."

He grinned, then turned serious. "Plus, your father wouldn't have given his blessing."

"Would you have cared?" I asked playfully.

"It's not ... even for a dragon, being married to a guardian is ..." Warner trailed off with a shake of his head.

I wondered if he was thinking of his parents' marriage. Dragons lived a long time, but guardians were practically immortal — right up to the moment they decided to pass on their responsibilities.

"What happens if Chi Wen tries to make Shailaja the next far seer?" I asked.

"They both die. Her, because she's too ... unstable. And him, because he must die to transfer his power."

"And the far seer's magic? Would it just be lost?"

Warner shook his head. "I don't know."

"When the guardians relinquish their mantles, is an alchemist involved?"

"I don't think so. But I know nothing of the ceremony. It's not written down or discussed. Only the nine know. I would go so far as to say that it takes the presence of all the guardians, but I'm not actually certain."

Heavy footsteps clomped up the exterior stairs of the jet, then Drake appeared at the head of the aisle. He was wearing a black parka and carrying two other identical jackets. Apparently, the items Kett had requested included cold-weather clothing. The fledgling guardian didn't speak, but I knew he was anxious to get moving.

Everyone was anxious. And I was dillydallying.

I brushed a kiss against Warner's lips, then turned away up the aisle. He tugged me back into his arms for a searing lip lock, only letting me go after my knees had turned to jelly and every thought had been wiped from my mind.

"After," he whispered.

Then we marched into battle.

Or rather, then we set out to scale a mountain. Same difference really, when you've never been big on hiking.

After climbing into two gray SUVs waiting outside the hangar, we made a beeline out of Chengdu. Assuming we'd even been in the city to begin with, that was. It was still so gray outside that everything I could see through the windows might as well have been the outskirts of any other big city I'd ever seen. Or perhaps I was just too distracted to notice any particular details.

Following Drake's map, we skirted the western edge of the Longchi National Forest Park — according to Kandy and Google Maps. Then, avoiding a small town at the end of the main road, we abandoned the SUV and struck off on foot. Though the trip was relatively quick, the area felt remote and alien ... mountainous but without the massive fir and cedar trees I was accustomed to being surrounded by. We continued on foot through the snow, clambering over rocks and skirting crevices, following a trail that only Kett and Warner seemed capable of seeing.

And if January wasn't off-season for hiking in Sichuan Province, it should have been.

It was cold. Seriously cold. Even wearing the heavy-duty parkas Kett had bought, I was probably as cold as I'd ever been. Thankfully, the vampire had also thought to source boots and weather-appropriate knitwear. I didn't bother asking how he knew everyone's shoe sizes. I left my pretty silk jacket in the SUV, pleased that I hadn't totally ruined it yet.

Bundled up and hooded, the six of us were pretty much indistinguishable. Though, perhaps that was only if you couldn't constantly taste all the different strains of magic whirling around us.

After comparing Drake's map with Google, we figured out that we needed to climb toward the summit of a mountain called Jiuding Shan. So ... we were somewhere in the mountains of China.

I wasn't sure what I was expecting. The last time I'd been hiking in the mountains Warner had practically carried me the entire way. And, as far as I remembered, there'd been less snow. Now he and Drake pushed ahead through deep-packed snow, along game trails identified by Kett. Blackwell and I kept our heads down in the middle of the pack while Kandy gleefully brought up the rear. The werewolf was in her element. The sorcerer and I were not. I wasn't a fan of having anything to commiserate about with the sorcerer, so I kept my complaints to myself.

According to Google Maps, the area was crisscrossed with roads and littered with mountain villages, but our path avoided them all.

As we climbed, Drake, Warner, and Kett kept stopping to argue — in Chinese — and gesture pointedly to the map. I assumed they were in disagreement about which peak was what, and whether or not we were on the path. But I was more interested in staying bundled up. Plus, looking at the map apparently required a huffy removal of gloves, though I wasn't sure the cold actually affected Kett.

I also seriously hoped that the climbing gear and snowshoes the vampire had strapped to all of us were going to be unnecessary.

After what felt like eons of stumbling blindly behind everyone else through the snow but might have only been an hour, the intensity of the area's natural magic increased. That meant we didn't have to consult the map for the last leg of the hike. Even in the snow, I could see strains of wild magic dancing all around us ... mostly from the icy granite, as there wasn't much vegetation.

The grid point portal was situated on a rocky plateau, halfway up one mountain and nestled between at least four others.

Warner immediately sent a message through to the nexus, apprising Haoxin of our progress. He didn't get a reply. Not one that I heard, anyway.

My heart sank just a tiny bit at the thought of my father and Pulou still bedridden. It wasn't that I was hoping they would swoop in and save the day. It was just freaking cold, and ... yeah, okay — I was kind of hoping the guardians would show up en masse and make Shailaja their problem.

A small, rather derelict hut was tucked against a sheer cliff face a few dozen feet away from the portal. At one point, the building might have been rather pretty and ornate. But time and extreme weather hadn't been kind to its hip-and-gable roof and red-columned entrance.

At least it was a place to get out of the cold. Warner wasted no time breaking apart a piece of furniture that might have been a table at one time and building a small fire on a flat clay surface at the center of the hut. The smoke miraculously vented out of a hole in the roof. When it was warm enough for me to take my gloves off, I sat down to see if I could trigger the dragonskin map to reveal whatever secrets it held.

After about fifteen minutes of studying the map, I'd been abandoned by everyone but Blackwell and Kandy. Warner, Drake, and Kett had left to walk the perimeter, but it was obvious that they hoped the rabid koala — the heretic, as Drake called her — would reveal herself now that we were stationary in a remote location. Shailaja might be crazy and consumed by her desire to achieve immortality, but she wasn't stupid. If she knew where we were, she'd know we were at an impasse, and either gathering information or awaiting reinforcements. The grid point portal's magic would speak to her just as much as it did to Warner, Drake, and me. Maybe even more. She was the daughter of Pulou-who-was, after all.

Kandy was pretending to be enthralled in some first-person shooter game on her phone, while standing sentry between Blackwell and me. The sorcerer was poring over his own notes.

I sat cross-legged in the middle of the floor, near enough to the fire that I'd unzipped my jacket and stripped off my hat and scarf.

Blackwell had risked sitting on a low bench that was the only intact piece of furniture in the place, though he'd dragged it away from the open window first. Tattered cloth stirred at the edge of the window frame, and snow had built up at its corners. The door to the shelter was missing as well, if there had even been one in the first place. But its walls held the warmth from the fire eagerly, making it cozy enough. It was like sitting in the middle of ancient history, though. I wasn't a fan.

The map still wouldn't reveal anything of substance. Not that I could understand, anyway. Frustrated that I was missing some fundamental clue, I attempted to curb my self-loathing and give myself a second to think by watching Blackwell. He was carefully copying a sketch from his ancestor's journal into his own Moleskine notebook. From my viewpoint, it looked like a variation of the flower-and-leaf motif on the map, but with fewer blossoms and more bare branches.

I closed my eyes, reaching my dowser senses out beyond the walls of the hut and casting my awareness into the mountains and snow outside. I was looking for dragon magic that tasted of cinnamon-spiced carrot cake and smooth cream cheese. Or even Chi Wen's spicy magic. Though I'd witnessed two displays in the last three or so days of how well guardians could mask their magic, so I imagined I'd only sense the far seer if he wanted me to.

I tasted Drake's and Warner's magic nearby, then Kett's peppermint farther beyond. But I didn't pick up any hint of the rabid koala or the far seer.

I opened my eyes.

Blackwell was watching me.

I scowled at him.

He offered me a tight-lipped smile. "You broadcast your magic loudly, alchemist."

I almost said something flippant back, but then thought to question him instead. "All the time?"

"No. But when you do whatever you were just doing, you are difficult to ignore."

I looked over at Kandy. Her attention was on her phone, but she was listening to us. She shrugged non-committally in response to my silent question. Which meant either that the smell of my magic didn't intensify for her, or she wasn't interested in talking about it in front of the sorcerer.

Adepts were annoyingly close-mouthed about such things. They treated secrets as power, when I'd only ever known secrets to be weaknesses.

I reached up, tugging my jacket half off my shoulders and unwinding my necklace.

Blackwell watched me intently.

I placed the wedding-ring-laden chain on the floor beside me, nearer to Kandy than the sorcerer.

"And now?" I asked.

Blackwell closed his notebook, then tucked it and the journal in his jacket pocket. He was still wearing his suit underneath his parka and knitwear. It was an odd combination, but the suit was clearly — and quite heavily — spelled, not only with protective wards but also with some sort of expansion magic on its pockets.

Apparently, a man purse wasn't Blackwell's thing.

With his expression carefully impassive, the sorcerer shifted off the bench, closed the space between us with a couple of steps, and carefully folded his long frame into a lotus position across from me.

Kandy dropped the gaming pretense. Though it seemed unlikely she would have been wasting her battery by playing the entire time anyway. I doubted the sorcerer had been fooled. She folded her arms and leaned back against the wall by the door, looking deceptively relaxed.

Blackwell glanced down at my necklace pooled on the floor about a foot from my right knee. He nodded. "Stunning. Years of work?"

Though it shouldn't have, impressing the sorcerer gave me a slight thrill. He had centuries' worth of artifacts in his collection — including some that were exceedingly dangerous in my estimation. He knew what he was talking about.

"Do you think the necklace impedes my own magic? As well as deflecting it?"

Blackwell tilted his head, looking at me thoughtfully. "I wouldn't think so. Certainly, you would know by now if you can use it as an amplifier."

"I mostly use it to absorb or shield me from magic."

"Your sister was eager to get her hands on it." Blackwell's statement was carefully measured, but placed before me without judgement or emotion.

I forced myself to not bristle at the mention of Sienna. I was asking the sorcerer for help ... circumspectly, but still. Listening, rather than ripping his head off was the better choice. For right now, at least.

Some sort of amusement flashed across Blackwell's face, as if he could sense my inner struggle. But it was gone before I could react.

"She used my trinkets as anchors for her binding spells," I said.

"You create them as empty vessels?"

"Not intentionally."

Blackwell nodded, returning his attention to my necklace, then looking at the map spread on the floor between us. "You were wondering if the necklace was hindering your ability to manipulate the map?"

"Yeah."

"Has it done so before?"

"No."

"So logically ..."

"Do you want to just hang out here in the freezing cold for days, or do you want me to figure out the issue?"

"Show me."

I reached forward and triggered the map. It shifted to the aspect I'd practically memorized — the fields of green surrounded by black triangles.

"Clearly the Himalayas with the Daxue Mountain range descending to the east."

"Sure, easy for you to say, now that we're here."

"But you are expecting something else?"

"In the … other collections …" I hesitated, not sure how much I wanted to divulge to the sorcerer.

He smirked, lifting his hand to indicate that I could continue if I wished, but that he didn't much care either way.

"The map shifted aspects the closer we came to the instrument."

Blackwell frowned. "Did you have to trigger it in a different way?"

"No."

"So why would it change now?"

"I don't know … unless …"

The image of Blackwell's sketch surfaced in my mind. The drawing was reminiscent of the detail on the door of the shrine we were seeking. Blackwell had referenced it as the image he recalled having seen among his ancestors' journals when he'd studied Rochelle's sketches in Westport.

"May I see the sketch you were working on? Compare it to the map? And to Rochelle's sketch?"

Blackwell pulled his notebook out of his pocket. I dug Rochelle's sketch of the door out of my satchel. We laid all three items on the floor, grouping them as closely as we could without obscuring the images.

I pointed to the top left corner of the door in Rochelle's sketch. "Do you think that looks similar to your ancestor's sketch?"

Blackwell leaned forward and carefully compared the two. Rochelle's sketch didn't have as much detail, but the curve of the branches was similar.

"I should have taken pictures of the other sketches," I said. "The door appeared in others, right?"

Blackwell fished his phone out of his pocket, opened his photo app, and flipped through the images. Of course he would have thought to take freaking pictures.

"I don't want you hanging me on your bedroom wall, sorcerer," I said gruffly. "I know you buy sketches from Rochelle."

Blackwell chuckled. "I do. But they don't adorn my bedroom walls," he said. "I'd be pleased to show you. Perhaps ease your mind."

Kandy made a harsh gagging noise.

The trace of playfulness that had crept into Blackwell's demeanor disappeared. He found the picture he'd been looking for and zoomed in on it.

He handed the phone to me, confirming my suspicion about his ancestor's drawings.

"It's unfinished. If it's a detail of the door. Your ancestor saw only half the image."

Blackwell harrumphed thoughtfully, returning his attention to comparing all four images.

"What if ..." I glanced up at Kandy. "What if Pulou-who-was died before he finished the map? What if the tattoo was just a work in progress?"

Blackwell glanced down at the dragonskin tattoo between us. He looked suddenly disconcerted, as if he was just putting together that it was an actual tattoo skinned from a dead guardian.

Kandy hunkered down beside us, joining the conversation while continuing to block Blackwell's path to the door. "You think he was still searching for the final instrument? Why wouldn't he have mentioned it? He ... bequeathed Pulou the map but not the reasoning behind it?"

I glanced at Blackwell, who, of course, was eating up every word. I'd have to worry later about what damage having him around was going to do in the long run. "I'm not sure he was ... all there when he passed on his mantle."

Kandy nodded. "Old wolves can get like that too. Highly and irrationally territorial, usually resulting in an ill-founded challenge. It's better to die at the teeth of a younger wolf than to slip away into the unknown, only half aware."

"Okay ... say the map isn't finished," I said. "We're seriously lost in the middle of China, then. We can't just wander around the mountains for the rest of our lives, hoping we bump into the shrine."

Blackwell tugged his ancestor's journal out of his pocket and began flipping through it. "I might be able to get us closer." Eyeing me, he grinned slyly. "Then you can do whatever it is you do when your magic fills the room, dances across my skin, and beguiles my senses."

"Creepy much, sorcerer?" Kandy spat, before I could express my own dismay.

Attracting Blackwell was seriously low on my to-do list. As in, nonexistent.

"I have to know what I'm dowsing for," I said.

"In the middle of nowhere? You just have to find something new."

"Right. While we freeze to death. Easy-peasy."

Blackwell's transcribed notes actually proved useful. The sorcerer quickly identified an existing, snow-covered trail that branched off from the grid point portal and carved its way through the mountain. Warner and Drake broke the path ahead of us, plowing effortlessly through what looked like months of accumulated snow. And after finding two magical landmarks — both of which had to be literally dug out of the snow and ice — and more consulting of Blackwell's journal, we stood in a somewhat sheltered spot at the edge of an icy cliff. I was trying really, really hard to not think about the drop behind us.

Though, thankfully, it wasn't currently snowing, Warner had insisted on roping Kandy and me to him when the wind had intensified and the path began to narrow. Blackwell was similarly tied to Drake, and neither of them was pleased about it.

No one suggested roping the vampire up. I think Kett might have gotten a good laugh out of the idea, though.

Blackwell carefully unfolded a parchment rubbing that had been hidden within the pages of his ancestor's journal. He held the delicate document up to an eroded etching on the rock outcropping we were huddled beside. Warner, Kett, and Drake were attempting to create a wind block, but they were only partially successful.

"It's a match," the sorcerer said.

"About freaking time," Kandy snarled.

The werewolf's and Blackwell's lips were tinted blue, so I had to assume my own were as well. I wasn't beyond cold yet, though. Which was good, because I thought I remembered that being one of the first signs of hypothermia.

This was the third time Blackwell had pulled rubbings from the journal. He had offered up each translated clue one at a time, keeping the rest to himself in a bid toward making himself invaluable. Unfortunately, with a deal in place and no working map, there wasn't much I could do but follow the sorcerer's lead.

I was tired enough that I had long since stopped caring. Whether the extreme cold and the perilous conditions were forcing Blackwell and I to bond to maintain our sanity, or whether I was actually just freezing to death, I didn't know.

"You're up," Blackwell said. As he turned his dark-eyed gaze on me, he carefully refolded the rubbing and replaced it in the journal.

"That's all you have?"

"The rest is conjecture," the sorcerer said. "My ancestor had to turn back before he found the next gatepost. Then he died. After he wrote the final section of the chronicle, but before he could pursue it further." Blackwell flicked his thumb across the last pages of the journal. They were blank. "He was searching in far less inclement weather, of course."

"We are not here of our own choosing, sorcerer," Warner said. His tone made it exceedingly clear that he was more than ready to toss Blackwell off the cliff we were currently perched on.

"We have about two hours of daylight left," Kett said.

"Really helpful, vampire," I groused.

Kett laughed quietly.

"Could you all step back a little?" I asked.

"No," Warner said.

I eyed the sentinel. He stood stoically, blocking me from the worst of the wind, and didn't elaborate on his objection.

Kandy unclipped her belt from the rope that held us a few feet apart, pivoting and clipping onto the rope that Drake anchored.

Then everyone else shuffled back the way we'd come.

After they had disappeared around a curve in the cliff face, the sentinel grinned down at me wolfishly. "You know my magic well enough to seek beyond it."

Well, that was a hard point to argue. Being intimate with an Adept — skin to skin, exchanging touches and bodily fluids — might have multiple benefits. One of which was warming me with the remembrance of the last time I'd been curled around the man who was now shielding me from the windstorm.

"Hmm," he said. "That look isn't particularly appropriate when you are wearing so much clothing, alchemist."

I laughed, then turned back to study the carvings Blackwell had found. Like the other two sets the sorcerer had uncovered and matched to the rubbings his ancestor made, they were smoothed from centuries of weather. But if I studied the curves and edges carefully, I could superimpose an image in my mind's eye — something similar to the leaf pattern on the dragonskin tattoo.

"I wonder if this is what the treasure keeper saw." I shucked off my glove and reached for the cold stone before me. "But for some reason, he couldn't find the shrine of the phoenix."

"If seeking out evidence connected to the legend of the phoenix is even what we're doing," Warner said, still doubtful.

"Worship can exist without evidence," I said. "We could simply be seeking out a sect of sorcerers or a coven of witches who based their worship on the idea of the phoenix figure. Peacefulness and healing doesn't sound like a bad thing to base your faith on."

Warner grunted in acknowledgement but said nothing else, letting me concentrate on running my fingers over the ice-cold carvings before me. I had to bend slightly forward. The carver had apparently been shorter than me. The stone was so cold that my skin was sticking to it. I tried to ignore the sensation as I focused my dowser senses away from Warner's magic — even as dampened as it was — along with the hints of Kandy, Kett, Drake, and Blackwell that I could still pick up.

I thought about how the sorcerer had talked of using my necklace as an amplifying device. Certainly, I had coaxed magic from it on many occasions, and I used it as an anchor, or to ground or focus myself. But I hadn't really figured out how to amplify my own magic with it. Maybe it just did so naturally.

"I can taste … subtle fruit … but I can't place it. Sweet, with an acidic finish. Almost like melon, but nothing I've eaten before. Not that I can recall."

"Pear," Warner said.

"I've eaten pears before," I said, pissy about being interrupted.

"Asian pear," Warner said evenly.

I had a fleeting memory of seeing light-brown-skinned, round fruit at a vendor's in the Granville Island Market.

"They'd be crisper than the pears you'd be accustomed to," Warner said. "More like an apple. Juicy too."

"I don't really pick up texture like that. Just taste. I mean, unless it's a memory … like how your magic tastes creamy and smooth like the gelato from Mario's."

Warner chuckled quietly, possibly recalling me feeding him said gelato in bed about a month previous.

I blew on my hands to warm them, then returned my attention to the carvings.

"We don't even know if this is going to help," I muttered. "I might just be picking up the magic of the carver …"

"And if that Adept carved more gateposts, it will lead us forward." Warner was in patient mode, which usually drove me a little batty. But I was too cold to be feisty.

"I can also taste some kind of toasted grain, and … maybe tea." I shoved my hand back inside my glove, then into the pocket of my parka. I buried my chin and nose behind my scarf, exhaling a few times to warm my face.

I looked up at Warner. At least an inch of icy snow had gathered on his shoulders while he stood there blocking me from the worst of the wind.

"You take me to the best places," I groused.

He lifted one eyebrow at me. "You take me to the best places."

I laughed, then sobered. "I'm going to have to lead."

He nodded, not happy about it. I didn't want to be the one pushing through the snow either.

Warner stepped around me, then tucked his hand up underneath my jacket to grab my leather belt.

I was instantly assaulted by the wind and blowing snow, and now my back was cold. "Don't do that," I cried. "That's just mean. You already have me tied to you."

"I'll hold the rope as well," Warner said. "Regardless of whether I can drag you back, I don't want you falling in the first place."

I huddled deeper into my jacket without further protest, likewise wanting to avoid taking a wrong turn. I stepped forward into the virgin snow, beyond where

Warner, Drake, and Kett had been standing. It came up to my knees. I slid slightly into the step, then felt my hiking boot find purchase on the icy rock beneath it.

Delightful.

Kett had deemed the snowshoes too cumbersome early on, and having never used them before, I'd been glad. But now … well, no true West Coast girl wanted to be trudging through snow up to her knees. Not without a ski lodge and a spa nearby.

"We're moving," Warner yelled back over his shoulder.

The others moved forward to gather behind us. We were going to have to advance single file.

I cast my dowser senses forward in search of tart, juicy pear and roasted grains.

I picked up a hint of carrot cake and cream-cheese icing instead.

"Shailaja," I said, tugging my hood closer around my face until I had absolutely no peripheral vision at all. But better that than my nose freezing off.

Warner huffed. "I expected her sooner."

"Would you hang out in this?" I gestured around us as I took another knee-high step through the snow. "It's faint. She's just checking in."

"And the leeches?"

I shook my head. "I can't taste them."

"As in their magic doesn't have a taste?"

"No taste I understand, at least."

Kett's peppermint magic brushed against me.

"You heard?" Warner asked quietly.

"Yes," Kett said, slipping by me.

I looked for the vampire but saw no evidence of his passing in the snow, either around or before me. I cranked my head sideways and got a face full of icy flakes for my trouble. I also got a glimpse of the crazy vampire scaling the cliff face running alongside us to the left.

I started to protest.

Warner interrupted me. "Let him do what he's good at," he whispered, practically pressing his mouth to my ear.

"He's no match for her alone," I hissed back.

"Not true," Warner said. "He was no match for Shailaja the first time. Now he's drunk from her. That changes the game. Plus, he has us to back him."

I shivered, but not from the cold. Someone wasn't making it through all of this alive. I just hoped it wasn't one of us.

"Pears …" Warner prompted.

I nodded and focused forward.

Chapter Twelve

We stood before the door to the shrine of the phoenix as the sun began to wane. Why it was that we always approached our darkest deeds at the beginning of the darkest part of the day, I didn't know.

I gazed up at the deepening gray of the sky. The windstorm that had pressed us throughout our slog up the mountain from the final landmark had abated, so that only a few stray snowflakes swirled around us now.

"It didn't seem so snowy in Rochelle's sketch," I murmured.

"You just need to look closer, alchemist," Blackwell said.

I ignored the sorcerer, watching instead as Kett dropped gracefully down the side of the cliff. He stepped out of the ever-deepening shadows to our left and approached the door.

Blackwell flinched at his appearance.

Kandy chuckled, a disturbing sound that raised the hair on the back of my neck. I turned to glare at the werewolf.

She flashed me her predator smile, but she toned down the creepy vibe.

The ornately etched door was carved into the side of the mountain — as expected. It appeared larger in person than it had in Rochelle's sketch, but I realized that it was my sense of self that was skewed rather than the oracle's perspective. Apparently, I felt more insignificant than I actually was … at least when seen through someone else's eyes and rendered in charcoal.

The narrow path we had been following beneath the snow and ice widened as it approached the door, extending twenty feet across and terminating at a dead end.

With the door sheltered on two sides as it was, the snowfall before it hadn't accumulated as much as on the trail, coming up no higher than our ankles.

As we stood arrayed before the door, the sun broke through the light cloud cover. An orange-red ray brightened the top left corner of the door for a brief second, before the sun dipped below the snowcapped mountains spreading endlessly to the west.

The touch of the sun triggered a wash of magic tasting of tart pear tea. It rippled across the etched leaf-and-flower motifs on the edges of the door, filling every furrow and ridge with a deep amber glow. The gleaming magic flowed through the stone, illuminating the carved branches until they stood out like magic-filled veins. The main lines of the design twisted and curled, meeting and pooling around a two-foot-wide circle at the center of the door.

Then the accumulated sun-triggered magic flared into the image of a majestic bird in flight. The deep amber energy blazed across the center stone, then washed forward into the open path where we stood.

Positioned directly in front of the door, Kett flung his arms across his face. Twisting his body away, he threw himself into the shadowed face of the cliff.

Warner and Drake both spun to the side, allowing the magic to wash across their backs.

Blackwell grunted as if in pain. He stumbled back a few steps.

Kandy stepped up beside me, blinking into the magic as I was. She pushed back her hood, lifting her face to the dying rays.

I felt ... sun kissed and chosen. Just for a brief moment.

Then the magic was gone. Depleted.

The door stood before us, as inert as before. But even though it wasn't physically carved into the stone in any way, I could still see the image of the bird etched across the center of the door when I blinked.

Our extremely different reactions to the sun-triggered magic were perplexing and disconcerting.

Drake and Warner were staring at the door, completely shocked. Then they looked at each other.

"It can't be," Warner said.

"And if it is?" Drake asked.

"Then we stand on the edge of our own doom," Warner said, turning to catch my gaze. "I've slept through centuries. Woken to find a warrior with whom I can celebrate the ages. Only to face the final extinction of the guardians."

A tendril of cold fear shot through my belly.

Inexplicably, Drake laughed. "You and I have been told very different bedtime stories."

Warner stiffened his shoulders. "My mother — Jiaotu-who-was — was an exceedingly able teacher. As was the treasure keeper."

"Cool." Drake shrugged. "Suanmi and Chi Wen see things differently ... and if I understand the succession properly, they have both walked the earth for many more years than your mother had when you were under her tutelage."

"Different guardians carry different beliefs."

Kett appeared on my left, slipping out from the shadows. His face, neck, and hands were crimson, as if he'd been severely sunburned.

"Jesus," I said, momentarily distracted from Warner and Drake's disturbing conversation.

Kett grinned at me. His cheeks cracked. A few layers of his skin crumbled into ash. "It's been over a millennia since the sun has burned me so badly." He sounded oddly pleased.

"I told you he was old as ass," Kandy groused. "How old does a vampire need to be to walk outside even on a cloudy day?"

Kett's gaze was fixed on the door as Drake crossed over to examine it. "Old," the vampire said.

Awesome. I loved it when all the deepest secrets came to light at exactly the wrong time.

Kandy snorted, then turned to start pacing the perimeter, keeping Blackwell hemmed in. Not that the sorcerer noticed. He had his nose buried in his notebook.

Ignoring Kett's revelations for a moment, because I wasn't sure I could process that he'd somehow been burned by the magic amplified through the door, I stalked up to Warner.

"I don't get it," I said. "So whatever you and Drake get, you need to share with the group."

Warner glanced past me. I turned to see Blackwell madly scribbling away in his journal — recording our conversation, maybe?

"I'm overreacting," Warner said, pitching his voice low. "It was just a shock. Drake is correct. We've been taught different versions of the same myth."

"It's still flummoxing to me that dragons even have myths."

Warner chuckled halfheartedly. "Some knowledge is retained for guardians only. Prophecies, objects of power, and such. Apprentices are usually selected within their first hundred years, but training begins in childhood in the form of stories and magical puzzles. Talents are uncovered. Apparently, since we're standing before what the sorcerer claims is the shrine of the phoenix, the myth of the phoenix is a truth wrapped within a childhood story."

"Nice to know it's not just me constantly left in the dark."

Warner raised his eyebrow.

"What?" I snarked.

"Perhaps not the best time for a bitch session," he said dryly.

I glowered at him. "Screw you, sixteenth century."

Warner laughed, much more wholeheartedly. I struggled to maintain my faked pissiness, but I loved to hear him laugh … especially in my darkened bedroom …

I sighed. My bedroom felt like it was an epically long way away right now. "So … moving forward, what do I need to know?"

We turned to face the door together, just as Drake reached out to touch the smooth center stone where the image of the phoenix had appeared.

The fledgling hissed in pain, ripping his hand back.

Literally, ripped. Whatever magic guarded the entrance to the shrine had tried to ensnare Drake.

"Ouch," he said, shaking his hand and looking back at me mournfully.

I wondered how long it had been since Drake felt any pain on a level that actually made him acknowledge it.

" 'Where dragons dare not tread,' remember?" I said sternly. Hanging around Drake made me channel

Gran, apparently. I tried to not think about how often I ran around constantly touching magical objects I shouldn't touch.

He sulked, then hunkered down to shove his hand into the snow at his feet, treating the wound like a burn.

I glanced back at Kett. Taking my look as a summons, he stepped close enough that I could see that his magic was already repairing his pink-hued skin.

"I didn't know dragons were allergic to the sun," I murmured.

"We're not," Warner said. "Just naturally nocturnal."

"Evolution," Kett said.

Warner nodded.

"Because you used to be beasts of tooth and claw who dwelled in caves and hoarded gold?" I asked.

Kandy snorted appreciatively as she paced by me. I could always count on a laugh from my BFF.

Kett smirked, then quickly wiped the expression from his face. Vampires who lived in glass houses and all that.

"If you will," Warner said, but his attention was on the door behind me.

I touched Kett's cheek, wondering if I could distinguish the magic that had burned him as distinct from his natural peppermint. I couldn't.

"This phoenix character is powered by the sun? Or controls it?" I asked.

"No," Warner said.

"Yes," Drake said.

Kett laughed.

"You go first, vampire," I said. "What do you think you know?"

Kett flashed his teeth at me.

I narrowed my eyes at him threateningly. "Looking a little pointy there, friend."

"A side effect of being injured," he said nonchalantly. "A phoenix is a large immortal bird that dies, then rises from its own ashes. Its tears have healing powers. It's able to carry great weight. Aspects of the phoenix myth have permeated many different cultures and religions, taking the form of any number of gods that die and are perpetually reborn."

"And the connection to the sun?"

"From Greek mythology. The sun sets each night, only to rise again each morning. It's associated with the deity the Egyptians named the Bennu, with the Native American thunderbird, the Russian firebird ... even in Christianity, with Christ's resurrection."

"But we're in China."

"In Asia, the phoenix is the symbol of the empress and feminine grace, as well as the sun," Drake said. "The sighting of a phoenix is a sign that a wise leader has ascended to the throne, and a new era of peace will reign for a thousand years. A phoenix is goodness personified."

"A mythical creature signifying eternal life, destruction, then creation," Warner said. "From the ashes, a new civilization will rise. But what do you think the ashes are from? What do you think the phoenix destroys to usher in an era of peace and tranquility? Us."

Drake straightened from his crouch, grinning up at Warner. "And that is where our bedtime stories diverge."

They all turned to look at me expectantly, as if they'd just gifted me with a wealth of knowledge and were expecting me to do something with it.

I turned, catching Kandy's gaze. "Kandy?"

The green-haired werewolf shrugged. "If I wanted to go to school, I wouldn't be freezing my ass off on the side of a mountain in the middle of freaking China."

I snorted. "Sorcerer?"

Squinting in the ever-darkening evening while still jotting down notes, Blackwell didn't bother to look up at my question.

"A light might be beneficial," I said snidely. "I'm sure you have an appropriate magical gadget in your pocket."

"Indeed, if I wanted to attract whoever is hunting you to our location." The sorcerer smirked at me over the edge of his journal. "You know, the person who you won't admit is following you, but who you were concerned would attack the oracle after you left?"

I opened my mouth; then realizing the sorcerer was just fishing for information, I snapped my mouth shut on my retort. "The phoenix?" I prompted instead.

"I have nothing to add to this particular discussion." Blackwell returned to his journaling.

Freaking sorcerers. Ever so helpful. For a price.

"So ..." I turned to eye the door. "Is this a shrine or a prison?"

"Demigods don't typically build either," Kett said.

Warner snorted as if he'd known a few demigods who liked to build shrines for themselves.

"The chronicle that allowed the sorcerer to lead us here is the clue," Kett said, continuing as if the sentinel hadn't scoffed at his conjecture. "As are the first two instruments."

"Because you think that a demigod wouldn't need a magical instrument with which to kill other demigods," I said, putting a few of the pieces together. "So we're looking for something associated with the phoenix that can kill guardians. Something created by the phoenix's followers, perhaps. Not something created by the phoenix itself."

"Exactly."

"You're guessing, vampire," Warner said wryly.

"And superstitions are a solid foundation on which to build a hypothesis?" Kett sneered uncharacteristically, allowing the edges of his teeth to show. "Your vision is clouded with ancient, fear-based teachings, dragon."

The gold of Warner's magic rolled over his eyes.

Ah, delightful. Apparently, getting kissed by sun magic made the vampire rowdy. Good to know.

I spoke up, injecting myself into the pissing contest before any male members got pulled out for real. "So when I open this door, I won't be, like … releasing hell on earth or anything like that? Because, you know, this has been a lot of setup."

"Assuming you can open the door," Kett said.

Warner, Drake, and Kandy all snorted. It was good that three of my four BFFs had my back.

I smirked at the vampire.

He shrugged. "You assume I underestimate your talents, when perhaps I simply prescribe caution. You are facing an unknown magic that burns vampires and dragons, and causes even sorcerers to flinch."

"But not werewolves," Kandy said proudly.

"Not werewolves wearing cuffs of unknown alchemist origins," Kett said, blithely undercutting Kandy's magical prowess.

I eyed Blackwell over my shoulder. He was still fervently making notes.

"Maybe the power of the door only makes sorcerers flinch who dabble in dark magic," I said, expanding Kett's interpretation.

"Then you would have flinched, alchemist." Blackwell didn't even bother to lift his eyes from his notebook. "You carry blood magic with you. And I doubt you've confined the practice to your knife. No. The magic simply bothered those of us who are hereditarily unaccustomed to the sun."

Kandy snorted. "Because you're from Scotland?"

"Exactly."

"Excuse me while I die laughing."

"We're delaying the inevitable, and rapidly losing the remaining light," Kett said. "Neither I nor the dragons can touch the door. That leaves the sorcerer, the werewolf, and you, dowser."

Kandy strode up to the door, shucking off her gloves and stuffing them in her pockets. Without a hint of hesitation, she placed her hands in the smooth center of the door and pushed. Her feet slid back on the snow-covered granite.

Blackwell joined her, scanning the edges of the door. Then he brushed the snow away from the base, apparently looking for a handle or a latch. Maybe even a hinge.

"No runes," I said. "Is there a pattern in the leaves or flowers? Perhaps a sequence that needs to be triggered? What does the chronicle say, Blackwell?"

"Nothing about the door. It was simply the similarity of the markings in Rochelle's sketch that reminded me of the rubbings in the journal."

The sorcerer and Kandy stepped back to gaze at the carvings. Then the green-haired werewolf started tracing the branches with her fingers.

I sighed. Blackwell's mention of Rochelle reminded me that I was ignoring the obvious.

"It's me," I said. "I have to open it. I'm not sure how, but in Rochelle's sketch, I'm standing in the center with all of you winged out around and behind me."

I hated following any sense of predestination, but we were wasting time. Being ignorant and scared were way different than being willfully stupid. I was done with willfully stupid behavior.

Drake and Kandy stepped up behind me. Warner and Kett crossed to either side. Blackwell hung farther back, hovering between Kandy and Kett with his notebook still in hand. It was somewhat amusing that he deemed a werewolf and a vampire — both of whom had reasons to hate him — safer companions than two dragons.

I palmed my jade knife, feeling the magic contained in the sharpened stone flow together with my own magic. The blade was really just an extension of my alchemist power ... a deadlier aspect. I strode up to the door.

"You're going to try to cut the magic with your knife?" Drake asked.

I couldn't answer because I wasn't sure. I had cut through magical wards before. But as I reached out with my dowser senses to the power coating the door looming over me, I knew instantly that I was dealing with something different.

I didn't think — or, rather, instinctively feel — that the pear-and-toasted-grain magic could simply be severed from the stone. Tracing in my mind the route it had followed, I recalled how the magic adhering to the door had rippled, then flared when the sun hit it. I got the sense that the magic was permanently anchored, not just triggered by the touch of the sun ... or by Drake's hand. It had simply been revealed on a visual level. If we'd arrived before sunset, the door might have been fully lit when we'd happened upon it.

"I don't think this is defensive magic," I said.

"What about it burning the vampire?" Drake asked.

I shook my head, though I was only guessing. "Just a powerful reflection. It might be witch magic by the way it's embedded in the stone rather than simply wrapping around it. But not from any sort of witch I've ever met. And there's nothing malicious here. Not like the stone warden powered by metallurgy in Peru. Or the defenses Shailaja stripped away from the temple in Hope Town by sacrificing her sorcerers."

I paused, trying to figure out what my senses were telling me. It was so quiet that all I could hear was the scratching of Blackwell's pen again. I probably shouldn't have been thinking out loud.

"Who visits a shrine?" I asked.

"Worshipers," Kandy said.

"Mourners," Warner said.

"Supplicants," Kett said.

I stepped back from the door. "But we aren't any of those. So the door doesn't want to open for us."

"We can't muscle or trick our way in," Kandy said thoughtfully.

"What about searching for another entrance?" I asked, clinging to a sliver of hope that I wasn't simply doomed to follow destiny's path as dictated by the far seer and the oracle.

"In the dark?" Warner said. "That puts you and the sorcerer out of commission, and eventually Kandy."

"The moon will be up soon."

"I looked as I was climbing," Kett said. "This is the door we are seeking."

"Okay." I sighed.

Then I did what I was created to do. What I was born to do. What I did best. I reached out to the magic embedded in the door with my dowser senses, grabbing hold of it with my alchemist powers.

The flavor of tart pear and tea instantly overwhelmed my taste buds. My mouth watered from the acidity carried within the unknown witch magic as I gathered it toward me. And when I'd gathered too much without even having dented the power flowing over and through the door, I claimed it as my own, channeling what I could into my necklace and knife.

I began to sweat beneath my multiple layers of clothing. I kept pulling the pear-tea magic toward me.

My head began to ache. I gritted my teeth.

"Jade?" Warner whispered.

"It's endless." I gasped. With a shudder, I was forced to release the magic I had gathered. I was panting, exhausted as I leaned forward to rest my hands on my knees. "I can't hold it all."

"Magic doesn't have weight," Kett said. "Or fill only a certain space."

"Then you do it," I snapped. "Because it's too much for me to hold. I didn't even dent it."

"Then don't," Kett said. "Don't try to just dent it."

"Speak plainly, vampire," I said, still breathing heavily. "Or forever hold your peace."

"Do you remember the ward the sorcerer held against us in the Sea Lion Caves in Oregon?"

Blackwell shifted uncomfortably in my peripheral vision, but I kept my focus on Kett.

"It's difficult to forget," I growled, straightening from my undignified bow. Now was not the time to re-open old wounds.

"The alpha, rather majestically but ill advisedly, cracked that ward."

"With his head," I said, remembering. "I don't think any of us should run headfirst into the freaking door."

"I assume that was the ill-advised part?" Drake said.

"Shut your trap," Kandy snarled. "Like you were even there."

I turned my attention back to the door, shutting out Kandy and Drake's playful bickering.

Simply cracking the pear-scented magic wouldn't let us pass. And I'd already figured out that I couldn't cut it with my knife … unless maybe I thinned it first.

I reached out to the magic again, foregoing all the foreplay and instantly claiming it as my own. I gathered the power to me with full force until I could actually see the deep amber energy writhing and coiling around my hands and arms.

I was shaking with the effort. I just needed the magic to thin, even slightly. I should be able to pull enough to dilute it or … maybe …

Maybe it was like making a pie. I never made pie, because I always screwed up the pastry. I always rolled it too thin, and then it broke, and I had to piece it together into a lumpy, thick crust. I wasn't a fan of lumpy. Or pastry in general, actually. Mostly because I found the insides of pastries tastier than the outside.

If I was crazy careful, took my time, and the surface I was working on was well floured, I could roll pastry very thinly without breaking it.

But if I was harsh, hasty, and unfocused …

I clumsily ripped the magic away from the door, screaming with the effort of doing so. I managed to slash my knife forward at the same time. Using the door's own magic against it, I slammed all the power I'd gathered into me back against the stone door.

A crack shot through the door from top to bottom, splitting it in half.

Drake whooped.

The magic I'd torn away from the door roiled around me. I tried to channel it into the knife and the necklace, but no matter what the vampire claimed, both vessels felt as if they were at full capacity.

Unable to contain or hold the power, all I could do was scream again.

Warner reached for me, but I shied away from him.

The pear-tea magic was coating me, smothering me. Swallowing me whole. So I did the only other thing I could do. I reached out for every source of magic I could sense on the open path around me. Then I shoved all the pear-tea power I couldn't hold toward it.

Kandy and Blackwell flew back, slamming into the cliff face and dropping to the ground.

Drake spun, pivoting and falling to one knee as if a giant had grabbed him by the backpack and shoved him down.

Beside me, Warner grunted. He stumbled a single step back as if someone had pushed him.

Kett didn't move.

And I was free of the magic.

Half of the sundered stone door tipped toward me and crashed to the ground.

"Took you long enough," Kett said, sounding as pleased as he ever did. Then he strode forward and through the gap I'd created.

"Keep an eye on the vampire," Warner said curtly.

The order was for Drake, who scrambled to his feet. He approached the door more cautiously than Kett had, though.

"Jesus H. Christ," Kandy said as she stood. "What the hell was that?" She touched the back of her head, then looked down at her hand. It was bloody.

I was still shaking, not quite in control of my limbs yet as I reached toward her.

Then the shadow leeches flooded across the open path, taking all sight and sound with them.

Kandy screamed.

I could taste the magic of Warner's blade even as I drew my own. Then I tasted baked potato with sour cream and butter. Blackwell's amulet.

The maelstrom of shadow demons blew through and around us, then funneled through the open door.

Then nothing.

I blinked, momentarily seeing the afterimage of the phoenix against the dark sky. Stars were starting to appear.

"Shailaja," I whispered. Though if the rabid koala had been among the shadow leeches, I hadn't tasted her magic. That wasn't disconcerting at all.

Kett and Drake dashed back through the door, both with swords in hand. I had no idea where the vampire's blade had come from. I'd never even seen him wield a weapon before, other than my knife in Peru. He preferred to fight with the teeth and claws he kept carefully hidden behind his human visage.

"The sorcerer's gone," Kandy snarled. "A blast of magic from you, a few shadow demons, and he tucks tail? Freaking coward."

"I guess he didn't want to renegotiate," I said wearily. "He's probably the sanest one among us."

"Speak for yourself, dowser," Kandy said, but there wasn't much heat in her retort.

Warner sighed, grim-faced. He sheathed his knife, crossing toward the sundered door. "Nice sword," he said to Kett as he stepped past him.

"I was examining it when the leeches passed through. There are … remains inside the door."

Warner nodded as if he'd expected that news flash. Then, with one foot through the doorway, he glanced back at me. "She's ahead of us now."

My stomach bottomed out at the darkness in his tone. He had made it clear that he thought pursuing Shailaja and seeking the final instrument was insanity. But he'd stayed by my side against his better judgement then, and he would stay now.

I nodded, swallowing my fear.

He disappeared through the door, willing to take the lead where he didn't want to walk.

Pulling my thoughts and fears back to the present moment, I reached for Kandy. I wanted a closer look at her head.

She batted my hands away as she strode after Warner. "It's a scratch, dowser."

With Kett and Drake close behind her, she crossed through the broken door, leaving me alone in the snow underneath the stars.

Almost every person I loved had just walked before me into unknown danger. And I'd opened the door.

I hadn't even said sorry for hitting them with the excess magic.

I guessed the time for talking was over.

I sheathed my knife and reached up to brush my fingers over my necklace. I was as ready as I could be. We all were.

Then I followed my friends into whatever trap lay ahead of us.

That it was a trap, I had no doubt — whether it was Shailaja's creation or just the power of the shrine itself.

All I could do was tear through it until I could go no farther … or I found the other side.

As I stepped through the door, I was expecting a tunnel, or maybe a series of chambers replete with traps and puzzles. I wasn't expecting the barren wasteland that stretched out before us. Or the mummified remains of the sentries that Kett and Warner were currently examining on either side of the door.

A faint glow illuminated the slick stone floor that spread from the doorway as far as I could see. Winter-bare trees were inexplicably growing out of the stone, rising ten to fifteen feet high. An intricate sprinkle of bright stars decorated the darkness above us, except I was fairly certain I wasn't looking at the night sky. At least not at the sky I'd been gazing at before I stepped through the door.

I hadn't felt any sort of portal magic or magical barrier as I crossed through. As such, I was pretty sure we hadn't stepped into a pocket of magic like the one that had concealed the temple of the braids.

Except, of course, I might have just clumsily and ignorantly ripped through that barrier.

Not a single snowflake decorated the bleak landscape. Not a single hint of life. Everything appeared to be encased in a thick layer of ice. Except I wasn't sure it was actually ice.

Kandy had crouched down a few steps beyond the door, taking in the scene before her. "Smells like magic," she said, looking up at me. The green of her shapeshifter power flared across her eyes.

"Tastes like it," I murmured in agreement. "A slightly different power from whoever constructed the door, though. Muted."

Kett crossed the half-open doorway to examine the second sentry. The mummified guard was wearing elaborately decorated, plated-leather armor and what was possibly a bronze one-piece breastplate. It looked ancient, but there was no way to even guess at how old it was through the maybe-ice that coated and perfectly preserved the sentries. Whatever it was that had mummified or frozen them ... and perhaps the trees as well.

"When we discussed the collection of the first instrument, you indicated you encountered an encasement spell in the temple where you found the braids," Kett said. He was still holding the sword he had taken from the first sentry. "Is this similar?"

I shook my head, but Warner responded before I could.

"No," he said curtly. "That was constructed out of stone." He had paced ahead to stand just inside the edge of the grove, about a dozen steps ahead of us and staring out into the darkness.

I couldn't see Drake, but by the taste of his magic, I imagined he was scouting the interior wall behind us.

I crossed to the nearest tree, deeming it way less creepy to examine that than the dead bodies. Warner turned to watch me.

I removed my glove and carefully touched the lowest branch. "The coating is cold," I said. "But it doesn't melt underneath my fingers. Magical ice? This is a fruit tree of some sort, isn't it? By the shape? Or it was. It looks dead, not just preserved."

"Apple?" Kandy had straightened from her crouch and was silently padding across the slick ground between us.

"Pear," Warner said flatly.

"Conjecture," Kett said coolly as he joined us. He had set the sword he'd taken back beside the dead sentry.

"Logical," Warner said. "Given the magic the dowser tasted previously."

"Let's all stand around being pissy about it," Kandy said, laying on the sarcasm. "That'll accomplish so much."

Warner turned his back on all of us. He was holding his knife at his side, and even from a dozen feet away, I could feel how pleased the blade was to be in play. It was creepy that I knew that about the weapon — which was why it was in Warner's hand, not mine.

"Drake," the sentinel said.

The fledgling guardian appeared to Warner's right.

"The wall extends in a gradual curve in both directions," Drake said, dutifully reporting his findings. "Smooth faced, unscalable, even if there was anywhere to go. No doors or magical loci. Not that I could feel."

"Loci?" Kandy asked.

I was always glad when the werewolf took one for the 'slow' part of the team. Namely, me.

"Manifestations," Kett said. "Points or beacons."

"And Shailaja?" Warner asked.

Drake, Kett, and Kandy turned to look at me. Warner shifted his grip on the hilt of his knife, twisting it in his hand. But he didn't look over his shoulder.

"What did you think would happen?" I whispered.

Warner turned to me. The gold of his dragon magic briefly flickered across his eyes. "This," he said. "This is what I thought would happen. Her ahead of us and with the upper hand."

I reached up, lightly touching the rings on my necklace. I hadn't zipped my jacket back up yet, though I was cooling down after the exertion of ripping a hole in the wards. I instantly identified the rune-marked betrothal bands by feel. Curling two fingers through those rings, I smiled at Warner.

"I'm glad you're here," I whispered, not caring about the distance between us or that we weren't alone.

"I wouldn't be anywhere else," Warner said.

"Holy Jesus," Kandy groused. "Have sex on your own time. We have the old man to rescue. That's why we're here, right?"

Warner shook his head, then huffed out a sigh. "Can you locate Shailaja?" he asked me.

I nodded. Then I stepped ahead into the twisted shadows cast by the starlit trees, placing the familiar magic of my companions behind me. I closed my eyes and sought out the rabid koala with my dowser senses.

"There," I murmured, pointing toward the taste of spiced carrot cake that I could taste in the distance.

My stomach rumbled loudly enough to echo back through the cavern.

Kandy and Drake burst out laughing. They were quickly joined by Kett.

I spun around, glaring at them all. I eyed Warner as he fought the impulse to join in. "It's not my fault she tastes like *Serenity in a Cup*."

Drake was the first to sober. "That is terrible."

"Yeah." Kandy was actually weeping. "You might have to rename that cupcake, Jade."

I turned my back on them, but only to hide my own smile. "She'll be able to search the area quicker than we can," I said, focusing once again on the problem at hand.

"How?" Drake asked.

"The leeches are sentient," Kett said.

"Enough to communicate with her? Like, individually?" Kandy asked.

"To some extent."

"So our best course is to follow her," I said, looking over at Warner. "I'm sorry. Though whatever defenses the shrine holds might slow her down."

He nodded. "Drake on the right. Jade in the middle with Kandy and Kett flanking. I'll take left point."

"Protecting me doesn't make any sense," I said as the others quickly shifted into formation around me. "The rabid koala wants me in one piece."

"You're also the most capable of standing against her," Warner said. "Which I believe you proved in Peru."

He glanced over at Kett, who nodded.

"Those were specific circumstances —" I said.

"Exactly," Warner said to cut me off. "Moving forward."

He took off through the trees, setting the pace at a light jog that everyone but me would probably have been able to maintain all day. I would likely be okay for an hour or so.

"I should take point, Warner," I said, reiterating my objection. "It's harder to sneak up on me."

He glanced back. His features were just a dark wash under the fake stars. "There won't be any sneaking this time."

Unfortunately, he was right.

Shailaja hit us with the shadow demons in waves. On their first assault, the leeches appeared without warning. They swirled and twisted through our ranks, siphoning whatever magic they could grab. Then they disappeared.

It was a reconnaissance pass.

The second time, they targeted Kandy and Kett specifically.

"She's dropping them on us through her miniportals," I cried out as I pivoted, slashing at the writhing mass of shadow swarming the werewolf and the vampire.

I couldn't get an accurate count, but it felt as if maybe a dozen leeches were pressing two Adepts who relied on their strength, stealth, and speed in a fight. With the demons having no real substance to gouge at with claws or shred with teeth, Kandy and Kett were ineffectual against them.

Plus, Kandy couldn't even see the soul-bound, demonic energy of her attackers, because most shifters related to magic through scent, not sight. She could feel them, though, sucking on her skin and consuming her magic. As could Kett. It hurt them both.

Utterly frustrated and completely blanketed in seething, malicious shadows, Kandy screamed.

The magic of one of Shailaja's miniature portals bloomed over our heads, literally vacuuming up the masses of leeches. As they vanished, we were left peering at each other through the starlit, frozen landscape, our weapons pointed at nothing.

"Fucking shit," Kandy snarled. Red welts crisscrossed her face and neck. Her jacket was shredded, as if she'd clawed at herself in an attempt to get the leeches off. "I can't fucking see or smell them!"

She glanced at Kett, whose reddened skin was slowly fading back to its typical paleness.

"I can see them," he said. He lifted his hands before him and twisted his lips wryly. "And I can feel them. But I can't touch them."

"She's playing with us," I said.

"No," Drake said. His golden broadsword gleamed brighter than anything else within the frozen emptiness around us. "Her force isn't strong enough to overwhelm all of us, so she's focusing her attacks. Further weakening what she perceives to be the weakest links."

"Speak for yourself," Kandy spat.

"Tighten the formation," Warner barked, before Drake and Kandy started seriously tussling. "Kandy and Kett center. I'll take point. Jade and Drake at the back. And dowser? Some warning?"

"I'll try." I turned to Kandy. "Here." I reached up to lift my necklace off, ready to offer it to the werewolf.

"No." She pushed my hands back. Anger had paled her face. "No sense in weakening you before the big finish."

"But ..." I looked at Kett, hoping he would take my knife as he had in Peru.

"No, dowser," he said icily. Then he turned his back on me, standing shoulder to shoulder with Kandy.

Warner took off again through the trees. I had no choice but to follow at the rear of the formation.

I opened my senses as wide as I dared, focusing forward through all the potent magic ahead of me. Realizing that Shailaja had moved, I veered to the right slightly. Everyone moved with me without question.

My companions were so silent that if not for the taste of their magic and the occasional brush of clothing against icy branches when I corrected our course, I might have been running alone.

Sugared cinnamon tickled the tip of my tongue. "Incoming!" I yelled, waiting for the leeches to drop from above us.

Instead, they hit us from the right, rolling in underneath our feet, buffeting our legs, and attempting to rip Kandy and Kett away from our protective triangle. Warner, still running, spun and yanked Kandy around by the arm, flipping her up and onto his back. The leeches immediately assaulted him, creating a whirling storm of darkness around them. The sentinel slowly twisted, methodically slashing through the shadows with his knife.

Drake and I sandwiched Kett between the two of us, facing out and attempting to skewer any shadows that flitted too close.

Frustratingly, they wouldn't come near me. If I lunged too far, they'd slip in and around my legs, leeching onto Kett behind me. If I stood still, they simply stayed out of reach.

Then they were gone.

Kandy was hanging off Warner's neck. The sentinel looked as frustrated as I felt.

"How many of them are there?" Drake asked.

"A dozen, maybe. Not as many as they seem to be," I said. "But even slashed to bits, they can keep coming."

"Or they regenerate quickly," Kett said. "Which is why she keeps pulling them back."

Kandy slowly swung down from Warner's back.

"You need shields," I said, glancing around me as if I was expecting to uncover some useful artifact in the ice.

"We need to keep moving," Kandy growled. "The sooner I have my hands around her neck, the better." She slashed her wolf claws across her shredded sleeves, freeing her hands from any loose fabric they might get tangled in. "Why do you think the far seer gave me these cuffs? I'm going to strangle the skinny bitch."

"How do you know she's skinny?" Drake asked.

"Chubby people are always cheerful. They get to eat whatever they want."

Under any other circumstances, I would have bantered with Kandy over that statement, but it wasn't the time or place to be playful. Not even for me.

Kett had a series of demonic hickeys across his neck. I reached up to touch his shoulder, but he warned me off with a shake of his head. A red sheen rolled across his eyes. The marks faded.

Everyone was getting hurt but me.

I turned away, dowsing for Shailaja. "She's nearer," I murmured. "The shadows are just a distraction. Let's provide one of our own." I glanced over at Warner. "She expects us to come straight at her, en masse."

He nodded, apparently following my train of thought.

"So … we need to be more … random. Maybe the shadows won't know who to concentrate on if we weave back and forth quicker than they can follow. So … stay close. But, you know, zigzag." And with that brilliant bit of strategy declared, I took off at a run.

Kett slipped up beside me, then split off into the trees.

Drake outpaced me. "There's a cliff face up ahead," he said, pointing, then darting off in the direction he'd indicated. "Forty-five degrees."

I still couldn't see anything but rows and rows of skeleton trees. I focused on the taste of Shailaja's magic ahead of me. The others flitted back and forth, weaving between and around the trees.

Monsters in the dark.

A tree splintered somewhere in the darkness to my left.

I kept running.

Kandy howled off to the right.

Shadow demons blew by me. I snatched one out of the air as it passed, but it had built up enough momentum that it dragged me off my feet and slammed me into a stone wall I hadn't seen in the starlit darkness. I lost my hold on the leech and my footing on the slick ground at the same time.

I scrambled to right myself, keeping my knife at the ready. But nothing else moved in the starlight. I ran my hand along the wall that stood behind me. More pear-tea magic filled my senses and clung to my hand. The entire freaking place was covered with whatever magic shielded the door.

Delightful.

Though I'd apparently found the chamber's far side.

Reorienting myself by tracking the taste of my companions' magic, I attempted to run along the edge of the wall, keeping it to my right. But the stone of the floor there was uneven and slippery, as if the ice had built up more along the edges of the chamber. There was also less light. And unlike the dragons and the vampires, my eyesight penetrated the darkness only so much.

I stepped back through the row of trees nearest the wall, homing in on the magic of the rabid koala just ahead. I held my knife at the ready, slowing my pace and attempting to not announce my presence like a rampaging elephant.

Warner slipped up out of the darkness beside me.

"It's odd that the shrine itself has no defenses, isn't it?" I whispered. "Not that I can taste."

He grunted. "It does for me, and probably for Drake."

"Probably Drake what?" the fledgling whispered to my left.

"You can probably still feel the magic of the door," Warner said.

"All around," Drake said. "It doesn't like me very much. But it isn't painful or anything."

"More like a warning pulsing in my hindbrain," Warner whispered.

Ice and wood cracked in the darkness behind us, the noise radiating out as a dozen or more booming echoes.

We slid to a halt. Well, I slid. Warner and Drake just stopped.

Then we waited in the dreadful silence.

Kandy screamed.

Warner dashed to the left. Drake and I followed.

We found the werewolf about a dozen hurried steps away. She was in her half-beast form, kneeling with her head bowed. As we approached, she melted back into her human visage, looking up at us with glowing green eyes. Her clothing was torn and stretched. She was bloody and bruised.

All the trees within ten feet of her had been shattered, their pieces spread across the ground. Drake hunkered down to examine the petrified-looking wood at the edge of the newly cleared area.

Kandy cracked a grin. "They didn't like that," she cackled.

I laughed. I couldn't help it. She looked dreadful, but she was still joking.

Kett appeared beside her, not looking much better.

"There's magic in the trees?" I asked.

"Yup," Kandy said. "They acted like it was poisonous or something. I think I got three of them."

Drake hastily withdrew his hand. He'd been about to pick up a piece of the shattered wood. "I've taken out two. I think. Sentinel? Jade?"

Warner shook his head. "Three or four maybe. It's difficult to tell."

"None for me," I spat with frustration. "They won't come near me."

"That leaves the heretic with what?" Drake asked. "Three or four shadow leeches?"

No one answered him.

"This isn't working, Jade," Warner said softly. "The werewolf and the vampire cannot continue."

"Shailaja is near," I said. "We're almost done. And if we can use the trees as weapons, then ..."

Warner shook his head, looking pointedly over my shoulder as if trying to force me to see something.

I turned back toward Kandy.

She shifted forward into a starter's crouch. Her glowing green eyes were fixed on Warner. "Says you, dragon," she growled, straightening as her shifter magic rolled around her once again.

But before Kandy could take on whatever form she was attempting to manifest, a shadow demon appeared between us, slamming into the green-haired werewolf's chest.

She screamed, arching forward on her tiptoes as if her heart had exploded.

I lunged, grabbing the leech's magic and ripping it from Kandy. Kett caught the werewolf before she could hit the icy stone floor. He swayed, almost losing his footing as he cradled her in his arms.

I held the shadow demon fast, seething with all the anger and frustration I was trying so hard to keep at bay.

"I'm done, Shailaja," I screamed toward the taste of carrot-cake-and-cream-cheese magic that was mocking me in the distance. "I'm done with the games and the manipulations."

Then I tore the shadow demon writhing in my grip to rags.

I ripped.

I shredded.

I destroyed its magic until it was a pile of nothingness at my feet.

"Jesus, dowser," Kandy muttered. "There's murder in your heart."

I locked eyes with my best friend. She hadn't protested the vampire's hold. As I stepped over the tattered demon, she didn't even lift her head.

"Maybe you should turn back," she said.

"I love you." I attempted to smile through the tears filling my eyes and spilling over my cheeks.

"Fuck you, Jade," Kandy snarled. "Fuck. Fuck. Fuck you."

I locked my gaze to Kett's. His eyes were bleeding. Actual blood, not simply the red of his magic. I looked past the blood and the red welts on his face, peering deeper into his icy core. "I love you."

Kandy grabbed me harshly, getting a fistful of curls along with my neck. She tugged me closer, pressing a fierce kiss to my forehead. The embrace was hard enough that I knew it would leave me bruised, but I took it gladly.

She released me. "Go," she said, unyielding and harsh. "I'll save the vampire."

I lifted my head, leaning across Kandy and pressing a kiss to Kett's ice-carved lips. I closed my eyes, breathing in his peppermint magic. I held it in my chest, refusing to exhale.

He brushed his thumb against my neck, checking my pulse. My heart beat once underneath his touch.

Then I opened my eyes.

They were gone.

A single sob ripped its way through my chest and out my throat.

"They will survive." Warner was standing behind me, but he didn't try to touch me or pull me away.

"Shailaja won't let them go," I whispered through the chokehold of my grief.

"They're not the endgame," Warner said. "You are. She wants you alone."

"Let's finish this," Drake said fiercely.

I lifted my arm, pointing in the direction we needed to go. Then I turned my back on my best friends and followed Warner and Drake through the last few rows of skeleton trees between the rabid koala and us.

The best way to distract Shailaja from Kandy and Kett was to stab her in the freaking heart. And I had just the knife for the job.

Chapter Thirteen

We found a second ornately carved door situated directly opposite the entrance — according to Drake, anyway. I had absolutely no sense of direction, which meant I would never find my way out of this place on my own. But that was okay. I wasn't sure that leaving under my own power was even going to be an option. Foiling Shailaja's plans, then walking away only to get lost would be a nice problem to have.

Except I couldn't taste the rabid koala's magic anywhere nearby, and the clean-edged holes that had been bored through one side of the door were giving me heart palpitations. Dozens of six-inch-wide stone circles littered the ground at our feet, discarded and useless like champagne corks. The scalloped-edged gaping hole in the door revealed a dark corridor leading deeper into the mountainside.

It had taken just about everything I had to rip enough magic away from the exterior door that I could crack through its stone. These pieces of granite screamed of precise, focused magic.

"You were right," Drake said, hunching over to span his hand across one of the discarded stone plugs. "The leeches were a distraction."

"She used her portal magic to bore through stone," I said. It was a mind-numbing idea. "Through stone. Solid stone. Spelled stone."

"Slowly," Warner said, sounding unimpressed. "And I doubt the warding here was as intricate as it was on the entrance to the atrium."

Drake straightened, stepping through the damaged doorway.

I tried to call him back, but I couldn't speak the words.

"Jade?" Warner's voice was distant.

I turned my head to him, scanning the dark night and the stone door as I did ... so, so slowly.

I was shutting down.

"Jesus," I murmured. "I'm having a panic attack."

"You don't appear to be panicking," Warner said.

"Don't laugh," I cried, suddenly sobbing and screaming at the same time. "Don't laugh at me! She can bore through stone! Through stone! That shouldn't be possible! Right? Not without a tool ... or a magical drill ... or something. What else could she bore through? And what about Kandy and Kett? What if the leeches —"

Warner grabbed my arms. I fought his grip, attempting to twist away. I needed to run. I had to run.

No.

First, I had to grab Drake. Then I had to run.

Warner was shouting, but I couldn't hear his words.

Drake stepped back through the door. His face was etched with worry. I was the one who was supposed to take care of him, not the other way around.

But I couldn't stop melting down ... I couldn't gain control of my limbs ... my brain was overloaded mush.

Then Warner was kissing me. His grip was brutal, punishing. His magic flooded my senses ... deep, dark chocolate with a hint of smoke in the finish, followed by sweet, explosive cherry, and topped with smooth, thickly whipped cream.

"You're not stone, Jade," he whispered. "You're not stone."

I wrapped myself around him, feeling the strength of his limbs and hearing the conviction of his words. Parting my lips, I thrust my tongue into his mouth. Holding him harder and rougher than I ever could have held anyone else I'd ever been intimate with.

Gradually, I became aware that I needed to be standing on my own two feet. I unwrapped my legs from him and stood. I loosened my embrace.

Warner responded in kind as he rubbed his thumbs across my cheeks. He wiped away my tears, placing teasing, light kisses on my lips.

"I'm sorry," I murmured.

"No," he said, stopping my apology with another all-encompassing, brain-scrambling kiss.

Then he stepped back from me and looked toward the door.

I followed his gaze.

Drake was standing in the rubble, his head bowed and partially turned away from us. His dark hair had fallen across his forehead. He looked utterly dejected.

A low fire began to burn in my belly. I stepped away from Warner, holding on to his hand until I had to let go. Then I took three deep breaths.

"Meltdown," I said. "Check."

Drake lifted his head, grinning at me.

I nodded as I looked back over my shoulder at Warner. "Thank you."

"Any time."

I chuckled. Crossing through the stone plugs littering the ground, I followed Drake through the hole bored in the door.

"Well," I said into the utter darkness stretching out before me. "Here's the tunnel I was expecting."

Drake laughed somewhere ahead of me.

I reached to my right, taking two tentative steps before my fingertips brushed against the wall. I waited, expecting the flavor of pear tea. But I couldn't taste anything. "The leeches have been here."

"Also as expected," Warner said behind me.

I spread my dowser senses along the wall, seeking out dormant magic. "Watch your eyes," I said. Then I pushed at the pinpoint of power I had sensed just above my head.

An amber light flared. I squinted up at it. The glow was emanating from the center of a sun embossed on the stone wall.

Warner grunted, shielding his face.

I reached farther, triggering more lights every few feet along the tunnel and illuminating Drake about a dozen steps ahead of us. Other than the stone light fixtures, the walls of the tunnel were bare, and constructed of smooth charcoal granite. The magical ice stopped at the threshold behind us.

"Installing lights always makes sense," I said flippantly. "Practically no one can truly see in the dark."

"Thank you, dowser," Warner said. "The leeches will have a difficult time sneaking up on us now." He palmed his knife as he stepped ahead of me.

We traversed the tunnel slowly and diligently, checking for magical traps every step of the way. The eight-foot-high passage curved and narrowed periodically, so that we couldn't see as far ahead as I would have liked. We spread ourselves single file about six feet apart, following the path cutting deeper and deeper into the heart of Jiuding Shan.

In the stillness — and despite the constant anticipation that the next curve would reveal the chamber that held the final instrument and Shailaja waiting for us — I began to replay all the thoughts that had given rise to my panic attack at the mouth of the cave.

We hadn't seen or felt another hint of the shadow demons since Kett and Kandy disappeared, and my dread grew with each step I took away from my best friends. What if the leeches had followed them? What if we weren't drawing them away?

Then there was Shailaja's ability to bore holes through stone.

I stopped walking. The corridor continued before me, its lights luring us ever deeper into the mountain.

Drake continued forward, his golden broadsword glinting as he turned to glance back at me.

"I've been here before," I murmured. "Again and again."

Warner looked back over his shoulder at me, concerned.

"What if this is it?" I asked him rhetorically. "What if this is life?"

"I don't understand." The sentinel glanced toward Drake. The fledgling had paused at the curve of the corridor a dozen feet ahead of us. Then he looked back at me.

I let go of my knife, feeling it slip into its invisible sheath at my right hip. I reached my hand toward him.

A frown creased his brow as he stepped back, taking my hand. I curled my fingers around his, feeling his strength.

When I was lost inside the golden magic of the portal, I'd felt trapped by that magic. Smothered. Now, I was deep within a mass of stone that felt as if it had always surrounded me ... physically and metaphorically.

Maybe I was doomed to repeat the same challenges — to learn the same lessons — over and over again. Maybe none of it was within my power to change.

Nothing was within my control ... except my own actions.

"I'm having an epiphany," I said.

"Right now?"

"Ask me again," I whispered, smiling up at him with my heart ready to burst. "Warner, ask me now."

He didn't even blink. He swept me up, twirling me around. Then he set me down, kneeling before me. "Jade Godfrey, I love you with every ounce of my being, with every drop of my magic. I would be yours till the end of my days. At your side. At your back. Whenever and wherever you'd have me. Will you marry me?"

"I will."

He straightened, rising to sweep me into a kiss.

I reached for him. My fingers brushed the hair just above his ears.

Then I tasted cinnamon. Shailaja.

"Warner!" I cried.

The sentinel shoved me hard enough to crack my ribs. Pain exploded in my chest as I flew backward, smashing into Drake and dragging him another twenty feet along the curve of the corridor.

Then the ceiling collapsed on Warner.

Let me be more specific.

Then the mountain collapsed on Warner.

Within all the destruction and ruin raining down around us, I felt the portal magic dissipate almost as quickly as it had appeared.

Shailaja must have set up some sort of magical delayed charge. Or maybe she had worked to slowly undermine the entire tunnel as we advanced. Instead of shoving the shadow demons through her miniature portals, she'd used them to bore out chunks of stone from the foundations of the passage, compromising its integrity.

I untangled myself from Drake's long limbs, heedless of everything else. I shoved the fledgling guardian away from me. Dust and rock cascaded off us.

I rolled forward onto all fours. I crawled over the edge of the cave-in, dragging myself to my feet. I could feel my ribs healing, leaving only a dull ache in place of cracked bones.

I ran the last few steps, climbing a mound of debris to press my hands against the pile of granite that now stood between us and the tunnel entrance.

I shoved at it.

Smaller rocks shifted, undermining my footing. But I didn't so much as dent the wall.

Scrambling for purchase, I slammed my shoulder and hip against the wall of jagged stones. I dislocated my shoulder in my grief-fueled effort. Pain streaked up my neck and into my right temple.

I hit the wall again, shoving my shoulder back into place with another burst of pain.

I wasn't going to break through with force. I wasn't strong enough.

I clawed my fingers at the rock, tearing my nails in an attempt to find a grip on any stone, any single piece. If I could move one, maybe it would shift the others.

But the jagged boulders were too large for me to move. Too difficult for me to grip.

My breathing was ragged, my heart a piece of lead in my chest when I finally stopped. I pressed my ear against the wall of rock.

I couldn't hear anything.

I couldn't taste a single drop of Warner's magic.

He had just stood there.

He could have grabbed me and run.

But he'd been so ... so stupid. So fucking stupid. Sacrificing himself. For me ... and Drake. He'd thrown me in a way that he knew would save both of us.

I stumbled back from the wall of stone. Then I froze, staring at that mountain of shattered rock that separated me from Warner.

I fell to my knees.

I would stay. I would watch. When Warner was ready, he would shift the rock himself. And I'd be there to help dig him out.

"Jade ..." Drake whispered from behind me. "We must continue. The oracle said it might come to this ... on the beach in Washington ... she said I might have to force you to continue."

I didn't listen. I wasn't interested in anything Rochelle had to say or anything she'd seen.

"Jade Godfrey!" Drake bellowed. "You will continue. You will get me close enough to lay my blade at the heretic's neck."

I screamed as I shot to my feet.

I screamed as if I were ripping out my heart and flinging it to the ground. I screamed a sharp, shattering shriek, filled with a dreadful magic so strong that it hit the wall of stone before me and cracked it.

The cave-in shifted, slumping to one side. Loosened rock tumbled down to strike my feet, bouncing up and battering my shins. It drove me back a few more steps.

Numbness flooded through my chest and my limbs. I welcomed the sensation.

I turned away.

I left my love behind.

Facing Drake, I held my hand out. "Give me your sword," I said.

His dark eyes were full of sorrow, and a promise of vengeance. He flipped the golden weapon, holding its hilt toward me without question.

I stepped forward to grab him by the wrist, seizing him with every ounce of strength I had.

He flinched, his eyes widening with what might have been the first hint of personal concern I'd ever seen from him.

Good. He needed to be wary.

Neither of us could stand against a dragon who could hold a guardian hostage. A dragon who could bore holes in stone and throw weapons through portals. Not apart and not together. Yet we were about to forge ahead, with everyone I loved scattered and battered and possibly even dead behind me.

I wrapped my hand around the hilt of Drake's broadsword. Pulling the weapon sharply toward me, I sliced his hand open, coating half the length of the blade with his blood.

He winced but didn't pull away.

Pumping my alchemist magic into the razor-sharp weapon, I snared every bit of magic in Drake's blood, holding it in place.

Loosening my grip on the fledgling guardian, I flipped the sword over, then ran the opposite edge of the blade along the palm of my left hand. I sliced open my own skin even as the wound on Drake's hand healed.

I raised the sword before me, drawing all the magic from our blood around it. I coaxed the power stored in my necklace up my arm and through my hand, then into the sword. Using that power as mortar, I wrapped every drop of the combined power of our blood around and along the blade. Sharpening it. Fortifying it. I whetted its golden edges with all the magic I could give it.

Drake's broadsword absorbed every drop.

"It's glowing," he whispered.

"Is it?" I asked. But I wasn't even remotely moved by the feat of magic I'd just performed.

My heart was nothing but a husk. My thoughts and feelings were dampened ... gone. I would continue. I would protect Drake as best I could. But only because there was nothing else left for me.

I flipped the sword in my hand again, offering it hilt first to Drake.

He wrapped his fingers around it reverently, lifting the weapon between us. A golden glow flared, flowing up the blade, then back down. "Thank you," he whispered.

I glanced down at the wound on my hand. It was already knitting together. I gathered my fingers into a fist.

"It won't be enough. Not against my mangled katana. The chakram."

Drake nodded. "It will be enough to give you an opening."

"So you'll sacrifice yourself before me too?" I laughed harshly.

"Why would I do anything different than what you do every day, Jade? Why would I give any less? Why would any of us?"

"I'm not a fan of being schooled by a fifteen-year-old."

"Sixteen today. And you never seem to not need it. You are blind to yourself."

I reached out, wrapping my arm around Drake's neck and shoulders in a tight clench. I pressed a harsh kiss against his temple. Then I released him, catching his dark-eyed gaze with mine.

"Let's go slay a dragon, then."

He nodded, slipping in behind me.

Striding forward in silent determination, we turned the corner only to see an archway at the far end of the tunnel.

We'd been a few dozen steps away.

Shailaja had perfect timing.

I would have hated her for it, but I was beyond all feeling.

Perhaps I was walking to my death ... or my re-birth, as Rochelle had called it.

And if these were the steps I was meant to walk? Well ... who was I to argue with destiny?

I was so damn tired of being scared of what was to come.

So I would surrender.

Right after I carved out Shailaja's freaking heart.

Drake and I stepped through the archway together, pausing and scanning the large chamber opening up before us.

No, not a chamber. A tomb. Though I'd never been in one — or even seen pictures of one this large — the stone sarcophagus placed along the far wall was an un-mistakable giveaway.

Yes, a sarcophagus. I pulled out the big words when my life was in imminent danger.

While the tunnel had been carved out of plain stone, the tomb of the phoenix was anything but. The image of an enormous orange and red raptor covered the wall behind the stone coffin. The bird's wings were spread in flight and its wicked talons poised as if to strike. Its multicolored feathers and scales were constructed out of some sort of jeweled tile mosaic. Its bright yellow eyes were trained on the archway where Drake and I stood.

The walls were constructed in similarly tiled fashion, though I wasn't sure of the material. The floor around the coffin was a mosaic in the form of a setting sun, whose horizon was the coffin's base. Its tiled rays radiated out toward the walls and the archway in alternating shades of light and dark orange.

Shailaja stood just to the right of the tomb, at the origin point of one of those inlaid sunrays. She'd changed into a fur-trimmed beige jacket and skinny-legged brown pants tucked into fur-lined boots. Apparently, she had been following us through the mountain though I hadn't picked up on her magic. She'd ditched the tote bag but was holding my mangled katana at her side. Three leeches clung to the tiled ceiling above her head, huddling between the amber lights.

Chi Wen sat on the sarcophagus, swinging his legs and smiling in our direction. I couldn't pick up a drop of his magic.

As his gaze settled on his mentor, Drake exhaled a soft sigh of agony, then fell silent.

The pain in that brief noise pierced my numb heart. "We don't know yet," I whispered to the fledgling. "We don't know that it's his doing that brought us here."

Drake didn't answer.

"Are you just going to stand there?" Shailaja asked.

Ignoring her, I shifted my head to get a better look at the one object that stood out even among all the glittery glamour of the crypt.

A single sparsely leafed branch speckled with pink-tinted white flowers hung suspended over the right side of the coffin. I recognized the distinctive pattern of leaves and flowers from the map. Apparently, we'd found the third instrument of assassination.

Though what flowers and leaves could do to a guardian dragon, I had no idea. Other than burn them, based on the first two instruments. But even Shailaja wasn't crazy enough to touch the branch. Poison maybe? Like Kandy thought the trees in the atrium might have poisoned the shadow leeches? The ramifications of the entrance of the shrine potentially being filled with leaves and flowers that could poison every single guardian dragon was chilling enough to crack the numbness that muted my thoughts and feelings.

I shook off the terrifying thought. I could only take care of what was in front of me right now.

Chi Wen and Shailaja were positioned an equal distance to either side of the branch. If I turned my head to just the right position and looked from the very corner of my eye, I could see that some sort of iridescent magic held the branch suspended. The same magic also appeared to be wrapped around the far seer.

"He's behind a ward of some sort," I said.

As Drake nodded, I could feel his relief.

"That's what happens when you try to get grabby with an instrument of assassination," Shailaja said snarkily, conveniently ignoring the fact that she'd grabbed an instrument herself and gotten her magic locked away for it.

"Is everything okay, far seer?" I asked.

Chi Wen responded with a cheerful nod.

"Where's Warner?" Shailaja asked crossly.

It took a concerted effort to not simply lunge across the room and rip her throat out, but I didn't answer her, scanning the tomb for possible exits and magical traps instead. I saw no sign of either.

The rabid koala tilted her head. One of her leeches stretched down from the ceiling to touch her shoulder. Her expression grew irate as she locked her gaze back on me. The leech squelched in on itself, shooting back up to the ceiling.

"And you just left him there?" Shailaja spat. "I suppose he got caught in it to save you. You are both so annoyingly weak. Standing around feebly waiting for the world to collapse on you. I expected better from the far seer's apprentice."

Drake started forward, but I slammed my arm across his chest, holding him back.

"Why cave in the tunnel," he whispered fiercely, "if we weren't supposed to be caught in it?"

Shailaja's only answer was a curled-lipped smirk.

"To block the exit," I said.

"To block the entrance, you twit." A smile spread across the rabid koala's face. "Never mind."

Then the shadow demons dropped from the ceiling and streaked toward us.

Drake and I raised our weapons, more than ready to slash the final three leeches to shreds. But, blowing past us like a hurricane of shadow, they exited into the tunnel instead of engaging us.

A smirk spread across my face. So apparently, I wasn't completely devoid of emotion yet. I still commanded all the ugly ones. Hate. Anger. Bitchiness.

"Only three?" I said tauntingly. "It's utterly stupid to send them away, Shay-Shay, whatever your master plan. Drake and I against you? Even with the katana, that isn't a fair fight. Not even remotely."

"The disgraced apprentice will come forward and relinquish his claim on the far seer's mantle." Shailaja ignored my snide remarks.

Drake lifted his sword.

"I don't think so," I said. "You don't have any right to call him out. No, we'll do this my way."

Tired of bandying words, I charged along the golden-orange ray that created a perfect path between me and my prey.

Shailaja looked surprised, then concerned.

Concerned?

The floor dropped out beneath my feet.

I tumbled down into darkness, slamming into solid, craggy ground and shattering my still-healing ribs. My skull cracked. A kaleidoscope of bright dots exploded before me.

I lay there for a second, catching my breath. Then, just as I decided I needed to keep moving, the hole caved in.

Darkness swallowed me.

When I awoke, I was in terrible shape. At least that was the thought screaming through my brain. My sense of self-preservation was babbling about staying still and waiting for help.

Then I heard grunts and footfalls above me.

I couldn't move. Not an inch. I wasn't even sure if my eyes were open or closed. My limbs were so, so heavy.

Maybe I was dead.

Then agony radiated through my head, chest, and limbs. So, unfortunately, I was still alive. Though probably barely.

One of the sources of footsteps above me fell so hard that the ground around and below me shook.

The pain in my head exploded, radiating back to front. I tried to scream, but I couldn't actually open my mouth or move my jaw.

Whoever had fallen scrambled to their feet. A clang of steel hitting steel sounded out.

I tried to focus through the pain. People were close enough that I could hear them, and my hearing wasn't that acute.

I couldn't move. But I might be able to dowse. I reached out with my magical senses, catching the taste of honeyed almonds and carrot cake before another avalanche of torment slammed through my body.

I pulled back the tiny tendril of magic I'd reached out with. I focused on my necklace. The chain was pressing against my chest so harshly that I thought it might have embedded itself into my ribs and collarbone. That had to be bad.

I could also feel my knife sitting on my right hip.

Okay, so I was armed. Just not remotely dangerous.

I thought about staying there. About just giving up. Then Drake fell again — I heard him cry out the second time — causing the ground underneath me to shift. I screamed, managing to voice a strangled sort of noise.

The fledgling guardian couldn't hold off Shailaja for long. No matter that he was destined to become the far seer, she still had years of training on him ... and my katana.

Ah, damn.

I attempted to sit up. My right arm and leg responded, but my left didn't.

Right. The walls of whatever pit I'd fallen into had caved in.

Slowly — painfully slowly — I began to feebly kick and shove at the stone that apparently covered me from my left shoulder to my left foot.

The sounds of metal striking metal got louder above me.

Drake grunted in pain.

Shailaja cackled.

Goddamn freaking rabid koala.

I kicked myself free of the stones that held me. Somehow, I managed to roll to my hands and knees. Then I threw up. And then I threw up again and again, until I had nothing else to evacuate.

My head swam. Blinking rapidly, I realized that I could see. The amber light from above was faintly permeating the pit I'd been half-buried in. My hands were covered in sticky blood, which didn't make any sense until I realized that must have been what I was throwing up. That couldn't be a good sign.

I pushed back into a sitting position, so that I could look up. I could see the ceiling of the tomb. I was maybe twenty-five feet below the floor.

The tomb apparently came with pit traps — one of which freaking Shailaja had set just for me. And I, not tasting anything magical in the area, had walked right into it.

My left leg and arm were shattered. I tried to ignore them, but the pain was almost incapacitating. I pulled more magic from my necklace and knife, coaxing it to flow through my body. My only hope was that it would stir up and accelerate my healing.

From above me, I heard Drake fall.

The ground heaved. The edge of the pit cracked and loose stone pelted my head and shoulders.

Then there was only silence.

Get up. Get up. Get up.

No one moved above me.

Ignoring my left arm and dragging my left leg, I reached for the rocks before me with my right arm. Pushing forward with my right leg, I attempted to climb out of the pit.

I got about halfway.

Shailaja peered down over the edge. "Ah, good. You're alive."

The rabid koala reached for me. Her fingers brushed my raised arm.

I threw myself away from her.

My left leg buckled, collapsing underneath me.

I fell back onto the craggy stone, cradling my left arm in an attempt to not injure it further.

Shailaja dropped down into the hole, reaching for me again.

I had nowhere to go.

I urged my knife into my right hand, but she pinned my wrist without effort. Then she grabbed my left arm, wrenching it up around her neck.

I screamed.

"Gadzooks," Shailaja said under her breath, continuing to lift me up and across her shoulders.

Agony flooded my entire being. I threw up blood again, splattering the rock wall as I tried to shift myself off the rabid koala's shoulders.

She pivoted, finding hand and footholds with no apparent effort. She climbed the craggy walls of the pit with me hanging across her shoulders.

The pain was too much.

I was dying.

Again.

Darkness took my eyes, then blotted the pain from my mind. I welcomed it.

Everyone else had fallen. Why not me?

Dying would make it all better.

And if I believed, if I could just believe in a world beyond this one, then maybe ... maybe ... I would see Warner again.

Damn it. I wasn't freaking dead.

Oh, God.

I was going to have to wake up.

Again.

I was going to have to fight.

Again.

I was lying on my back on a hard surface. My limbs were splayed out as if I'd been dumped unceremoniously onto the ground.

Right.

Shailaja.

I tried straightening my arms. Then when that failed, I simply pulled them closer to my torso. My left arm responded sluggishly, then exploded in a flood of painful tingling that set my entire left side on fire.

Moving was a bad idea.

I opened my eyes instead.

Warner was lying beside me.

Hope bloomed in my chest, pushing away the pain in a wash of euphoria. I didn't know what was going on, but we'd survived it all somehow ...

Except ... he wasn't moving. I wasn't even sure he was breathing. He was badly beaten ... almost crushed looking. And his magic was a faint note of smoke in the back of my throat ... like the memory of a taste.

Maybe we were dead. Maybe this was some sort of limbo.

No.

I could see the image of the phoenix rising on the back wall.

We were still in the tomb.

Shailaja nudged me in the ribs with her foot.

I screamed.

Yep, I could still feel pain.

She muttered something impatiently, then stalked off.

Though I really didn't want to, I turned my head away from Warner. Scanning the ceiling, I spotted the remaining three shadow leeches and clicked the pieces of Warner's appearance together. The demons had dug him out somehow. Or maybe they transported him as they did Shailaja.

I kept turning my head, catching sight of Chi Wen's sandaled feet still dangling off the sarcophagus.

Then I saw Shailaja standing over Drake at the far side of the room.

The fledgling guardian's chest rose, then fell. He was still alive.

"Do you think I have to kill the apprentice?" Shailaja called out to me. "For the ascension ceremony to work?"

Focusing every part of my body and mind, I attempted to leap up, race across the chamber, and rip her heart out.

The only result was a low growl and a mouthful of bloody spit.

Shailaja laughed at my feebleness. She deliberately pointed her finger at me, then pressed it to Drake's forehead. "Get up, Jade," she said. "I'm sorry about the collapsing floor. It was for the fledgling, not you. Tricky you. I thought you always let those more powerful lead."

I sat up. It hurt. I still couldn't use my left arm. I spat a mouthful of blood onto the pretty mosaic tiled floor. The bright red complimented the orange perfectly.

"That was Warner's idea ... him leading," I said. Shifting my weight onto my right leg and arm, I attempted to stand. "When Drake and I train, he always follows. So as not to impede my dowser senses."

Shailaja straightened, stepping away from Drake and widening her stance. She held my mangled katana loosely at her side.

"I really don't care," she said. "Your heroes are down. And if you don't want them dead, you will free the final instrument of assassination and aid in my ascension."

"You should care." I carefully shifted weight onto my left leg, testing it. It held, though barely.

"We're running tight on time, sweetling," the rabid koala said.

Then I lunged to the side, startling Shailaja enough that she raised the katana. Except I wasn't going for her.

I slammed my hand into the iridescent magic that surrounded the far seer. Then, in the hastiest bit of alchemy I had ever performed, I ripped it asunder. The flavors of pear and toasted grain filled my mouth even as the magic coursed through my limbs, burrowing into my arteries and veins.

The flowered branch fell, landing softly on the stone coffin.

I twisted around, fighting to force the foreign magic I held into my knife and my necklace. I raised my blade to meet the overhead blow I was expecting from Shailaja as she raced across the chamber toward me.

She kicked me in the gut instead.

I flew across the tomb, over the pit, and crashed into the far wall near the archway. I fell in a tangle of limbs, still too injured to be graceful about any of it.

I rolled over onto my belly. Looking up through the tangle of my curls, I tried to organize my thoughts.

Chi Wen slid off the coffin.

Shailaja shied away from him, raising the mangled katana before her.

But the far seer was watching me, not her.

I struggled to stand, knowing as I made it to my feet that I wasn't going to survive another hit.

I couldn't understand what the far seer was waiting for …

Then I realized.

Me. He was waiting for me.

And I had no idea what to do.

I looked at Shailaja.

The rabid koala was livid. She was wary of Chi Wen and completely pissed, all at the same time. She stalked back over to Drake, laying the edge of the katana at his neck.

"Dragons don't kill dragons," I said.

"They do when they're ascending," Shailaja sneered.

"No," I said. "That's by mutual agreement. Not force. Not trickery."

"We both know you're going to do this, alchemist. We both know you won't stand there and let me kill anyone." Then she turned just her head, glaring at Chi Wen. "Look at him!"

The far seer continued smiling cheerfully at me.

"He's gone!" Shailaja snarled. "He's walking around with all that power, and he's nothing. Useless. The more powerful I am, the more you are."

"No."

"We'll take Warner to Baxia. She's next in line to relinquish her mantle."

"He'd never do it."

"I swear I will kill him!" She pressed the blade to Drake's neck. As it had when it hit my father, it sliced through his skin with no effort.

I let go of my knife. It sheathed itself before it hit the ground. Tears began to slip unchecked down my cheeks.

Disbelief flitted across Shailaja's face. Then anger. She straightened. Spinning on her heel, she stomped across the chamber to stand over Warner.

"Fine," she said. "Him, then." But there was an edge in her voice as if she was convincing herself. "The sentinel is a worthy sacrifice."

I began to sob. Terrible, racking cries tore out of my hollow chest. My heart was in tatters, and my mind wasn't far behind. But I wouldn't do it. I wasn't going to hand Shailaja any more power. Warner wouldn't want me to.

"Goddamn you, Jade Godfrey. You will do this!"

"He's already dead …"

"What?"

"He's already dead to me!" I shrieked.

Shailaja threw the katana.

It spun toward me.

I took a deep breath, closing my eyes and reaching out with my dowser magic. I sought the stolen magic held within the mangled blade.

Then I claimed the darkness I had sealed in the weapon with my own blood. I claimed the magic of all the Adepts sacrificed by my sister. I acknowledged their deaths. I accepted responsibility for the creation of this dark blade, as I should have that night on the beach in Tofino.

I opened my eyes.

The sword heeded me, zigzagging away from the portal that Shailaja was in the process of opening.

Her jaw dropped.

The circle of folded steel spun toward me. I reached for it. I let the blade slice across my open palm, then twisted around to clamp my bloody fingers around the hilt. The weapon came to a halt in my hand.

I met Shailaja's surprised gaze. My face was sticky with the tears I hadn't bothered to wipe away.

Chi Wen grunted with satisfaction.

The rabid koala lunged sideways, sliding across the tiled floor and grabbing Drake's gold broadsword from where it lay beside the fledgling. Then she rolled to her feet, facing me with the pit trap between us.

It was my turn to smirk.

"What?" Shailaja snapped.

"That blade owes you no allegiance. It was forged for the fledgling."

"No matter what dragon weapon you hold, alchemist, I will always outclass you."

I snorted, slamming all the power in my grasp into the mangled katana. Under that onslaught, the blade unfurled. All the damage done to it when I'd twisted it around Sienna's neck unwrought itself, as the blade re-formed into its original twenty-eight inches of straight, strong steel.

"You stupid bitch," I said. "This is my freaking sword."

I shifted my right foot behind me, falling into a classic forward lunge pose as effortlessly as I'd claimed the pulsing magic of the katana. I leveled the blade at Shailaja, offering a challenge.

"And they call me dragon slayer now," I whispered.

Shailaja snarled.

I leaped forward, pushing up and over in an attempt to clear the pit between us. But I understood even before I'd completed the leap that she was faster and stronger than me.

Whether I'd reclaimed my katana or not, I wasn't going to land a single blow.

Still, I held the sword over my head, primed for a futile downward strike. Knowing that when that attack was thwarted, I was only leaping toward my own death.

That thought was a relief, actually.

Because what else could I do?

As I'd expected, Shailaja ducked underneath my strike. In my gamble to get there fast enough, I'd left myself open.

I waited for her to gut me.

Then Chi Wen appeared beside Shailaja. He laid his hand on the back of the rabid koala's head, as if to tousle her hair and congratulate her on an imminent victory.

She screamed as the far seer's golden-white, spiced magic flared within her eyes.

The rabid koala convulsed, lowering her blade and arching forward and upward, directly into the path of my strike.

My katana sliced off her head.

I hit the ground hard, landing on my weak left leg. I collapsed. Crashing into the far seer's legs, I felt my ribs snap — again. Or maybe it was my spine. The sensation was like slamming into two steel poles.

I screamed. My vision blackened from the pain for a moment. But I regained my sight in time to watch Shailaja's headless body fall to the floor in front of me. Blood flooded from the ghastly wound that was her neck.

I was still screaming. I couldn't stop. Screaming with the terror of what I'd done, and of the life I'd snuffed out. It was Chi Wen who silenced me, yanking me up onto my knees.

"Hurry, hurry, Jade Godfrey. Hurry, alchemist."

"What?" I mumbled through the pain of being hauled up so abruptly.

"Take the magic now. Take the magic. Claim your kill."

"What?" I shrieked.

"You must take the magic of the daughter of Pulou-who-was. It is your destiny."

"What?" I repeated a third time. And then my brain finally clicked in. "No!"

"You will not allow such a gift to go unclaimed. Take it now, alchemist."

"You've seen this? You see me taking her magic?"

Chi Wen gently turned me, so that I was looking at him instead of Shailaja's beheaded corpse. Even with me on my knees, he wasn't much more than a foot taller than me.

Then I realized he wasn't moving me with his hands on my shoulders. He was moving me with his mind.

Utter terror filled my already overwhelmed brain.

"I will see this," Chi Wen said simply.

"What do you mean?" I forced the words out, trying to push past the horror in an attempt to understand what was happening.

"Do this, alchemist," he insisted. "You must not allow this power to fade."

Completely disoriented but still attempting to obey the far seer's concerned urging, I grabbed the magic that coursed within Shailaja's blood. I tried to channel that intense power into my necklace and knife, then into the katana.

I failed.

"The sword can't hold any more," I cried. "My necklace, my knife … I can't."

"You, Jade Godfrey. You are the vessel to hold the power of the daughter of the mountain."

"No."

"This is how you ascend. This is how you become."

"Become what?"

The far seer crouched down before me. He ran his hand through the blood pooling by Shailaja's severed neck. "If you were a fledgling guardian, you would need to actually drink her blood and consume her heart and brain."

My stomach squelched with revulsion. "But I'm not a fledgling guardian."

"You are not. And as such, the physical consumption is not necessary for you."

"I can't do it," I mumbled, still not completely understanding what he was asking of me. "I won't."

Chi Wen lifted his bloody hand, catching my chin and forcing me to look in his eyes. I waited for his brain-searing magic to destroy what was left of my mind.

"When I was a boy, my mother was the far seer," Chi Wen said. "She saw me, as I see Drake." His guardian magic rolled across his eyes, yet I knew his vision wasn't clouded. He saw most clearly in those moments when he used his seer powers.

"The day my mother saw me no longer was the day she knew she was to relinquish her guardian mantle."

"I don't understand, far seer. We must call the other guardians ... Drake ... Warner ..."

He released my chin, wiping a single bloody finger across my face. Then he dipped down to Shailaja's blood and back up again, making another pass on my other cheek. It was as if he were applying slashes of war paint. He was painting me with Shailaja's blood.

"That is not how I see Drake."

"I don't understand ..."

Then the far seer's magic flooded my mind, wiping out everything in its path ... my thoughts ... my memories ... myself.

I was an empty shell.

Then Chi Wen showed me ... he showed me Drake.

Drake older ... but not old enough.

Drake was standing over Haoxin. The petite guardian was lying across a gold altar surrounded by nine ornate chairs, arrayed in a semicircle.

"No ..." I moaned.

Drake was lifting a jewel-crusted chalice filled with blood. He looked across Haoxin's body at someone I couldn't see ... someone even Chi Wen's sight couldn't see. The fledgling's face was etched with fear.

A five-colored silk braid was wrapped around Haoxin's neck.

"No!" I cried.

Chi Wen released his hold on my mind. The tomb of the phoenix swam back into view.

"That can't ... happen ..." I was dizzy and so, so sick. I wasn't sure if I was sitting or standing, but I could see Drake still lying on the ground just beyond Shailaja. The pool of her blood was slowly creeping toward him.

"You can unmake what you have seen," Chi Wen said. "I'm sorry, Jade, but you must hurry."

Something stung my right wrist. I looked down to see blood there, then to watch the far seer drag my jade knife across my left wrist, then up my forearm. "No," I muttered. "That's mine. That's my knife. You can't be touching it without my permission."

"Now ... become."

He wasn't listening to me. He sliced my right wrist and my arm again.

Why wasn't I moving? Why wasn't I stopping him?

He was killing me ... with my own knife.

Oh, God.

He was still in my head.

The magic in Shailaja's blood tingled against my face ... then it began to itch ...

Then it burned.

"Ow ..."

I couldn't do anything but speak. I couldn't wipe the blood from my face or move away from the far seer.

"No," I said again as I watched blood pour from my slit wrists. "This is so wrong."

"Who are you to say so, fledgling?"

"Me. I'm me."

"Yes," Chi Wen said, sounding overly satisfied. "Now you are you."

"This was my destiny?"

"It is now. If you are to survive, you have to take it all, alchemist. Every last drop."

Then he nudged me forward — not with his hand or foot, but with his mind.

I fought back. "Magic isn't blood ..." I screamed the words as I rose stumbling to my feet. Somehow, I managed to shove the far seer away from me.

He grunted, pleased and full of satisfaction.

My head swam. I was standing, but I didn't think I could move without falling down again. It was too late. I'd lost too much blood. I was too badly injured.

"Take the magic. Make it your own," Chi Wen whispered. "Or die. I cannot force you, Jade. But do this. For Drake. For you."

As if woken by the far seer saying his name, the fledgling guardian groaned and turned his head toward me.

I looked over at Warner. His chest rose as he drew breath. He was alive. He would live … without me …

"I don't want to die," I murmured.

Chi Wen pressed my knife into my right hand. I took it. Then he pressed the katana into my left. I took that too. Though I wasn't sure why I needed them.

"Take it all, dragon slayer," Chi Wen coaxed. "You will need it to stand before your next foes. You will need it to stand at Drake's side. You will need it to alter the future."

So I took it. I reached out for the dragon magic of the woman I'd murdered. I took it for my own.

I sought out the power swirling within the blood at my feet. Then I pulled at it. It rose eagerly, coating my feet, ankles, and calves in a golden sheen. I pulled it higher, coating myself with it as I'd seen Shailaja do twice. I gathered all the rabid koala's magic, along with the magic in my own blood that Chi Wen had drained from me.

I wrapped the power from every last drop of blood around me like a full-body shroud … like a spinning net that sparkled with gold. It settled on my skin, then was absorbed into it.

I was the abomination I had always been accused of being.

"Forget now." Chi Wen brushed his fingers across my cheek.

...

...

...

"Forget what?"

A massive boom sounded through the archway, cracking the tile mosaic on the wall and shaking the ground underneath our feet. I stumbled away from the far seer, falling to my hands and knees, then crawling the rest of the way to Warner as more stone exploded somewhere deep within the tunnel.

A plume of rock dust flooded into the crypt. Coughing and barely able to hold myself up on my arms, I tried to shield Warner's nose and mouth with my body. Just as I'd triggered the earthquake and flood in Hope Town and the centipede in Peru, I assumed I was about to face the final security measure of the shrine. Though I hadn't tried to remove the instrument. Maybe compromising the magic that had been holding the instrument was enough.

Then the fire breather walked through the archway. I thought Suanmi had been scary in cashmere and braids. But she was a much more terrible and awesome sight in shiny black samurai gear. Her dark hair was slicked back in a tight bun. Her katana was easily a foot longer than mine.

Her gaze swept the chamber, taking in the sight of all that had happened. Then that gaze turned toward me. "What have you done?"

A portal blew open behind her. And the seven remaining guardian dragons stepped through its golden magic into the tomb behind the fire breather, fanning out around the pit. The portal remained open at their backs.

I'd been praying that the guardians would show up and save the day. And here they were.

Except I had a sinking feeling that I was now the big bad they had come to save the world from.

Qiuniu went to Drake, crouching to briefly touch his neck. Then he straightened with a nod in Suanmi's direction.

Pulou stepped over Shailaja's body without a second glance, sweeping the instrument of assassination off the sarcophagus and into a mesh bag constructed out of platinum and cinched with jeweled ties. The entire side of the treasure keeper's face was badly scarred.

Yazi, appearing fully healed, immediately stepped toward me, but Chi Wen shuffled into his path, lifting his hand to stop the warrior. Frowning, my father stepped back to fall into line with the other guardians. They turned, looking toward me.

Not knowing what they wanted, I struggled to my feet and attempted to bow.

No one spoke.

The pit and Shailaja's decapitated body stood between them and me.

"Please," I whispered. "Healer ... the sentinel ..." The combined magic of the guardians was wreaking havoc on my senses. I was injured and overwhelmed.

Hell, I'd just murdered someone.

Qiuniu looked to Chi Wen. The far seer raised his hand a second time.

I felt my grip weaken, and I lost hold of my katana. It hit the floor. I couldn't find the strength to pick it back up.

So I just stood before the nine most powerful beings in the world. I'd done so before, but this time, each of them was arrayed for battle with dragon armor and weapons. Swords ... knives ... bows ... Jiaotu carried two deadly axes. I was pretty sure I couldn't have lifted either one of them.

Jesus.

Their power flooded the chamber, blowing through and around me.

"May I present Jade Godfrey, alchemist, wielder of the instruments of assassination, dragon slayer," Chi Wen said, bowing formally in my direction. "We have been awaiting her awakening."

No 'granddaughter of Pearl Godfrey' ... no 'warrior's daughter' ... no 'treasure keeper's alchemist' ...

Just me. Me and all the terrible I was capable of.

Dragon slayer.

Drake sat up with a groan, rubbing the back of his head. "What did I miss?"

I started laughing. I couldn't help myself. I felt hysteria burble up to override my terror and pain.

The magic of the guardians continued to weave in and around me. They stood arrayed before me, armed to the teeth.

They were the nine most powerful beings in the world. And they ... paused.

Paused.

As weak and terrified as I was, I gave them pause.

Then, without a word or a glance exchanged between them, their guardian magic finally broke through the shielding I was desperately trying to hold against it. Their power boiled around me, causing me to lose my grip on my knife.

I swayed.

I was going to die. Again. Or maybe I had already done that. I was losing track.

The far seer stepped forward and swept me into his arms. He was at least seven inches shorter than me, but it was like I weighed nothing to him.

He held me as if presenting me to the rest of the guardian nine.

I continued to fight the onslaught of guardian magic. I lost. Darkness folded around me.

"Dragon slayer," the far seer repeated, utterly satisfied.

I'd been set up.

I'd been manipulated every step of the way. Perhaps right from the first moment Pulou had handed me the map and sent me to collect the instruments of assassination.

But did it even matter? I wasn't sure I would survive long enough to find out.

Darkness shuttered my eyes, then my mind.

There was nothing I could do about it.

Chapter Fourteen

I remembered killing Shailaja.

I remembered taking her magic and filling my necklace, my knife, and my katana to capacity ... or at least to their limits as I understood them.

I remembered talking to Chi Wen. He had showed me ... something wrong, or bad, or dangerous. Something about destiny ... and Drake? But it felt distant and unreal now. A story I could barely recall ...

I remembered gathering and absorbing Shailaja's magic for myself instead of allowing all her power to fade.

I just couldn't remember exactly why. Except ... maybe we'd unmade the future.

I woke up.

I was surrounded by white.

The ceiling, walls, and floor of the room I was in were constructed out of white tiles, each about eighteen inches square. They looked like some sort of metal, and were glowing softly. No doors, no windows, and no furniture decorated my white box.

I sat up.

I was wearing white brushed-cotton drawstring pants, a white cotton tank top, and a long-sleeved white cotton scooped-neck T-shirt. My feet were bare. My toenails — which had been prettily painted before — were naked now. No knife, no necklace, and no katana.

And not a drop of magic.

I couldn't taste anything. I couldn't feel or see any sort of energy. I wasn't sure if something was wrong with me, or if something built into the white room was stripping all the magic away.

I pushed my sleeves up. Then I pulled up each leg of my pants. My arms and legs were clear. I didn't have a bruise on me. I didn't feel any pain …

Yet something was wrong.

I rolled onto my feet easily enough … but not as quickly or smoothly as I'd become accustomed to moving since my dragon training started. The floor felt neither cold nor warm, as if it was somehow heated to my exact body temperature.

I scanned the walls, looking for a door. But the white room was a perfect square box, twenty tiles across in all directions.

It was a prison cell.

That realization hit me hard, deep in my gut. A flush of knee-weakening fear washed through my body.

They had taken my clothes.

They had taken my weapons.

They had taken my magic.

And locked me away.

Alone. With nothing and no one. I didn't even know if Warner was okay … or if Kandy and Kett had survived … or Drake …

A terror like nothing I'd ever experienced before threatened to choke me. I wanted to scream … to lash out against the walls ... to pound the floor. I was shaking from my need to freak out.

But I wasn't going to give them the satisfaction.

I sank to my knees, then shifted back into a lotus position. I closed my eyes and breathed.

I was alive. I was whole. I wasn't going to break down. I would figure everything else out. They might control my body, but they couldn't control my mind ...

Control my mind ...

Had Chi Wen done something to my head?

I pushed the thought away. I focused on my breathing. What was done was done. I couldn't change it.

I slept.

I dreamed of Warner, of chocolate cosmos ... and of laughter.

When I woke, I was curled on the floor with my head on my arm. I sat up to discover that my arm had fallen asleep. I couldn't remember the last time something so benign had happened to me.

I laughed at the sensation of my limb reawakening. That rush of almost-painful tingling just beneath the skin.

Had they really taken my magic? Was I wholly human now?

Either way, I really needed to pee.

"A bathroom would be nice." I spoke out loud, wondering if someone was watching me. If so, I'd been a rather boring subject so far.

One floor tile in the corner of the room suddenly rose to become a white cube. I stood, crossing to stare down at it suspiciously. The inside of the cube was shaped similarly to a toilet, but it was made out of the same metal that tiled the floor, walls, and ceiling. It didn't hold any water, nor was it equipped with any sort of flushing mechanism I could see. And though it had appeared out of nowhere — just like magic — I still couldn't taste or feel a single drop of energy emanating from it.

"You can't be serious," I said. Again, speaking to no one. "What about freaking toilet paper?"

No response.

Damn it.

I really needed to go, though.

And … apparently an invisible bidet came installed in the magical toilet, as I discovered when I was done.

Yikes.

With that taken care of, I wandered back into the middle of the room, wondering what else I could demand from it.

"How about some food?" I asked.

Nothing happened. Maybe I needed to be specific?

"Chocolate? Preferably a 70 percent single origin cacao from Madagascar or Ecuador?"

Again, nothing.

"Cupcake? Cake of any kind? Icing?"

I spun around. The room ignored me. Or maybe the plan was to slowly starve me to death. At least my body would give out before my mind … I hoped.

"Jesus, not even a piece of freaking fruit? An apple or a banana or an orange?"

A white platter constructed out of the same metal as the tiled room appeared at my feet. It held a Granny Smith apple, a mandarin orange, and a banana.

Apparently, the room got to decide what qualified as food. Or it was some shot at my weight. No matter what dragon genes I dragged around every day, I was never going to be skinny — and I was seriously okay with that. "A freaking prison should just keep its snotty nose out of my business."

Yeah, I was mouthing off to a cube.

I ate the banana first. It was delicious. So were the apple and the orange. The flavor of the fruit was most likely heightened by my hunger, and by the fear of being locked away alone for any extended period of time.

As I ate, I tried to lift the platter from the floor but couldn't. Either it was seriously welded there, so that I couldn't use it as a potential weapon, or I was really, really weak.

The platter disappeared with my discarded peels and apple core the instant I swallowed my last bite.

So ... that was done.

What the hell else was I going to do?

I paced.

I slept.

I attempted to meditate.

I thought I might be going slowly insane ...

What if the room didn't actually exist? What if it was a product of my mind? But again, I really didn't want to give whoever was watching the satisfaction of seeing me freak out, so I kept my thoughts tightly contained. Though I caught myself talking out loud more than once.

What felt like eons passed, interrupted only by another summoning of the disconcerting toilet and the appearance of a bowl of tasty ramen. When I ordered the second time, I figured out that the room would present the food normally served in the nexus. But then, another platter appeared without my requesting it.

A silver ice bucket with a lid, a silver spoon, a chocolate bar, a bottle of nail polish, a stick of peppermint candy, and a handwritten note sat on the platter.

My heart was beating wildly as I sank down before the offering, first reaching for, then reading the note.

I recognized the barely discernable scrawl even before I read the words.

We have all survived.
I won't let them keep you. — W

My hand was shaking as I reached for the lid of the ice bucket. Inside, packed in dry ice, was a half-liter carton. The waxed cardboard container looked identical to the tubs that Mario's Gelati used to custom pack their in-store flavors. I snatched the container — careful to not touch the dry ice — and pried the cardboard lid off.

It was my favorite flavor. Black-forest-cake gelato.

Happy tears leaked out from the corners of my eyes, but I ignored them. Delicately running the edge of the silver spoon through the smooth, creamy top of the gelato, I made sure to scoop up a bit of each flavor — vanilla, chocolate, and cherry. Then I reverently slipped that cold, creamy goodness into my mouth.

The taste of Warner's magic, minus the smoky finish, flooded my tongue. I still hadn't figured out how to duplicate that flavor combination in a cupcake. Not yet, anyway.

I brushed the tears from my cheeks and ate half the carton, thinking of nothing else other than Warner. His grin, his stubbornness, his fierceness ... how even when he was tender with me, I could feel the strength that lay underneath.

I wasn't alone at all.

Then I cracked the chocolate bar — Amedei Madagascar Cru, 70 percent cacao. Its ripe red-berry finish was similar to Kandy's magic, but without the bitter edge.

The peppermint stick was predominately white, with a simple swish of red. It looked handmade. I held it underneath my nose and inhaled Kett.

Sucking on the tasty candy in between squares of chocolate, I took my time painting my fingers and toes with the gold OPI nail polish. The color — *Rollin' in Cashmere* — was from a two-year-old collection, and must have taken some effort to find. It was also almost the same color as Drake's magic.

Apparently, my boyfriend knew me freaking perfectly.

Correction … my fiancé knew me perfectly.

Huh. That was going to piss off some people — though who exactly would be against us would be interesting to discover.

I ate the rest of the gelato while I waited for my nails to dry.

I had just licked the last of the creamy goodness from my spoon when the platter disappeared. The bottle of nail polish and the remainder of the chocolate and candy went with it.

"What the hell?" I yelled at the white tiled ceiling.

Then a door slid open behind me.

I shot to my feet, whirling around and holding the silver spoon between me and whoever had appeared at my back.

Chi Wen stood in the doorway. He was clothed in his typical gold-embroidered white robes and gold sandals, but at least he had the decency to drop his ever-present Buddha-inspired smile.

I couldn't see anything but a solid white wall in the short corridor behind him.

"You set me up." I brandished the spoon in his direction.

"Events were to transpire that, when given a slight correction, resulted in a better outcome," he said.

"For whom?" I asked. "You?"

"Drake. You." The old Asian man was completely calm in the face of my rising anger. "And, ultimately, the guardians. Though I'm not completely satisfied on that front. It is difficult to discern the events that weave around the nine. You, Drake, and the sentinel provide some clarity for the moment."

"You made me murder someone." But even as I pronounced that as a fact, I knew it wasn't true. "Shailaja was destined to die?"

Chi Wen nodded. "By the warrior's blade."

"And you thought I was a fine substitute?"

"I cannot cause things to happen. I can only make suggestions."

"Like Pulou giving me the map."

Chi Wen smiled.

"Like Suanmi persuading me to unlock the last layer of Shailaja's magic."

"That last one was … difficult."

"And how do the other guardians feel about your manipulations?"

Chi Wen tilted his head, thinking. "They are not all yet convinced of the necessity. But they understand that only I see."

He stepped away from the door. It remained open.

I hesitated. And for a brief second, I thought about staying in the white room. I thought about how I deserved to be punished for my actions. Whether or not I'd been manipulated, no one had forced me to do anything. I'd been presented with options and I'd made choices.

That was life, wasn't it?

It was safe in the white room. Safe and clean and easy.

"You are expected, Jade Godfrey," Chi Wen called from somewhere off to the left of the door.

I crossed to the opening. I couldn't see any hinges or casings or pockets that the door would slide into when opened. The tiles that had been there before were simply missing, creating an opening large enough to walk through.

I glanced to the left. I was standing at the end of a white corridor. About a dozen white-tiled doors lined either side of the gold-carpeted hall.

Still holding the spoon before me, I stepped onto the plush carpet and instantly tasted dragon magic. I was in the nexus — or someplace created with the same magic that had birthed the nexus.

I turned down the hall, tasting Chi Wen's magic wafting down the corridor.

The door to the white room reappeared behind me, sealing it closed.

I wandered after Chi Wen. With each step that took me farther away from the room, I felt myself becoming stronger, as if my magic had been dampened before and was now flooding back.

By the time I saw Chi Wen open the intricately carved, Asian-inspired, dark wooden door at the end of the corridor, I realized that I felt … different somehow. I felt stronger, like my own magic was … embedded within me. Not just simmering somewhere, waiting to be called forth and utilized.

"I'm … changed," I whispered.

Chi Wen glanced back at me with a nod. "Transformed by the power of the daughter of the mountain running through your veins. As expected."

"Expected by you, maybe."

Chi Wen grinned, then gestured for me to precede him through the door.

I stepped through into the chamber of the treasure keeper. The massive piles of artifacts and gold coins, along with the onslaught of magic, were a dead giveaway.

Except none of it felt quite as intense as before. Even without my necklace, I was able to walk across the cool floor without feeling overwhelmed. Though I still had the urge to snatch up random magical objects and mess with their magic.

Once a magpie, always a magpie.

I paused. I wasn't sure what I was walking away from — or what I was moving toward. Either way, I needed a moment.

Beside me, Chi Wen shifted back into my peripheral vision. He was just standing, staring ahead. Waiting.

Waiting for what? For someone to come around the far pile of treasure? Or waiting for me? Maybe for me to slot certain missing pieces together in my head? Maybe for the questions I hadn't yet formed?

"What was in the sarcophagus? Who, I mean?" I asked without really knowing I was going to say anything at all.

"It was empty."

"What does that mean?" I whispered. "That the phoenix has risen?"

"If she has, she is hidden from my view. But that is not for you to fear."

"And the instrument? The flowers and leaves? Are they poisonous?"

"A good guess."

"So you really know nothing?"

Chi Wen chortled. "Perhaps you are asking the wrong questions, dowser."

I thought about that for a moment. "Was it like … golden fire?" I whispered, recalling what Rochelle had told me in the cramped confines of the Brave. "Was I washed away in a fire of gold? Reborn?"

Chi Wen looked at me. The white of his far seer magic flared in his eyes.

I didn't flinch at the sight. I didn't feel fear curling in my belly at the thought of being shown a future I couldn't control. I didn't desperately want to be anywhere else but near him.

"Yes," he said. "Though 'reborn' is a simplification."

"It doesn't sound simple to me."

"You are young." He patted my shoulder, then said, "You go that way." He pointed ahead of us. Then he did his old-man shuffle off to the left, slipping between two piles of treasure that I swore hadn't been separate piles a moment before.

"At least tell me you're done with me," I called after him.

"I am not your concern, Jade," he called back. "And you are not mine. Take the gift. Be strong. Love who you love. The rest will fall into place as it will."

And with that oblique-yet-somehow-completely-clear pronouncement, he turned out of my line of sight.

I took the path he'd pointed out to me. For the first time in a long while, I felt that every step I took was by choice.

I was also fairly certain I knew where I was going. And who would be waiting for me.

I might have meandered on the way. Not deliberately. But I was surrounded by so many pretties that I couldn't help but brush my fingers against all their different flavors of magic as I passed. I'd felt so alone in the white room, without a single taste or glimmer of magic. It was a terrible punishment for any Adept. Which was most likely the point of the prison.

Of course, I might have just been feeling pissy because I could taste my father's and Pulou's magic ahead. Apparently, absorbing a crapload of power didn't make me any less of a brat.

As I rounded the final pile of artifacts that separated me from whatever awaited me in the core of the chamber, I remembered Warner saying that the treasure keeper kept more than just treasure. I felt slightly sickened, wondering how many of the other cells along the hall had contained prisoners. Then I wondered who exactly would be deemed dangerous enough to be locked in a guardian prison.

Most Adepts were overseen by the Convocation, or the Conclave, or whatever organization governed their type of magic. Even Sienna hadn't been a big enough threat to garner attention from the guardian nine. Well, not until she'd unleashed a demon horde on Vancouver Island. And even then, it was Yazi who'd come. Not Haoxin, though it was her territory. Which probably meant my father had come for me. Not Sienna at all.

So, again, who was so powerful that they had to be locked up in a magic-dampening prison hidden somewhere in Antarctica and guarded by one of the nine?

Um, yeah. That was one of those thoughts best confined to my 'never needed to know' list.

Pulou and Yazi were waiting for me beside the stone table where the sentinel spell had been stripped from Warner. My jade knife, my necklace, and my katana were laid out on that altar. The katana was sheathed in the flower-etched black leather case that the sword master had given me. I had been assuming it was long gone, swallowed by the raging sea in Tofino when I fell to Sienna.

The treasure keeper stood slightly to the left, with the warrior slightly to the right, both of them framing the tableau of the magical items on the altar.

The chamber bore no evidence of the fight with Shailaja. The marble floor that had cracked underneath the fallen guardians was unblemished.

Pulou and Yazi were glowering at me as if I were a naughty puppy. So I glowered back at them. The scars that had marred Pulou's face in the shrine had disappeared.

Then, realizing I was still holding a silver spoon like a weapon, I tucked the utensil behind my back, cursing the fact that I didn't have any pockets.

My father fought a smirk for just a moment.

"Yazi has secured a majority vote for your release," Pulou said. His British lilt was more clipped than usual. "A full council will be convened, and you, Jade Godfrey, will stand trial for the death of Shailaja, daughter of the mountain."

"I won't hold my breath."

"If it were solely up to me, you would have been contained until the nine could be gathered once more."

"Yeah? Who were the five yea votes?" I asked, vaguely surprised at my own capacity to be glib. "It's always good to know who has my back ... you know, like how I had yours when I stopped Shailaja from murdering you. Unless she scrambled your brain so completely you can't remember that."

My father chortled, then coughed to cover his laughter. "You are released under the guardianship of Haoxin, Chi Wen, Qiuniu ... Suanmi, and me."

I didn't miss the pause before he said the fire breather's name.

"You aren't to enter the nexus without invitation or permission," Pulou said.

"You can keep it. It clashes with my lifestyle. As in, I prefer to stay alive."

"On the subject of Warner Jiaotuson ..."

An insane grin spread across my face. I could actually feel the crazy in it. In me. Maybe I hadn't walked away from murdering Shailaja — or from the white room — with my mind wholly intact. Epic anger and frustration seethed behind my expression. I had wondered who would be against the idea of Warner and me. Apparently, my former mentor and boss topped the list.

The treasure keeper paused, as if he was rethinking whatever he'd been about to say.

"My consent remains unaltered," Yazi said. His tone was even and nonconfrontational. "Not that the sentinel would heed any directive. I believe he has made that exceedingly clear in the last two weeks."

Pulou's jaw clenched. His large hands curled into massive fists.

"What do you mean?" I said, suddenly uncertain. "I've been in that room for two weeks?"

"No," Yazi said. "Only since you've awoken. Your healing was extensive and took the bulk of that time."

"Your stolen magic was incompatible with your own," Pulou spat.

"The healer believes you simply hadn't had enough time to absorb it fully," Yazi said. An edge was creeping into his even tone.

I eyed the treasure keeper. "You put me in that box."

"I did."

With our gazes locked, tension built between us. I could feel the weight of it in my heart. I had saved his life. I couldn't understand the hate he was pouring my way.

"You may go," the treasure keeper finally said.

"Sure." I shrugged to cover my frustration and confusion with nonchalance. "I'll just collect my things."

I stepped forward, reaching for my necklace and knife on the altar.

Pulou moved to block me. "Your magical artifacts have been collected, and will be held pending your trial."

His words threw me completely off balance. I looked to my father for clarification.

He nodded. "A condition of your release."

Anger overtook my confusion and frustration. I spun on my heel, ready to flee the room.

Then I paused.

It was my freaking necklace. My knife.

Mine.

I turned slowly, raising my chin and locking my gaze to the treasure keeper's again. "I've been manipulated and used. By you."

"It is you who has colluded against me, alchemist."

"Don't be a freaking moron," I sneered.

Pulou flinched, then lifted his hand slightly to the side. He was showing me that he was armed with his wicked blade.

"Treasure keeper," Yazi said, aghast.

"You would strike me down unarmed?" I asked.

My father took a step away from Pulou. "Of course he would not, Jade." Then to the treasure keeper, he said, "My friend, my daughter is young. Perhaps even disrespectful. But she is upset."

"She is dangerous," Pulou said.

All my frustration and anger was boiling in my belly. I could feel my chest and face flushed with it. If I was going to be condemned — or even face death — for something that had to be done, I wasn't going to do it unarmed.

I lifted my arms, reaching for my magic. Reaching for those items that didn't belong under glass, lock, or key. My creations weren't going to be tossed into the treasure keeper's garbage pile.

My knife appeared in my right hand, already raised against the treasure keeper. Its invisible sheath twined around my hip and thigh.

My necklace settled across my collarbone, unfurling as one long loop around my neck and over my breasts. I didn't have time to loop it a second time and get the chain out of my way, though. Because as it settled, the treasure keeper's stance shifted.

He was going to attack me.

My father stepped forward. Not between us or blocking the treasure keeper, but a step ahead — so he could turn and face Pulou. Physically indicating that he was firmly on my side. Yeah, my demigod dad had my back. I was going to have to open his Christmas present now.

My katana appeared on my back. I felt it settle across my shoulder in its leather sheath.

Pulou paused.

Then, inexplicably, the sound of creaking metal rang out from somewhere behind the altar.

A pile of treasure there collapsed.

My father and the treasure keeper spun to face the avalanche. Two more mountains of treasure followed suit.

Gold, silver, and platinum relics collapsed in against each other. Swords, bowls, amulets, and untold other types of magical artifacts crumpled in waves of bright metal and glimmering jewels, first blocking, then erasing the passageways behind the stone altar.

Three more items flew toward me. I didn't know their intent, or whether it was some sort of attack. But even as I stumbled back, I reached out toward them with my dowser senses. The taste of their magic flooded my senses. Moss and honeysuckle ... metal ... and pear tea.

Jesus.

The treasure keeper ducked as all three of the instruments of assassination blew by him.

They drove directly for me.

And all I could do to stop them was to claim them. Once and for all.

"Mine," I whispered, opening myself to their sweet, deadly magic.

They slammed into my chest. All three at once.

"Jade!" my father roared.

I staggered back, my sternum feeling as if it had imploded.

But I didn't fall.

I ensnared the moss-, metal-, and pear-flavored magic. I fused it with the power in my necklace.

"Mine," I whispered again.

The centipedes clicked — once, twice, three times — over three wedding rings to the left of Warner's betrothal bands.

"Mine," I said, my voice and resolve growing stronger as I quelled one of the three.

The three rainbow-colored silk braids wove themselves through the links of the necklace's chain, then were still. The magic of the necklace flowed over them, then receded. My claim had encased them in gold.

"Mine!" I cried.

Leaves and flowers exploded from the branch that was the third instrument of assassination, spinning around me like confetti. The now-bare branch fell to my feet, completely dormant. The shredded foliage adhered to the necklace, clinging to every link and ring. I coaxed another wash of golden magic to run through the chain, absorbing the leaves and flowers and embossing every inch of the necklace with a finely imprinted leaf-and-flower pattern.

I swayed on my feet. A flood of utter weariness almost took my legs out from underneath me.

I brushed my fingers along the necklace. It was mine. Every link. The individual magic of the instruments of assassination had been absorbed into the whole.

I lifted my gaze to meet that of the treasure keeper's. He stared at me, utterly aghast.

Movement drew my eye to my father. He'd pulled his sword at some point. The magic of the blade was potent, but no longer on the edge of unbearable for me. He didn't look horrified, as Pulou did. He didn't even look frightened. He looked wary, but proud.

He glanced at the treasure keeper, then loosened his hold on his weapon. The broadsword disappeared.

"A masterful display of alchemy," my father murmured. But he wasn't speaking to me.

"Until she loses control of the instruments," Pulou said.

"I believe it has already been made clear that the instruments of assassination were not as well contained as you thought. The wielder will wield, as the far seer has foreseen."

"As the far seer has contrived."

"Perhaps. That doesn't change the nature of the wielder."

Pulou nodded once. Just a tight, tiny movement of his chin. When he spoke, his tone was stilted and seriously stressed. "While she awaits further instruction, the wielder will remain at the treasure keeper's disposal."

I wasn't big on being talked about as if I wasn't still in the room. "Nah," I said. "I quit. Next time clean up your own mess."

Then, armed to the teeth, I turned and walked out of the treasure keeper's chamber.

No one tried to stop me.

I stepped through the portal into the bakery basement. Relief flooded through me the instant I felt dirt instead of cool marble underneath my feet.

I was home.

The portal snapped shut behind me. As it did so, I realized that its magic felt different. More substantial, as if I might be able to touch it. Perhaps even manipulate it into other forms. In my rush to leave the nexus, I hadn't noticed anything odd about the crossing. But now … it felt as though I might be able to seal the portal. Maybe even disconnect it if I wanted to.

I reached out to test my theory. But before I got any further, I tasted dark chocolate, sweet cherry, and thick, creamy whipped cream behind me.

Warner was in the bakery.

I crossed the space between the brick wall that held the portal and the wooden stairs without another thought, leaping up the stairs and into Warner's arms a split second after he'd slammed open the door to the pantry.

I crashed against his chest, already kissing him.

Then I tasted Kandy's and Kett's magic.

Keeping one arm looped around Warner's neck, I reached out as my BFFs squeezed into the pantry. Wrapping my free arm around their necks and shoulders, I hugged the werewolf and the vampire fiercely.

They gave as good as they got.

Drake slipped through the door behind Kandy and Kett, grinning madly. Even though the pantry was crammed to capacity, he burrowed his way into the Adept sandwich.

My mother, then Gran, appeared in the kitchen beyond the pantry door. They both looked weary and red-eyed. Also fierce and overjoyed.

I closed my eyes and inhaled. Cherry, chocolate, peppermint, almonds, strawberries, and lilac mingled with vanilla, cocoa, sugar, cinnamon, and all the other delicious aromas of my pantry and bakery.

The magic of everyone I loved combined with the scents of all my favorite flavors in the world.

I was home.

Acknowledgements

With thanks to:

My story & line editor
Scott Fitzgerald Gray

My proofreader
Pauline Nolet

My beta readers
Terry Daigle, Angela Flannery, Gael Fleming, Desi
Hartzel, and Heather Lewis.

My cupcake recipe testers
Angie Bartley, Diane Castro, Karie Deegan, Temperance
De'lonkcra, Kimberly Dicken, Megan Gayeski, Andrea
Guido, Amy Lynn Haskins, Amanda Hendrix, Coreen
James, Kendall Jarish, Traci Leigh, Gina Loss, Lisa
Moody, Wendy Novak, Theresa Russell, Johanna Sol

For their continual encouragement,
feedback, & general advice
Angela Brown – for finding an error that no one
else saw in Dowser 3
Jodi Maguda – for the Alberta weather report
The Office

For her Art
Elizabeth Mackey

Meghan Ciana Doidge is an award-winning writer based out of Salt Spring Island, British Columbia, Canada. She has a penchant for bloody love stories, superheroes, and the supernatural. She also has a thing for chocolate, potatoes, and sock yarn.

Novels
After The Virus
Spirit Binder
Time Walker
Cupcakes, Trinkets, and Other Deadly Magic (Dowser 1)
Trinkets, Treasures, and Other Bloody Magic (Dowser 2)
Treasures, Demons, and Other Black Magic (Dowser 3)
I See Me (Oracle 1)
Shadows, Maps, and Other Ancient Magic (Dowser 4)
Maps, Artifacts, and Other Arcane Magic (Dowser 5)
I See You (Oracle 2)
Artifacts, Dragons, and Other Lethal Magic (Dowser 6)

Novellas/Shorts
Love Lies Bleeding
The Graveyard Kiss

For recipes, giveaways, news, and glimpses of upcoming stories, please connect with Meghan on her:

Personal blog, www.madebymeghan.ca
Twitter, @mcdoidge
Facebook, Meghan Ciana Doidge
Email, info@madebymeghan.ca

Please also consider leaving an honest review at your point of sale outlet.

Catch a glimpse of
    the dowser universe
        through Rochelle's eyes...

The day I turned nineteen, I expected to gain what little freedom I could within the restrictions of my bank account and the hallucinations that had haunted me for the last six years. I expected to drive away from a life that had been dictated by the tragedy of others and shaped by the care of strangers. I expected to be alone.

Actually, I relished the idea of being alone.

Instead, I found fear I thought I'd overcome. Uncertainty I thought I'd painstakingly planned away. And terror that was more real than anything I'd ever hallucinated before.

I'd seen terrible, fantastical, and utterly impossible things ... but not love. Not until I saw him.

41142373R00209

Made in the USA
Middletown, DE
05 March 2017